THE SORCERER'S REVENGE

MICHAELA PETERS

THE SORCERER'S REVENGE

Interior Graphics/Art Credit: Aranwen's Jewelry

iUniverse books may be ordered through booksellers or by contacting:

iUniverse
1663 Liberty Drive
Bloomington, IN 47403
www.iuniverse.com
1-800-Authors (1-800-288-4677)

ISBN: 978-1-5320-1549-6 (sc)
ISBN: 978-1-5320-1551-9 (hc)
ISBN: 978-1-5320-1550-2 (e)

Library of Congress Control Number: 2017903716

Print information available on the last page.

iUniverse rev. date: 04/28/2017

Beginning

When envy and selfish ambition are allowed
to rule in the kingdom, then disorder and
every evil practice will be sure to follow.
—high king's law

Concealed by shadows next to an upper window, the sorcerer stood in his private chambers listening to the angry cries of the mob gathered in front of the palace. He could clearly smell the acrid smoke from their torches as it hung thickly in the warm night air. The sorcerer's sightless eyes smoldered darkly. He yearned to use his power against them, but he knew the attempt would be futile. Earlier that day, they had sent a prophet to evoke the law of banishment over him, leaving him powerless to use his dark magic.

In frustration, he tugged at the amulet on the chain around his neck. Held within the amulet was the single eye that provided his magical means of vision. Necros still found it hard to believe the captives of Amuron had the courage to confront him, but he should have guessed they would. They were now feeling bold because they were temporarily protected by the law. The sorcerer thought he had subdued them with fear; but fear, it seemed, had not been enough.

The distorted light from the torches danced across the face of a young boy standing among the crowd on the lawn. Shouts from the noisy throng caused the small figure to flinch protectively, as if he were taking personal blows. They were ordering Lord Necros, at the height of his reign, to leave the palace in which he had been born, the kingdom in which he had grown, and the city he had eventually come to rule. The boy hunched his shoulders, dearly wishing he had some sort of power to make them stop. Glancing up at the sorcerer's chambers, he longed to catch a glimpse of his master, but he could see nothing beyond the open casement.

Unheeded by those around him, the boy moved cautiously, maneuvering his way closer to the palace. A sudden shift in the restless crowd caused the furtive figure to accidently bump into the person beside him. Startled, the boy quickly backed away, keeping his head down. Now that he was getting close to the high king's palace, he would have to take even more care not to be seen.

The press of the crowd was like a solid wall in front of the building. It took all of his cunning and concentration to move unnoticed to the specific spot he had chosen next to the side of the palace. He waited for just the right moment and slipped like a shadow down a narrow lane and stopped in front of the servants' entrance. It was a door he knew well, and one he had used before. Hoping he wasn't too late, the boy took a deep breath and entered the dimly lit corridors, leaving the mob behind.

The dark hours of the night were becoming fewer, and consequently little time remained for Necros to stay in the city. His only recourse was to leave Amuron and never return. Otherwise, according to the law of banishment, by sunrise his power would be gone forever. For a sorcerer, being stripped of sorcery was a sentence worse than death! No! He would not be defeated by those he thought of as little more than chattel. He would make them pay—but not yet! Taking a long, slow breath, the sorcerer strengthened his resolve for revenge.

A soft knock came from the door, and Necros turned in the direction of the sound. A small, thin-framed boy with short, stringy hair entered the room unbidden. The boy had tear streaks on his pale face, and he fell trembling to his knees in front of the sorcerer. "They are threatening to burn you out of the palace, my lord," the frightened child choked out. "I beg you to leave and take me with you."

"I will leave," the tall, dark figure answered him, "but you must stay." His handsome features were strong and hard edged, giving the sorcerer a forbidding look. Reaching out a hand, he raised the boy's face to meet the eye staring out from the middle of his amulet. The sorcerer felt no love for the scrawny and unattractive boy. He knew of the boy's desire to learn of the black arts, and he could readily use the boy's desires for his own purposes. "The time will come when I will return, and I will need you here when I do. You must serve this kingdom and the high kings who rule it, unfailingly. Obtain an honored position within this household, and then you will be ready."

"But I want to serve you, Lord Necros. I want to be your apprentice," the boy protested, trying to look away as more tears ran down his face. But the hand holding his chin held him firmly.

"To do that, you must obey me without question."

Dropping his eyes in submission, the boy stopped crying, and Necros released him. "Will I see you again before you return?" Looking earnestly at the sorcerer with his dull green-brown eyes, he wiped the sleeve of his tunic across his face to clean his running nose.

"Yes. Many times you will come and visit me in the days and years ahead, and together we will plan my return to this city," his master assured him. Comforted by these words, the boy managed a weak smile. "Now shut the window and lock the door; there is something I must do before I leave."

Scrambling to his feet, the boy hurried to obey his master's wishes. He then stood watching wide-eyed while the sorcerer prepared the room. Never before had he been allowed in the sorcerer's study when Necros practiced his sorcery. Pressing his insubstantial frame against the back of the door, the boy watched in eager anticipation.

Pushing the heavy wooden table covered with items used for the black arts against the back wall, the sorcerer cleared a space in the center of the floor. Then he beckoned the child to come forward. He took the black sash from his fitted gray robe and tied it tightly around the boy's eyes. "Listen to me carefully! I am calling a spirit from the eternal realm. If you were to look at this spirit, you would be blinded by its light. Because I am already blind and see only by a magical device, I shall not be harmed."

Necros then led him to a corner in the room and faced him toward the wall. "You will be tempted to remove the blindfold by the flashes of colored light you will still be able to see," the sorcerer cautioned. "But you must not for any reason look at the light! Do you understand? If you fail me in this"—his tone made sure there was no misunderstanding—"I will kill you."

The boy nodded, straightening his back with determination.

With a look of grim amusement, the sorcerer set about his task. With some powder he took from a pouch on the table, Necros drew a large circle on the floor. He then took a pointed dagger from the table and cut cleanly into his index finger. As the blood flowed from his wound, he patiently drew a symbol in the center of the circle. When that was done, he pulled a hair from his head and tied a knot in it. The sorcerer then put the knotted hair on top of the blood symbol and backed away, careful not to disturb his work.

Keenly aware of the unpredictability of calling on spirits, Necros once more consulted the information in his red leather spell book on the table. Confident that there was nothing he might have missed, the sorcerer knelt in front of the circle. Removing the amulet he used to give him sight and placing it by the circle, the sorcerer uttered the words of the incantation with a voice of calm authority. In response, a being of intense white light appeared. The spirit had no recognizable shape, but when it spoke, its form broke into a dizzying kaleidoscope of colors.

"Who has called me forth to this realm and holds me captive within this circle?" The spirit's voice was high and sharp, like the tinkling of many little bells.

"I, Necros, the adopted son of Kareishalla the Witch Queen. I have called you to do my bidding as a seer."

"What would you have me see?"

"I wish to know—will I have my revenge on this city?"

There was a pause before the answer. "Yes."

The law of banishment was clear. Only one of royal blood could break the banishment and allow him to return. Necros needed to ask another question. "And who is it that will break the banishment?"

"Release me from this circle and I will answer." The sound of the high tinkling bells deepened an octave, and the shifting colors stopped suddenly and changed direction.

"If I release you, you will then return to the eternal realm and my question will go unanswered," Necros said with strained patience.

"Your question will be answered if you give me something in return."

"What do you ask?"

"I would take your power to call on spirits."

The sorcerer had been anticipating something like this, so he was ready with his response. It did not pay to offend a spirit, but he did intend to get his answer. "What you ask I will not give. But consider what would happen if you did not return to the eternal realm." He was sure the spirit had heard his intended threat and understood his meaning. The sorcerer could not see the reaction of the dancing colors, but he could still feel their intensity.

The spirit did not fear death, as it was immortal. It was possible that its power could diminish until its light was nothing more than a spark, but the thought of being contained forever within this realm was what caused the spirit to change its offer. "Then I will hold your power until you are freed from your banishment."

This was the very reason he was leaving the city—so that he would not lose his power. Yet, here again, he was being asked to give it up. Necros disliked playing these games. He was used to giving an order and being obeyed. This banishment had already cost him more than he would care to admit. He must have revenge! He could work on breaking his banishment by using his servant, but that would be much more difficult, and his need for calling on spirits would not be essential until the time came for him to return. There is a difference between giving up your power temporarily and having it taken from you forever. He would be a fool not to know the difference, and besides, he would gain what he wanted in the end. "The power is yours," he agreed, "until the banishment is broken."

A shard of white burst from the body of light and flew toward the kneeling sorcerer, piercing his chest. He gasped, his face contorting in pain, until the sharp piece of light emerged again, exiting slowly from the place it had entered. It pulsed to the tempo of the sorcerer's beating heart and then plunged into the amulet lying at the side of the circle.

Feeling the drain in his power, the sorcerer strained to ask in a voice that was barely more than a whisper, "What is the name?"

"His name will be Prince Naibor. The future is not constant, and you will have to work hard to turn the prince against the beliefs he will learn as a child. He will be the son of a high king, and he will be the seventh of royal blood who hopes to rule."

Satisfied with the answer, Necros leaned forward and, feeling with his hand, opened a part of the powdered circle. "You are released."

The creature's light soared to the top of the room. It spoke again before fading. "Your power is being held within the amulet and cannot be released until you return from your banishment. During that time the amulet must remain in the city, or your power will be lost to you forever."

After the spirit had gone, the sorcerer quickly gathered the few belongings he would take with him in exile. Then he magically sealed the amulet and his other prized possessions into a carved wooden box. "Guard it well, and make ready for the day when I will return," Necros said, placing it in the hands of the young servant boy. Realizing the seriousness of the situation, the boy tried not to reveal his excitement at having the box placed in his care. Receiving the box was like a promise to him that someday all his own dreams of glory would come true.

Departing from the city, Necros took limited satisfaction in the fact that he had left a willing servant behind to do his bidding and set in motion the events that would one day lead to his revenge.

CHAPTER 1

Prince Naibor was disturbed from his thoughts by the tavern owner slapping a mug of ale down on the table in front of him, causing the froth to spill over the side.

"Yous gotta pay for th'ale now. I don't run no tab for strangers," the sour-faced, burly taverner said, shoving his huge hand in front of Naibor's nose.

The prince's thoughts were not kind as he put sufficient payment into the sweaty palm. "He doesn't even recognize royalty sitting under his very nose," Naibor muttered to himself with a frown. "I shouldn't wonder in this place." Shifting uncomfortably on the wooden bench, he looked around the dark tavern.

The smell of ale, sweat, and wood smoke from the fireplace hung heavy in the stale air. The dim light in the room helped to hide the grime on the walls and on the heavy cloth separating his table from the next. He was moderately pleased, however, that he had managed to escape recognition. He had come this far out from the main city for just that reason. He knew no one would expect to find the son of the high king sitting in such a place. Coming here allowed him to be alone for a while, away from all the false merriment of the Celebration Games. The very name caused him to shudder inwardly. Naibor didn't see the games as a celebration, just a poor excuse to rob him of his throne. Why did the people cling to such absurd traditions? His worthiness need not be tested. He was the rightful heir.

A group of four scraggly young men, already full of beer, burst into the room, creating a disturbance. Leaning on one another, they moved over to the bar to order drinks. There was some laughing and cursing as coins appeared from the pouches tied at their sides. It seemed apparent that a farmer must have just paid them for their work in the fields.

"I'll drink to the games, and who with me?" their leader loudly inquired, grabbing the ale he had just paid for from the busy tavern owner.

"Hear, hear!" his friends responded enthusiastically, each reaching eagerly for his mug before raising it in the air.

"Should be pretty exciting," continued the first, wiping the froth from his lips. "Who do you think will be the best of the lot?"

"Probably none of 'em can take it," spouted another, followed by a howl of laughter from the group.

"I'd like one of the princesses to become king," proposed the smallest of the group, a wiry youth who had not many teeth.

"They become queens, stupid," laughed the leader, rolling his eyes heavenward.

Unabashed, the other continued. "Anyway, like I was saying, maybe she'd take a fancy to me and—"

"You!" exclaimed the group with an uproar, laughing so hard they had to put their mugs down in order to slap one another on the back and wipe away the tears springing into their eyes.

"An' what makes you think a queen's goin' ta be interested in the likes of you?" broke in the leader, with a wink to the others.

"Charm—I got me charm."

"Yea, charmin', ain't he?" cracked the leader, elbowing one of his companions forcefully in the side before doubling over with laughter.

Another round of laughs ensued, this time with the rest of the house joining in.

"Now seriously," another patron began, when things had settled down a bit. "Who'd ya think's goin' ta win?"

"Princess Janii," shouted the large and well-rounded barmaid from the corner. "She's the prettiest." Smacking an empty table with a wet rag, she wiped up the spills left behind by the former occupants.

"We ain't 'ad a queen for at least three successions," answered a man from somewhere out of Naibor's sight.

"'Bout time for one then," retorted the barmaid. Making the best use of her size to intimidate the patrons, she stared about the room, daring anyone to disagree.

"Prince Baynor," put in another. "He's the strongest of the lot."

Most of the crowd agreed.

"How 'bout the high king's son, Prince Naibor?" another suggested.

The prince stiffened unconsciously in his seat.

"Ha, that good-for-nothin'? He'll come in last, behind Prince Ranor, Prince Tybor, Princess Sanii, and Princess Tayii."

The laughter that broke out caused Naibor's anger to rise.

"Yeah," agreed another. "He'd need a mighty powerful sorcerer to help him win."

The words "mighty sorcerer" echoed in Prince Naibor's head until he no longer heard the noise from the crowd. A forbidden thought came into his mind. The more he thought through the possibilities, the more Naibor became convinced that a sorcerer was what he needed to ensure his victory. The prince looked around at the crowd of people in the tavern. Now it was his turn to laugh. "Oh, how you underestimate me."

* * *

Seven days later, Prince Naibor stood contemplatively at the window of his private chamber overlooking the exercise grounds below. He held his lean body and muscled shoulders royally. Several of his competitors were practicing vigorously for the upcoming competition. Naibor's blue eyes and tight lips were set with determination while he watched them. One finger danced unconsciously at the corner of his mouth, and a line of worry creased his brow.

Elbanor, the court tutor who had taught his father before him, and whose father had taught his father's father, shifted impatiently next to the prince and continued with his plea. "You see, Prince, everyone is preparing for the games, except—excuse my rashness—seemingly you, my lord. And they are only four days away!

"There are rumors," he hesitantly stated after a stiff silence, "that Prince Baynor is an undefeatable warrior and that Princess Sanii excels in wisdom and counsel. Others boast of Princess Tayii, reminding the people of her athletic abilities and her personal integrity. And then there is Princess Janii, with her beauty and gentle spirit. Her generosity and humility have endeared her to many. She is what many envision to be a true princess. Prince Ranor and Prince Tybor have their supporters too. This is due to Ranor's acclaim among the economic world for his policies, and Tybor's knowledge of medicine and his ability to heal."

"So what you are telling me, Elbanor," Prince Naibor summarized, turning sharply toward the elder tutor, "is that I'm doomed to disgrace?"

Over the years, the prince had noticed that the tutor always had a way of pointing out his mistakes and shortcomings while politely making excuses for him when he didn't quite measure up to what was expected. No matter how hard the prince had tried during his lessons as a child, he always seemed to disappoint his teacher in some way. Eventually this had caused the young prince to lose interest in his lessons, feeling that his best was never enough for the master scholar.

Elbanor hastily took a step back from the prince, hearing the hostility in his voice. "Could I perhaps do something to help, my lord?" he inquired, squinting his eyes in an ingratiating smile.

Prince Naibor looked down with distaste at the elder tutor's gaunt face and shrunken body. "Yes," he muttered, making a conscious decision. "Yes, I think you can help me, Elbanor, but not in the way you are thinking. You are known as the greatest historian in the kingdom, are you not?"

"Yes, my lord." Elbanor's face was unable to mask his pride.

"Good. Then what I am about to ask of you, you must treat with the utmost confidentiality. Do you understand?"

The skullcap denoting Elbanor's position bobbed up and down.

The prince disliked having to confide in his tutor, but he could think of no other person who could help him find the information he wanted. He went to the door of his chamber and looked out into the hallway to make sure there were no servants about. When he was satisfied that they were completely alone, he motioned for the tutor to sit in one of the large cushioned chairs by the unlit fireplace. Then he sat in the chair opposite his tutor and secretively told him of his desperate resolution. "I intend to do whatever it takes to become high king, even if that means using a sorcerer to help me." Elbanor's eyes bulged from their sockets at the mention of the word "sorcerer," but Naibor continued nevertheless. "I need you to help me find that sorcerer, Elbanor. Will you do it?"

Naibor watched his tutor closely, waiting for his response. Elbanor sat dwarfed by the chair, gravely tapping his tented fingers together. After opening and hastily closing his mouth several times in quick succession, the court tutor stood up and addressed the prince. "I did say that I would help you if I could, Prince. In order to do that, we must go to my private study."

The elder scholar's reaction surprised Naibor. The prince had expected Elbanor to chide him like a foolish child. Not giving his tutor a chance to change his mind, Naibor hurried to the door and gestured for Elbanor to lead the way. Naibor, following behind Elbanor, did not see the gratified smile that fleetingly crossed the tutor's face.

On the main floor of the palace, they entered the large, high-ceilinged room where Naibor had been taught his lessons. The prince still found the library oppressive. Daylight weakly filtered through the thick curtains as they made their way past the heavy furniture in the book-lined room.

Elbanor's study was located in an adjacent chamber at the back of the library. The tutor briefly fumbled with the key in the lock before they went inside. Entering the small room, the prince looked around with bewilderment. The study overflowed with scrolls, books, and maps, which were scattered and piled and stuck in every available space.

"Descriptions of sorcerers and different types of sorcery were recorded on scrolls long before the beginning of this city," the master historian explained in an attempt to continue their prior conversation. Pinching up his wizened face in concentration, he rummaged through a pile of books near a table in the middle of the room.

"No, not that far back, Elbanor," Naibor replied impatiently, working his way through the cramped chamber after him. "I want to know about powerful sorcerers—ones that might still be around today." Elbanor's quizzical look caused him to continue. "I don't mean the kind that boast about their abilities and say they can read the future or talk to the dead. Those so-called sorcerers, who trick foolish and superstitious people into giving them money, I can find in almost any town outside of this city. I mean a real sorcerer: one who has real power—the kind of sorcerer whom people generally stay away from. Are there any who are really powerful and still alive?"

"Alive, you say?" Elbanor's voice rose with the question. "Sorcerers are banned from the kingdom, as you know, Prince, powerful or not. That type of information would therefore not be in the palace history books. It probably hasn't been transferred to a book of any kind, but I have heard tales of a sorcerer so powerful that he turned people into animals." Elbanor paused at this point and gave the prince a searching look. "He was known as Necros. What I know about him is mostly rumors. Now, rumors, as any historian knows, are not considered reliable sources; however, we can learn some truths from them when compared with other—"

"Elbanor," Naibor interrupted, his patience wearing thin, "just tell me what you do know, rumors or not!"

"Why, yes, I see." The tutor exhaled loudly, pausing to reflect. "The story goes as such: About eighty years ago, Necros was banished from the city of Amuron. He was the only son of a former high king. He supposedly learned his art from a foreign woman who had seduced his father. She was said to have been so beautiful that no man could resist her, including, unfortunately, the high king. Soon after, the high king's wife mysteriously died. This allowed the king to take the foreign woman as his wife, which greatly displeased the people. Soon she ruled in the high king's stead, and she became known as Kareishalla the Witch Queen. Under her tutelage, Necros grew up to become both powerful and cruel. Anyone who was said to have spoken out against the new queen was changed into an animal and slaughtered by Necros in front of the people. Then, one night, in a horrible fight, the witch queen blinded her sorcerer son. He, in turn, murdered both his stepmother and his father, taking one of his father's eyes for his own. With no one left to stand against him, Necros began to rule the kingdom. The people feared him and secretly prayed to Aii for deliverance. Shortly afterward, a prophet appeared, declaring that the city would be destroyed if Necros was not banished from the kingdom. Eager to have the sorcerer leave, the people came to burn the palace down. To the surprise of everyone, the sorcerer fled the palace without incident, and a new high king was quickly appointed in his place."

"Is all of this true?" Naibor asked wide-eyed.

"My lord, I have already told you most of this information is not very reliable."

"Thank you, Elbanor," Naibor replied with a sigh. "Can you tell me any more? What happened to him? Was he ever heard from again?"

"Well, most people believe that he traveled north into the Land of the Dead to live among the ancient ruins."

"Ah yes, the Ancient City," Naibor remarked. "I have heard of it, but isn't that just a rumor as well?"

"Oh no, my lord, the Ancient City does exist. Many historians have studied and written about it—even I have seen it."

"Good. Then you can tell me how to get there," Naibor responded eagerly, seizing the opportunity.

* * *

As the first signs of a new day dawned, Prince Naibor mounted his horse and set off on a journey of which even he knew not the outcome. He had with him provisions for several days, as well as a crude map in his head of the land that lay north and ahead of him.

North was a road seldom traveled, for it led to desolation and things unknown. Behind him, to the east, west, and south, ran a border of white stones marking the boundaries of the land ruled by the high king. The kingdom was large, and it encompassed pastures and streams, towns and villages, forests and lakes, and the main city of Amuron, from which he had come. The north, however, was a place outside of the kingdom—a region known as the Land of the Dead.

The path he was following soon disappeared, and Naibor led his horse toward a series of low hills on the horizon. The sun was hot, and gusts of dust swirled around him on the dry breeze. What little green there had been vanished, leaving only rock, stone, and pale dirt to greet the eye.

The bleakness surrounding the prince began to gnaw at his spirit. In his frustration, he cursed the years of training that had led him to this point in his life. The bitterness Naibor felt was so strong that he could almost taste it on the back of his tongue. His life seemed so futile, and he felt he was being taunted by the coming of the Celebration Games. His training would not help him become high king. Instead he would remain the servant of some other chosen in his place. How degrading!

His horse gave a big sigh as the prince dismounted for a short rest. Shading his eyes against the brightness surrounding him, Naibor looked off toward the line of hills to the north. He had already covered half the distance it took to reach them. They now appeared larger and more hostile than before. They seemed more a formidable barrier than a welcome relief from the flatness of the surrounding landscape. He could just make out the hard and rocky surface of the ridge, dotted randomly with sparse, thorny bushes.

The sun's heat seemed to have lessened when Prince Naibor resumed his journey. The breeze had become stronger and cooler. For the first time since he had set out from the palace, the prince began to almost enjoy himself.

His mind wandered to thoughts of his youth. Back then, he had dreamed of being a gracious king loved by all. These memories tugged at the emotions Naibor had worked so long to ignore. He was surprised by the strength of his feelings of disappointment. Why was being high king so important to him? Why could he not just let it go?

Lost in his musings as he rode across the parched land, the prince could think only of one thing that had kept him from realizing his dreams—*The High King's Law. The High King's Law* was a book that had originally been dictated by Aii, the god of the people, to the first king of this land. The high king's authority came from Aii through these laws. It had been handed down from one high king to the next as a method and guide for governing the people. Naibor regarded the book as a collection of archaic beliefs that strangled the high king's authority and limited his power. He felt that the book acted contrary to the high king's true position and purpose. Naibor did not understand how the high king could rule without having final authority.

Without *The High King's Law*, the prince knew there would be nothing to keep him from being high king. It was *The High*

King's Law that did not recognize his status as heir to the throne. It declared that all those of royal blood wishing to become high king must compete according to the guidelines set forth in the Celebration Games. Naibor knew one of the first things he would do when he became high king would be to abolish *The High King's Law* and, along with it, the Celebration Games. Then he could rule for life and make his own traditions.

Naibor's thoughts were rudely interrupted when a gust of sand smacked him sharply in the face. The breeze had become a strong wind that stirred the sand and dry dirt high into the air, flinging it about violently.

As the prince rode on, conditions became worse. The wind whipped the dirt around him with increasing volleys of strength, stinging his eyes while making it difficult to breathe. His exposed skin felt as if it were being rubbed raw, and he pulled the hood of his robe up over his head for protection. The hills that had been coming steadily closer now disappeared from view. All Naibor could see were particles of dirt gathering in swirling clouds, to be dashed by the wind around him.

A dead piece of brush suddenly blew by, startling his horse. The horse leaped in the air with a scream of fright and ran forward blindly in a wild burst of speed. Caught unaware, the prince was thrown roughly to the ground. He lay biting down on the grit in his mouth, with the wind whistling shrilly around him. He had lost his sense of direction and, with it, his horse and all of his provisions.

Some time later, the fierce wind abruptly stopped, leaving the dirt hanging in the air to resettle slowly back to the ground. It would be evening soon, but Naibor had not the will to get up. He half hoped that he would sink into the ground, ending his life, his struggles, and his unattainable dreams. He turned his head and saw with dismay the hills still off in the distance. He would not be able to reach them by nightfall.

Sitting up, Naibor wondered if his life was worth anything to anyone. Rising quickly, he tried to shake off the fine dirt that encased his body. He felt that he was nothing but a worthless fool, rejected as useless—a stain in the princely bloodline.

"Look at me!" he shouted defiantly into the air, "The greatest fool that ever lived." He shook his head in disappointment, laughing at himself. "I must be going mad!" His voice was swallowed by the surrounding bleakness. "Here I am, trying to find a sorcerer abolished from the kingdom almost a century ago, on some whim that I could find him among the ruins of an ancient city, still alive after all these years, and with the power to help me."

The prince was about to turn back and head for home when he realized he wouldn't be able to face living in the city—not if he wasn't voted high king during the Celebration Games. Feeling he had no other choice, Naibor continued with what he had set out to do.

As the night grew colder, the shoulder Naibor had fallen on began to ache, but this discomfort only urged him forward. He could plainly see in the starlight that he had not much farther to go. Elbanor had told him to head for the gap in the rock wall where there had once been a path through the hills. He could see the crevice just to the right of him, but the sight of the dark gash oozing blackness caused his courage to fail. Instead he searched nearby for some shelter for the night. At the base of the hill, he spotted a small ledge several feet above his head.

"It will do," he grumbled miserably to himself, and with that he scrambled up and lay down.

The prince was anything but comfortable. Throughout the night he was plagued by bugs which bit at him mercilessly, until he gave up trying to swat them away. The light robe he wore did not provide much protection against the cold or the sharp little stones from the ledge that dug into his body. Nevertheless, exhaustion conquered and he fell into a fitful sleep.

Naibor woke abruptly and sat up with a start. Something had touched him! Looking around, he could see nothing but the usual rock and stubble, surrounded by the shadows cast by the half-moon that had finally risen in the night. His heart beat furiously. He waited watchfully, listening for the slightest sound.

With the corner of his eye, he caught sight of something moving. A shape detached itself from the shadows and came rushing toward him. It was a floating head. The face was grotesque and misshapen, with oversize staring eyes and a cavernous mouth. Terrified, the prince threw his hands up to protect himself.

Another bodiless head appeared and came at him, and then another. They came at him from all directions—apparitions of death, some shriveled and some bloated, but all horrible to see. Naibor shrunk back against the rock wall behind him. They mocked him by floating up in front of his face and then quickly disappearing. He was pushed and poked at by unseen hands while the heads laughed shrilly with gurgles and squeaks.

"Who are you?" Naibor squeezed from a tight throat. "What do you want?"

His assailants only hissed loudly in reply.

Summoning what courage he could find, Naibor stood up, readying himself for their next attack. "I'm Prince Naibor, from the city of Amuron. I've come to see Necros," he called out boldly in an attempt to justify his presence.

His voice sounded surprisingly loud in the clear night, and for a moment it seemed that he was completely alone. Then face after face began appearing until there was one everywhere he looked. He was trapped!

Their hissing changed into a rhythmic chant of many different voices, the sound of which caused Naibor's skin to rise. He had to get away!

The prince was about to jump down off the ledge and run for his life when there suddenly appeared before him the most horrid face of them all! His fear paralyzed him. The hideous face was charred black. Its burning red eyes penetrated his soul and drained his strength. The mouth—a cruel, dark line—opened slowly in a deadly silent laugh, revealing a tongue that was pointed and black.

Naibor tried to look away but was unable to break from its gaze. A stench rose up, stinging his nostrils, leaving him gasping for air. An intense heat began radiating through his body. Naibor felt as if he were being burned alive from within, and he writhed in torment. A dismembered hand floated up in front of his face. The charred hand with long, glistening black claws reached toward Naibor's throat. The prince was still unable to get his body to respond. Helpless, he felt the fingers grab on to his neck and the nails begin to sink into his flesh.

"Noooo!" he screamed out. Throwing himself backward against the rock face, Naibor jerked himself free from the deadly grasp. Before he could regain his balance, the prince felt his feet slip out from under him and his body fall. Shattering pain exploded inside his head. He heard the words "Necros lives" before he descended into the dark abyss of unconsciousness.

* * *

Prince Naibor awoke to a great pressure pounding and surging inside his head. The pain was not unlike what he had frequently experienced after a night of overindulgence, courtesy of the wine cellar. When his vision cleared, he found himself lying on a cot in the corner of what appeared to be a shallow cave with walls of yellow mud. Specks of fine dirt floated in the sunlight lazily streaming through a circular window and the open doorway beside where he lay. In the middle of the dirt floor, Naibor noticed a fire pit surrounded by clay crockery.

His confusion concerning his whereabouts was interrupted by the movement of a figure almost hidden by the shadows on the opposite side of the room. In the dimness not reached by the light, he could see the back of someone dwarfed by a robe made from baggy brown sackcloth. A bald head scattered with strands of white hair that stuck out in all directions could just be seen over the hunch in the back. The figure turned slowly around and came out of the shadows carrying a bowl.

Naibor gasped as the face came into view. For a moment he imagined the horrible charred face in front of him, but this face was white and smooth and alive, and the eyes were discolored instead of burning red. He was not relieved, however. Hanging from a gold chain were two long and flat carved black stones that held between them an eye—very much alive and seeing. The eye focused on him.

"Ah, I see you have awakened. How is your head? You have a nasty bump on the back of it."

Naibor slowly reached up a hand and felt the bump, never taking his eyes from the eye.

"Do not be alarmed," the strange figure continued. "This is how I see. I have no other sight, and at best I see only forms and shapes. I know I am not a pretty picture, but someday, Prince, you will find that age is not a friend to many. Here, drink this. It will help to clear your head."

The prince sat up and obediently took the offered bowl, thinking the red liquid was just a bit of wine. Taking a sip, he made a disgusted face. Naibor was about to throw the bitter drink on the ground when he realized the aching in his head had completely cleared. Setting the bowl on the ground, Naibor warily took a closer look at who was standing before him.

"Well, at last we meet, Prince Naibor. I am Necros—the sorcerer whom you seek."

"I … I …" Naibor faltered. His mind wandered back to his strange conversation with Elbanor on the day before last. He was still not sure how he had managed to convince Elbanor to help him, considering the fact that both sorcerers and their dark arts were forbidden in the kingdom. He had followed Elbanor's directions to the Ancient City, and now here he was, face-to-face with this strange old man claiming to be Necros.

"Yes, I came north to live in the Ancient City," Necros said, interrupting Naibor's thoughts. "You are in it now, but not all you have heard about me is true."

Naibor was unable to hide his alarm, and the prince worried that the sorcerer could read his mind with the eye, as well as see.

The old sorcerer shifted his position and took his eye off Naibor. "You have come all this way, Prince, yet you still have not told me why you are here."

"I came because I need your help, Necros." Naibor's conviction grew as he stood to face the sorcerer. "I am the high king's son and heir to the throne, yet if I compete in the Celebration Games, I am sure to lose. The games are only two days away, and if you could stop them from happening, with the use of your powers, then I would surely become high king."

"Now, if I were to do this, supposing I still had the power to do so, what would you offer me in return?"

"I could reward you handsomely. How much would you like?"

"The price would be high. But tell me, Prince, what would I need money for out here?"

"I could offer you gold or even jewels."

"Pretty decorations, I am sure. I have no need for them."

"Well," Naibor said hesitantly, "you could come to the kingdom and help me rule. I could appoint you as my advisor."

"But I am content here. This is my home. It has been for a long time now, and I am quite comfortable right here where I am."

The prince bit his lip apprehensively.

Necros suddenly broke into a laugh. "Do not worry, Prince. I am quite flattered that someone of your stature has gone through so much trouble to inquire about my services. So I will help you if I can. Nothing would please me better than to be able to stop the Celebration Games. If the truth be known, they were not kind to me either. But I don't see how I can help you. Did you have something in mind? I cannot stop the games from happening with my power, for I cannot change time, nor can I improve your abilities. I could hamper the other competitors, but there is still no guarantee of the outcome."

A brief silence passed before Naibor spoke. "I know of a way to stop the games and still be guaranteed the throne. It would be simple—just eliminate the competition. If there is only one competitor, then that competitor is the obvious choice. That competitor will, of course, be me."

"What are you saying, Prince?" Necros sounded shocked. "You want me to—"

"Not harm them," Naibor blurted out. "Turn them into animals. You can do that, can't you?"

"I can," Necros assured him, but Naibor looked at him with uncertainty. "I think it's time we got some air." The sorcerer eyed the prince shrewdly. "Come outside for a moment."

The prince made a disapproving face but followed Necros through the doorway, intent on humoring the old man. The bright sunlight temporarily blinded Naibor, and he shaded his eyes until they adjusted.

With shock, Naibor looked around him from side to side. Necros was gone! *Where could he be?* He had been right behind the sorcerer when they had come outside. "Necros!" Naibor called out with concern for the blind man.

Looking around, the prince found he was in a canyon whose walls rose high above him. Carved into the canyon walls were grotesque faces of death, reminding the prince of the night before. Suddenly feeling ill at ease, Naibor's stomach hardened into a knot.

Behind him rose the Ancient City, all formed of the same yellow mud as the inside of Necros's home. Dug into the canyon walls, it hung suspended above the ground. The city must have been ancient indeed, for time had washed over it and left it looking like a sea-scrubbed surface. Not much remained but a random series of barren hollows as well as some narrow ledges left clinging precariously to the cliffs. The dusty, dry yellow walls were parched with staleness and age. Heat waves and nits danced in the empty silence. Set against the deserted city, the carvings on the canyon walls seem all the more overpowering. The faces leered down oppressively, and the chill from their gaze caused Naibor's heart to grow cold.

What a desolate place. The prince tried to shake off his uneasiness. "Necros, where are you?" he cried out desperately, unnerved by the whole situation.

Hearing a laugh come from above him, Naibor looked up to see Necros standing on top of a carved face at the rim of the canyon.

"I'm right here," Necros called down with a wave of his arm. "How do you like my home? Interesting, isn't it? The people who used to live in this ancient city worshipped these carvings as gods. Wait a moment. I'm coming down."

To Naibor's surprise, Necros threw his body forward in a dive, plunging downward off the top of the cliff from a formidable height. The prince watched helplessly as the body fell toward him, knowing the fall would surely kill the aged sorcerer. Then, as Naibor watched, the body of Necros righted itself and floated down unharmed to the ground in front of him.

"Necros, I thought you would be killed!" Naibor exclaimed, clearly amazed.

Necros chuckled in reply. "My dear prince, it is not that easy to kill a sorcerer."

The words were hardly out of the sorcerer's mouth when a giant boulder broke loose from the top of the cliff wall and came plummeting down on top of them. Naibor moved out of the way just in time as it crashed to the ground. Through the dust and rubble, the prince could see that Necros had not been as fortunate. Under the boulder, Naibor could see the remains of the sorcerer's crushed body.

With dismay, Naibor got up to remove the body from under the rock. As his hand touched the boulder, it burst into flames that roared up high above his head. Startled, Naibor jumped back, only to find himself surrounded by the fire. The intensity of the heat scorched him, and the flames flicked inward, trying to consume him.

"Necros!" the prince cried out, his voice full of panic. "Stop it! Stop it!"

Instantly the fire disappeared. Naibor checked himself over and found he was not harmed. A tap on his shoulder caused him to turn around. There stood Necros!

"You learn fast, Prince," was all he said.

Naibor, annoyed, didn't reply for a moment. "All right, you've proven to me that you are powerful, but how do I know I can trust you?"

Necros gave a gleeful look that did not secure Naibor's faith.

"You will have to trust me, Prince, if you are to become high king. Look!" he instructed, pointing to the ground.

There at Naibor's feet was the high king's amulet. Naibor reached down and picked it up. It was exactly as he remembered it! His father had only once removed the amulet from around his neck to let him hold it. In that brief time, Naibor had absorbed every detail about it so that it had become a part of his being. It was exactly as he remembered it! The gold chain felt like silk in his hands—and then there was the Stone of Wisdom. The Stone of Wisdom was a large, clear stone centered in the oval amulet. It seemed to radiate from within. Colors danced within its depths, as if it were alive and made from the purity of true color. The brilliance of this one stone alone made all the other jewels in the kingdom seem passive in comparison.

"It is beautiful, isn't it?" Necros asked, but the prince was too enthralled to hear. "Go ahead; try it on."

As if in a trance, Naibor began to raise the amulet to his head. Almost before he realized what was happening, the amulet changed into a dagger and plunged toward his throat. Naibor managed to stop it just as the tip pricked his skin. With all his strength, he pulled it back to about an arm's length, but the dagger fought just as hard to go forward.

"Necros!" Naibor said with a trembling voice, hardly daring to break his concentration. "Stop it!"

"I can't," the sorcerer stated calmly. "You have to stop it yourself."

Prince Naibor's anger rose as he continued to struggle with the dagger, but the compelling force was stronger than he.

"Necros! Do something! Help me!" the prince implored.

"Let go of it."

"What?" Naibor exclaimed, not believing what he had just heard. "It will kill me!"

"Trust me," Necros answered.

The dagger inched forward as Naibor's strength weakened. "I can't hold it back much longer."

"Naibor, trust me!" the voice of Necros rang with authority. "Let go of the dagger!"

Naibor's arms collapsed, letting go of the dagger. It dropped to the ground and vanished. Naibor had nothing to say.

"Come inside, Prince. We will have some refreshments and work out our plan in detail."

* * *

Prince Naibor rode swiftly and unhindered back toward the kingdom. The old sorcerer had found his horse in the canyon, nibbling at what little grass there was to be found, and had stabled him in one of the hollowed caves. When Naibor reached the remains of the North Road, he turned aside to the right and urged his horse toward the road that lead up to the West Gate.

Easing his horse to a walk, Naibor traveled beside the great wall of stone surrounding the city. It was a dark gray, almost black in color, but its shiny and smooth surface caused it to reflect the light and made it seem alive with colors. It was more than twice as thick as a man's waist, and at least four times a man's height. The top of it had been shaped into a gently curving arc, and a deep trench had been dug all the way around the outside of it to further its defense. He thought back to the time when, as a boy, he had asked Elbanor about it.

"What is the wall made of, you ask? Well, Prince, it is a secret substance that our ancient ancestors discovered long ago, before they started to build this city. The substance they found is a rock they named coa. When this rock is heated, it becomes a thick liquid that can be poured, but when it cools, the rock becomes twice as hard as it was in its original state and almost indestructible. In its new form we call it blackstone."

As the city had expanded over the decades, the wall had been extended to encompass the newer parts of the city. Subsequently, the inside of the city was divided into a number of separate sections.

The first section was the oldest and the most magnificent part of the city. This was where the main palace and the surrounding palaces of the lesser kings had been built. These palaces had almost become one because of the many connecting lanes, courtyards, and gardens. Not surprisingly, this section was known as the Palace Section.

By far the busiest and most crowded part of the city was the Market Section. This section had expanded during a time when bandits had plagued outlying villages, causing villagers with young families to seek refuge within the safety of the city's walls. To accommodate the swelling population, groups of small houses separated by short, narrow streets had quickly been built.

The central street of the Market Section was used by merchants to sell their wares. The Market was open six days a week from sunrise to sunset, except during holidays, when it was used for celebrating festivals. Everything that could be sold—from the freshest fruit and vegetables to the finest cloths and linens—was to be found at the market, and as a boy, Naibor had spent many happy hours wandering through it. He now avoided this section as much as possible, finding the crowds and noise of the place almost intolerable.

Next to the market area was the arena, where athletic contests were held and where he soon would be competing in the Celebration Games. Athletes were held in high esteem throughout the city. After a competition, the winners were thrown large amounts of coins by the appreciative crowd. This not only guaranteed a constant flow of competitors; it also guaranteed entertainment for the people.

He then passed the newer parts of the city, where the skilled tradesmen lived and worked. There were four of these sections, commonly referred to as the North Quarter, the East Quarter, the South Quarter, and the West Quarter. There was also a section devoted to the military, who, along with the Guard of the Gates and the People's Guard, helped to keep the city in order. Then, of course, there were the Outlands, which he would not be passing because they skirted the south side of the city. This was where the farmers produced their crops and stabled their livestock until it was time for them to be sold at the market.

There were only four gates into the city—one facing in each direction. Prince Naibor was fast approaching the one to the west. He and his horse were both exhausted when at last they came in sight of it. The West Gate was the main gate inside the high walls of the city. The road running up to it was used mainly for commerce, and it led to many outlying villages and on past the kingdom's boundaries.

The prince arrived at the gate during the lazy hours after dinner, and the guards jumped to attention when they realized who it was riding toward them silhouetted by the setting sun.

Naibor quickly dismounted and addressed the guards. "You—go find me the captain of the guard. And you—take my horse to the stable and see that he is well looked after. He has had a long, hard ride. And send someone to bring me some food as well. I will be waiting in the guardhouse."

Turning from the gate, the prince walked briskly into the brightly lit stone room. The last guard he had sent off followed him into the room. "Sir, should I call the alert?" the guard asked anxiously, confusing Naibor's hastiness for some unlooked-for trouble in this time of peace.

"No!" returned Naibor with a scowl of impatience, disappointed to find the guard still there. The prince began to wave the guard away with his hand, but then he thought of something else to ask. "Wait; where do you keep the ale in this place? I don't see the cask."

"Not in the guardhouse," the exasperated soldier answered.

"Well then, get me some of that as well!"

* * *

Striding briskly into the room, the stocky captain found Prince Naibor with a mug to his lips. "What seems to be the trouble, my lord?" he asked in a tone less respectful than was proper.

Naibor, ignoring the tone, smiled in his friendliest manner.

"Sit down, Captain." The prince motioned to the chair beside him at the end of the long table. "I'd like a word with you, if I may. Will you join me in a drink?"

Captain Regg tried not to sound annoyed. "Well, to be honest with you, Prince, you've caught me at a bad time. With the games being only a day away, I'm rather rushed. All day long travelers and caravans have been coming up this road. Most are people coming to see the games. We just managed to get everyone properly checked in before the sun went down. Now I still have to see that all our guests are in their appropriate locations and settled in for the night. As well, I have my troops to see to and the remaining preparations for the parade. I hope you will understand if I decline your offer—another time, perhaps?"

The captain turned to leave, but Naibor stopped the beleaguered man. "All that can wait, Captain; I need to talk with you."

Naibor knew Regg would not disobey, even though he caught a moment of anger flashing behind the captain's dark eyes. Regg was the captain of the guard, and his sworn duty was to the king and his family. Taking a seat in a chair across the table, the captain rubbed his large, strong hands over the rugged lines of his face.

The prince belched loudly when the beer in his stomach caused air to rise in his throat just as he was going to speak, but he ignored the captain's long-suffering look. "I am fully aware of how busy a time this is, Captain. I have some important preparations to make before the games as well, and for that I need some information from you." Naibor paused, licking his lips, unsure of how to find out what he needed to know. Then he asked straight out, "I would like you to tell me about the men in the guard, Captain—who they are and what they are like."

Captain Regg stared hard at the prince for a moment. "The whole guard?" the captain asked, disbelieving.

"I assure you, Captain," Naibor interrupted, suspecting the captain's thoughts, "I am not drunk. This information is of the utmost importance to me!"

"But I am in charge of over sixty men! That would take most of the night."

"Oh, all right then, tell me about the men who will be guarding the gates tomorrow."

"The guards at the gates will be increased during the games to ensure your safety, Prince. I have a list of who is on duty posted over here on the wall." Captain Regg walked over to the list hanging by the door and brought it over.

Naibor's anger toward the captain's presumptions and toward his own failure at not having noticed the list was quickly displaced as he greedily read over the list of names. *Nothing!* Naibor didn't recognize any of the names. *There must be someone.* He looked over the list again, noticing something he hadn't the first time.

"Captain? Why is this name crossed off the list?"

The captain looked where Naibor pointed. "Oh, Amon," he said, reading the name. "He is one of my errand runners, and his father is in the guard. Amon is a hardworking lad, and dependable, so I gave him an early chance at being a guard by posting him at the North Gate. I put him at the North Gate during the afternoon because I figured it was the place where he was least likely to run into any trouble. Unfortunately, Amon was found asleep when his relief arrived."

Prince Naibor looked delighted by the news.

"Maybe you do not understand, Prince. Any guard found asleep at his post is immediately dismissed from the guard. Amon's duty as a guard was short-lived, I'm afraid."

Naibor's face became unreadable. "I have a proposition for you, Captain. In order for the troops to become more familiar with me, and to reveal to them my interest with the military, why don't you give the boy another chance? He could be reinstated under my authority—with your approval, of course, if you think the boy is worthy."

"Amon is worth another chance, in my opinion. You might have guessed I'm rather fond of the boy. He has lost heart because of what happened, and it disturbs me to see him so. He would give anything to have a chance to make amends, but I could not allow him to do so on my authority. I think your offer will solve a lot of problems. You are gracious to give him another chance, although you surprise me by doing so."

"Well then, on my authority, Captain, Amon will again be placed as a guard at the North Gate. He can replace"—Naibor stopped to look at the schedule—"the two guards working tomorrow evening."

"Alone? I was going to put four men on tomorrow night because of the games. I don't think this is a good time for him to be alone on duty."

"But, Captain, you yourself said he was reliable. What better way for him to regain the trust of the guard? You can send some relief after it gets dark." Naibor saw the captain wasn't convinced. "At least give him the chance to be alone for a little while to prove himself."

"All right, I will let him guard the North Gate alone for one hour; after that, three other guards will join him. So if you will excuse me, Prince, I'll go and find Amon to see that he is prepared for duty."

"Captain, there is one more thing I need to know before you leave. Have many supplies come in for the games?"

"Supplies?" Captain Regg responded with a roll of his eyes.

"Prince, we have enough supplies to last this city a whole month of celebrating."

Satisfaction spread over Naibor's face. It would be easy for him to take what he needed for his own private celebration, and no one would notice.

"Thank you, Captain Regg," Naibor added, speaking to the back of the efficient man, watching as he left the barrack. "You have been more help than you could know."

CHAPTER 2

Prince Ranor was the last of the young royalty to arrive at the palace and gather with the others already waiting in the common room. Prince Baynor shut the large, decorative brass door behind him, knowing that the tapestried walls and thick woven rug would help to ensure their privacy. He had sent a message to the others, asking them to assemble as quickly as possible at his family's royal home. Princess Tayii and Princess Janii were standing in the middle of the room, talking quietly to each other while Prince Tybor and Princess Sanii stood intimately off to one side. Once they had greeted one another and seated themselves comfortably in the softly cushioned chairs, Prince Baynor thanked them all for coming.

Noticing that Baynor hadn't bothered to change his riding clothes, Princess Janii looked at him with her crystal-blue eyes and asked, "Is something wrong?"

"I'm not sure," he answered, knowing he couldn't fool her even if he tried. They knew each other too well for lies. She had been training as well; he could tell by the fact that her sunlight-colored hair was braided neatly down the back of her neck, away from the delicate features of her face.

"It doesn't seem as if there is, but that is what I'm hoping you can help me to decide. A messenger rushed this letter to me just before midday. It's from Prince Naibor. But it's addressed as much to all of you as it is to me. Let me read it to you:

> To my competitors in the Celebration Games,
>
> I have sent this letter to Prince Baynor, trusting that he will read this in your presence. I wish to extend my humble apologies to you all at my apparent lack of interest in maintaining a friendship with each of you. I sincerely hope that this will change hereafter. In the past, my rashness led to a rift in our relationships, and I would like to put an end to any differences we might have had. Please allow me the pleasure of having a banquet this evening, in honor of both you and the Celebration Games. I trust that you will not deny me this chance to set things right. I will expect you at the main palace when the bell tower announces the eve of night.
>
> Yours in Anticipation,
> Prince Naibor

No one spoke for a moment, and then Prince Ranor broke the silence. "He is an odd fellow, that Naibor. For the last few years, he has kept to himself and not been the least bit friendly toward any of us, and now he wants to throw a banquet in our honor. Even more surprising, he wants to honor the Celebration Games—an event for which he has loudly proclaimed his disrespect. I wonder why the sudden change of heart?" He raised a quizzical eyebrow. Ranor's black hair and beard were streaked with early gray, probably due to the stress of trade negotiations conducted in barbaric foreign lands. Set against his honest, dark eyes, it gave him quite a distinguished look.

"Perhaps he'd like a chance to flatter the next high king or high queen," Prince Tybor teased, looking over at Princess Sanii.

Her brown eyes danced merrily, and she looked back at him

with the trace of a smile on her lips. "What a thing to say, Tybor!" she said, unable to resist his charms.

Prince Tybor shrugged and looked the part of a mischievous child. It was hard for him to look otherwise with his baby face, wayward light brown hair, and good-natured grin. "You're right! He's much too proud to do something like that."

"You're positively unruly," Princess Sanii replied, giving him a lighthearted laugh. The gentle shaking of her head caused the rich brown hair that went all the way down her back to softly sway from side to side.

Prince Ranor looked at the couple that was soon to be married and laughed along with them. "Well, maybe he has changed. What do you think, Baynor?"

Prince Baynor had the instinct of a good commander, though he was still young enough not to have yet experienced a serious battle. The odd feeling he had concerning this matter perplexed him. "I'm not sure, but I think Prince Naibor is hiding something from us and that he has another reason planned for having this banquet. I do not think he is to be trusted."

"Surely you don't think that he intends any harm?" Princess Janii asked Baynor with a look of surprise.

"I can't say," he replied, "but I value each of your opinions about the matter."

"Prince Naibor has not been overly gracious toward us in the past, but I cannot believe that he would harm us," Prince Ranor pointed out to all those in the room. "After all, he is the high king's son and not a barbarian, and I've dealt with enough of those to know."

"If Prince Naibor did intend to harm us, what would he gain by doing so? The people would rebel against such a violent crime done by a prince, and certainly not reward him with the kingdom," added Tybor's sister, Princess Tayii. They both had the same hair and honey-colored eyes, but Tayii was generally the quieter of the two.

"What do you think, Tybor?" Tayii asked.

Tybor ran his fingers through his hair before giving his opinion. "I agree with my sister Tayii and the others. Prince Naibor would definitely not benefit by harming us, but perhaps he does have an alternative reason for hosting this banquet. He might want to size up his competitors, or something of that nature."

Prince Baynor waited until he had everyone's attention before he addressed his friends. His imposing figure received immediate results. Everything about him spoke of power and strength, except for the kindness in his soft brown eyes that allowed others to be at ease in his presence.

Baynor's eyes became serious before he began. "I do not doubt that you have given me good counsel, but I have decided against going to the banquet."

"It is not like you to be so mistrusting, Baynor," Janii said softly to the man she loved. "You know it is not beyond any man to have a change of heart—especially in times of great distress. We could hardly break Naibor's good faith by not going."

"A banquet would probably do us all some good, considering all the preparations and training we have been doing. Why not be good to yourself and come?" Tybor said, trying to encourage his friend. "While we are there, Baynor, I promise you that we will keep an eye out for anything amiss. You worry too much. Tomorrow will come and go, and we will have a new king or queen to celebrate in a feast."

"Tybor, you should know that I love a feast as much as any man—maybe more. My decision, however, has not changed. I hope I am wrong and all goes well with you tonight, but I will not be going. Please ask Naibor to forgive my absence; I have some things to take care of before tomorrow. Until then, my friends, my best wishes go with you all."

Not long after his guests left, Prince Baynor sat in his favorite chair and reread the letter. There was nothing in it to account for his uneasiness, but if he couldn't trust his instincts, then what could he trust?

Baynor thought back to the friendship he had shared with

Naibor when they were boys. The two of them had gotten into a fair bit of mischief together and at times had been inseparable. They had become even closer friends during the time when Naibor's mother was sick, and they had remained close after she died. They had always shared a lot of the same interests. The trouble in their friendship began when they both took interest in Princess Janii.

Prince Baynor remembered clearly the day when Naibor confided to him that he was in love with the princess. Nervously sharing a poem he had just finished, Naibor confessed that he had sent poems to Janii that had taken him hours to write. Baynor, concerned for his friend's feelings, was unable to tell Naibor that he and Janii were already courting. When Baynor finally told him the truth, Naibor, in a rage, accused him of stealing Janii's affection. Baynor asked Prince Naibor to forgive him for any misunderstanding, but Naibor refused, saying that their friendship was over. All subsequent attempts by Baynor to reestablish their friendship failed. Naibor made it clear that he would not forget what he considered Baynor's betrayal. Naibor declared that as long as Baynor and Janii were together, he and Baynor could never be friends.

Suddenly Baynor realized what was wrong with the letter—it did not acknowledge Naibor's true feelings. Prince Naibor would never give up without a fight!

* * *

Prince Naibor lay with his boots dangling over the end of his bed, staring at the designs on the smoky bronze tiles that covered the ceiling. He was feeling pleased with himself. Everything was going well. The preparations for the feast had all been taken care of, a letter had been sent to his fellow competitors inviting them to the feast, and Amon was to be alone on guard when Necros arrived at the gate.

Necros had told him that all would happen just as they had planned, but Naibor had not been so sure. Now he wondered if

Necros knew something he did not. Could it be that the sorcerer could read into the future as well?

Naibor was once again lost in his thoughts of being king when he heard a soft knock on his door. "Yes, what is it?" he lazily inquired.

"Am I disturbing you?"

"Father!" Recognizing the voice, Naibor sat up quickly in surprise before the high king entered the room.

"When I sent for a servant, I found that they were all busy running errands for you. So I decided to come and find out the reason for all the activity."

Naibor was about to bow low over one knee in the traditional manner when his father came over and embraced him in a tight hug. "You look good, my son. It has been too long since I last saw you."

It was not often that the father and son saw each other, although they lived in the same palace. The king was a busy man who spent his time attending court, listening to reports, and consulting with his advisors. Naibor was a grown man concerned with his own affairs.

There had been a time when father and son had been close, but that was before the death of Naibor's mother. She died when he was at the tender age of twelve. Just when Naibor needed his father most, the king withdrew from him in his grief, spending hours in private prayer and time alone with only his closest advisors. The young prince was left feeling he had lost both of his parents. For two years, the high king neglected both his kingdom and his son. When he tried to make amends, he was able only to reestablish a relationship with the people of Amuron. His son remained distant.

The prince examined his father carefully. His heavy build, broad shoulders, black hair, and blue eyes were like his own, with the exception of the trim beard. His father's movements were deliberate and steady, and his countenance calm. This was the way his father always seemed, but there was also a noticeable difference in him. He seemed to stoop under the weight of an invisible burden. The prince also noticed black circles under his father's tired eyes, as well as deep lines of worry creasing his forehead. Naibor had not seen his father look this distressed in a long time, not since his mother's sickness and death almost ten years before.

"Father, is something wrong? You look troubled."

The king dismissed the question with a reassuring smile. "I have not been sleeping too well lately. But now tell me, why is it all the palace servants are rushing so madly about?"

Naibor's confident mood broke out in a laugh. "Well, Father, tonight I am hosting a banquet, and I have invited my peers to join me in a feast of celebration before the games tomorrow."

"You are having a feast of celebration with your competitors? This is good news!" His father looked much relieved. "But forgive my surprise. It is the high king's job to worry about his people, and it is a father's job to worry about his son. I have inquired of Elbanor concerning you as the games approached, and his reports did not ease my fears."

"What did he say?" Naibor asked defensively. "I wouldn't take his reports too seriously."

"He told me only what I already suspected: that you were downcast and not preparing yourself for the competition. I have known for a long time about your desire to become high king and about your bitterness toward the Celebration Games. I feared that your anger toward the games would interfere with your chance to become high king. But you seem to be at peace with it now, and I am very much relieved. My heart has been heavy for several days now. A terrible foreboding came upon me, such as I have never known, and I feared something was terribly wrong—that some horrible disaster was about to occur. Do you think anything will go wrong during the games tomorrow?" The king studied his son, waiting for his response.

Naibor felt a sudden flare of anger toward his father's inquiry. "I think everything will go as planned," he answered dryly, looking his father straight in the eye.

"Good," his father responded with a sigh. "It is good we have had this talk."

In reply, Naibor knelt on one knee in a bow to the high king. The prince did not rise until his father's patterned robe left the room and the door closed behind him.

* * *

Prince Naibor began preparing himself for the events of the evening soon after his father's departure. It was not often that the high king's son bothered to dress in anything other than the loose-fitting clothes of a commoner, much to the court tailor's dismay, but tonight was different! Tonight he would proudly wear the tight-fitting formal attire of a prince.

Naibor pushed the gold buttons smoothly through the rich, deep blue cloth of his coat, admiring his reflection on the shiny metal inside the doors of the wardrobe. The family colors of blue, white, and gold looked good on him, though not much of the white satin from his pants showed between the length of his coat and his tall black boots. Smoothing the hair back from his face using scented oil, Naibor felt confident that even Princess Janii would be impressed.

Satisfied that he was ready, the prince left his room and went down the back stairs leading to the servants' quarters. Making a left-hand turn at the bottom, he continued down the corridor toward the kitchen and the banquet hall to check on the preparations.

"How is everything?" the prince called out to the head servant in charge of the banquet arrangements, who was at that moment rushing out of one doorway and into the next.

The servant stopped midstride to answer. "Everything will be perfect for when your guests arrive, m' lord."

"Good, and everyone knows that they have the night off for working so hard for me today?" Naibor inquired, walking over to stand beside the servant.

"Yes, m' lord. I shall be the last to leave after the arrival of your guests. There's bound to be some good cheer in town tonight. Everyone really appreciates the time off." With a nod of his head in the prince's direction, the servant quickly disappeared down the stairs to the wine cellar.

Naibor unconsciously licked his lips as his eyes followed the servant down the cellar stairs. A sudden thirst for a quick drink seized him. He paused, but only briefly. He looked forward to celebrating his victory later on.

Continuing down the corridor, he came to a door at the end of the hall that led out to the stables. Stepping into the fresh evening air, Naibor wondered if it was his imagination that the air tingled with excitement. The sinking sun hung low on the horizon and the warm wind gently blew into his face, tousling his hair. Smiling to himself, the prince walked toward the glowing sun along the dirt lane that went from the stables to the North Gate.

The North Gate was not a main gate. It was a private gate used exclusively by the royal families for their personal business. This gate allowed them the freedom to go where they wished without having to pass through the city. It was the least used of all the gates and was usually watched by a rotating guard of only one or two men.

Prince Naibor called out a greeting when he entered the small guardhouse on the opposite side of the road leading up to the gate. As he had hoped, only the youth Amon was on duty inside the wooden building. Captain Regg had reinstated him as a guard earlier that day.

Recognizing who it was that had entered the building, Amon immediately got up from his chair. Keeping his head bowed, the youth saluted the prince by holding his right arm to his side at the elbow with his left hand. The guard's salute meant "I will not draw my sword against you."

The prince was surprised at the age of the lanky youth. Amon possessed a fresh-faced honesty, fair hair, and a wide smile of white teeth. He could not have been more than sixteen or seventeen years old, but it was also obvious that his father had taught him well concerning the proper conduct of a guard.

"How is your guard duty going, Amon?"

"Very well, thank you, sir." The youth punched the words out formally, but then he relaxed a little before adding, "I am glad you came by, Prince Naibor. I wanted to thank you for giving me another chance."

"Well, Captain Regg assured me of your competence, and I trust his judgement. I told him that a guard needs to be reliable—someone you can trust. I think I can trust you, Amon."

"I'm sure you can," Amon replied with a confident smile.

"Good. I'm glad to hear it, because I need you to do something for me. I am having a banquet at the palace tonight. One of the guests will soon be arriving at this gate, but I would like to keep it a secret. If you could not record his arrival, then you will have done me a favor."

"But m' lord, I can't do that! My duties as a guard require me to write down everyone who comes or goes through the gate—even you, sir."

"Yes, I know that, Amon," Naibor told him, trying to stay calm. "That is why I have chosen you to do this for me."

"But sir, I can't! I just got this position restored to me after having failed to do my duty, and now you're asking me to risk my job again?"

"Really, Amon," Naibor said, annoyed. "I'm only making a simple request."

"Then why does it matter to you so much if I write down your friend's arrival?" the youth protested a little too boldly before he could stop himself.

"That's none of your business. You will do as I ask! If you are so loyal to the guard, then your loyalty should also be to me. I was the one who secured your second chance as a guard. I can just as easily have you dismissed again for your rudeness and disobedience. Do you not realize that the whole guard is bound to service under oath to the high king and his family? Well, I am the high king's son, and that means you are bound to serve me. Do you understand? I want all comings and goings through this gate while you are alone on duty tonight unrecorded, as I have requested, or you can be sure you will never set foot in a guardhouse again—on my order!"

Amon's look of genuine surprise was quickly replaced by a look of anger. "All right," the youth coolly agreed, with his lips pressed into a line. "I'll do as you wish."

"Good for you, Amon! I knew you wouldn't let me down. Don't look so melancholy. Everything will work out. No one needs to know you did anything wrong. It's our secret, remember? Now I must get ready to meet my guest. He should be arriving soon. Please come and open the North Gate."

Amon obediently followed the prince outside to the small gate in the wall made of heavy iron bars. Naibor then stepped back to allow Amon room to open the door with an iron key.

"Thank you, Amon. Just leave the gate open and return to the guardhouse. I'll call you when it's time to close the gate."

"But I'm not supposed to leave the gate open, let alone unattended!"

"Now, Amon," Naibor replied sternly, pointing a finger at the young guard's face. "Let's not have any argument over this. I said I'll call you when it's time to close the gate!" Amon stood up to the prince's gaze for a moment before backing down.

Naibor felt a little sorry for the boy as he watched the youth walk back and enter the guardhouse. Then the prince went through the gate and looked north along the route he had previously taken to meet with the sorcerer. There was no sign of him in any direction. "Come on, Necros," Naibor muttered impatiently, "you had better not be late. The evening bell will be ringing soon, and that's when the guests for the banquet will start to arrive."

A nagging doubt began to plague Naibor as he watched the sun slip slowly behind the tops of the trees, creating a warm orange glow in the sky. Perhaps he had been fooled and Necros never intended to come in the first place. It was a horrible thought, but Naibor began to fear it was the truth.

The wind blew a little colder, and a bird squawked in the twilight.

"That's it!" the prince announced angrily, scanning his surroundings for any sign of Necros. "I cannot wait any longer."

Turning to go back through the gate, he heard a voice behind him say, "I am here, Prince."

Startled, Naibor jumped. Behind him stood the sorcerer, where just a moment ago there had been no one. "Necros?! Where did you come from? How did you get here? I just …"

"I am here, Prince. That's all that matters." The two faced each other like opposing champions before a competition.

Prince Naibor eyed Necros warily. The sorcerer wore a heavy traveler's cloak that covered his head and fell to below his knees. Necros appeared to be hiding something beneath its folds. A timely gust of evening air opened the front of the gray cloak, pushing the hood back from the blind sorcerer's face. During that momentary glimpse, the prince saw nothing unusual. The misgivings came from somewhere else. Something in Naibor's subconscious fought to be heard—a voice of reason. The voice warned him that the sorcerer was not to be trusted—that Necros was not what he seemed. Disturbed by what he thought to be nothing more than childish fears, the prince reassured himself that everything would be all right.

"Good, but we had better hurry," Naibor snapped tensely. He walked briskly toward the gate, only to be stopped by the words "Not yet, Prince."

Surprised, Naibor turned back to find the sorcerer had not followed.

"What do you mean?" Naibor inquired. "The guests will be arriving any moment!"

"We will not be late. There is time yet before they arrive."

Seemingly unaware of Naibor's urgency, Necros carefully

scratched strange symbols into the dirt with a sharp stone. "There is something that we still have to do."

Naibor's muscles tightened with anxiety as the twilight steadily deepened, but Necros was deep in concentration. The sorcerer stared with his sightless eyes at the ground where he had drawn the symbols, as if he could will them to life. Drawn by curiosity, the prince moved over to the side of the old conjuror. Naibor then realized that Necros was without the strange device that gave him sight.

Still in deep concentration, the sorcerer pulled a small drawstring pouch from his robes. Muttering words too quietly for Naibor to hear, Necros sprinkled a fine dry powder over each of the harshly formed marks on the ground. He then returned the pouch to the pocket beneath the folds of cloth and withdrew a small ornate sheath containing his ceremonial dagger.

"Here!" Necros instructed, holding out the dagger. "Cut your finger with this. To break the law of banishment, I must be pardoned with blood. The law of higher powers states that in order for there to be a pardon, innocent blood must be offered as a sacrifice. Fortunately in this case, Prince, all that is required is a few drops of royal blood. I cannot enter the city unless you let me finish the ritual."

The prince took the dagger and made a tiny cut in his left index finger. A small line of red quickly appeared, followed by a growing bead of blood.

"Is it cut?"

"Yes."

Grabbing for Naibor's hand, Necros squeezed the prince's finger so that a drop of blood fell over the top of each of the symbols.

"There! It is done!" the sorcerer said with finality, releasing the prince.

Looking heavenward while raising both of his hands in the air, Necros called out triumphantly, "Never again, while I am living, can I be banished from this kingdom."

The surrounding darkness was now complete.

CHAPTER 3

A rich, deep note rang out from the West Gate bell tower, announcing the eve of night.

"We must hurry, Prince; your guests will soon be arriving."

Naibor snorted indignantly in reply. "It's not my fault that we are not already there to greet them."

Following Necros through the gate, a sudden thought caused Naibor to stop and question the mysterious man. "Necros, how can you see? You are not wearing the eye."

Necros did not stop to answer, so Naibor continued after him.

"There are many ways to see without the use of your eyes, Prince. Besides, have you forgotten? I used to live here. I know the place quite well. Oh, and Prince," Necros added in the same breath, "don't forget the gatekeeper. He is waiting to close the gate."

Naibor's anger rose quickly, reddening his cheeks. His heated thoughts flashed like lightning cutting though the center of a storm. Once again he was made to appear the incompetent fool, and Necros the superior. He was supposed to become high king, yet he was not the one giving the orders.

Raising his voice, the prince spoke to Necros with well-practiced authority, hoping to conceal the inferiority he felt. "You go on ahead.

I'll catch up with you in a moment and let the guests in." Naibor hoped that Necros understood that he wanted to greet his guests.

The old sorcerer kept on walking as if he hadn't heard, barely visible in the darkness next to the wall of blackstone.

Frustrated, Naibor jogged back to the guardhouse where Amon was already waiting outside in the shadows for him. As Naibor approached, the young guard stepped into the lighted doorway, startling the prince.

"You … you can lock the gate now, Amon." Naibor inadvertently gasped while trying to catch his breath.

"I already did," Amon responded flatly.

Naibor tried to fix his eyes on Amon, noting the change in his tone, but the light that framed the youth in the doorway completely overshadowed his face.

"What do you mean?" the prince asked, stiffening defensively.

"I heard you leave" was Amon's only explanation.

"Oh, well, thank you, Amon. I assure you, you have done yourself a service." Feeling he had wasted enough time, Naibor muttered a "return to your duties" and quickly made a return trip back up the lane.

The youth watched him leave, feeling his temporary boldness give way to dismay. Concerned about the amount of time the prince had taken in returning to the guardhouse, Amon had gone out to the gate. Hidden by the approach of night and the arching black stone of the wall, Amon watched in horror while Naibor and Necros completed their ritual.

After the prince and his guest had left, Amon had quickly shut and locked the gate. The thick iron bars, however, did not make him feel safe. Out in the blackness, Amon imagined he saw floating, lidless eyes staring at him, and he stumbled back to the guardhouse feeling cold and numb.

Falling into the well-used wooden chair, the young guard sprawled half his body over the table with his head between his arms. His mind reeled with the realization that Prince Naibor had brought a sorcerer into Amuron. Everyone knew that sorcerers and their evil arts were forbidden in the city. Amon could not believe this was happening. He had thought the prince was on his side, but now he realized the prince had only intended to use him for his own private purposes. It was obvious why Prince Naibor had not wanted him to record the entry of his special guest. The high king's own son had used him to go against the written law.

"Prince Naibor must think I'm a fool," Amon said, speaking his furious thoughts aloud. "Captain Regg wondered why he had me reinstated as a guard and put on duty by myself at the North Gate. I guess the captain had good reason to be suspicious. I was just glad to have a second chance. Prince Naibor must have thought it would be easy to sneak a sorcerer into the city while I was on duty, but he won't get away with it!" Amon slapped his hand down hard onto the table.

All of Amon's puzzled thoughts seem to fit into place except one: why was the high king's son sneaking a sorcerer into the city?

The youth knew that whatever the reason, it couldn't be good. He had to think of what to do next. Sounding the alarm was out of the question. The alarm was used only if the city was under attack. Amon wished desperately that Captain Regg would come by to check on him, but the captain was busy preparing for the games and would not be able to visit him tonight. *Preparing for the games!* Amon suddenly realized why the prince had brought a sorcerer into the city.

Scraping the chair across the floor in his haste, Amon pushed himself away from the table. He felt he couldn't wait for the relief guard to arrive. Every moment wasted could lead to disaster. There was only one person Amon could tell what he had seen. That one person had to be told, and he had to be told now!

An unsettling thought flashed through the youth's mind as he shut the door to the guardhouse. *Maybe I wasn't meant to be a guard after all.* Leaving his post, he hurried down the dark road surrounded by the shadows of seemingly innocent night.

* * *

Amon barely heard the waters laughing in the fountain on the lawn in front of the palace as he leaped up the steps to the Hall of Justice and entered the great hall—the Hall of Hearing.

Closing the large, heavy oak door behind him, Amon looked around the lofty chamber with astonishment. He had heard people talk about the size of the great hall, but it was even larger and more impressive than he had ever imagined. Giant pillars of white marched in two columns down either side of a central hall and rose to a vaulted ceiling made of burnished brass. The floor of blackstone, stretching out before the youth, appeared to be a long pond of still, deep water. The reflection cast by magnificent chandeliers from high above sat like a bright mist upon its shiny surface. At the far end of the hall, Amon could see the high king's throne on a dais. Behind the throne were tall paneled windows filled with colored glass. On either side of the throne were rows of chairs where the high king's advisors sat when the king held public audiences.

Amon hurried past the pillars quietly, afraid of disturbing the room's solemn peacefulness. The throne and the accompanying seats were empty, but Amon was not surprised at this. Instead he turned to the left and approached a small marble table that stood between two of the pillars. A round chime hung down from a stand that sat in the center of the table. A small stick with a round head also lay on the table. Without hesitation, Amon picked up the stick and struck the chime.

The note from the chime sang out clean and clear. It was a note that demanded attention and called for a response. Amon waited and was perplexed. No one responded! In the Hall of Hearing, everyone was guaranteed to be heard. Someone should have answered the call of the chime.

Letting go of the breath he was unconsciously holding, the youth wondered what to do next. *Why is nothing happening as it should?* After restlessly waiting a few minutes more, Amon decided to carry out his plan despite the setback.

Adjacent to the empty dais, he entered a hallway used to gain access to the palace. The walls were covered in panels of carved stone, each one depicting a different scene of the Celebration Games. At the end of this short passageway was a door. Boldly turning the knob, Amon entered the palace. Continuing onward, the youth passed several chambers with open doors and many others that were closed. These were the chambers belonging to the high king's advisors. He wished an advisor were there now to guide him.

Heading into the heart of the palace, the young guard's urgency increased. Amon passed scenic paintings, colorful tapestries, and quiet garden courts with sculpted statues, but he still did not find the person he was seeking.

The palace was an enormous building consisting of several smaller buildings joined together, and Amon found it strangely quiet and empty for what he imagined to be the center of the city. Where were all the people coming and going on important business? Where were the servants that worked for the high king? And, most importantly, where were the palace guards?

The main hall he was following eventually opened into a large oval chamber. Reverent paintings of past high kings lined the gently curving walls. In the center of the room, water cascaded down the sides of a small tiered fountain. Over on the right, a sweeping staircase of colored stone rose to the next level.

Open to his left were large, intricately carved wooden doors that revealed an open foyer. Turning from the double doors, Amon approached the remaining door under the staircase balcony. He could see a garden beyond the door's glass panels. Seeking to be refreshed, Amon opened the door and entered the secluded courtyard. It seemed to the youth as if he had been wandering around for hours, but it was still early evening and the moon had not yet started to rise into the sky.

Amon gulped down several big breaths of the fragrant garden air. Feeling his spirits revive, he followed a white stone path to a similar door on the other side of the courtyard and reentered the palace. Down the hall on the right were two palace guards standing beside a closed door. Amon knew he had found the high king!

"What is it you wish, sentry?" one of the high king's personal guards inquired as Amon approached.

"I have an important message for the high king."

"The king does not wish to be disturbed. I will pass your message to my lord."

Amon felt small and insignificant as he stood facing the highly trained and skilled fighters. Their crisp white uniforms contrasted sharply against the black of his own uniform. The guard waited patiently for Amon to state his message, but Amon remained steadfast. A sentry would not normally object to passing a message to a member of the Personal Guard, but Amon believed this to be a private matter.

"When do you expect the king to be free?" the youth asked sheepishly. "I … I … My message is for the high king only."

The other guard explained tolerantly, "The high king is at prayer and cannot be disturbed. I expect him to be busy for most of the night. He usually is. If you are not going to tell us your message, you had better leave and try again in the morning."

"But this is urgent!" Amon's voice rose in frustration. "I must speak with him!"

"Quiet!" the first guard ordered. "The high king is not to be disturbed! You will leave now, or I will take you to the guardhouse and lock you up!"

Amon was about to try to fight the guards to reach the door when the door suddenly opened and Amon found himself standing face-to-face with the high king. Each of the king's guards jumped to attention, and Amon immediately dropped down on one knee rather ungracefully.

"Your Majesty, I must speak with you!" Amon stated adamantly.

"I'm sorry, my lord, but this sentry has been quite insistent about seeing you, despite my warnings that you were not to be disturbed."

"Well then," the high king replied, "perhaps you have some

information that I was hoping to learn through my prayers. Come in, sentry, and tell me your news."

Amon got up and stepped through the door at the king's invitation.

The king remained for a moment longer to say, "Thank you, guards. Once again I must ask you for some peace." The door closed, and the personal guards resumed their positions on either side of the door.

* * *

No sooner had Prince Naibor stepped back inside the palace than he heard the chime announcing the arrival of his guests. He could not see Necros, but he had no time to search for him now. Tugging on his jacket and smoothing down his hair, the prince paused to take a breath before opening the door. "Welcome!" he exclaimed, inviting them in with a sweep of his hand.

Princess Janii entered first. "Good evening, Naibor," she said pleasantly, with just a hint of anticipation in her voice.

The light, floral fragrance from the oil she had bathed in tantalized Naibor. Her milky-white skin and delicate features, which were at once childlike and womanly, drove all other thoughts from his mind. Her silky pale blue gown complemented the color of her eyes and reflected her clean, elegant style. Gathered at the waist, it had delicate beadwork around the bodice and down the length of the sheer sleeves. Janii was beautiful. Naibor could have admired her all evening, but the other guests had started to follow her in, and he knew he must greet them as well.

Princess Sanii and Princess Tayii also looked lovely as they entered and warmly greeted their host, but Naibor only had eyes for Janii. Tayii's brother, Prince Tybor, entered next, quickly followed by Prince Ranor. Tybor and Ranor both handed Naibor the short swords that hung at the sides of their tunics as part of their formal attire. It was customary for guests to offer their swords to the host upon arrival, thus ensuring the host of his guests' good intentions. After taking their swords, Naibor noticed Baynor's absence. A worried frown creased his forehead. Momentary panic seized him. "Where is Prince Baynor?" he demanded anxiously.

"I'm sorry, Naibor," Janii said, catching the worry in Naibor's voice, "but Baynor was unable to come this evening. He sends his regrets."

Naibor quickly got his emotions under control. "Oh, I'm sorry to hear that. I was especially hoping that he would be here tonight."

This did not seem unreasonable. They all knew that Baynor and Naibor had been close friends as boys.

"This banquet is a splendid idea," Prince Ranor enthused. "It's just what is needed to break the tension before the games."

"Well then, let's get started," Prince Naibor said, leading the way.

The palace banquet hall was one of the most beautiful works of art in the kingdom. Opening the rose-colored glass doors, Prince Naibor revealed a marvelous garden created from carved stone. The white marble pillars were carved to look like a forest of slim trees with fine branches. These branches intertwined to support the crystal panels of the domed roof. Vine garlands of flowers, and fluttering birds made of colored stone and embedded with semiprecious stones, graced the pillar trees and accented the surrounding cornice. In front of the doors to the outside garden stood a gently flowing fountain. Carved delicately from rose-tinted crystal, it was shaped in the likeness of a freshly blooming flower. Water captured in the fountain glowed and shimmered, quietly reflecting the light that surrounded it.

Ushering his guests toward the table in the center of the hall, Naibor searched the room for Necros. He was waiting there for them. Standing off to one side of the fountain, he looked like a meek traveling musician cradling an instrument in his arms. Naibor himself was startled by the change in his appearance, even though he knew this was part of the plan. Traveling musicians were commonly blind, and this disguise was the perfect way for Necros to attend the private party.

While his guests were admiring their surroundings, Naibor took a moment to sneak over to the pretend musician. "Necros," Naibor whispered desperately, "Prince Baynor isn't here! He's not coming! What are we going to do?"

"Prince, calm down! Let's not make our friends suspicious. He'll come."

"But …"

"I said he'll come! Now go back to your guests."

"Look, Tybor," Princess Sanii said, leaning on his arm, "Prince Naibor has hired a musician for the evening. How thoughtful."

Naibor, overhearing what was said, walked over to the couple. "Let me introduce you to V—Vol …" he said, stumbling over the name.

Necros helped him. "Volkas."

"Volkas," Naibor continued. "He will provide our entertainment for this evening."

The blind musician took a step toward the sound of the group and nodded. "I'm at your service, m' ladies and lords."

"A foreign name," Prince Ranor commented, trying to place the origin of the name. "Strogarian, isn't it? I know many Strogarian families."

The disguised sorcerer responded with a humble grin.

Naibor cleared his throat with a loud "Ahem!" to draw attention, not wanting Ranor to delve into a family history that did not exist. "Volkas, why don't you play us a tune?"

Necros began to strum a lively tune on his instrument, and as if on cue from the music, the guests settled themselves comfortably around the table. Prince Naibor sat at one end, with the ladies seated to his left and the men to his right. Naibor noticed that Janii just happened to sit the farthest away from him.

When the friendly applause for the music ended, Prince Naibor addressed his guests. "Friends, I invite you to enjoy yourselves and help yourselves to whatever you desire." He gestured to the table in front of him, which was covered from one end to the other with a wide variety of delicious delicacies.

There were platters of succulent meat, some hot and some cold, accompanied by a variety of flavorful sauces. Sitting among the platters of meat were colorful bowls of favorite vegetable dishes and mounds of decoratively arranged fruit. Breads and sweets were not forgotten. There was a rich assortment of both of these, as well as golden pitchers filled with refreshing beverages. Decorative oil lamps sat on the table, adding a rich, warm glow over all.

Princess Tayii gratefully thanked their host. "This is wonderful, Naibor."

Prince Ranor added his praise. "This is truly a feast! You've got enough food here to feed the entire guard!"

"You forget he was expecting Baynor to come," Prince Tybor quipped, unable to resist.

"Nonsense, he just knows how to set an impressive table for his guests," Princess Sanii remarked, giving Tybor a warning glance.

"Of course, and tonight we all get to eat like royalty, courtesy of our host," Tybor replied innocently, returning Sanii's glance.

Naibor did not find his guests amusing, but he was relieved that they seemed to be enjoying themselves. It gave him confidence that his plan with the sorcerer would work. Seeing his guests helping themselves to both food and drink, he rose from his seat at the end of the table.

"A toast," Prince Naibor began, lifting his goblet. "A toast to beautiful ladies and worthy competitors." The guests raised their cups in reply and all took a drink.

When Naibor finished, Prince Ranor rose next to propose a toast. "To the new high king and a …" He stopped because of certain displeased looks. "Er, sorry. To the new high queen or high king, and a peaceful kingdom." Flashing the ladies a winsome smile, he took a drink from his cup. The others joined him, laughing good-naturedly at his slipup.

"I hope you saved some for me," announced a voice from the front of the banquet hall. All eyes turned to see Prince Baynor standing in the doorway.

"Baynor!" Prince Naibor exclaimed, jumping up in surprise. He hastily glanced over at Necros and caught his knowing smile. Stepping away from the table, he went to greet his newly arrived guest. "Baynor, how good to see you!"

"Naibor, I am truly sorry that I am late, but it turned out that I was able to come after all. I hope you don't mind that I let myself in, but there does not seem to be anyone about." Baynor looked at him closely, searching for answers, but Naibor held his gaze, unafraid of the scrutiny. He knew that Baynor's arrival was a sign to him that everything would go as planned. Nothing could stop it now.

* * *

"Come in, Baynor, and join your friends," Prince Naibor encouraged, smiling with pleasure. "The fun is just beginning." Turning to the pretend musician, he added, "Volkas, another tune, please."

Necros began to play a popular ballad from his seat on a stool behind Naibor, while Baynor eased himself into the chair opposite Janii.

"I'm glad you could make it, Baynor," Prince Tybor said, watching him pile his plate high. "You would have been disappointed if you hadn't come."

"I'm sure I would have," Baynor replied without mirth.

Janii leaned across the table and whispered, "What do you mean?"

Hoping the music would drown their conversation, Baynor replied, "Naibor is lying. He is hiding something from us. I came because I felt I can better help you here, if Naibor tries to harm you."

Janii frowned. "If he plans to harm us, he is slightly outnumbered."

Noticing that Naibor was watching them, Baynor asked Janii to pass some more food.

Naibor, however, was not concerned with what they were saying. All he noticed was the way Janii looked earnestly into Baynor's eyes. "Baynor, you missed our toast. Perhaps you would like to make one."

"All right," Baynor replied, standing to do so, "To good health, honest friends, and fair competition." Once again the others sipped from their goblets.

"Ooh," Princess Sanii moaned suddenly, putting a hand to her forehead.

"What's wrong?" Prince Tybor asked, getting up from his seat and hurrying around the table to where Sanii sat.

"Oh, I have such a pounding in my head," she answered, turning terribly pale.

"Let me see if I can help," Tybor said with concern, gently taking her head in his hands.

Then Prince Baynor watched as each of his friends sank unconscious to the floor. "Naibor, what have you done?" he demanded, for they were apparently the only ones not affected, besides the musician.

"It is too late now, Baynor," Naibor said, feeling strangely giddy.

"I suspected as much. You drugged the wine, didn't you?" Baynor accused, lunging toward Naibor with contempt in his eyes.

Naibor quickly stepped back, putting the table between them.

"You won't get away with it," Baynor continued, "because I didn't drink any of the wine!"

Lunging over the table, Baynor grabbed Naibor by the throat of his tunic with his large fist. Naibor struggled, but he was unable to pull free from the tight grip.

"No, Prince Baynor, you are incorrect. It is not the wine, as you suspect," the strange musician explained, stepping between them at the end of the table like a referee at the games.

"It is a powder mixed into the oil in the lamps. The magic in the powder is being released as the oil burns and fills the air. That is what has affected your friends. Since you have not been here as long as they have, it has not affected you yet. Prince Naibor has drunk the antidote, so he won't be affected.

Prince Baynor looked at the little man incredulously, loosening his grip enough for Naibor to break free. Thinking quickly, Baynor strode over to the patio doors to let in some fresh air, but Necros was quicker. Blocking his way, the tricky sorcerer blew some of the noxious powder into Baynor's face, causing the last guest of the party to collapse unconscious to the floor.

Naibor came out from behind the table, not knowing what to do next. "You were right, Necros! Everything happened just as you said it would."

"Of course," the sorcerer answered, as if he were speaking to a child. "Nothing can go wrong." Then, turning toward the entrance to the banquet hall, he spoke some strange and twisted words in a commanding voice. From the shadows on either side of the doorway, two figures emerged. Each figure was dressed in a black floor-length robe. Their faces were completely hidden by their overhanging hoods.

Naibor stared in disbelief. It looked as if the shadows had struggled free from the corners and come to life. He shuddered at their sinister appearance. "Necros, who are they?" Naibor asked, almost dreading to hear the truth.

"They are my servants—helpers, if you like. I need them to help me with certain tasks. Remember, Prince: I am not as young as I would like to be."

Both black figures stepped forward and bowed in unison to Necros. Silent instructions passed between them, and then the sorcerer dismissed them. Immediately they began to lift the unconscious guests, one at a time, and carry them away to the wine cellar.

"Don't just stand there," Necros told Naibor, while moving to the table to take a seat. "They will take care of things for a while. Come." He began filling a plate. "Come and enjoy yourself. Sit down and eat!"

The prince sat at the table, but he couldn't eat. He watched the dark figures as if he were watching a dream. They carried each guest effortlessly and without sound—even Baynor! It hardly seemed real to Naibor, and he suddenly felt things had gotten out of control. *Maybe this wasn't such a good idea after all*, he concluded.

"Having second thoughts, Naibor?" Necros asked, squinting his sightless eyes at him. Momentary silence followed. Putting down his forkful of food, Necros laughed. "The best is yet to come," he promised.

Necros's silent servants completed their task just as their master finished his last plateful. "Well," the contented sorcerer said, pushing away his empty plate, "that was delicious! I haven't had food this good for a long time—in fact, not since I last lived in Amuron. You can well imagine that food in the Ancient City is scarce. If I hadn't had a servant sending me provisions, I might not have survived."

Turning from the table, the sorcerer questioned the shadowy forms standing patiently to one side, as if he were questioning the cook about the next course. "Are our guests ready?" One answered with a nod of his head.

Looking from the sorcerer to the frightening figures, Naibor felt his stomach drop.

"It's time to go and look after your guests, Prince," Necros announced, rising from the table. The aged sorcerer stared powerfully at the prince with his discolored eyes, compelling him with his will to obey. Necros had spent a lifetime of plotting and planning, training his secret servant within the palace to cast spells against the prince in order to wear him down and make him obedient in a situation just like this. Bowing his head in a subservient manner, Naibor stood, and together they walked out of the banquet hall to the stairs of the wine cellar.

Reaching the same stairs he had earlier longed to go down, the prince now felt differently. A feeling of hopelessness began to slowly coil itself up and around Naibor's body, slowing his movements and constricting his chest, leaving him short of breath. He tried to swallow, but the lack of moisture in his throat made it nearly impossible. The voice he heard earlier in his head returned, this time more forcefully. Like the toll of a signal bell, it warned him to stop what he was doing, urging him to tell the sorcerer to leave. Naibor wanted to stop, but he felt it was too late. He had gone too far to back out now.

"After you," Necros said with mock politeness before following closely behind the prince as he went down the worn wooden steps to the cellar.

It was dark in the small stairway, but Naibor knew his way down these stairs so well it did not matter. Weak lamplight came from the doorway below on the left. Stopping on the bottom step, the prince realized that if he went any farther, he would have only himself to blame for what was about to occur. Sensing Necros shift impatiently behind him in the dark, he entered the awaiting room.

As he feared, his fellow competitors were no longer unconscious but awake and trying to free themselves from the posts they were securely tied to. Only Baynor remained unconscious, his head still drooped upon his chest from the strong effect of Necros's powder.

"It was the best I could do, Prince, seeing as this is not a proper dungeon," Necros commented while going over to check on the tightness of the knots.

"Naibor, what is going on?" Ranor demanded, but the prince did not respond.

"Well, what do you think of your guests now?" The disdain in the sorcerer's voice was clear. "Not much of a challenge," he scoffed, waiting intently for the prince's reaction. His power over Naibor's mind was increasing, and soon the prince would be entirely under his control. All Naibor had to do was succumb to his feelings of anger. Then Necros could use him fully.

Naibor looked at each of his competitors, and he felt an uncontrollable rage rising within him. They stood struggling against their bonds, looking so helpless and defeated. Was it his fault they were so easily captured? He realized they weren't so intimidating after all. He had spent so much time believing his fate during the Celebration Games rested in their hands, and yet here they were, at his mercy.

"What are you doing, Naibor?" Princess Janii demanded. "Why are we tied up down here?"

"The prince has arranged for you to miss the games tomorrow," Necros explained, smiling guilefully.

There was silence while the captives tried to figure out what was meant by this. They didn't like the look on Prince Naibor's face or anything about their situation.

"I hope you don't mean this as some kind of joke." Prince Tybor frowned with disapproval. Naibor's replying scowl assured Tybor that he didn't.

"Naibor, be sensible!" Princess Sanii cautioned. "The games will just be postponed if we don't arrive as expected. You would be wise to let us go now, before this goes any further."

Janii tried another tactic. "Naibor, we are your friends. We all understand the strain of the Celebration Games. Untie us, and together we can try to resolve this situation."

"You won't get away with this no matter what you plan to do; therefore, there is no sense in continuing," Prince Ranor added, impatient with Naibor's silence. "I see you're an accomplice to this, Volkas. Why don't you talk some sense into him before you get too deeply involved?"

"I've known you all my life, Naibor," Tybor began persuasively, "and you have always seemed rational …"

"Enough!" Prince Naibor shouted, ending any further arguments. All of their pleas and words had just made him angrier, not changed his mind. "You are all fine speechmakers, and I'm sure your speeches would have impressed the crowds during the Celebration Games. But I realize now that none of you are any better than I am and that none of you really care about me. Necros, cast your spell and turn them into animals. I am tired of listening to them."

"Very well, Prince." Necros nodded approvingly, pleased with the way the events were progressing.

Ranor spoke up again. "A sorcerer! Is that what the musician Volkas really is?"

"Yes, a sorcerer! And one who is very powerful. Let me introduce you to Necros, a sorcerer powerful enough to turn you all into animals and ensure me the throne."

The meek traveling musician they had seen in the banquet hall vanished. The rough-looking old and blind man standing before them now was much more menacing and proud.

"Naibor! No!" Janii cried out against Prince Naibor's intended betrayal.

The sorcerer lifted a hand and used his power so that the prisoners could no longer speak. Necros then reached inside his robes, bringing out his eye and the necklace that held it. The eye seemed to squirm out of control until he placed the necklace over his head and it hung down properly in front of him. Reaching into his robes again, the sorcerer withdrew his pouch of magic powder. With the pouch in his hand, he walked over to each of the captives and sprinkled some powder on top of their heads.

"There!" Necros took a satisfied step back. "All that remains now is for us to decide what animals they should become."

Necros walked over to where Prince Baynor was tied to a post close to the door and lifted his unconscious head by the chin. "This one has been such a bore. Don't you think? Ah, perfect!" he said with hideous glee. "A boar you shall be." Letting Baynor's head drop, the sorcerer reached up and placed his hand on top of Baynor's head. He then muttered the words of the incantation.

"Who's next?" Necros asked, moving to the other side of the rough wooden pillar. It was Prince Tybor. "You know, I never liked healers," Necros said, looking into Tybor's face with scorn. "They pretend to possess the power of healing but really know nothing about power at all. Any suggestions for this one?" Necros asked, looking over in Naibor's direction, but Naibor remained quiet.

"Look at those warm, sensitive eyes! Let me think a moment. I know! A mongrel. This healer will be a dog." Necros let out a crude laugh. Reaching up a hand, he again spoke some strange words.

Princess Sanii was tied to the next pillar, facing Tybor. Tears rolled down her cheeks as she watched her betrothed be humiliated. She hurried to conceal her tears from the sorcerer, but her attempt was in vain. "Tsk tsk," Necros chided, turning toward her. "Tears are for cowards, and cowards are nothing more than chickens, so the children say. That's what you shall be—a worrying hen."

When Necros had finished his incantation with Sanii, he walked around to the other side of the post and said two words as soon as he laid eyes on Prince Ranor. "A rat."

Although Naibor hated to admit it, he found the idea of the others being turned into a pig, a dog, a chicken, and a rat distasteful. He decided Necros was being overly cruel. Worse, Princess Janii was tied to the next pillar, and the prince could see that Necros was thoroughly enjoying himself. "Um, Necros." Naibor's voice faltered as the sorcerer walked up to her.

"Yes, Prince, you have a suggestion?"

"How about a bird? A dove maybe?"

Necros turned and scowled at him. "Don't be such an ass, Prince, or you'll spoil my mood. Ha, you've given me an idea! You, pretty thing," he said to Janii, "will be a donkey."

Naibor groaned as he watched Necros place his hand on Janii's head and say the incantation.

"And last but not least, we come to this silent beauty," Necros said, speaking to Princess Tayii. "And why has this beauty remained so silent? I see the reason." He tightened the ropes that held her hands. "She has managed to almost slip her hands free of these knots. Clever girl! She is standing so poised and so calm, so sleek and so slender. She reminds me of a black cat—The perfect pet for any sorcerer." Necros flashed a wicked smile.

"There!" Necros gloated when he had finished the last incantation.

"But Necros," Naibor said, somewhat confused, "they haven't changed!"

"No, not yet, but they will. The process takes time. I'm having them change from the inside out rather than the outside in, which would have killed them instantly. By morning they will have transformed."

CHAPTER 4

The warmth and peacefulness of the king's prayer room made it hard for Amon to tell the high king of his son's betrayal. Encouraged by the king's patience, Amon was able to tell him of the events he had seen and heard at the North Gate.

Leaving the comfort of the large cushioned chair, Amon looked down at the high king, who was sitting lost in thought. Amon still felt as though he had to help in some way, but he wasn't sure how. The cheerful light coming from the lamps on either side of the fireplace was not enough to dispel the heaviness in the room as he turned to go.

Stepping into the hallway, Amon paused, realizing something was wrong. The guards were gone! *Where could they be?* The high king's Personal Guard never left the king unattended. One might take a few moments of leave when necessary, but two guards would never leave together. Amon had an uneasy feeling about this, and he quickly shut the door behind him in an attempt to protect the king. Just then, two black-robed figures materialized in front of him. Amon had no time to defend himself or cry out. He felt their icy hands grip his shoulders with an unimaginable strength. One of the shadowy figures leaned forward and breathed into his face, releasing a black mist. The icy darkness turned Amon completely numb, and the youth fell unconscious into the arms of the other dark servant of Necros. Together they silently lifted and carried him away.

Following Necros up the narrow stairs out of the cellar, Prince Naibor fingered the small bottle of port he had secreted in his tunic pocket. He hoped it would help settle his nerves. His head pounded, and his body felt drained of energy, as if he had fought a long, hard battle with a skilled enemy.

Necros turned to Naibor when they reached the hallway at the top. "Console yourself with these thoughts, Prince. Tomorrow you shall become high king. You have participated in your own Celebration Games. In your own way, you have fought for your right to be high king, and you have won." Necros gestured toward the banquet hall. "Come. Let us work out our plans for tomorrow."

"Can't it wait until the morning, Necros? I just want to rest. I've had enough to think about for one day."

The sorcerer was about to tell the prince to go upstairs to his room when his dark servants came down the hall carrying something black and bulky between them.

Prince Naibor frowned at the sight of the eerie figures and the darkness that surrounded them. "Amon!" he gasped in surprise, recognizing the unconscious figure they carried. "What is he doing here?"

"You know who this is?" Necros asked, turning on the prince suspiciously.

"Yes, I do. This is Amon, the guard who was at the North Gate."

Satisfied with Naibor's answer, the sorcerer turned to question one of his black servants. "You found him in the palace?" A black hood bobbed up and down in reply.

"He must have told my father you are here," Naibor said with dismay. "What are we going to do?"

Necros closed his sightless eyes and stood deep in concentration. Opening his eyes, the sorcerer smiled with satisfaction and said, "It is of no consequence. Nothing will come of it."

"What should we do with Amon?" Naibor asked nervously.

"Take him downstairs and bind him," Necros ordered his servants. They immediately obeyed.

"Are you going to turn Amon into an animal too?"

"No. He will be sacrificed with the others tomorrow night," Necros replied indifferently.

"Sacrificed!" Naibor exclaimed, wide-eyed. "What do you mean sacrificed?"

"Tomorrow I will make a sacrifice to the god who has given me the power to help you, Prince. I am a sorcerer, after all."

"But you weren't supposed to kill them, remember—just turn them into animals. I don't want them killed!"

"Prince, Prince, remain calm. You must stop thinking of them as your friends. Tomorrow they will only be dumb, witless animals, the same as you would find at any animal market. I'll be sacrificing only a few animals to my god for making you high king. The worst is already over. The rest is just in your mind."

The prince felt a strange calm creep over him, despite his uneasiness. "Yes. Yes, that's fine," he found himself saying, with a thick and slow-moving tongue.

"Good. Now I want you to go upstairs and get some rest," Necros instructed.

Yes, that was what he needed—rest. But he was unable to get it just yet, for another sight caught his eye. It was a sight far worse than that of Amon—one that filled him with dread. Walking toward them down the hall was his father, the high king of Amuron.

"Necros, quick! Get out of here! Don't let my father see you," Naibor said, trying to hide the sorcerer behind him.

"It's too late for that!" Necros objected, stepping out into full view, and he hurriedly spoke to the black figures who had returned to his side. "Go and find my servant and have him bring what I need." They vanished as if they had never been.

Naibor braced himself and desperately tried to think of something to say. His father, however, spoke directly to Necros. "So you are the evil that has entered the city."

Necros smiled a wide smile and bowed his head with mock humility. "Yes, your son has allowed me that pleasure."

Facing the sorcerer, the king's eyes flashed with a bright light. "My son does not understand, as I do, what he has done; nor do you fully understand the consequences of your actions."

"You do not have the power to stop me," Necros snapped in a threatening tone.

"It is not my power that you have to worry about," replied the high king.

"Yes, you are right. I do not have to worry about your power, high king of Amuron, for you and your entire city are already under my control." Necros seemed to grow larger and more hideous as he said these words.

With a deft hand, the sorcerer reached into his tunic and pulled out something long and thin that gleamed evilly. It looked like a sliver of silver and was as sharp as death. Before Naibor could say or do anything, Necros threw the dart at his father. The poisoned silver plunged into the king's chest, melting into his flesh without leaving a mark. There was no sound—only the sight of the high king's shocked expression before he sank to the ground.

"Father!" Naibor cried out, rushing to his side.

Bending down, he felt his father's face and hands, but they were already cold. The prince's throat tightened, and tears blurred his eyes as he stood up. "What have you done to him? Why have you killed him?" Naibor shouted at Necros in a rage. "Why?" Tears of shock and grief flowed down Naibor's face while he stood before the sorcerer, searching for an answer.

"There cannot be two kings in the kingdom, Prince. Did you think the people would let you take the high king's place while he was still living? No, they would have let your father remain king. They would not have chosen you. You would have remained the pitiful son of the high king, living a worthless life full of shattered dreams."

With a groan, Naibor sank to his knees. There was nothing he could do. His father was dead, and it was his fault. Being high king did not seem important to him anymore. "Help me, Necros," he murmured, for he felt he had no one left to turn to.

* * *

"I have brought them, Master," Naibor heard a familiar voice say. Looking up from where his father lay, the prince saw Elbanor coming down the hall, accompanied by the black figures.

"I have awaited this day for many years, and now the promised day of your return has come!" The elder tutor's eyes gleamed excitedly as he bowed to his master.

"Elbanor, quick! Go and get a cot and some linen."

"Is the high king dead?" Elbanor interrupted.

"Yes," Naibor said morosely. "Quickly, please; I want to put him in his bed."

"I don't take orders from you," Elbanor hissed contemptuously. "I am no longer your servant. I have more important things to worry about than a dead king."

"You served my father for years, Elbanor, and he thought well of you," Naibor commented, bewildered. "And now you don't have time for him?"

"I served your father so I could aid my true lord and master. I have been sending news and food to Necros for most of my life. I served Lord Necros when I was a boy in the palace and he was high king. So I knew all about Necros when you came to ask me about a sorcerer."

"And now the time has come for Prince Naibor to see the lord that you served. Give me what you have hidden for so long, awaiting my return." Reaching out, Necros took the ornate black box that Elbanor held in his hands. Saying an incantation, the sorcerer opened the lid and removed a silken bag.

From the bag Necros retrieved a small red leather-bound book with painted gold symbols upon it. This he quickly secreted within his tunic. Next he removed a necklace—a replica of the Stone of Wisdom, except that it was entirely black.

Necros spoke and caressed the necklace as if it were a prize he sorely missed. "Too long I have waited to have you back around my neck and feel your power race through my veins. Even now as I touch you, I can feel the power that you hold. Once again we shall be one, and my power shall be made whole." He placed it around his neck, over the stones and the eye that he already wore.

Naibor watched as the sorcerer did this, amazed by the transformation he saw taking place before his eyes. When the eye and the stone in the center of the necklace came together, the stone became alive with the presence of the eye and the eye became the heart of the stone. While this happened, the sorcerer's body became erect and he began to change. Within the blink of an eye, Necros was tall and strong in body. His hump was gone, and he was no longer bent with age. His hair grew in thick and black, and his sightless blue-gray eyes were now dark and smoldering. When the transformation was complete, Naibor shuddered.

Falling to his knees before the restored Necros, Elbanor worshipped him. The two eerie figures beside him joined in the worship with a slow chant. While they chanted, Necros grabbed the original black chain, breaking it from around his neck. Throwing the useless object into the air, along with the bag he had been holding, they vanished in a burst of flames.

When the chant was finished, Necros spoke to Naibor, who still knelt beside the body of his father. "So now you see me as I was with all of my power returned—a true ruler and high king." Clenching one hand into a fist, he raised it toward Naibor. "Do you still see yourself as king, Prince? Do you see yourself as my equal? Do you have the power to overthrow me and regain the throne? You were already my servant long before now, and I tolerated your insolence, but no more. Now you will serve me."

"No. No, I will not serve you, Necros." Naibor spoke with little energy.

The sorcerer laughed. "You will serve me. I can crush all of the bones in your body by just thinking it. Call me Lord Necros!"

Naibor said nothing, keeping his head down.

"I'm waiting, Naibor; don't push my patience."

Feeling an unseen weight crushing him, Naibor clenched his teeth. The pain increased, and he struggled to get to his feet. "Kill me, Necros; I want to die," he forced out between tight lips, waiting for the sound of his bones to crack. "I have betrayed my people and my friends and destroyed my father. I deserve to die."

"Yaah!" Necros yelled angrily, sending the prince flying with his power into the wall. "You have more to you than meets the eye, Naibor," he told the unconscious heap lying on the floor next to the wall.

"Master, why don't you just kill him?" Elbanor urged.

"He's such a tortured soul, is he not? And so helpless against me. I will enjoy making him suffer, but he must not be killed yet. We must wait until the appointed time."

Elbanor answered with a self-satisfied chuckle.

"Take the king to his bed like the prince suggested," Necros instructed his dark servants. "Set up the room as though he is dead, cover him with a shroud, and light the appropriate candles and incense. Remove the prince to his bed as well."

"The high king is not dead?" Elbanor asked, looking at the white face of the unmoving figure lying at his feet.

"No, he is not truly dead. I have not the power to kill him while he is protected by the Stone of Wisdom. His soul is imprisoned in his body, and therefore he appears to be dead to all who are concerned. For now it is useful to me that Prince Naibor think his father is dead."

Bending down, Elbanor stretched out his hand toward the Stone of Wisdom. He yearned for the stone's power. It lay so close to his reach.

"I wouldn't," Necros cautioned. "The stone is cursed." Elbanor drew his hand back suddenly, as if burned. "Anyone who touches it without the high king's or Aii's consent will instantly die. Amuron's court historian should know this."

Elbanor dropped his eyes, embarrassed. He had known.

Taking a moment to appraise the shriveled court tutor standing before him, Necros said with little emotion, "Elbanor, you have served me well. The power that you desire shall be given to you tomorrow night at the sacrifice."

"Thank you, my lord. I did everything that you asked. Using the incantation you taught me, I poisoned the prince's thoughts. It worked, just as you told me it would, locking his soul in despair. Eventually he came to believe that he deserved to become high king and that the Celebration Games were unfair. He was the one to come to me asking for the name of a sorcerer to help him win the games. I didn't even need to make the suggestion. He fell right into my—uh, your hands, Master."

"Go to your bed and dream sweet dreams, Elbanor. I wish to be alone."

"Yes, Master," the tutor muttered, lowering his head before shuffling away.

* * *

Amon awoke to find himself tied securely to a pillar in the wine cellar. He tried everything he could think of to break free, but his struggles only managed to dig the rough rope cord farther into his wrists. Looking around from his corner at the side of the room, the youth could see that he was not alone and not the only one in pain. Tied to the other large support beams of the cellar were the young lords and ladies of the city. All of them looked as if they were enduring something horrible.

"Lord Baynor," Amon called out softly. "Lord Baynor, are you all right?"

Snapping his head up, Prince Baynor tried to focus on who was speaking. "Who are you?" he asked with a deep, throaty voice.

"My name's Amon, sir. I am a sentry in the guard. I was working at the North Gate."

"Why are you here, Amon?"

"I discovered that Prince Naibor betrayed the city, so I went to the high king to tell him what I knew. I must have been captured, because I don't remember what happened after I left the king, and I seem to be a prisoner now."

Prince Baynor was unable to reply. Amon watched, horrified, as he writhed in pain, gasping raggedly while trying to breathe.

"Prince Baynor, what is wrong?" the youth cried out with compassion.

"Amon," Princess Janii answered in a wavering voice, from the opposite side of the room. "Please avert your eyes and don't watch us. We are being changed into animals because of an accursed sorcerer, and I am afraid it won't be pleasant to watch."

Before Amon could respond, a small but colorful light appeared in the center of the room between the pillars. It grew quickly in intensity and size. Taking the form of a woman's face, the glowing features rapidly kept changing into various animals. Remaining suspended in the air, the face changed dizzyingly from a rabbit to a deer and then from an owl to a horse.

"I am Nagala, Spirit of the Animals," the apparition said, continuing to change from common creatures to ones rarely seen.

"What do you want with us, Nagala?" Prince Tybor asked, feeling his pain ease.

"Our great Lord and protector, the Lord Aii, has sent me to help undo the evil that has befallen you. The power used by the sorcerer to cast his spell cannot now be stopped, but it can be altered. Our Lord and Creator has chosen to intercede in your transformation in two ways. I have been sent to change you from the humble creatures you were to become into those that will be more suitable for you in the future. As beasts, you will retain your ability to talk. This means that your personalities, intelligence, and memories will remain as they are now, united with the spirit of the animal.

"As well, you will not have to suffer while you are changing. You will fall asleep and awaken changed. As beasts, it is hoped that you will be able to escape from the sorcerer and travel to Berroc, the Place of the Stones, to meet with a messenger from Aii. The lives of the people of the city Amuron depend on it." As soon as Nagala finished speaking, she faded from view.

Finding the other prisoners already asleep, the exciting events of the evening finally caught up with Amon. With hardly enough energy to yawn, he too fell into a deep slumber.

* * *

The next morning was a difficult one for Prince Naibor. He could barely tell which banging was louder—the banging on his chamber door or the banging of his head.

"Prince Naibor! Prince Naibor!" an urgent voice called to him through the door. His body felt heavy and sore, and it did not want to respond when he tried to move.

"Open the door!" another voice demanded with authority.

Naibor managed to recognize the next voice, despite his jumbled thoughts. It was the now all-too-familiar voice of Necros. "Move aside; I'm a physician."

Hearing the voice of Necros jarred Naibor's mind, and he suddenly remembered the events of the night before. He groaned at the recollection.

"The prince is suffering from shock and grief. I must see to him," the voice of Necros continued.

Naibor heard the click of the lock on his door. Looking up, with his vision blurred, he saw the door open and a figure step inside.

"How did you do that?" a curious voice from out in the hallway asked. "The door was locked."

"Your banging must have knocked the lock open," the pretend physician answered smoothly before closing the door again on those outside.

Walking over to where Naibor was lying, the sorcerer quickly assessed the situation. "Here. Chew on these," he ordered, handing

Naibor the pungent leaves of an herb while helping the prince to sit up.

"Leave me alone!" Naibor refused, pushing away the offered herb. "Why do you need me, Necros? You seem to be looking after things quite well by yourself. I just want to be left alone."

"Today is a glorious day, Prince! It is a day of celebration! A new high king shall be named. For you, however, there are still duties to be performed. You have the palace servants to address. They are waiting patiently outside of your door. Their king is dead, and you need to take charge of things."

Necros again offered Naibor the herb, and this time the prince took it, despite the fact he knew he was the sorcerer's pawn. Immediately after Naibor put the leaves in his mouth, his nose and throat came alive with tingling. The more he chewed, the less his head ached. Eventually the pain in his body eased and his mind cleared.

Another knock sounded at the door. "Is he all right, doctor?" a concerned voice asked.

The prince got stiffly up from his bed and walked over to the door. When he opened it, he found cooks, servants, and members of the high king's Personal Guard standing in the hall.

"We found the king's memorial when we took him his morning meal," a servant said sadly. "How did it happen?"

"When did it happen?" another servant asked.

"I want to know how he died!" A fierce-looking guard in white demanded. "And where are the personal guards who were with him?"

The questions swirled around in Naibor's head, and he was completely at a loss about what to say to them. Reaching up a shaky hand to his forehead, he swayed unsteadily on his feet. It was obvious to all who were present that the prince did not look well.

Taking the prince by the shoulder, Necros securely grabbed the swaying prince and answered for him. "Prince Naibor sent for me early this morning. He had gone to talk with his father about the games today. When the prince entered his father's private chambers, he regrettably found the high king lying dead in his bed. I examined the king and found that he died peacefully in his sleep. His personal guards were still standing outside his door, and they had not heard anything to alarm them."

"Again I ask"—the guard looked suspiciously at Necros—"where are the guards now?"

"After the memorial was set up, they were sent away to grieve. The prince wanted to be alone with his father, so I left as well. Now I have come back to attend to Prince Naibor's needs."

"I will take over from here, then," the shrewd guard stated. "The prince is not well. I must make sure that things are handled properly and that there is no disorder to disgrace the high king's passing."

Naibor felt a sharp pinch from the fingers that supported his shoulder. Catching Necros's gaze, the prince knew what he wanted. "No. Thank you for your offer, overseer; I am well enough. I will see to these matters myself." The guard seemed about to object, so Naibor continued. "It is my right. I am the king's heir."

The overseer looked at Naibor for a moment and then bowed his assent. "Your will is mine, my lord," he said. And with a quick turn, he marched away from the small crowd around the door.

All eyes were again on Naibor. "I will announce the high king's death today at the Celebration Games. I ask you, please, not to mention this to anyone until I have made the announcement. The funeral will be tomorrow. Those of you who do not have pressing duties may be dismissed to go to the arena with your families as is customary. The rest of you, carry on with your work." On finishing his instructions, the prince waved them away. "I will call on you if I have a need."

The servants, in shock and grief, left to carry out Naibor's instructions, leaving the prince to return to his room, followed by the sorcerer.

"Good. Very good, Prince," Necros said, closing the door behind him. "You see, you can take control when you want to. And we will follow your plan just as you said. Now we must see what has become of your guests in the cellar."

CHAPTER 5

Prince Baynor woke with a stretch and a yawn. It was a very natural act, but everything about it felt unnatural. His mouth felt too big, and his tongue too long; his eyes seemed blurry, while his nose felt alive with strange smells. His arms stretched out instead of up. He shook himself. "What is this?" he asked with surprise, looking down at the long, thick shaggy fur that covered his body.

"I always pictured you as a bear, Baynor," Princess Janii said with a quiet nicker.

Turning his head, Baynor saw a glistening white unicorn standing behind him. "Janii?" he asked, although he was no more surprised to see Janii as a unicorn than she had been to see him as a bear. Janii, with her fair complexion, bright blue eyes, and grace, were reminiscent of a unicorn. He couldn't help but admire her beauty.

"I'm not sure I like this," Baynor grumbled, conscious of how he must look to Janii.

"This will take some getting used to," Princess Sanii commented to herself from the top of the nearest wine rack. The others saw an eagle perched there, testing her wings by giving them a gentle flap.

A wolf eagerly strode forward into the group. "What's up?" he asked, cocking his head.

"Tybor, is that you?" Sanii asked, ruffling her feathers.

"I suppose so; however, I'm not quite myself this morning."

"Uhmf," Baynor snorted. "I'm convinced!"

"So am I," Sanii agreed.

"Come on out," a woman's voice softly encouraged from behind the pillars next to the cellar wall. All eyes turned to see a sleek black panther trying to coax something out from the shadows.

"No! I'm too embarrassed," a muffled voice replied mournfully.

"You can't dig yourself into a corner for the rest of your life," Princess Tayii teased, purring with amusement.

"Very funny," the other creature replied dryly.

"Ranor, is that you?" Prince Tybor inquired, moving closer. "Show yourself, my good friend. What are you afraid of?"

"Well, for one thing, you are all animals that you can be proud of. Baynor's a grizzly bear, Sanii's a golden eagle, Tayii's a panther, Janii's a unicorn—of all things—and you, Tybor, are a wolf."

"I must say I am a bit surprised, Ranor," the wolf responded. "I've never known you not to stand up for yourself in any situation."

There was the sound of some disapproving grunts and snuffles, and a badger popped out of the shadows. "Well, go ahead and have your fun," Prince Ranor grumbled impatiently.

It was hard for the group not to laugh when they saw him. Despite the fact he was now a badger, the change seemed to suit their friend. The markings on the badger's coat fitted in quite well with the streaks and specks of gray that were so common in Prince Ranor's hair and beard.

"I think he looks as dashing as ever," Princess Janii said, in an unsuccessful attempt to ease his hurt feelings.

Prince Ranor gave a resigned sigh at his fate.

"We seem to have become animals that more or less reflect our personalities," Tybor observed, looking from one animal to the next, and his friends had to agree.

They couldn't deny that they all had become animals they had resembled as people. Tayii, with her independent personality, slender build, and deep golden eyes, made a perfect panther. The sorcerer's spell to turn her into a black cat had left her with the dark velvet coat. Baynor's wavy brown hair, fearsomeness, and strength gave the impression of a bear. Tybor's love of people and outgoing personality could be translated into the social animal of a wolf. Sanii's poise, as well as her contemplative and quiet spirit, was reminiscent of an eagle.

"Good morning," a strained voice said.

The animals turned and saw Amon in a rather uncomfortable position. He was still tightly tied in the opposite corner, and the rope around his wrists had dug into his flesh.

"Amon!" Janii cried out in distress. "We've got to free him."

"Here, let me," Baynor said, lumbering over to where Amon was tied. The large bear raised a heavy paw and brought it down upon the rope, tearing it in two.

Amon flinched unconsciously, closing his eyes at the sight of the bear's menacing claws. It was hard for the youth to believe that something as fierce and frightening as a grizzly bear was not going to hurt him. "Thank you," Amon said gratefully before immediately sinking to the floor with a groan.

"We must have either broken or slipped out of our binds when we changed into animals," Prince Tybor remarked, coming over to see how he could ease the youth's discomfort.

Cautiously and tenderly, Tybor licked one of the raw and bruised wrists of the youth. Amon pulled his arm away and stared at him in wonder.

"Don't worry," Prince Tybor reassured him. "I won't hurt you."

"I wasn't afraid you were going to hurt me," Amon blurted out honestly. "It's just so strange—seeing you as animals, I mean."

"I understand all too well!" Tybor said, sitting down beside him. Lifting a hind leg to his ear, he scratched at an itch.

The animals were all wondering what to do next when Ranor scuffled into the center of the room. "It's time we made some plans.

We've still got to get out of here and get to Berroc while we can. I have been scouting around a bit, and I've found—"

"Quiet!" Tybor interrupted, jumping up toward the doorway with his ears alert and listening. "Someone's coming!"

Everyone in the room froze for an instant. At the sound of the cellar door opening, they hurried to find a vantage point where they could watch, hidden, and wait to attack. This was not hard to do in the dim cellar. It was stacked with barrels and crates and was filled with long wooden racks of wine.

Dashing behind the wine rack closest to the door, Amon had one thought in mind. The animals could deal with the sorcerer. He was going after Prince Naibor. For this purpose, the youth selected a large, heavy bottle from in front of him and held it ready in his hand.

* * *

"Come, Prince, let us see what your friends have become in the night," Necros said, with a slight smile curling upon his pale lips. The smile did not touch the dark depths of his eyes.

"Necros, can't this wait?" Naibor hesitated, trying desperately to avoid what was imminent. "I didn't sleep well last night, and it's still early morning."

"Do not forget your place," Necros said in a low tone.

Following him slowly down the stairs, Naibor entered the room and stopped abruptly. The prisoners were gone! Whatever animals had been tied down here had disappeared. The ropes that had tied them lay loosely on the floor.

Naibor sensed the tension building around him until it crackled in the air. Bracing himself for the sorcerer's wrath, Naibor risked a glance in his direction. He saw no anger in the sorcerer's face—only watchfulness. The sorcerer's cold black eyes searched the shadows with piercing intensity. Naibor's heart beat wildly while time passed achingly slowly.

At the sound of an angry snarl, they were attacked! To Naibor it seemed like some childhood nightmare. Wild beasts leaped out from the shadows toward him. Their sharp teeth and deadly claws gleamed savagely in the eerie half-light. He froze in fear, not having anything to defend himself with, but Necros was ready.

Using his power, the sorcerer spoke some twisted words in a commanding voice. In response, the ropes lying on the floor jumped into the air, alive and alert. Wriggling momentarily in anticipation, the ropes flew with great speed at the animals and began wrapping themselves tightly around their legs and mouths. The animals' attack quickly turned defensive. They snapped, swatted, kicked, and clawed desperately in an attempt to keep from being recaptured.

Jumping out at the same time as the animals, Amon rushed at the prince with his bottle raised high. Hearing a sound from behind, Naibor turned just in time to avoid being hit in the head. Before the youth could swing again, several ropes swiftly wrapped themselves around his hands and feet. The youth struggled briefly, but it was no use. The only thing to escape was the red wine, spilling like blood from the broken bottle at Naibor's feet.

It seemed to the prince that he was watching some sort of frenzied dance, but it soon was over. The animals began to fall to the ground, tripped by their own momentum, until even the eagle lay on the dirt floor with her wings pinned.

"Someone has interfered," Necros said with restrained anger, after he had inspected the prisoners. "These animals are not as they should be."

"Does that matter?" Naibor naively asked.

Necros spun to face him. "If you had anything to do with this …" he threatened menacingly, his cruel gaze promising pain. Naibor clenched his teeth, waiting to feel the heat of the sorcerer's power, but it didn't come.

"No, I see you did not," Necros stated calmly. "You have not the understanding, and you have not the power. After the sacrifice tonight, it will not matter."

The sacrifice! The words fell like a stone that hit the water in the well that was his stomach. The prince unconsciously looked down, only to find himself looking straight into the eyes of the bear. Something wasn't right. These were not the eyes of a wild animal. These eyes had a look of understanding and a look of intelligence that Naibor had not seen in wild beasts before. Confirming his fears, Naibor looked quickly into the eyes of each of the other animals. There was a difference! These were not the eyes of ordinary witless animals he had seen sold at the market. They truly had not changed in the way Necros had planned.

"Come, Prince, there is still much to be done. We shall leave your guests resting comfortably," he taunted. With a final look at the prisoners, they left the cellar.

The sound of the door closing signaled another attempt at escape. But, as Amon expected, the attempt was futile. Feeling helpless, he lay despairing on the cellar floor. They had lost their chance at freedom and all hope of reaching Berroc.

In the hallway above the cellar, Necros again instructed the prince. "I want you to do what is necessary to prepare yourself for the games. When the parade arrives to take you to the stadium, I will accompany you. If you are asked questions concerning the whereabouts of your competitors, act as if you know nothing." The sorcerer paused to scrutinize Naibor. Satisfied with his assessment, he continued. "Do not look so worried, Prince. My plans are going well. Everything will happen just as it should." Necros then turned his attention to the two black figures that had approached Naibor so silently from behind that the prince jumped when he finally realized that they were there.

"You found Elbanor?" the sorcerer inquired. "Good. Take me to him." Necros then left, escorted by the shadow figures.

* * *

Naibor's mind seemed to clear as soon as the sorcerer was gone. Walking with purpose, he went toward the high king's chambers.

He found his father lying peacefully in his large wood-framed bed. A lamp of spicy incense burned at each bedpost. Dimly lit flames solemnly danced behind their orange-tinted globes hanging on the wall. A coverlet bearing the family crest lay tucked underneath the king's arms and across his chest. Resting on top of the coverlet was the Stone of Wisdom. The entire room seemed to reflect the quiet.

The prince looked longingly at his father. Reaching out, Naibor lifted one of his father's hands and held the chilled fingers in his own. The colored light took the pallor from his father's face, making the prince want to believe that he was just sleeping.

"Father, I'm sorry," he whispered. "Everything's gone wrong." Momentarily overcome, the prince tried to push his grief aside so he could continue. "Ever since I was a little boy, I dreamed of being a king like you. You always seemed so content, so at peace with yourself, and I thought that being high king would solve all of my problems. That's why I brought the sorcerer into the city. I thought he would help me to become high king. I lied to myself, telling myself that everything would be fine and that it would all work out for the best. I don't know what came over me. I suddenly became obsessed with being high king, and nothing else seemed to matter. I never meant for anyone to get hurt, but I just couldn't stop myself. Please forgive me, Father.

"For so long I've worried about myself, but now I'm worried about what Necros is planning to do. You knew something horrible was going to happen, didn't you, Father? I could see it in your face that morning when you came to visit me. I promise to try to stop whatever he's planning." The prince paused for a moment, his heart filled with sorrow, but he knew he didn't have much time. "I have to go now, Father," he added regretfully. "I'll return as quickly as I can." He then kissed his father's hand and gently placed it over the Stone of Wisdom before leaving the room.

Prince Naibor then went to his own chambers, but he spent even less time there. After grabbing the dagger he had hidden under his mattress, he hurried back down to the cellar.

The animals and Amon remained just as they had been before—tightly bound on the ground.

Taking a couple of steps over to the youth, Naibor whispered, "Don't worry, Amon. I'm going to cut you free."

Slicing the ropes from around the youth's hands and feet, Naibor threw them aside. Amon began to get up but stopped when the cut ropes began to move. Seeing the same thing, Naibor prepared for the attack with his dagger. This time, however, the pieces of rope squirmed and turned like the bodies of headless serpents. Becoming lifeless, they turned black before smoldering away into a foul-smelling gas.

Amon gave a small cough from the gas and tried to stand.

"Let me help you," Naibor offered, holding out his hand.

"I'm fine," Amon replied, getting up without his help. "What do you want from me, Prince?" he asked sharply.

"I've come to help you escape, Amon—both you and the animals."

"Why?" the youth asked, eyeing him warily.

"I know you don't trust me, Amon, and I understand why, but the truth is I don't want you or the animals killed tonight at the sacrifice."

Despite Amon's angry feelings toward the prince, there did seem to be an honest change about him. "Maybe so," he cautiously replied, "but your friend the sorcerer won't like it."

"No, I don't suppose he will, but what he wants no longer matters to me. And he's not my friend. Necros doesn't have any friends—only servants. He used me to get inside of the city, just as I used him to try to become high king. What I did was wrong, I know that now. I didn't realize it before, because I was blinded by my own foolish ambition. So what happens to me is not what matters. He can do whatever he wants to me; I deserve it. But you have suffered enough!" He paused, looking sadly around at the animals who were once his friends. "My only hope is that I can find some way to get rid of Necros before I am no longer useful to him and he kills me. But it's time for you to go now.

"Here," Prince Naibor continued, handing him a small key. "This key opens the door at the back of the wine cellar, where they bring in the beer and wine. It leads to a small courtyard used by the cooks. The door outside, next to this one, is the food cellar. From there you will be able to get some supplies. Once you are out of the courtyard, you can see the wall and find your way to the North Gate. My advice to you is that you leave the city at once. While Necros is here, your life—and everyone's in the city—is in danger. There are lots of small villages along the West Road and you should be safe in one of them. But before you go, I want you to have this." The prince held out the small dagger in its sheath to the youth.

Amon could see that the knife was finely crafted. It had large precious stones embedded in both sides of the handle, and the small bone sheath it sat in had the royal symbols etched into it.

"It's the dagger my father gave to me as a boy. I want you to have it. It's a gift given in restitution for the way I treated you."

Amon hesitated and then took the knife. A gift of restitution was never given lightly, and it was a way of asking for forgiveness. Amon, worried that his emotions might show, tried changing the subject. "Aren't you going to free the animals?"

"Yes, but I was still trying to think of a way to get them out of the city."

"That's okay," Amon answered without thinking. "I'll take them with me when I leave."

"Amon, these are wild animals. The bear alone will tear you to pieces."

"I don't think the animals will hurt me, Prince," he said quickly, biting his tongue. "They didn't hurt me the last time they were free."

It was obvious that Amon felt confident about his safety with the animals. Once again Naibor looked at the animals, feeling there was something strange about them.

"Well then, I will leave it to you. But be careful and try not to be seen. Necros is able to see with more than just his eyes, and I'm sure he has spies watching the city."

The prince stood looking at the youth for a moment. Then, not knowing what else to say, he said an ancient blessing that soldiers used when parting company. "May goodness guide you and keep you safe until the day we meet again."

The blessing was something the men in the guard now said casually to one another, but for some reason it seemed relevant to this situation. Amon smiled when he heard it. "And to you, Prince," he returned.

Naibor smiled too, replacing the small bottle of port he had been carrying on a shelf before leaving the cellar.

* * *

Immediately after Prince Naibor left, Amon hurried to cut the ropes that held the animals. Once free, they all stood by the open doorway at the back of the cellar and looked outside. The bright morning sun filled the whole courtyard with light, leaving little room for shadow.

"Not much cover," Baynor noted, his bulk almost filling the entire doorway.

Looking at his companions, Amon realized that sneaking out of the city was not going to be easy—especially with a bear, a panther, a wolf, and a unicorn at his side.

"I'll go next door and get some supplies," Amon volunteered.

"I'll go with him." The badger prince, wanting to be useful, followed closely at his heels.

"Me too," the wolf stated.

"While they're gone, I'll fly around and see which will be the safest way out," Sanii offered.

"Be careful," Tayii cautioned her friend while her large tail flicked nervously behind her. "Fly where you won't be seen."

Beating her wings, the eagle quickly rose into the air. Gaining height in the open sky, she circled high above the palace, away from the eyes of anyone who could be watching from open windows.

At first Sanii had been worried about her flying skills. Once she was in the air, however, her animal instincts took over and she maneuvered herself expertly among the air currents until she was at the height she wanted to be at. With her keen eyes, she was amazed at what she could see. She watched as her friends and Amon went into the storage room to get supplies before she wheeled around and set about her task.

Amon entered the food cellar with Ranor and Tybor right behind him. Without a word, they split up and began looking for things they might need to take with them on their journey.

"The meat is over here," the wolf said, letting his nose lead him.

"And look over here!" the badger called out from beside an open cupboard.

Amon grabbed some sacks and some waterskins and went to see what the others had found. "Hey! Cut that out!" he quietly scolded when he saw what they were doing.

Ranor had found some eggs in a basket on the floor and was just finishing his third one, while Tybor was busily enjoying some smoked sausages that he had pulled down from where they had been hanging.

"You both should know better," the youth reminded them, speaking to them as if they were a couple of disobedient domestic animals. "We've got no time to fool around."

"Sorry." Tybor licked his lips, finishing off his last mouthful. "But that saying about being as hungry as a wolf is true."

"He's right, you know," the badger said regretfully, looking over at the wolf. "We should have controlled ourselves, even though those were the best-tasting eggs I'll probably ever eat." He smacked his lips contentedly.

"Okay," Amon began, returning to business as he started to fill his bags. "I'll take some fruit, travel bread, lots of dried meat—"

"Amon," Prince Ranor interrupted as his more practical side

surfaced. "Just take what you will need for yourself. We will have to hunt for our own food. You would never be able to carry enough food to feed us all, but bring along some extra water; we might still need that."

After packing his bag with food, Amon slung it casually over one shoulder. He filled two large waterskins and gave them to Tybor and Ranor to carry back to the others. Then he filled a second bag with what he thought would make a nice surprise breakfast when they had left the city and were nicely on their way.

On his way out, Amon's eyes fell on some travel bags packed with items designed to be both efficient and lightweight for travel. Inside there was everything he would need for the journey: a good, strong length of rope; a protective blanket and a traveling cape; a cooking kit; medical supplies; and a long-bladed knife. Satisfied that he had everything he would need, the youth rejoined the others just as Sanii came back with her report.

"Our main concern will be getting through the North Gate," the eagle explained after landing and neatly folding her wings against the contours of her body. "As you know, the stables are on the far side of this courtyard. From there, a small road leads to the gate. Most of the palace servants seem to be busy down at the arena, but there are some getting the carriages ready for the parade by the fountain on the front lawn. Although our chances of not being seen are good, we will be traveling for the most part in the open. I didn't see any guards at the North Gate. They must have been inside the gatehouse, but there should be four. I saw their horses tied behind the house."

"That's right," Prince Baynor agreed. "Captain Regg always doubles the guard on important occasions. What about the East Gate?"

"Not good. We would have to pass through the Palace Section and pass by the arena, where most of the people are, before reaching the East Gate."

"I should have thought of that." Baynor gave his big head a

shake. "And to get to the West Gate, we would have to pass by the North Gate anyway. I'm not used to secretly moving around a city where I am accustomed to being a prince. We will just have to chance it, whether we are seen or not."

"Now all we have to worry about is how to open the gate," Tybor commented. And looking straight at Sanii, he teased, "We can't very well fly over it."

Sanii flapped a wing at Tybor, and Tybor responded by cocking his head innocently and wagging his tail. "Except, that is, for you, my darling."

"If you can create a diversion of some sort," Amon proposed, having gotten caught up in the sense of adventure, "I can slip into the guardhouse and grab the key."

"I like the way this boy thinks," Ranor approved. "Gets right down to business."

"That shouldn't be too hard to accomplish with a pack animals like us, Amon. What kind of diversion would you like?" Princess Tayii inquired.

"Let's not make it too big of a diversion," Baynor cautioned.

"Is there some place by the gate where most of us could hide?" Janii asked, thinking aloud.

"The gateway is too small," Amon mused. "But there is a space between the guardhouse and the wall that should do if the guards are still inside the house when we get there."

"Perfect!" Janii tossed her glowing white mane. "Then I will be the diversion."

"What?" several voices asked.

"You all know the old rumor that if you catch a unicorn, you get three wishes. Well, I am going to trust that these guards are superstitious enough to try to catch me. Even if they aren't superstitious, unicorns are so rare that they're going to think I must be a present for the new ruler and that I've escaped. Either way, I'll let them chase me until you have all gone through the gate. Then I'll come and join you."

Baynor hesitated, but he knew they didn't have many options. "All right, we will give it a try. Sanii, would you be good enough to keep watch from above and keep an eye out for any trouble?"

"My pleasure," she replied, and once more she took gracefully to the skies.

"Then it's time we got out of here," the bear advised.

CHAPTER 6

"I'll go first," Ranor suggested. "I'm the least conspicuous. When I get to the other side of the courtyard, I'll check to see if the road is clear. If I see someone coming, I'll signal to you by digging."

Amon's heart was pounding while he watched the badger trundle across the courtyard. His silken fur rippled softly in the sunlight with every step. It seemed to take the badger prince forever to get to the other side, and then even longer for him to come back after he had gone through the open doorway. But when he returned, everything seemed fine, because he stood patiently waiting for them to follow.

"Okay, let's go!" Baynor signaled with a throaty howl, and they all made a mad dash across the courtyard, straight toward Ranor—who barely missed being trampled.

"Lead on, Ranor; we'll follow you," Baynor informed him.

As swiftly as he could, the badger prince led them past the stables and between the other assorted buildings containing harnesses, carriages, and the like. But before they made it to the end of the buildings, Sanii dropped down swiftly in front of them.

"Get back!" she urgently whispered. "Someone is coming!"

The animals desperately looked around for cover, but there was none. They were standing in the lane next to a storage shed. They did not even have time to move back behind the building before they heard voices and approaching footsteps. Pressing themselves against the side of the building, they tried to remain still.

Holding his breath, Amon listened as two men in conversation came increasingly closer. Stopping just short of the corner, they went inside the building.

"Here it is," Amon heard one of the men tell the other. "Just where I left it."

"What's the matter with you today?" the second man asked. "You haven't seemed yourself all morning."

"I just got a bad feeling, that's all," answered the first.

"A bad feeling about what?"

"I don't know," the man replied. "When I was in prayer last night, I got this strange feeling that something bad was going to happen. Then I had this nightmare about the Lord of the Dead calling the dead to rise. Normally I don't let dreams bother me, but this dream was so real."

"Sounds like one of those scary stories a passing traveler might tell to your children in the market. You believe in that kind of stuff, but I don't," Amon heard the second man say with a laugh. "Come on; let's go. You look so scared you almost got me spooked. Today is Celebration Day, and I'm going to have a good time no matter what you say."

The animals and Amon all breathed a sigh of relief when they heard the men retreat. The eagle once again took to the air, while the badger left the cover of the last building and went down the lane toward the guardhouse. The guards were all inside the house, and no one else could be seen, heard, or smelled, so Ranor turned and waited for the others to follow.

"We'd better go one at a time," Tayii advised. "I'll go first." And off she went, as quiet as a cat stalking its prey.

"Baynor, why don't you go next?" Tybor suggested. "Amon and I will follow behind you."

Baynor agreed, sensing the youth relax at Tybor's suggestion.

"Are you ready?" Prince Tybor asked Amon after they had watched the grizzly lumber confidently over to the gap between the wall and the guardhouse. The youth nodded.

Amon didn't know why he was suddenly so nervous. Perhaps it was the excitement from all the recent events. For once he just wanted everything to go smoothly. Trusting the wolf to be on alert for anything amiss, they crossed the road and joined the others.

Princess Janii came next, prancing merrily down the lane. She stopped, stood on her hind legs, and gave a terrific neigh when she was directly in front of the door.

The senior guardsman got up from his chair to see who was outside, thinking that someone had ridden up silently on a horse. "Hey!" he called out to the others behind him in the room. "You won't believe this!"

The other men, bored from their inactivity, immediately came to the doorway. What they saw made their mouths hang open. Janii proudly paced back and forth on the road in front of the dazzled men, making eye contact with each of them.

Amon thought she looked fabulous. Her white coat gleamed like cut glass in the sunlight, and she danced around on her light feet—which were more like a deer's than those of a horse—as if she were dancing on air.

"Now, that sure is a fine sight," commented a stocky guard with brown hair and a trim beard, to no one in particular.

"A unicorn! Where in the world …?" his taller friend with red hair asked, mesmerized by the sight before him.

Now that the princess had everyone's attention, she stopped a little way down the road from the guards and stared at them invitingly with her big blue eyes.

No one moved.

"Well," the first guard began slowly, while stroking the gray stubble on his chin, "I guess we should try to catch her. Easy now!" The others all jumped into action. "Don't scare her. One of you quickly find me some rope."

The bearded guard scratched his head with a puzzled expression. "Where do you think it came from?" he asked the one giving orders.

"Don't know," the other answered simply, but he was wondering the same thing himself.

Everyone knew that unicorns existed in the wild, but they were untamable and almost impossible to catch. This was because they ran faster than any horse and could climb up and down steep cliffs like goats.

The princess unicorn stood looking at them innocently, occasionally flicking her tail.

The fourth and youngest guard, who had gone for the rope, returned and handed it silently over to the first. "I wonder if that old rumor is true. You know, the one about a unicorn granting you three wishes if you catch it."

"Have to catch it first," said the greying guardsman, running the rope through his hands. Getting a good feel of its weight, he deftly made a slipknot.

"I doubt it," the red-haired guard muttered under his breath.

Without warning, the senior guard holding the rope let it fly.

Waiting for just that moment, Janii leaped toward them at a run, easily avoiding the rope. When she was close enough for them to be almost able to touch her, she swerved away and ran down the road away from the gate. The guards ran after her, trying to corner her and cut her off, but she let them get only so close before she kicked up her heels and ran off again.

Seeing his chance, Amon dashed into the guardhouse and out again with the key. "So far, so good," he said to the others, letting them know he had been successful. In less than a minute, he had the gate open and they were standing together on the other side.

Baynor, rising up on his hind legs, quickly looked around before speaking to his friends. "The rest of you go down the old North Road until you come to a rocky gully where there once was a river. Wait for me there. I'm going to wait here to make sure that Janii makes it through the gate."

Without question, the others began to run north, but Amon hesitated. "Aren't we going to Berroc?" he asked, knowing that Berroc was to the east and not to the north.

"Yes, Amon," Baynor patiently answered. "We are going to follow the gully east, until we are in the forest," he explained, lowering himself to the ground. "But you had better hurry if we are to escape without being seen." Feeling his cheeks grow hot, Amon turned and raced after the others.

Wanting to give her friends as much time as possible, Janii led the guards as far from the gate as she dared. The distance she had put between her and the guards was rapidly lessening, and she had now run out of road. If she went any farther, she would be too close to where Sanii had said they were preparing for the games, and she could not risk being seen by any more people.

Thinking quickly, the unicorn princess ran to where the main houses of the royal families were located. She knew of several side paths with low gates to gardens that she could jump over. This gave her the chance to double back down the road while still evading the guards.

After several attempts at these dodges, the men began to split up and anticipate where she was going to come out. As Janii was running toward the end of a statue-lined path, the guard with the rope suddenly stepped out in front of her. She zigged to avoid the rope and then made a quick turn back down the path, nearly knocking down the two guards that were coming up from behind. Realizing how close she had come to being captured, Janii bolted straight down the road for the open gate.

Just as she reached the gate, the fourth guard—whom she hadn't noticed missing—jumped out of the guardhouse with another rope and flung it toward her. In his eagerness, he overthrew his target. Janii easily checked her stride and veered as the rope hit her side. While she was distracted by the first rope, the senior guard skillfully threw his rope neatly over her neck and tightened it firmly from behind.

Not now! The unicorn thought with dismay, her nostrils flaring. *Not when I'm so close to freedom!*

Stopping for a moment to catch her breath, Janii looked behind her at the triumphant guard's smiling face. With all her might, she unexpectedly leaped toward the gate. The senior guard securely holding on to the rope was thrown off balance, and she pulled him with her through the opening. But that was as far as she could go. The other guards had now grabbed onto the rope, making it impossible for her to pull away. Drawing in on the rope, they began closing the gap between them.

"We've got her now!" the red-haired guard shouted excitedly.

Hearing the angry roar of an animal, the guards looked with amazement at the savage bear running straight toward them.

"Look out!" the youngest guard cried, and all but one ran for their lives back inside the gate.

The older guard still clutched the rope. Waiting one brave moment longer, he tried to coax the unicorn to come with him. "Come on, pretty thing. Come this way to get away from the bear."

"Let her go!" the others shouted frantically at him.

Finally dropping the rope, he ran for the gate just as the bear rose onto his hind legs to swing a mighty paw at him. Once safely back inside, the others quickly shut and locked the gate—which for some mysterious reason had been open in the first place and for some bewildering reason still had the key in the lock. In frustration, the graying sentry watched the bear challenge them with one more howl before turning and running northward after the prized unicorn.

* * *

Amon and the animals had made it safely out of the city, but they still had a long journey ahead of them. Not far up the North Road, they found a narrow gully that an old stone bridge crossed over.

"This must be the gully Baynor was referring to," Tybor said, panting.

Leaving the side of the road, the youth and the others climbed down into it. Sitting down among the rocks and the white dust from the now dry clay bed, Amon waited with the wolf, the panther, and the badger in the silence of their own thoughts for their missing companions.

Amon was swatting away some bugs when the shadow of a bird floated across him. In a flurry of rising dust, Sanii joined them.

"Janii and Baynor are on their way," she informed them, momentarily relieving their anxiety. "But there is something strange heading toward us from the north, and I don't like the look of it." The rest of them looked northward, but for now none of them could see anything out of the ordinary.

Slowing her pace, Janii let Baynor catch up with her. "Pretty impressive," the unicorn teased her powerful friend as they walked to where the others were waiting. "You looked so mean, I almost ran back inside the gate with the man who was holding the rope."

Baynor gave a grunt for a response and then said, "I wouldn't have hurt him. He's a friend of my father. I even bought my horse from him. But I would have knocked him over if he hadn't let go of the rope."

Reaching the side of the gully, Janii and Baynor looked down to see their friends intently looking toward the north. "Not much of a lookout," Baynor commented to Janii before scrambling down the side of the bank.

"Or a welcoming party," she added. Slipping the loose rope from around her neck, Janii easily leaped down beside him. They then joined the others in scanning the northern landscape.

"What are we looking for?" Baynor asked Tayii, who was beside him.

"Sanii said she saw something coming our way," the panther answered. "But we haven't … Wait! I think I see something."

Soon they could all see what appeared to be a black cloud that hugged the ground. It had been traveling swiftly south, but it stopped on the edge of the kingdom's border and lingered there as if waiting for permission to enter.

A cold wind blew into their faces, and the animals catching the scent shivered with revulsion.

"What is it?" Amon asked, feeling the hair on the back of his neck stand up.

"Whatever it is, it sure smells bad," Tybor commented, wanting to get the stench out of his nose.

"I'll go and have a closer look," Sanii volunteered.

"Maybe you shouldn't," Janii cautioned.

"I agree," Tybor added, a whine of concern escaping his throat.

"Don't worry; I'll be all right," she assured them, rising swiftly into the air.

The animals and Amon watched Sanii circle high into the sky, far above their heads, before heading off toward the darkness. She was just beginning to glide over the black fog beneath her when they heard her cry of distress.

Responding instinctively to her cry, the animals felt a nameless fear hit them. Baynor rose up on his hind legs, and Janii reared, tossing her horn high in defense. Tybor's hackles rose, and his lip curled back in a snarl, while Tayii flattened her ears and her body into a low crouch. Ranor, resisting his urge to dig an escape, hugged the ground with his body and bared his teeth. The reaction of the animals made Amon's mouth go dry, and his heart pound wildly in his chest.

Sanii quickly returned and dived down out of the sky, landing beside Janii.

"Sanii! What is it?" Janii asked, deeply concerned, but Sanii was still breathing heavily because of her fright.

"What is it, Sanii? What did you see?" Baynor asked impatiently, feeling frustrated because his bear eyes were of no help to him in this situation.

"Let her catch her breath," Tybor growled in her defense.

"It's … it's …" she said, hardly able to get the words out. "It's the evil spirits of the dead. I saw their faces. They're all dead—and all evil!"

CHAPTER 7

Captain Regg, like Prince Naibor, was not fond of the Celebration Games, but for different reasons. To the captain, the games meant extra work. Not that he begrudged a day of hard work; it was the sleepless nights that set him on edge. The events of the day before and last night's two-hour rest were the things that made the captain less enthusiastic about the games.

The day before, one of his main concerns had been the disappearance of Amon. For some reason, Captain Regg assumed, Amon had left his post. But no one had seen or heard from him since. Then, as the evening wore on, some Ix people had shown up at the West Gate, wanting admittance to the city.

The Ix people were a barbaric and hostile tribe who enjoyed cruelty, and were known to bathe in the blood of their sacrifice victims. Captain Regg had not wanted to let them into the city; but their leader, named Volkas, had been quick to remind him that all visitors were welcome to watch the Celebration Games. It was well known that the Ix people scorned Amuron and anything to do with the city. The captain therefore doubted their interest in the games. Following city policy, he had allowed them to enter—but not without misgivings, and not without several guards being ordered to keep an eye on them.

No sooner had they been admitted to the city than it seemed to the captain that he began to hear rumors of missing people, animals, and even mysterious deaths. With what was left of his frayed nerves, he then had to spend a good deal of the night trying to settle a dispute between two of the visiting camps.

Now it was morning, and Captain Regg, tired as he was, saddled up his freshly groomed horse and rode to the front of the palace. It was his duty as one of the captains to escort the high king's carriage on its way to the arena. The ride in the bright, warm sunshine was pleasant, and when he arrived, everything looked in order.

"Good morning, Captain," one of the guards greeted him as he rode past the ranks of men in the parade.

Everything gleamed: saddles, horses, uniforms, carriages, bells, musical instruments, and men's faces. It looked like it might be a good morning after all.

It was still early—two hours before midday, when the games would begin—but the parade to the arena would be starting soon. Captain Regg checked with his commander and the other captains and found that they were all ready to start. Now they had to wait for the competitors and the high king to come and join them by the front lawn.

They did not have to wait long. The parents of the competitors arrived in a tight group and approached the captains solemnly. Captain Regg, watching them come forward, knew something was wrong.

"The rumor is true, then," Zai, the first captain of the People's Guard, whispered to him.

"What rumor?" Regg whispered back.

"The rumor that …" Zai began, failing to finish when one of the lesser queens broke stride with her companions and came up to speak with them.

"Our children are missing," Dame Lucianii said straightforwardly and without embarrassment.

This was the last news that Captain Regg wanted to hear. *Not more missing people!* Captain Regg looked over at his friend and could tell by his raised eyebrows that this was not the rumor he had heard.

"Your children are missing?" the first captain repeated, hoping to get further information.

"As unlikely as that may seem," Baynor's mother continued, "it is the truth. Our servants informed us that they all went to a banquet together last night. They have not been seen since. I do not know what has happened—only that they are missing. Normally we would not be concerned about our children's overnight absence. The fact that they are competing in the Celebration Games and have not arrived home for the last-minute preparations is what has us worried."

There was silence for several moments while both the captains thought through various possibilities for their apparent absence.

"Look! Here comes Prince Naibor. Maybe he can inform us of something," a guard pointed out. Leaving the front entrance of the palace, accompanied by Necros, the prince approached the small gathering.

"Prince Naibor, were you invited to a banquet last night?" Captain Zai asked diplomatically when they reached the carriages.

"No. But I did have my own banquet last night," Naibor replied truthfully.

"Were the other competitors at your banquet?"

"Yes. Why?"

"Well, they seem to be missing," the captain answered, sounding somewhat apologetic for this line of questioning.

The prince glanced uncomfortably at Necros, trying to look shocked by the news. "They all left the banquet well before midnight. Did they not arrive home?"

When several people started to ask Naibor further questions, the imposing figure of Necros stepped in front of the prince. "Captain Regg, why don't you sound the horn announcing the start of the parade?" the sorcerer suggested. "If the other competitors don't respond, a search can begin. The high king is not here yet, and he should be so we can consult him."

Everyone became quiet and stared curiously at the dark man, including Prince Naibor.

"And who are you, sir?" Captain Regg inquired, looking dubiously at the mysterious man.

"I helped Prince Naibor train for the games," he replied innocently.

"Blow the horn, Regg, and let's see what happens," Captain Zai encouraged his friend quietly.

Captain Regg signaled to one of his guards. The guard obeyed by raising a curled horn to his lips and releasing a strong, unwavering note.

The crowd grew restless quickly, but the first captain said, "Let's give 'em some time."

After a few more minutes had passed, an anxious Captain Regg began to go over in his mind what the best strategy for a search would be. He was about to put the guard on alert when he heard Dame Lucianii say with relief, "They were with the king!"

All eyes turned toward the main door of the palace to see the high king and the six missing competitors come through the door and step out onto the terrace. A cheer rose up from the awaiting crowd, and Captain Zai slapped Captain Regg on the back with a merry laugh.

Naibor looked with astonishment at Necros. The imposters came down the stairs and moved toward their awaiting carriages. Not one of them said a word. They only nodded their heads in acknowledgment of the crowd or smiled benignly when asked a question.

With horror, Naibor knew who the imposters were. He recognized those silent movements all too well. They were the black servants of Necros! Necros had somehow managed to make his servants appear to be his father and the other royal competitors.

Holding his breath, the prince watched while the crowd chatted gaily with the silhouette figures of Necros. He waited for someone to notice something different about them. Naibor hoped that this might be his opportunity to expose the sorcerer and defeat him.

Then he realized that Necros must have put a spell of some sort on the crowd. They not only believed that these representations were real; they also believed they were being answered by them!

"If you would step into your carriage, my lord," he heard Captain Regg say next to his ear. "The parade is ready to start."

Naibor looked around and then took the step up into his open carriage. Everyone else had already taken their places, while he had been watching the maddening charade. The sorcerer stood in the decorated carriage in front of him, along with his servant king. "Once again, Necros has everything under control," the disheartened prince murmured to himself.

Captain Regg, surveying the lines, signaled for the horn to be blown again. At the sound, the parade began to move forward down the road on its way toward the arena.

An older woman who helped to keep the palace clean was looking out of a window in order to watch the parade leave. When she saw the high king come out of the palace and walk toward the carriages, she gasped in shock. She knew that this was not the real king! She had seen the high king lying dead in his chambers, and she wondered what kind of trick this might be. She wanted to shout out the window, "That's not the king! That's not the king!" But she knew they wouldn't believe her any more than if she went down and told them in person. Who would believe a woman of her age when a false king was standing right there in front of them? Knowing they would rather believe their eyes than their hearts, she clutched her robe in sorrow because she was able to do nothing.

* * *

The parade followed its usual route. After going through the Market Section, it went down through the North Quarter, passing by the West and East Quarters before returning to the stadium. During the journey, the prince thought back to the first time he had participated in the parade. He had only been a young boy at the time. His father had been competing to be high king, so he and his mother had ridden in the back of one of the carriages. He remembered having been so excited that he had hardly been able to sit down. The crowd now was like the crowd then. Lining the streets, cheering and waving, they threw flower petals as the parade passed by. As a boy, Naibor had waved back and tried to catch the flower petals to give to his mother. He remembered feeling important while watching as the crowd followed the carriages through the streets to the arena, and then marveling at how many people there were in the city when they had gathered together at the stadium. But that was as far as his memory went. Exhausted from the parade, he had fallen asleep during the games and missed seeing his father compete. Thinking of these pleasant memories made Naibor uneasy. The prince wondered what games, if any, he would be witnessing today.

Horns blew merrily, announcing their arrival as they entered the arena. Musicians played music beside the platform for the high king while the carriages circled the stadium. This gave the people following the parade time to climb into the stands. When everyone was settled, Necros led the substitute king up the steps to the king's platform at the end of the arena. Then, as tradition dictated, he invited the competitors to come up to be blessed.

Climbing the steps to the platform, Naibor noticed the false competitors walking with him in unison. This mockery angered the prince, and questions crowded his mind about what Necros was planning to do. If only he knew what the sorcerer was planning, then he could plan his own strategy against him.

When the prince reached the top of the platform, he stood waiting for the proposed blessing, but it didn't come. Hearing a shout from behind, he turned to see who had called out. Rushing toward the stairs of the platform was a group of the king's Personal Guard, led by the guard who had challenged him in front of his chambers that morning.

"To me, people," the white uniformed guard cried out. "Listen to me! You know me as a faithful servant of the high king, long held in high respect. Listen to me and know that you have been deceived! This is not your high king!" He pointed an accusing finger toward the imposter. "The true king lies dead in his chambers at the palace. Do not let your eyes be fooled. Who knows the high king better than his Personal Guard?"

The sound of anxious muttering rose from crowd, and Prince Naibor looked over at Necros to see what his reaction would be. Thinking that the sorcerer's plans had finally been spoiled, the prince was surprised to find Necros silently laughing.

"It's true," the sorcerer said with amusement, growing more frightening with each passing moment. "This is not your high king. Your king is, as the overseer tells you, dead. Come, overseer, arrest your imposters," Necros goaded.

The crowd became hushed as the guards, with bright swords ready in their hands, rushed up the stairs toward the king and the sinister man in black. Naibor watched as the false images wavered and changed back into the eerie black figures he knew them to be. When the guards reached the top of the stairs, they found themselves facing a line of frightening silhouettes. The leader of the group, with great courage, took his sword and swung it at the black figure closest to him. His sword passed right through his opponent, as if it had swung through air. The overseer looked at his sword and then at the figure with amazement, not really sure what had happened. He raised his sword again for another attempt, but the ghostly figure did not give him another chance. Using his numbing power, the black servant leaned forward and breathed his black breath into the guard's face. The overseer fell unconscious and tumbled awkwardly down a few of the steps. It was deathly quiet. The rest of the Personal Guard began to slowly retreat, moving toward their fallen leader as they did so.

"People of Amuron, you are without a high king, so I now declare myself your leader. I am Necros, the new high king of Amuron. I assure you I am worthy of the right, for there is no one here who can defeat me in any kind of competition."

The evil king paused, but the only response from the crowd was silence. An infant's cry was quickly muffled. "Is no one here going to worship the new high king?" Necros raised his arms in the air, staring hostilely at the crowd.

From somewhere down at the far end of the stadium, Naibor could hear the faint echo of a low drum. Soon he could hear the sound of voices and the ringing of tiny bells. Then he could see the Ix people and hear their chant as they moved through the arena toward the king's platform. "Necros! Necros! King of Amuron!" they chanted, while the women danced vulgarly and the men sprayed blood from the carved horns they held in their hands. Louder and louder the chant became, until Naibor's whole mind was filled with the sound of it.

When the chanters reached the platform, a chill wind began to blow, blocking out the sun's heat. Naibor found the chant repeating itself over and over in his head until his tongue was forming the words inside his mouth. Many people in the crowd had joined the chant, but the chant had changed. "Necros! Necros! King of the living! King of the dead!" A fear seized Naibor when heard what the chant had become, and he knew in his heart that Amuron was lost.

To the right of the platform, a horn blast sounded. A group of soldiers from the military charged into the stadium on horseback, but they came too late! By the time the soldiers reached the chanting Ix people, the wind had turned into something foul. It whistled eerily throughout the arena, bringing with it a malevolent mist that clouded the senses and darkened the mind. The horses began to rear and snort with fright, and the soldiers tried desperately to regain control of them. The mist then began to take form, and when it did, screams of terror and cries for mercy rang out throughout the crowd in the stands.

Naibor found that he had fallen trembling to his knees. In the mist, he had seen the faces of the dead, and he suddenly realized who the servants of Necros were. They were the captured spirits of the dead, and now they were seeking out bodies to inhabit.

"What a wonderful sight," Necros said into Naibor's ear, gripping hard onto his shoulder. "And long awaited."

Naibor watched as the horrible spectacle before him continued. Nothing was left of the military's bold rescue. The horses had run screaming in every direction, and a number of soldiers lay dead from Ix knife wounds at the bottom of the platform steps. The rest had scattered or, worse yet, been possessed.

People in the arena around him were trying desperately to escape, running frantically from one end of the stadium to the other, only to find the exits blocked by more of the savage Ix people. Others in the stadium fought violently among themselves or tried to hide from those who had been possessed. Panicked children huddled together in groups, some crying in confusion, while others sought protection from the surrounding scenes of madness.

A private sob shook Naibor's body. Necros responded by whispering vengefully, "And you can do nothing to stop it!"

The king of darkness then straightened up and called out in a booming voice, "Stop! Listen to me, my servants, and obey. I have given you an eternal life as promised from long ago, and have provided you with these new bodies. I trust you will make good use of them, but now is the time for order. Any who are dangerous and not followers should be captured and locked up as prisoners. The women should be gathered to cook for us, and the children should be kept separate from them. Tomorrow work details will begin. Those of you who are not followers and who hear this, do not think of rebelling. Those of the dead cannot be killed. If they are in a body, the person's body will die—but not the spirit in it. You will only hurt your own people and former friends. There are other reasons why I would advise you not to do so, but I will only say this—don't put me to the test."

Necros then ran off a list of names of who was in charge of what. Finished with the formalities, he grabbed Naibor by the hair at the back of his neck and took him to a carriage that had somehow managed to remain upright at the foot of the platform.

"Come, Volkas," he called to the Ix leader, who was standing close by, wiping his bloodied knife with the ceremonial cloth intended for such use. "Come meet with me at the palace that was once mine and is now mine again. We shall feast together." Volkas gave a bow of his head in reply, and the carriage with its occupants wove its way through the confusion and out of the arena.

Captain Regg's eyes followed the carriage holding the sorcerer as it left the stadium. He had managed to fend off an attacking Ix woman by knocking the knife from her hand. Now he lay bleeding on the field of the arena with a gash in his thigh. His friend Captain Zai had been less fortunate. He lay unconscious and badly beaten not too far away.

The two captains had climbed into the stands after the parade, along with the rest of the crowd. They had felt confident about the city being secure, and both were looking forward to a time of enjoyment. Captain Regg had placed some men at the gates and around the stadium for crowd control. Captain Zai had some men patrolling the city to watch for thieves, as well as a small unit on horseback behind the king's platform in case of trouble. The rest of their men had been free to enjoy the games with their families.

When Necros had claimed himself as high king, the two of them had tried to round up as many men as they could and had run down onto the field just as Zai's men on horseback had charged in. When the foul mist had fallen upon them, Captain Regg found he was no longer leading an attack. It seemed that over half of their men had been possessed, and some of them had violently turned against their own group. Now all he could see were frightened people weeping in shock while those possessed were trying to round them up.

"Get up, Captain," he heard a cold voice say, and looking up, he saw a face that he knew.

"Kybor, is that you?"

"He is no longer as you knew him," the man informed him. "Now, get up!"

"I cannot use my leg," Captain Regg replied, motioning to his wound. To his surprise, the guard reached down and with amazing strength lifted him to his feet.

"You!" he barked to a passing soldier, who was being pushed with a group of men toward a bedraggled carriage that had flipped over a few times. "Assist the captain!" The soldier came over and put his arm around the captain to give him support.

Regg took the opportunity to use the sash from his dress uniform to apply a tourniquet to his leg to stem the bleeding.

"I will take care of this one myself," Kybor growled, and leaning down, he lifted the still unconscious Zai over his shoulder. "Move!" he grunted at Regg and the soldier. Together they slowly hobbled toward the carriage, following the line of prisoners.

Struggling to fit into the already crowded carriage, Regg grabbed Zai under the shoulders from Kybor and heaved him inside. When the carriage arrived in the Military Section, above the West Gate, the prisoners were shuffled off in the direction of the jail only to find it already full. Kybor spoke to another of the possessed, and they were quickly moved into one of the barracks normally used by the guards. The barracks were long, low buildings made of strong masonry bricks. They provided a perfect alternative.

After being locked in, Captain Regg went to get some medical supplies, linen cloths, and some water in a ceramic basin from the washing area at the back of the building so he could attend to his wounds and to those of his now conscious friend. "They can't be too concerned about a counterattack if they put two military captains together in one barrack," Regg remarked while washing the tear in Zai's cheek.

Zai winced. "You can't do much against the dead anyway."

"We will have to wait and see. I have some ointment to help heal your wound, but I think you are still going to have a scar," Regg said after assessing the damage to his friend's face. Besides the slash in Zai's cheek, his face was swollen and bruised. "How do you feel?"

"I'll live," Zai grunted, sitting up.

Checking his own wound, Regg grimaced. "I am going to have

to sew this closed to stop the bleeding," he noted, grabbing a needle and thread from the supplies.

After Captain Regg had stitched and rebandaged his leg with a clean cloth, one of the prisoners unexpectedly announced, "Someone's coming!"

All eyes in the room turned toward the door. There was the sound of a scuffle outside, and then the door burst open with a bang. A small, wiry man was thrown roughly inside.

"You have no power," the elderly man yelled, shaking his fist with anger at the door that had been quickly shut and locked after his entry. "You are fools to think that you and your Lord Necros will not suffer judgement."

Captain Regg and Captain Zai looked at each other, knowing their situation had just changed for the better. The man thrown inside the door was Graypah.

Graypah was a well-respected retired military captain who had been an advisor of the high king. There was very little that Graypah didn't know. He was soon surrounded by the inhabitants of the barrack.

"What is happening, Graypah?" one man asked.

"Tell us what to do," another pleaded.

The two captains both moved their way politely to the front of the crowd. "Let's move back and give Graypah some room," Zai told them, gently motioning the others away from the door. Graypah had not moved. He still stood facing the closed wooden door with his head down.

"Are you all right, Graypah?" Captain Regg looked anxiously at the advisor.

"The Daimos caught me giving food to some children on their way to where they are keeping them as prisoners. The children received a beating for it," Graypah confessed sadly, waiting a moment longer in sorrow. He then looked up with a tired sigh. "Come now, captains." He gestured toward the beds. "I see you have a lot of questions. Let me tell you what I know."

The captains settled on the nearest bed while Graypah sat facing them. The others in the room arranged themselves on the remaining cots and against the walls so that they could listen intently to what was being said.

A look of calm assurance now rested on Graypah's face as he spoke. "Regg, captain of the Guard of the Gates, and Zai, first captain of the People's Guard, I know of you both. You are good men and are loyal to our high king. He will have need of your services."

"Graypah, have you not heard?" Zai solemnly inquired, surprised that the advisor did not know the news. "Our lord, the high king, is dead."

"Is he?" Graypah asked, turning to Zai for confirmation. "What source gave you this information?"

"The sorcerer Necros."

"Not a very reliable source, Captain, but I'm sure he would be dead if Necros had the power. You do not know the high king like I do. He would have known about the arrival of his enemy, and you forget he wears the Stone of Wisdom. The stone is empowered to protect the high king, so therefore I do not think that the king is dead, but that Necros has done something to make it seem so." There was silence as this news registered around the room, and a new hope began to shine in the eyes of the men.

Captain Regg thought back to something Graypah had said earlier. "What was it you said captured you, Graypah?"

"The Daimos captured me."

"The Daimos?" Regg hoped for more clarification.

"The Daimos are the evil spirits that Necros has called from the dead. They were once the worshipers of evil gods and users of evil power. Long ago they were promised eternal life by their priests. What they did not know while they were still living was that their promised eternal life could be lived out only by inhabiting another's body. These are the Daimos of Necros."

"Is there nothing we can do?" Captain Zai said, trying to

remember the ancient laws. "Is there not something we can do to make Necros and the Daimos leave the city?"

"You are thinking of the law for banishing evil," Graypah answered.

"Yes, that's right!" Zai interrupted, "the law of banishment!" The forgotten law suddenly flooded into his memory. "If those whose faith and hope rest in the ruler of all fast and pray together as one to rid the city of evil, then that evil shall be cast out and never able to return."

"Unfortunately the law has been broken and evil has returned to the city," Graypah explained, "for Necros was once banished from this kingdom."

"But how can that be?" Zai muttered out loud.

"There is more to the law than what you recited. It goes on to say that the evil will never be able to return to the city unless one of royal blood invites the evil back and donates his blood to break the banishment."

"None of our royalty would do such a thing!" Captain Regg objected.

Graypah did not answer him. He only looked searchingly into Regg's eyes.

Different occurrences began to sort themselves in Regg's mind, coming together like the pieces of a puzzle. He thought of Prince Naibor asking Amon to be placed at the North Gate alone, and the replacement guard telling him that Amon was missing. He remembered that Naibor had come out of the palace with the sorcerer after Dame Lucianii had said that their children were missing, and he had seen the prince being taken away by the sorcerer after the Daimos had fallen upon the city. He knew who it was. "Naibor!" he said with anguish. "It was Prince Naibor."

"Yes, it must be Prince Naibor," Graypah agreed sadly, "for he was the only one of flesh and blood with the sorcerer at the arena."

One of the fellow prisoners jumped up. "Prince Naibor?" he said from between clenched teeth. "I'll, I'll ..." He choked on his rage.

"My family ... my friends ... the city!" Several others joined him in his anger, and they raised their voices, crying out against the prince.

"Enough!" Graypah said with authority, rising to his feet. "Your anger should be toward the evil that has come to our city, not toward the prince. He was foolish and listened to the lies of the enemy. Any of you could be guilty of the same offense, for any number of reasons—some even worse than those of the prince. We must stand together if we are going to fight this evil. The prince is suffering at the hands of the sorcerer, and that is punishment enough!"

Graypah looked around the room and into the eyes of those condemning the prince. All of them dropped their eyes before his stare and sat quietly back down.

"But what can we do against the sorcerer, Graypah?" Zai asked again.

"There is little now that we can do against the terrible evil that has befallen our city. Our sorrow is great and our losses many, but we must not lose hope. It is the only thing Necros has not taken from us. We must not let him. If our faith does not fail, then he is powerless to rob us of our spirits. We can pray for our loved ones and for Amuron, but the only one who can do anything against the sorcerer is Prince Naibor."

Several gasps of surprise sounded around the room, and this new information left Captain Regg feeling bewildered. Graypah, sensing their confusion, continued. "There is always a price to pay when you use the powers of darkness. The prince and Necros are held together by a blood covenant. This provides the prince with some limited protection. If the sorcerer were to kill the prince, Necros would be sent back into banishment. The covenant also gives Naibor another advantage. He now has the power to destroy the sorcerer. The prince only needs to find the means to do so."

"Does the prince know all this?" Captain Regg wondered, speaking his thoughts out loud.

"This I cannot say."

CHAPTER 8

The seven travelers marched eastward through the gully toward the outskirts of an old forest. Baynor took the lead, followed by Janii, Tayii, and Ranor, with Amon and Tybor at the end of the line. Sanii flew high over their heads, mostly gliding at an even pace.

The uncomfortable feeling that they were being watched lessened as they traveled farther away from the vile black cloud. When they reached the boundary line of stones that marked the border of the kingdom, Amon felt a strange tug at his heart. He had never before been outside of Amuron, let alone outside of the kingdom. Passing the boundary, he looked back toward the city feeling that things would never be the same for him once he returned home, if he ever did.

"It won't be the same when we go back, you know," Tybor commented from behind him, almost as if he knew what Amon had been thinking. "It never seems quite the same once you leave it."

"Oh," Amon replied despondently. He didn't find what the wolf had said very comforting.

"No, it certainly won't be the same," the badger added over his shoulder with a note of caution in his voice, "especially since Amuron has been taken over by a sorcerer with enough power to command the dead."

Not long afterward, the old waterway they were following entered the less open cover of a forest. Climbing easily up the northern side of the ditch, the troop stopped their march. Princess Sanii took the opportunity to swoop down to a low tree branch to join them.

"That's better," Janii sighed. "I'm glad we are out of the open."

"Sanii, do you think you can find the first gate and fly back to meet with us?" Baynor asked. "I want to be sure of the way."

Sanii nodded her head. But before she could fly off, she heard Tybor say with dismay, "Again!"

"Don't worry, beloved," she said, gliding down to face him. "I can fly high, away from any danger, and still see enough below to be able to find my way."

"This situation is not going to be easy on me," Tybor muttered to himself, watching as she took to the air. "I worry when she is separated from us."

Tayii looked at her brother compassionately and replied softly, "We all do."

After a short scout ahead, Baynor informed those traveling with him, "There does not appear to be a path through these trees, aside from a few animal runs. It would be best if we continued following the gully as a guide." The dry waterway had deepened, and the bottom of it had become rocky, but the edge of the ditch was relatively clear of obstructions, and they could make good time walking beside it.

"Can any of you tell me about Berroc?" Amon asked as they continued their journey.

"What do you know about it?" Baynor replied over his shoulder as the common trees of beech and ash began to be slowly replaced by the thick gray-trunked trees belonging to an ancient forest.

"All I know is that every high king or queen travels to Berroc before his or her coronation."

"Well then, let me tell you what I know," Baynor began, waiting for Amon to catch up with him. "All children of royal lineage are taught that the pilgrimage to Berroc takes six days of travel from the first gate and that there are seven gates in total. All the gates have names we must memorize; however, we are never told what the names mean, because we are supposed to learn that on our pilgrimage. We are told that it is a very solemn pilgrimage but that it is the greatest experience of a high king's or queen's life. We are also taught that Berroc, the Place of the Stones, is a most holy place. It is a place of communion where each new ruler must go to receive his or her blessing from Aii, to whom the new ruler must dedicate his or her life. There are rumors and great discussions about what exactly happens at Berroc, but we do not know for sure, because it is a personal experience that is not shared with others."

"Maybe nothing happens," Amon carelessly suggested, "and that's why nothing is said about it."

"Well, if that is true, then there is not much point of our going to Berroc," Baynor responded gruffly. "But I know differently," he continued. "My father told me that every high king that has gone to Berroc has come back to Amuron ready to rule. I remember Prince Naibor telling me in secret that his father had changed when he came back from Berroc. When I asked him what he meant, he said that he did not know how to describe it except to say that his father was now a true high king."

"I wonder if I should come along then," Amon blurted out suddenly, his eyes to the ground. "The spirit creature said you were to go to Berroc—not me."

"Don't worry," Janii spoke from behind him. "I do not think Nagala meant to exclude you."

"I don't know," Amon continued dejectedly. "It doesn't seem like a place for someone like me."

"None of us are high kings or queens, Amon," Baynor sympathized, inwardly smiling at the youth's humility. "We are going to see if we can do something for Amuron, and we are going to need your help. But if you feel uncomfortable when we get to the last gate, you need not enter with us; you can wait on the other side for us to return."

"Thank you, Prince," the encouraged youth replied, and he returned to the back of the line just in time to see the badger collapse in an exhausted heap.

"Prince Ranor!" Amon cried out, calling for the others to halt.

Tybor quickly dashed back from where he was walking beside his sister to check on Ranor's condition.

"I can't go on at this pace," Ranor said between pants. "I haven't got the long legs the rest of you brutes have. I cannot go another step!"

"How is he, Tybor?" Baynor's bear eyes clearly showed concern. The others gathered around, waiting tensely.

"I'm not trained in the healing of animals, but I'd say we should stop here." The wolf paced around his friend, appraising the situation. "He needs to rest. Amon, could you give him some water, please."

While Amon was giving Ranor some water, Baynor confided with Janii and Tayii a little to one side of their chosen path. "I was hoping to make the first gate by midday tomorrow, but I was forgetting that Ranor and Amon cannot keep the same pace as the rest of us."

"Janii, can you give Amon a ride on your back?" Tayii asked. "I am sure he would not be that heavy."

Baynor flashed a dubious look. "I don't know—"

Janii interrupted enthusiastically. "What a good idea, Tayii. I was forgetting I'm half horse."

"Well, that may solve Amon's problem," Baynor said, with a slow shake of his bear head, "but that still does not help Ranor any."

"You could carry him on your back," Tayii teased, giving Janii a quick look. "You're as wide as a horse." Janii gave a whinny that could be interpreted as a laugh, while Tayii purred softly with amusement.

"And your sense of humor hasn't improved over your brother's," Baynor replied with a snort. "But I don't think it will work. He would never be able to stay on."

Amon, catching the last part of their conversation, spoke up. "I can carry Prince Ranor. He can't weigh any more than my little brother, and I've carried him lots of times. I know it's not the proper way for a prince to travel, but if you don't mind, then I don't."

"That is very kind of you." The badger graciously accepted the boy's offer while unpleasant pictures of him being carried around like the family pet went through his mind.

"Now that we have all stopped for a rest," Amon began, looking toward the bear for approval, "how about a little breakfast?" Baynor looked at each of his friends and nodded with agreement, finding that he was suddenly hungry at the mention of food.

"It's not much," Amon said. "I tried to find a little something for everyone. I have some roots and bran for my lady." Amon gestured to the unicorn. "I have some smoked fish for you, sir." He nodded to the bear. "Some mussels wrapped in a damp cloth for you, Sir Badger, and some smoked meat for the rest of us."

"Amon, you are wonderful," Janii exclaimed, quietly munching on the bran he had poured into a pot for her.

They chatted while they ate, seemingly indifferent to their situation, but in their hearts they worried about what was happening back in Amuron and whether they would be able to help or not.

After finishing their quick meal, the bear gave a vocal yawn and said, "Time to get moving."

Tybor, watching Amon shake out the empty sack he had used to carry their breakfast, suddenly got an idea. "Ranor, why don't you climb into the sack that Amon is holding? Then he can carry you on his back like the merchants do with their wares." Although it was not a very flattering way to travel, everyone recognized the idea as a good one.

"That way, Ranor, you do not have to worry about scratching Amon," added Janii, "and Amon does not have to worry about you slipping. The only problem is what to do with the rest of the supplies that Amon has been carrying?"

"I think I know of a way," Amon stated, and after consulting with Prince Ranor, he soon had tied together the water pouches and the traveler's pack and secured them to the back of the grizzly's neck.

After resuming their journey, the winged princess returned, telling them that Baynor's information had been correct. If they stayed by the old waterway, it would eventually lead them to the first gate.

They were now heading into the heart of an ancient forest, which was as lifeless and barren as an old forgotten tomb. The forest of stone-gray trees was not dense, but the air was stifling and stale. Even the bright sunlight coming down through the long tree branches seemed to have paled. Fortunately there was little underbrush, so it was not difficult to travel quickly or keep to the side of the ditch they were following.

Amon looked up at the tall, smooth trees that seemed to be made of living stone. Their gray-white leaves did not move, and they provided little or no shade. "This forest seems very old," he commented.

"Indeed it is," Prince Ranor answered into his ear, from his seat on Amon's back. "Some say this forest was here long before any people ever existed on this world."

"How can that be?" Amon replied with a bit of a laugh. "We have been here for hundreds and hundreds of years."

"As strange as it may seem, in all of our earliest records, ancient maps, and writings, this forest has always been recorded as being here just as it is now."

"But that doesn't make any sense; the forest hardly looks alive." The youth was clearly puzzled.

"It does seem strange, I agree. There is an old story about this place that I can tell you as we travel if you would like to hear it," the badger proposed, hoping to lighten the oppressive mood.

"I sure would," Amon answered enthusiastically.

"It is the story of Andril and the crystal cave, and I will tell it to you as I heard it told to me. A long time ago there lived a man named Andril, who was well known throughout the world for being a learned man and a good thinker. For many years, Andril questioned the existence of the old forest and how it could have survived for so long without ever changing. One day the answer came to him.

He concluded that the water running by the roots of the trees must have the power to grant eternal life. He studied to find the source of the trees' water and discovered that the Sand Sea (which we will be crossing over) used to be a lake that was fed by mountain streams. He believed that the water from that lake must now run under the ground, and that this water would give eternal life to whoever drank it. So, leaving all that he knew in the world, he went in search of it.

"For many weeks, the villagers talked excitedly of Andril's return and of him finding the secret of eternal life. But he never returned, and the villagers soon lost interest, many believing he had found death instead of longevity."

Prince Ranor paused while Amon readjusted the weight on his back. "Some fifty years later, a traveler passing through the old forest heard the sound of someone crying. Finding an old man sitting on a rock, he asked his name. The man claimed to be Andril, the once well-known scholar. The traveler asked Andril why he had remained in the old forest and not returned to his village. Andril's answer was a strange tale. The scholar explained that for many years he had searched up and down the mountainsides, hoping to find a cave or an entrance to what he believed was an underground waterway beneath the old forest. After ten years of searching, he had found no clue, and so, discouraged, he had decided to return home. When he reentered the old forest on his final journey, his heart was so heavy that he had sat down on a rock and cried with grief. As he cried, he heard something move at his feet. Noticing he had disturbed a snake warming itself in the sun, he was about to hurry away, fearful that the snake might be poisonous. But the snake spoke to him and asked him why he had been crying. He explained to the snake that he had tried unsuccessfully for ten years to find the water that ran under the old forest they were in, because he sought eternal life. The snake hissed with laughter. 'You need only follow me into the hole under the rock you are sitting on. This will lead you to a most beautiful crystal cave containing a marvelous waterfall. If you but taste the water that issues forth from the waterfall, you will live forever and have the wealth of knowledge that comes from eternal life.' The snake then disappeared into a small gap under the rock.

"Overjoyed, Andril found a strong piece of wood to help him pry away the rock. Uncovering a small lair, the scholar enlarged the hole with his hands until he had dug his way into a low cavern that he had to crawl through on his belly. The cavern began to slope steeply downward until Andril found he was sliding headfirst into the darkness. It seemed to him that he had fallen a long way when he came to a sudden stop in some moist earth at the bottom of a large open cave. The snake had been right. He found himself in a cave lined with shards of hanging crystals, which seemed to radiate dazzling colors from an unknown source of light. Through the center of the cave ran the underground river for which he had been searching. The river shone a honey-gold and issued forth from a waterfall surrounded by clouds of bright mist. The waterfall was the most wonderful thing that Andril had ever seen. The scholar tried to explain it to the traveler, but Andril found that words failed him. All he could say was that the waterfall contained within the depths of its shimmering curtain all eternity, where the existence of time as they knew it did not exist. He further explained that as he stood watching the waterfall for what seemed to him but a moment, he grew old. He would have died standing there, without ever tasting the eternal waters, if he had not heard a strange conversation behind him.

"Unable to take his eyes off the cascading waters, he heard a voice telling the snake that it had disobeyed by bringing the man down to where no mortal had a right to be. The voice then told the snake that because of its disobedience it was banished from the crystal cave forever and that the man would take his place as the guardian and be allowed to drink from the eternal waters.

"Andril then told how the snake, with a hiss of anger, bit him in the leg so that he would die as the snake had originally intended. The pain and dizziness from the bite, however, caused him to fall into the river. While in the river, he swallowed some of the eternal waters and consequently lived after all.

"The puzzled traveler then asked Andril why he had been crying, since he now had the eternal life he so desired. Moaning in his sorrow, Andril explained that it was not as he thought it would be. He was now cursed to live forever on the mortal plane, where everything around him died. It was a life full of loneliness, and because of his foolishness he had to spend eternity as an old man with the pain of a snakebite in his leg. The only thing that helped him endure his endless days, Andril told the traveler, was keeping away those who wanted in life to make the same mistake as he. The traveler, after thanking Andril for telling him his story, then moved on, continuing with his own life journey."

"That's a good story, Prince," Amon said to the badger after he'd finished. "But I hope you don't expect me to believe that Andril is alive in this forest, keeping people from finding the crystal cave."

"Stranger tales have been told," the wolf added, jogging over to join them with a mysterious glint in his eyes. "I've heard it said that Andril has become mad over the years because of his loneliness and pain, and that he attacks anyone who enters here."

"That may be so," Ranor laughed, his sharp badger teeth showing in the wide grin. "But he should be wise enough to stay away from a group of talking animals." Tybor and Amon both agreed, laughing along with him.

Amon and the others enjoyed the story that Ranor had told. It was the kind of tale that travelers liked to tell to earn lodgings for the night as they wandered from town to town. It made them seem special in the eyes of ordinary citizens, who could not imagine the world beyond their own city or town. Some of the stories they told were scary, while others were silly, but they always gained a favorable response from the crowd. Amon's father, having been in the guard, had learned many of these tales. He entertained his family with them on stormy nights when they were gathered together around the hearth for warmth.

Amon noticed the trees getting thicker and the ground becoming steeper as they left the mysterious old forest behind. The trees surrounding them now danced gaily in the fresh breeze, laughing musically as their green leaves were tickled by the sunlight. Rocky outcrops sprang up around them, the first sign of the mountains they were steadily approaching, and they found they had to travel around large boulders that lined the deepening gully they were following on their right.

The warm sun was now at their backs as evening was drawing close. Although they had been traveling all day, with but a few short rests, the animals felt their spirits lift when the sun began to lower toward the horizon. Instinctively they began to yearn for the night's hunt, but they also knew that Amon would lag behind. They would soon need to find a place to stop and shelter for the night.

Feeling Amon's fatigue, Prince Ranor asked the youth to let him down so he could stretch his legs when the others decided to call a halt.

"If only I knew this trail better, then I could recommend a place to rest," Baynor commented, feeling frustrated that he had not had the time to properly prepare before they set out on their journey.

"I noticed a large outcrop of rock not too far from here. It is to the left of our chosen path, but I think it would be suitable," Sanii suggested from where she had perched on a young, leafy branch.

All agreed that this sounded like a good place to try, so they turned and headed off in the direction that Sanii led them. The eagle guided them to a rock face that jutted out from a hill, facing westward. The flat ledge of rock was almost level with the tops of the trees and sliced across the steep rise, making a natural shelf. To reach the top of it, they would have to climb up the side of the hill.

"This looks like it will do nicely, Sanii," Baynor said with approval, his nose twitching as he tested the air around him for signs of anything unusual. "Let's go up and have a look around."

Amon watched as Janii, Tybor and Tayii led the way, nimbly climbing up the slope with leaps and bounds to the top. Baynor, because of his bulk, took a little longer, but he soon joined the rest at the top.

"Ready, Prince Ranor?" Amon asked the badger at his feet.

"I'd rather stay down here, where I can dig myself a den for the night and be quite comfortable. But I suppose it would be best if we stayed together." Ranor gave the youth a nod and repositioned himself once again in the bag.

Lifting the badger prince onto his back, Amon began scrambling up the hill on all fours much like his companions before him. Normally the youth would have enjoyed the climb; however, his tired limbs felt heavy and clumsy as he grabbed for each new handhold and tried to secure his footing.

On reaching the top, Amon sat down momentarily to catch his breath, and he freed the badger from his back. Prince Ranor took the opportunity to thank the youth for getting him this far. Replying good-naturedly that he was glad to help, Amon stood up to have a look around. The outcrop they were on was wedge-shaped and nicely sheltered from the wind by an overhanging lip. Behind them the hill sloped gently over the remaining distance to the top of the rise.

"Good choice, Sanii. I couldn't have picked a better spot," Baynor said with approval.

Now that their need for shelter had been met, the eagle glanced conspiratorially at her friends with a gleaming round eye. "Even better, I know where I can get us some dinner." Hopping lightly to the edge of the cliff, she raised her wings. Hesitating before taking off, she added over her shoulder, "I'll expect a nice cooking fire for when I get back."

At the mention of dinner, the animals could resist their urges no longer. One by one they began to depart in search of food. Tybor, one of the last remaining, asked Amon, when the youth made a gesture to leave as well, "And where do you think you are going?"

The youth gave a shrug. "I thought I could look for firewood."

"Don't worry. Tayii and I will bring the firewood. You stay and rest. Better yet"—he looked at Amon's uniform with laughter dancing in his brown eyes—"You can be on guard while we are gone. After all, you're the most suited for the job." Not waiting to see Amon's grimace, he sprang away after his sister.

Amon sat with his feet dangling over the edge of the cliff, left alone with his own thoughts on the dark and silent rock. The setting sun spread a warm, honey-colored glow over all that was below him. The uneasiness he had felt earlier when they left home was gone; instead he felt an excitement stirring within him and a strange longing he could not name.

As the night deepened, Amon started a warm cooking fire with the wood Tybor and Tayii had brought to him. Sanii was one of the first to return, bringing with her a rabbit, which Amon quickly set about preparing. One of the duties of a guard was to cook, and Amon's father had showed him all he needed to know about the craft. As the other animals returned, several more rabbits were added. Soon they were cooking nicely on sticks over the fire, along with some ground squirrels roasting at the fire's edge. The animals all looked on eagerly, their eyes brightly reflecting the fire's light. They knew they did not have to cook their food, but their humanity would not allow them to eat it any other way.

When the meat was ready, Amon cut it into pieces so that each could take what he or she wanted. Baynor, having foraged in the forest for some sweet flowers, berries, and nuts, took only a tasty morsel or two. The others, being much hungrier and less polite, tore into their dinner with wild fervor until everything was devoured.

Seeing that Janii was the only one who could not join them, Amon quickly mashed some fruit onto a hot rock. Mixing it with some grain, he made her a meal of warm cereal. He then poured water into depressions in the rock's surface, creating small pools for those of his companions who needed a drink.

Not much was said during dinner, so the youth watched as the stars began to light the night sky. "It is time to get some sleep, Amon." He heard the bear's throaty voice from the other side of the fire after the meal was finished. "We will be rising before the sun tomorrow."

Shaking himself, Amon realized that the air had turned chill. He dug out from among his things the light traveling blankets, which were woven tightly to hold in the heat while keeping out the wind and rain. Wrapping himself snugly, he lay down close to the warmth of the low fire and closed his eyes.

"May I join you?" Tybor asked, and Amon smiled to himself when he felt the warmth of the wolf at his back.

If a traveler had been passing by that night and had been able to see those that slept together on the rock ledge, he would have had a strange tale to tell. The story would have begun with a youth sleeping next to a wolf, but the wonders of the tale would not have stopped there. The story would have included a unicorn lying beside its natural enemy, a panther, along with a badger curled up in a bag near a bear that slept protectively close by. The traveler would have embellished the story greatly, resulting in a tale full of dangers and perils that caused these seven travelers to come together in companionship. Then the traveler would poetically finish the story with moonlight outlining the silhouette of an eagle that was resting peacefully on an outcrop above them all.

* * *

Prince Naibor sat at the banquet table and absentmindedly chewed his thumbnail. Time was going by too quickly. He tried desperately to think of something to do against Necros, some sort of plan, but he feared that instead he would lose control and be lost in despair. Different scenes of horror that he had witnessed at the stadium kept pushing themselves into his consciousness. He tried to get them out of his mind so he could think straight.

At the table with him sat Necros, Volkas, and several Ix people, as well as some of the possessed people from the city, whom Volkas referred to as the Daimos. Elbanor, with great delight and humility, served them a meal using food that appeared to be left over from the previous night's banquet. Naibor had tried to listen to the conversation between the sorcerer and the Ix leader, but he was unable to concentrate. He picked up only snatches of their conversation, such as, "… at the sacrifice," "… build the new temple," and, "… revolt in the women's camp."

Elbanor kept a close watch on the prince throughout the dinner. At Naibor's request to leave, the sorcerer's servant took the opportunity to accompany him and further rub salt into his wounds.

"Why do you still fight Necros?" he asked, not waiting for a reply. "You know it is useless to oppose him. Serve him as I do and you will regain your power. I am sure he would give you a place of honor if you worship him, being the one who allowed his return. Necros might even let you rule under him, as you have dreamed of so many nights in the past. Think it over, Prince. Tonight at the sacrifice you can join with us in exalting the powers of evil, and your mind can become at peace. What can you gain by fighting us—your honor? You have no honor. You have betrayed your people and disdained and destroyed your friends, and now your father is dead. You have already served Lord Necros. Now is the time to serve him fully."

In walking quickly down the halls Naibor had hoped to discourage Elbanor from following him, but the elder tutor had managed to keep step with him the whole time. Now they had reached the upper level and were nearing his bedchambers. The prince reached out a hand to stop the horrid little man from pursuing him further. Looking down at his former tutor, he said, "You used to come to me as a sheep, meek and mild, but now I see you were really a wolf in disguise."

"Yes," Elbanor answered shrewdly, pushing away Naibor's hand to grab onto his coat. Drawing himself nearer, he looked up and vehemently whispered into the prince's face, "And you used to come to me as a prince, full of pride and arrogance, but you were really just a fool." With a strength that surprised the prince, Elbanor released him with a shove and walked away.

Entering his room, Naibor fell to his knees a broken man and did the only thing left in his power to do—pray.

CHAPTER 9

The time for the sacrifice had come. Naibor was summoned from his room by two of the Daimos and escorted to the Great Hall, where the ceremony was to take place. The Daimos that walked beside him were dressed in crimson robes that flowed out and down from the neck in a bulk of cloth. Before he was allowed to enter the hall, the prince was taken to a small antechamber. Once there, he was wordlessly instructed to put on one of the ceremonial robes.

The Hall of Hearing was, as always, silent and waiting when Naibor entered, but it was no longer inviting. In the center of the hall, a slab of black stone had been set up as a table to lay the chosen sacrifice upon. Stands holding smoky torches had been placed around the table. The oil that burned in the torches was at the same time both sweet smelling and repugnant. Naibor thought he was one of the first to arrive, until his eyes caught sight of more red robes among the shadows between the pillars.

At the sound of a single but steady drumbeat, a wordless procession began to move forward in the dim light from the far end of the hall. The first Daimos in the procession came forward carrying a golden basin. The second, following two steps behind, held a golden chalice on a round tray covered by a black cloth. The next Daimos carried a black knife with an inscribed golden handle on a pillow of red. Behind this Daimos came Necros. He carried a small inscribed urn with a lid.

Normally the black sorcerer was frightening enough to look at, with his piercing, empty eyes, but now he sent a shiver of dread up Naibor's spine. The sorcerer's face appeared deathly pale, in stark contrast to the red symbols he had drawn on his cheeks and the black he had painted on his lips. The robe that he wore was a colorless grey, the edges of which were outlined in a cold red that seemed to seep out from the lifeless fabric. The hands that carried the urn had been stained a crimson color, and Naibor shuddered to think with what they had been stained.

The procession continued. Another Daimos followed Necros, this one carrying a raven perched on top of a carved pole of ebony. Two more followed in succession, each carrying a large white porcelain urn etched with red markings. The leader of the Ix people came last, dressed as a raven, in black feathers and a headdress.

After those in the procession had taken their places around the table, those attending the ceremony began to come forward from the shadows and draw into a tight circle around the smooth slab. The prince gasped when he saw the faces of those previously hidden. Each face was covered with a gray burial mask, reminding Naibor of those controlling the bodies from within.

"Bring the prince," the sorcerer ordered, and Naibor was roughly moved over to the table by one of the robed servants. "You should witness the final result of your treachery." The prince silently prayed that his knees would not buckle.

Taking the ceremonial knife from the pillow, Necros cut deeply into his wrist, opening a vein. His blood ran freely, pouring into the awaiting basin held by a Daimos to catch every precious drop. When the sorcerer was satisfied with the amount, he nodded to another servant. This Daimos quickly opened the small urn that Necros had been carrying and sprinkled some of its powdered contents onto the flowing wound. Before Naibor's eyes, the blood began to slow and the ugly gash to close, healing into a tiny line.

The sorcerer then chose several others, and the process of bloodletting continued. When the basin was almost full, Necros placed it on the table in front of him. The room began to resonate with mounting anticipation as the sorcerer stirred the warm liquid with his hands. Using the blood on his fingers, Necros wrote an inscription on the table. The strange letters sat upon the surface, almost pulsing with a life of their own. Extending his hands over the writing, the sorcerer whispered an incantation, and the red letters disappeared into the table as if swallowed whole.

"Bring me the sacrifice!" Necros commanded, suddenly breaking the silence. There was a flurry of activity and a rustle of robes, and Naibor saw Elbanor and several Daimos hurrying toward the sorcerer.

Naibor then realized that Elbanor had been missing from the ceremony, and he guessed why. The elder servant must have gone to the wine cellar to get the prisoners. The moment of truth had come. Now Necros would know what he had done. The prince involuntarily shivered, awaiting some horrible end brought about by the angered sorcerer.

"The animals and the boy are gone, my lord," Elbanor informed his ominous master. "We searched and found no sign of them in the palace. The Daimos say they are not within the city."

Necros turned toward the prince. Naibor tried in vain to look brave, but the sorcerer only looked at him and smiled a smile that was anything but pleasant.

"You were right, Elbanor," Necros said, looking momentarily at his dutiful servant. "The prince can no longer be controlled by fear, and he can no longer be trusted. He must be watched from now on. But we still need a sacrifice!" He turned his attention back to the ritual. "I can feel the hunger of the table as it draws power from our blood. It must be fed, or the incantation will work against us."

"We will sacrifice the prince," Elbanor suggested, eagerly taking a step toward Naibor.

"No!" Necros's voice was stern. "You forget about the higher laws." Elbanor dropped his head in subservience, but his eyes remained on the prince, promising revenge.

"Shall we bring a baby from the city?" Volkas inquired, ready to give the command to his people.

"No, we have not the time. I can already feel my power being drawn by the table." Going over to his faithful companion, Necros grabbed Elbanor by the shoulders. "You will be the sacrifice, and tonight you shall have immortal life!"

Elbanor tried to shrink from both the sorcerer's piercing gaze and his touch, but he was helpless. "M-M-Master!" The elder tutor stumbled over the word. His eyes were wide, and his bottom lip trembled ever so slightly when he continued. "I have only desired to be always at your side and to learn of the art that you, many years ago, said you would teach me as your apprentice."

"I can give you nothing greater than the honor of being one of my immortal servants, to know my thoughts and to experience my power through death. Do not disgrace me, Elbanor; time is short. Place your life in my hands, and I will give it back to you; displease me and I shall make you suffer so that death will be something you can only dream about."

Elbanor looked pleadingly for a moment into the sorcerer's eyes. He saw no mercy. Unable to match the will of his master, Elbanor's body slumped into the red-stained hands of his lord.

Laying the chosen sacrifice on the stone slab, Necros opened Elbanor's robe, exposing his chest. Those within the hall began to softly hum a chant. The sorcerer then moved to the head of the table and dipped his fingers once more into the blood. Speaking arcane words, he placed some of the red liquid on Elbanor's closed eyes, under his nose, on his lips, and upon his left breast. The wordless chant of the Daimos continued, increasing in volume each time it was repeated. Necros then took the knife and dipped it into the small urn, ensuring the black blade was covered in the fine powder. The chant rose to a fever pitch, ending in a scream, and Necros plunged the knife down.

Naibor averted his eyes, but the dead silence filling the hall caused him to bring his gaze back to the table. Once again Necros was holding the knife, but this time only the handle remained.

Putting aside the handle, Necros lifted the golden chalice. "Now we will drink to our unity." Taking the cup, he dipped it into the basin and filled it with blood. Those around the table began to spread out, holding on to one another's hands, until a large ring was formed. The prince watched, feeling his stomach lurch, as Necros took a drink from the chalice before passing it to Volkas in the circle. The Ix leader also took a drink and then passed it on to the next person. This continued until it had gone all around the circle and every Daimos had taken a drink.

When the cup was returned to Necros, he raised his arms for silence, although those in the room had not made a sound. "Hear me!" the sorcerer boomed in a voice that rocked the unseen chandeliers overhead. "I, Necros, command the spirit of the sacrifice to walk upon the earth. The ritual is complete. We are in unity, and you have my blood to give you power. Come forth! We await you!"

A chill wind began to wail within the hall. Naibor saw, or thought he saw, the thin black outline of a robed figure appear at the foot of the table. The figure wavered like smoke in a breeze, and it seemed much less permanent than the black figures the prince had previously seen. Shadowy and silent, it bowed its head to Necros, and they exchanged unheard words.

Breathing a sigh of relief that the ceremony was over, Naibor hoped he could return to his room. But Necros spoke again. "Daimos, your brother is weak. Although his spirit was mine, he did not come as you did as a willing sacrifice. Elbanor, therefore, has not the strength to take possession of a human body, and he is useless to me. Rather than have his spirit removed from the earth, he has chosen to take the body of an animal. I have agreed. In honor of death and the power that we serve, the spirit of Elbanor shall possess the animal we use to represent these things. He shall take the body of the raven."

The raven, after sitting so quietly throughout the ceremony, suddenly gave a loud squawk. Flapping its wings violently back and forth while holding on to the perch, it looked as if it were trying to fight off an unseen foe. After several hoarse cries, it flew from the ceremonial pole to the shoulder of Necros. Once there, it ruffled its feathers triumphantly.

"It is done," the sorcerer proclaimed darkly.

The solemnness of the ceremony suddenly changed. The robed Daimos started laughing and hugging one another. The Ix people began to play music, and their leader, dressed as a raven, began to dance. Turning his head from side to side, he made the dull yellow eye on the headdress catch the light. Then, jumping forward in a pretend attack, he beat his wings rapidly, sweeping them up high and down low. The music was wild, and the Daimos began behaving as if they had lost control. Waving their arms in the air, they ran around the hall screaming and yelling. Other Daimos did flips and somersaults or jumped up and down. All seemed to be in a fit of hysteria. All except for Necros, that is, who stood watching the entire proceedings without moving from his position at the head of the table.

When the revelers were at the point of exhaustion, the music slowed to a stop. The Daimos then began to disperse, returning silently to whatever task they had been assigned within the city.

Volkas and some of the Ix people waited patiently in a group by the end of the table. "Volkas, you may have the body for your rituals," the sorcerer said, gesturing with his arm as if releasing those remaining from a spell.

The immense hall was almost empty when Necros finally approached the weary prince. Two of the red-robed guards remained standing faithfully by Naibor's side. The king of the dead gazed menacingly at the prince, perhaps looking for a reaction, but the prince had nothing to give.

Turning abruptly, almost causing the raven Elbanor to lose his footing, he gave his last instructions before striding from the great hall. "Take the prince to his room, and keep constant watch at his door."

* * *

"Amon," the youth heard a resonant voice say in his ear. "It is time to go."

Amon felt the cold around him and the hard ground beneath him. It was still dark because the sun had not yet risen. Pulling the blankets high over his head, he instinctively gathered himself into a tighter ball.

"Come on, Amon; get up or I'll tell Baynor to get you up," the wolf threatened with the hint of a growl.

"All right." Amon gave in, pushing the blankets away with a shiver. "I'm up."

Every muscle in Amon's body protested stiffly as he got to his feet. The cold and wetness in the air clung to him, and he could make out only vague shadows in the surrounding darkness.

"What's wrong?" the badger asked from close by as Amon groped around for his bag.

"It's too dark," the youth replied, putting his hand into the cold ashes of the fire. "I can't see."

"Clouds moved in during the night; that is why it is so dark. Have you a torch?"

"Yes, it is in my bag, but I can't find it," he answered in frustration.

"I will get it," the nocturnal badger offered.

There was the sound of some shuffling and dragging, and then Amon felt the bag pushed against his feet. Within moments, a spark from Amon's flint caused the light of a flame to spring up from the torch in his hand. The light was not far reaching, however. As soon as it left the flame, it became encircled by the thick mist.

Amon could now dimly make out the animal forms of his companions and see the glow from the torch reflected eerily in their eyes. Setting the light down carefully against a rock, the youth splashed some cold water onto his face before hastily gathering up his belongings into the sack. When he was ready, he signaled to the others with a nod. Picking up the torch, he followed as they climbed over the hill of the ridge and down into the forest on the other side.

Morning came to greet them as they left the forest to walk among a valley of rolling hills. The fog began to lighten, as well as the world around them, but there was no sun. The day would remain gray. Once again they met up with the former gully, which had changed to a wide streambed holding a slow-moving, shallow stream.

Hot breath steamed from their mouths while the seven companions stopped for a short rest huddled together in an open stretch between two of the larger hills. The hills surrounding them were covered by short wild grasses and various flowering shrubs that hung down, wet from the fog. The damp and raw air made Amon long for a warm drink.

Prince Baynor approached the youth just as he was adjusting the badger prince on his back. "Amon, now that we are in the open, we, as animals, can travel faster." Ranor gave a snort in his ear when he heard this. "Seeing as this seems like a good time to stretch our legs in a run, Janii has offered to let you ride on her back."

Janii swung her magnificent blue eyes around to look at the youth, and he fancied that she gave him a big smile. "That is, if it is all right with you?"

Replying with a wide grin, Amon flung himself agilely onto the unicorn's back. Janii shied a little, first this way and then that, until she was used to the feel of the weight on her back. "There, that's better," she said when everything was under control. "No doubt you, Amon, will be the first and the last human to ever say he has ridden a unicorn."

Getting an idea, Janii stomped her nimble hoof onto the soft ground to get everyone's attention. Raising her horn high, her eyes gleamed with enthusiasm. "I challenge you all to a race to the first gate."

"I accept the challenge," the winged princess, wolf, and cougar said, with their animal voices rising in excitement.

"All right," Baynor agreed, speaking to Janii. "You give the signal to start."

Looking over her shoulder, the unicorn warned the youth, "Hold on tight. I feel as if I could outrun the wind." Then, with a loud neigh and a toss of her head to clear the mane from her eyes, she leaped forward at a run, with the others racing swiftly behind.

Amon leaned forward excitedly, the wind whistling in his ears. The unicorn's gait was smooth, and her footfalls light, as she galloped over the lush green hills. The speed at which she ran made Amon's eyes water, blurring the hills and the valleys in a swirl of fog.

"Prince Ranor," Amon shouted over his shoulder, caught up in the excitement of the race, "where are the others?"

"Baynor was close behind us, but now he has dropped back and is behind the last hill. Sanii is above the clouds, and Tybor and Tayii are competing against each other far behind us."

Janii ran on, invigorated by the pace. The soft grass and the cool air made her heart race with joy. She wanted to leap and to roll, to climb and to dance—but to run was enough. Then, as she ran, she saw a flash of white on the hill to her left. She called out with her unicorn voice, almost despite herself, and her call was answered. Could it be that a wild unicorn was coming to race with her among the hills? In her mind she pictured them running together in harmony, sharing in their joy and companionship as they urged each other forward. Checking her stride, Janii waited for the young unicorn to join her.

Janii imperceptibly heard a shout from her rider while concentrating on the other unicorn. "Princess!" Instead of running toward her, the young unicorn wove an erratic pattern over the ground.

Slowing to almost a stop, Janii realized that the other unicorn was not running in joy. It was running in terror before a mountain lion that was chasing it. The predator lunged in a mass of fur and muscle. Its teeth were bared, as it longed hungrily to taste flesh, and its claws were extended. Janii froze, trembling, as she smelled the other unicorn's fear.

The tiring unicorn, with wild terror in its eyes, suddenly ran straight toward them, attempting to get away from the horrid creature at its heels. Amon kicked at Janii as if she were a stubborn mule. "Princess, please!" he pleaded in her ear, but to no avail. The young unicorn raced past with the angry cat following.

Seeing death in the lion's eyes, Janii reacted instinctively. Jolted into action, she kicked out at the cat and leaped away at high speed. Thrown off balance, Amon could not hold on. He and the badger were sent tumbling head over heels to the ground.

The mountain cat shrieked in outrage when a new perceived assailant fell down almost on top of its head. Having its path blocked, the cougar flattened its ears, preparing to attack the half dazed and defenseless youth. Ranor, after freeing himself from Amon's bag, ran in front of the youth to protect him. Snarling viciously, the badger challenged the savage animal. The wildcat hissed loudly in return, hesitating in a moment of indecision.

Seizing this opportunity, the badger snapped wildly in a violent flurry at the lion's face. Janii, still running in fright, heard the sounds of the conflict behind her and suddenly came to her senses. "What am I doing?" she cried aloud, her anger rising to take away the numbness and fear. Turning in midstride, she stormed back to join the fray.

The lion, engaged in a vicious battle with the tenacious badger, was totally unprepared for the attack of an adult unicorn. Trumpeting a battle cry, Janii charged with her horn lowered. The mountain predator turned in time to fend off Janii's assault, unwittingly exposing its side to the badger. Ranor's sharp, pointed teeth quickly found their mark. With a scream of pain and frustration, the lion tried to shake the badger off while continuing to dodge further attacks from the unicorn. Then the wildcat began to run, having had enough. The lion was leaving with or without the badger still attached.

Ranor let go, and Janii made the pretense of chasing after the cougar, to make sure it did not change its mind. The mountain cat, however, was going away to nurse its wounds and to ease its hunger with easier prey.

"Is everyone all right?" Janii asked anxiously, looking at each of her friends while trying to catch her breath.

"I think so." Standing up, Amon brushed himself off. Unable to look the unicorn in the eye, he busied himself with a rip at the elbow in his shirt.

"I'm all right," Ranor told her, giving his body a shake, "but, Janii! What happened?"

"I'm so sorry," she apologized, her head hanging down. "I don't know what came over me. I guess I let my animal side or my instincts get the better of me. I'm not really sure. My emotions seemed to be controlling me, and it wasn't until I heard you fighting with the lion that I came to my senses. My thoughtless actions could have seriously hurt someone!"

There was a pause before Janii continued. "Let's see if we can find some way out of the mess I've gotten us into."

The three looked around in dismay. They stood at the bottom of a grassy bowl, encircled by hills on all sides. The reality of their situation began to sink in. In her excitement, Janii had left the shallow gully they were using as a guide some time ago, and now, in all the confusion and fog, they were not really sure in which direction to travel and had little hope of being found.

"I cannot believe I have been so foolish," Janii scolded herself. "I cast all caution to the wind and ran wild, leading myself and others into danger. Baynor will be so angry with me."

"We might have used the sun as our guide, if only the fog had not thickened as we climbed higher into the hills," Ranor commented, searching the skies above him. "Even Sanii will have a difficult time trying to find us."

"Maybe we can get a better view of where we are if we climb up the hill in front of us," Amon suggested. "It is the highest of the hills surrounding us."

The others nodded their affirmation, and together they walked up the gentle slope. They each secretly hoped to find something to guide them when they reached the top, but they were disappointed.

Standing at the crest, there was not much to see but the silhouettes of more hills through the swirling clouds of wet gray. At the bottom of the hill lay a quiet pool of clean, clear water. Its mirrorlike surface reflected the endless haze of the sky and the ever-so-green hills surrounding them.

"Well, it isn't what we were hoping for," the disheartened unicorn sighed. "But it sure would be nice to have a drink." She had become suddenly aware of her great thirst after her long run.

"That sounds good," the badger agreed, longing to get the cat hair out of his mouth. "And you could refill your water bag, Amon."

As they went down the hill toward the water, Amon began to feel apprehensive. He looked around, trying to find some reason for his uneasiness, but he could find nothing. "What is bothering me?" The youth questioned, speaking aloud. "There are birds feeding by the waterside. They would not be here if there was any danger." As they approached, the small flock of birds rose quickly into the air before landing a safe distance away on the opposite side of the lake.

The unicorn's lips were just about to touch the water's surface when Amon cried out, "Janii, don't!"

Reacting quickly, Janii brought her head up with a jerk. "What is it, Amon?" she inquired with a tremble, hearing the edge of fear in his voice.

"The water! It changed when you went to drink it!"

"What do you mean?" she asked, taking a step back from the lip of the serene pool. "I didn't notice anything."

"The sky was no longer reflected in the water. And I saw something else," he explained.

"What did you see?" Ranor demanded, his lip curling back.

"I don't know," Amon replied honestly.

They all stared at the water, but they could see nothing unusual.

"I did not see anything either," the badger said, echoing Janii's words, and he moved closer to the water to get a better look. "It was probably your imagination. Maybe it was the reflection of a fog cloud passing by."

"I don't see anything now," Amon said defensively, "But I get a strange feeling from this place, don't you?"

The two animals exchanged glances. They could sense nothing out of the ordinary. The badger sniffed at the water, but he could smell nothing wrong with the water.

"What is it you feel, Amon?" Janii asked, perplexed.

"I don't know how to explain it."

"Try," she urged.

"It is a kind of tingling feeling, as if something is going to happen. It's not a scary feeling—just an unusual feeling. Just to be on the safe side, I would be happier if you did not drink the water," he added, and out of respect for the youth, his companions chewed the wet grass instead.

Feeling suddenly impatient with himself, Amon dug a stone out of the earth and threw it into the water. Nothing happened! The water rippled normally until the disturbance subsided. "I guess it is just my imagination," the frustrated youth muttered, and stepping up to the water's edge, he prepared to fill his waterskin. Looking at his reflection, he saw himself as a young boy looking back.

"Aaaagh!" Springing back from the water, he fell over backward in fright.

"What?" Janii and Ranor both asked with concern.

"There *is* something strange about that water! I just saw myself as a boy!"

Janii went over to try to calm the youth, while Ranor went over yet again to look into the pool.

"You must be the only one who can see anything," the badger surmised. "Come. Have another look and tell us what you can see. It might be important."

"It could be dangerous as well!" Janii cautioned, reading the fear on Amon's face.

"I think it's a descrying pool," Ranor said excitedly, licking his badger lips.

"A what?" Janii asked.

"A descrying pool. Ancient tribal documents talk about still pools of water in which elders used to learn of events to come—especially if they were going to war."

"Ancient tribal documents! How do you know this is a descrying pool?" Janii asked Ranor dubiously.

"I do not know for sure, but it sounds like what they used to describe in their writings."

"Well, what do you think, Amon?" Janii asked the youth softly. "Do you want to take another look?"

Amon did not really want to. He wished this were not happening to him. He wanted everything to be the way it used to be before the sorcerer had come to the city. He was worried about his family and what was going on back home, but now he was here and there was no turning back. Not wanting to let his friends down, he got up and said, "I'll take another look."

Going back over to the side of the lake, Amon got down on his hands and knees and bent over the edge of the pool to stare into the water. The water was like liquid glass, reflecting the cloud-filled gray sky in its smooth and tranquil surface. Amon's racing heart slowed. A deep calm came over him as the sereneness of the pool rose up around him almost as if he were floating within the richness of the cool water. The image of the misty sky slowly swirled and cleared until an endless deep blue sky could be seen in its place. A young couple appeared, bringing an infant to one of the city's temples to be blessed by a priest, as all firstborn children were. He watched while the priest anointed the child with fragrant oil before praying silently with the parents for the child's well-being. The couple looked familiar to Amon, and he pondered who they might be until he heard the priest address them. They were his parents, and he was the infant!

"There is a prophecy for your son," the priest joyously told them, opening his eyes. "But it is for your ears only, and even the child must not know of it, so that the prophecy of his life will not be changed." Amon then heard the prophecy. "Your son will be a great and guided servant—one who will bring you both sorrow and joy."

"Is this a good prophecy?" his mother inquired of the priest, puzzled by what he had told her.

"I can tell you no more about it," he answered simply. "But I can tell you it is a privilege to receive a prophecy concerning your child. It is not common."

The picture began to fade, and the water's glassy surface returned. Amon, disappointed that there was no more to see, started to move away. He quickly stopped when the water began to swirl again. It filled this time with rolling black clouds. He saw a violet-colored sunset stretch endlessly within the depths of the pool. Then he was looking into a dark room lit only by the flame of a candle, but even in the dim light he recognized his parent's room: the bed and its marriage quilt; the patterned tiles behind it on the wall; the table beside the bed, where the candle burned; and the shuttered window with the woven curtains. He assumed the room was empty, until he could just make out the shape of a figure sitting in the shadows by the window.

"Mother." Amon mouthed the word, not daring to speak aloud for fear of losing the picture. Her face was hidden by her hair, which fell forward from her tilted head and drooping shoulders, and alarmed, Amon realized she was crying.

The picture faded quickly into blackness before growing lighter and becoming so bright that the light was like the brilliance of the sun. Amon shaded his eyes, but the brightness did not last, and he found himself looking into a large room made dark by shutters closed against the sunlight. At first he could not see much of what was happening in the room, because of the intensity of the light from moments before. When his vision adjusted to the dim light, he was shocked to find the room full of children of different ages. There were children everywhere he looked. One or two were on chairs, but most were on the floor or together on beds. The worst of it was that Amon had never seen children so unhappy. Most of the young ones were crying. The older children were making attempts to look after them, but all of them together looked so lost and lonely as they sat unnaturally quiet with vacant stares.

As Amon watched the pitiful sight, a door at the end of the long room opened, and in came two adults, one carrying a large pot and the other a sack. Instead of the children hurrying forward to get the food, most cringed in fear or huddled together for protection. The adults, however, paid no attention to them, and leaving the food on the floor, they went back out the door. Some of the larger children then came forward. The sack contained dishes and bread, but when one girl did not find what she hunted for, she cried out in dismay, "No milk! How can we feed the babies? They cannot live on water alone!"

Amon was confused by these images. He did not understand what was happening or even know who these children were, but he did know it made him uncomfortable. He continued watching, hoping to find some clue as to why he was seeing this vision. When he found out, his sorrow was so great he felt as if a permanent rend had been made in his heart.

While the children were being served their meal, one of the girls went to draw a boy from the corner, where he sat rocking himself for comfort. Amon gasped when he saw the child's face for the first time released from the shadows. It was his younger brother! She sat the young child down in a space on one of the beds and attempted to feed him some broth from a bowl, but every time she brought the spoon to the boy's mouth, he turned his face away in refusal. The young girl continued to try in desperation to get him to eat, but his brother could only cry his grief to her, and eventually she had to give up and try with another child.

"No!" Amon cried out, and in anguish he hit the water with his fist, causing the vision to disappear into ripples of water before returning to its natural state.

Janii shivered, but whether it was from a chill as her body cooled down or from nervous anxiety she did not know. She waited quietly with Ranor while the youth dealt with his emotions, giving him a chance to sort out what he had confronted in the descrying pool.

"Amon," Janii called softly to him.

"They have taken the children away from their homes and locked them up together somewhere," Amon explained, looking up into the large, liquid blue eyes of the unicorn, with tears still visible on his cheeks. "My younger brother," he began, choking on the words in his sorrow, "he is so upset because he has been taken away from my parents that he is refusing to eat. He does not understand. I need to help him! He is so pale and he has dark circles under his eyes. I've got to do something!" Amon got up from his knees and looked at his companions imploringly.

"As upsetting as it is, Amon, we can do nothing more right now than help ourselves," Ranor pointed out, speaking calmly.

"I should not have come!" The youth spoke angrily in his frustration. "You should have gone to Berroc by yourselves. I should be back in Amuron with my family."

"Even if you were in Amuron right now, you still might not be able to help your brother. There is no point in wishing for things that cannot be changed," the badger added with a sigh. "Sometimes it is easier to deal with feelings of regret than with the situation you find yourself in. I am sorry I made you look in the descrying pool. It seems it would have been better if we had left it alone."

"No," the youth said resolutely. "I am glad I looked."

"Good," Ranor replied, proud of the youth's courage. "Now, are you able to tell us what you saw?"

Amon nodded his reply and then began to relate all that he had seen in the pool. Janii and Ranor listened closely to everything Amon had to say, hoping to gain some insight into their situation. Surprisingly, all the visions Amon had seen in the descrying pool were of a more personal nature than Ranor had anticipated. Ranor had thought Amon would see more global events—events relating to the city of Amuron, such as the visions recorded in the ancient scrolls. This did not mean, however, that nothing could be learned from the visions. Ranor intended to learn as much from them as possible.

Just as Amon finished speaking, the sun made a hazy appearance in the sky. Finally they were able to gain a sense of direction. Eager to be reunited with their companions, the three of them set off in an eastward direction, heading up the hill on the opposite side of the pool and down the other side into another shallow valley. This time Amon and the badger traveled on foot so that they would be sure not to pass by the old waterway or any signs left behind by their friends.

There was little time now for reflection on the visions Amon had seen, but Ranor found the images the youth described occupying his mind. The first vision was the one Ranor felt the most comfortable about interpreting. Amon either had, or was now, fulfilling his role as a great servant; therefore, he had been allowed to hear the prophecy. That much seemed clear. The vision of his mother weeping also went along with this prophecy, for the priest had said Amon would bring his mother both sorrow and joy. Ranor presumed this second vision was from the present. *Amon's mother must fear her son dead, thereby explaining her sorrow.* Of this he was not positive. He was unsure how joy fit into this vision or whether it even should. The last vision was as insightful as it was disturbing, but he felt certain he could make some assumptions from it.

"It must be assumed," he said quietly, thinking aloud, "that the sorcerer has somehow taken over the city and has certain people in the city helping him. I must also assume that he is using the children as hostages to control the citizens. But just what the sorcerer wants to use the city for and why he has summoned the dead still remains a mystery."

"I must admit," Ranor continued, muttering in a low tone. "I'm a little bit disappointed in myself. I've studied ancient lore, tribal customs, and foreign cultures, but I just do not know enough about sorcerers to have even the slightest idea of what this one might be planning."

While the badger talked to himself, he failed to realize that his companions had stopped several paces behind him. Hearing his name, Prince Ranor turned his head but kept on walking for several more paces until he found himself standing in a small stream. Janii and Amon had stopped where they could just make out the tracks of a bear having gone by.

"At last!" Janii gave a sigh of relief, feeling that things had changed for the better.

CHAPTER 10

"Baynor, stop pacing! You're making a hole in the ground in front of the gate," the wolf complained tiredly, raising his head from where it rested on his front paws.

"I never should have agreed to the race. It was an unwise decision," the bear grumbled aloud, not heeding what the wolf had said.

"You were the closest behind her. And you say she just began to run off, away from the old stream marking our route? It hardly sounds like a thing Janii would do," the panther commented, catching the bear's attention from where she lay on the ground with her tail nervously twitching.

"Well, that is what happened. And there was nothing I could do to stop her. I could not run any faster, and she soon outdistanced me."

"There is a good possibility she could have run right past the gate then," the wolf considered seriously. Rising to his feet, he gave himself a shake.

"There are many different possibilities, and there is not much any of us can do with the fog still as heavy as it is," the bear replied, finally coming to a stop.

"Sanii, you did not see her?" Tayii asked the eagle.

"No. I saw very little and probably would have missed the gate if not for these two giant trees marking its location. I did not know anything was amiss until Baynor arrived."

"And Tayii and I did not see any sign of them as we came up from behind," Tybor added. "But we have been over all this before, and we still have no solutions."

"How long do you think it has been now?" the eagle asked, fluffing her feathers.

"I don't know—an hour, maybe two. It seems longer waiting here like this," the restless panther said, trying to cover up a yawn.

"Tybor, try calling again," Baynor requested. "Even though the sound echoes off the hills, it is better than doing nothing."

Tybor obliged to ease Baynor's worried conscience. Standing on all fours, he raised his head and let his throat sing out a cry.

* * *

Not far from the first gate, a unicorn and her riders stopped to listen to a wolf call that drifted like a spirit toward them within the trailing mist. "That must be Tybor," Janii told her companions, with her ears reaching forward. "We must be getting close!"

"Yes. Just as long as he is the only wolf this low in the hills," Ranor reminded her.

Amon, concealing his fears, looked about with furtive glances, not finding the wolf howls comforting.

"Well then," Janii said, after considering the possibility of leading them into further danger, "We will proceed cautiously."

At a trot, it did not take them long before they broke through the fog and into the circle of friends before the first gate, the Gate of Silence.

"Janii! Ranor! Amon!" the others exclaimed all at once.

"Is everyone all right?" Baynor asked, carefully inspecting the latecomers.

"Yes. We are fine," the badger answered while Amon dismounted and helped him to the ground.

"What happened?" Baynor inquired after his initial concerns were eased.

"We got lost in the fog," the youth said hastily, wanting to protect Janii from embarrassment.

"No, that is not quite right," the unicorn politely corrected. "Behaving rashly, I let my animal instincts take over. It was only later that we became lost in the fog." She gave a wink to the youth and then proceeded to explain what happened when she chased after a unicorn, only to run into the jaws of a hungry lion. "These animals' instincts can obviously help us in the wild, but they can also be a danger to us if we do not control them carefully," she summarized, feeling exhausted from the whole ordeal.

Later, when Janii, Ranor, and Amon had rested for a bit and had some refreshment, Baynor announced it was time to continue their journey. Overall they had lost only about two hours, but Baynor was still eager to press forward. The gate they were resting beside was supported by two enormous trees that stretched to great heights into the sky. The trees were a wonder to see, whereas the gate was plain and not even fancy enough to have been a simple garden gate in the city of Amuron. It was arched at the top, with the two sides meeting at the center. Baynor asked Amon to open it for them.

Amon, feeling proud of the honor, reached forward and pulled on the two knobs where the doors joined. To the youth's dismay, the doors did not move no matter how hard he strained.

"It won't open," Amon explained, his face red from his physical exertion and embarrassment.

Baynor tried with his heavy claws to pull at the doors, but they still remained closed. "I wasn't expecting this to happen," he grunted. "I haven't heard of the gates not opening."

"That, of course, does not mean it doesn't happen," Ranor pointed out, wondering if he should dig a hole under the gate and attempt to push it open from the other side.

"There must be a reason why it won't open," Tayii mused, trying to think of the answer. Her large cat eyes looked intently at the obstacle before them, willing the doors to open.

"What is the name of the gate?" Amon inquired, curious.

"This is the Gate of Silence," the bear replied gruffly, utterly frustrated.

"Are there any words that you have to say to make them open?" Amon asked.

"No, I don't think that is it," Baynor answered, puzzled. "I could understand it if the gate didn't open for us, because we are animals, but it should have opened for you, Amon."

"But I'm not a high king," Amon pointed out.

"Maybe he needs to be wearing the Stone of Wisdom," Tayii suggested.

"I cannot believe we would have been sent here only to find out we need the Stone of Wisdom to pass through the gates," Janii countered, giving her mane a shake.

"Well, maybe we should go around the gate," the youth proposed, knowing it would not be hard to find their way through the short brush and scattered hickory trees surrounding it.

"No, that will never do," Baynor said impatiently, rattling on the gate once more. "To get to Berroc, you must always pass through the first six gates. Otherwise, the seventh gate will not open, leaving Berroc inaccessible."

"What a strange group we have here!" a tiny, sleepy voice said with a yawn. "Nita, you must come and see this."

"Go back to sleep, Ari," another little voice answered. "It is too early to be up."

"Who said that!" Baynor demanded with a growl, searching the branches of the trees. The animals sniffed the air and strained their ears, searching in vain for who owned the voices.

Suddenly, giggling erupted above them. "Oh, I see what you mean, Ari. It was worth getting up to see."

"Who is there?" Baynor again demanded.

"Ooh, and talking beasts. Imagine!" was the only reply heard from a small, high-pitched voice.

"Maybe it's the trees or the gate that talks?" Tybor said, trying to trick whoever was speaking into revealing themselves.

A multitude of giggles came as an answer.

"Well, if it isn't the trees or the gate, then it must be something terribly clever to be able to hide from the eyes of all these different creatures," Tybor continued, perking up his ears and cocking his head slightly in the direction of the voices.

"How is it you animals can talk?" one of the little voices boldly inquired.

There was silence for a moment as the animals tried to think of a way to answer this question. "A sorc …" Baynor began somewhat hesitantly, but Tybor came to his aid and finished for him. "Nagala, the spirit of the animals, blessed us."

"Nagala." "Nagala." The spirit's name was whispered back and forth.

"You lie!" one of the voices said. "Nagala has not the power to do such a thing."

"Excuse me," the wolf replied. "I meant to say that she was sent to give us the ability to speak from the Great Lord, Aii. We are on a mission to Berroc to meet with a messenger from him. Please show yourselves; we mean you no harm."

More giggles came forth, but this time they seemed to be closer. "We were not worried that you would hurt us. We are not afraid of you. We would have shown ourselves to you before, but there is a human with you. We do not usually show ourselves to humans. However, because we have made our presence known to the youth already, we will reveal ourselves."

There appeared before them, on top of the gate, two tiny transparent figures with merry impish faces, wispy bodies, and delicate wings. They could have not have been bigger than a woman's forearm.

"Who are you?" Janii asked in awe.

"We are wood fairies," the male fairy said, making the introductions. "My name is Ari, and this is Nita." He pointed with his small hand toward the female fairy.

"But there is no wood here," Tayii said, feeling the wood fairies were misplaced.

"There used to be a marvelous wood here many ages before, to which these two trees belonged," Nita told them with a sigh. "These are the last two remaining trees. And when they are gone, so shall we be."

There was momentary silence in response to the gravity of this news until Baynor spoke up. "Maybe you can help us with a problem. As you know, we are on our way to Berroc, but we cannot open the gate. Can you tell us how?"

Once again the two wood fairies broke out in a succession of giggles. "You tell them, Nita," Ari piped, unable to control his laughter.

"Oh, no! You must, Ari," Nita managed to say between giggles as she shared in their private joke.

The animals waited patiently, and eventually Ari was able to solve their riddle. "The gate," he informed them, "cannot be opened until the sun has gone down."

"Well, I guess we wait until sundown." Baynor, disappointed by the setback, heaved a sigh before thanking the wood fairies.

"Don't be sad, friends," Ari announced, seeing the companions' discouragement. "Why don't we have some refreshment? I'll get the food. Nita can play you some music on her wood pipe."

"Splendid!" Nita cried out joyously, clapping her hands. "A party! We haven't had a party in ever so long." Then, with a giggle of delight and a flutter of her wings, the tiny fairy disappeared only to reappear a moment later with a miniature reed pipe on which she played the merriest of tunes.

"Ah, well done." Ari clapped approvingly, disappearing before reappearing again a number of times in succession while bringing with him various things to eat and drink. "We will need a fire and some water for boiling, so we should move away from the front of the gate to a more suitable location," he concluded after surveying the scene with his arms full.

Guided by Nita, they moved off to one side of the gate where there was an open space in the brush. In the blink of an eye, the fairies had a fire going. A sweet aroma arose from the fire, caused by scented herbs they threw onto it. Within the same blink, a natural spring burst through the ground, and a pot of water was soon boiling over the fire. Nita continued to play her music, flying and dancing and laughing among her guests. An unexplainable joy began to well up inside of those who listened to the whimsical sounds.

For their meal, the fairies showed Amon how to spread a sweet paste made of ground nuts onto thick green leaves which were boiled in the water to soften them. Berries could also be packed inside, or the juice of berries poured over top to make the meal more succulent.

"Will all the animals be able to eat this?" Amon asked Nita as he made up several of the moist packets.

"Why, yes!" Nita responded with surprise at the question. "Fairy food is suitable for all to eat. You need not worry." She smiled sweetly, flying up and fondling the youth's hair before flying away again.

Amon handed out the food to his friends, and while they ate, they shared who they were and stories of their adventures with the wood fairies. As the travelers talked, all of their different worries and cares seemed far away. The unexpected refreshment filled their bodies and cleared their minds, providing them with a sense of comfort while renewing their hope for the journey ahead.

When the companions had eaten all they could of the delicious food, Ari announced that it was time to drink. From several awaiting jugs, he poured out richly colored nectars into bowls for the animals. "But I advise you to add water," he added with a smile and a wink to Amon. "Fairy nectars are always potent."

Amon's time with the wood fairies was like being awake inside of a magical dream. The dream was wondrous and serene, intoxicating to the senses. Whether it was an illusion or not, Amon found himself suddenly surrounded by a magnificent forest of wood fairy trees filled with vibrant greens, and colorful wildflowers bursting with life. The gray of the day vanished, replaced by shafts of glowing honey-yellow sunlight. The warm glade became alive with the glimmer of tiny wings and the laughter of merry voices. Happily reclining with his companions, Amon watched as groups of wood fairies lightly danced through the perfumed air. Other fairies perched randomly among the trees, singing music that awoke all of his emotions at once. For the first time in his life, Amon felt truly alive.

Outside of the world of the wood fairies, however, the sun had dipped behind the cloud-filled horizon, and so one of the most unusual parties ever to occur in the history of that land came to an end. The doors to the gate opened just as the wood fairies said they would, and the group parted company beneath the two trees where they first had met.

* * *

After the gaiety and liveliness of the party, Amon found the grayness of the evening light and the deep purple-blue shadows of the Sand Sea, which the travelers now stood upon, lonely and quiet. As they set out across the sand, the carefree chatter between the travelers was soon replaced by a pervasive silence. The evening shadows deepened. Low clouds lay like a dark blanket above their heads, and the thick carpet beneath their feet turned into a sea of black. It seemed to Amon that he walked within a world of hushed stillness that was empty of all but him and his companions.

"This certainly is a silent place," Amon muttered aloud, referring to the name of the gate.

"It seems a silence of anticipation to me," the panther answered from Amon's right. Amon secretly wondered what there was to anticipate, except maybe an end to this dark desert.

The hours marched by in a repetition of nothing except the

quiet darkness. Then, slowly, almost imperceptibly at first, the desert began to pulse with an unseen energy. Amon and the animals immediately noticed the change. The sand was cold beneath their feet, but it wasn't the cool that sent a tingle of excitement coursing from the ground up their legs and through their bodies. There was sweetness in the night air that Amon could almost taste on his lips. A light breeze blew, causing the air around them to vibrate with the hint of a song. The song remained just at the edge of their awareness, tantalizing the animals' sensitive hearing. Finally the clouds above began to stir, and a single white light was revealed. The star pierced through the darkness, a point of intense brightness. Then, as the sky began to clear, star after star and clusters of stars began to join the first star, filling the canopy above their heads with lights. It was a glorious sight—one that caused Amon's heart to ache with joy.

"Wow," Amon breathed. Standing in a close group, they all raised their heads to view the unfolding spectacle.

"Now we have something to guide us," Baynor said appreciatively, with his muzzle pointing heavenward. "We have come too far east," he concluded after a moment's inspection of the stars and their familiar patterns. "We will have to turn to our left. We should be heading more toward the north." With the lights to guide them, they continued across the sea of sand.

"It's beautiful!" Amon said to the wolf, cheered by the marvelous sight, looking up at the vast expanse above him. "I can imagine that I'm on a world floating within a sea of endless lights."

"I think you drank too much of the wood fairies' nectar," Tybor quipped, laughing with the starlight glowing in his eyes.

When the travelers stopped for a rest, they did not stop for long. They were eager to finish their night's journey, as well as to keep themselves warm. To pass the time, Amon began humming a tune. He watched the silhouettes of those he traveled with against the starlit sky. The grizzly bear looked even more powerful now than in the daylight. His muscular shoulders rolled from side to side, while his large head swayed to the rhythm of his strong stride.

Somewhere above him, floating on the warm currents that rise into the night sky, was the eagle, and if he strained his eyes, the youth thought he could catch a moment when a dark spot sailed by. Eagles do not normally like to fly at night, but Sanii found she could still see enough to be able to do so. The wolf's coloring mirrored the mixture of light patches among the dark in the starlight overhead. Next to the wolf, the panther moved as one with the night. Her rich black pelt melted into the shaded shadows on the sea of sand so that she could only be seen when the occasional flash of starlight became caught in the reflection of her eyes. The badger prince was eager for a run and loped along horizontally to the ground, gently rippling like a whisper of the breeze over the top of the sand. While all the rest of them moved like dark figures through the night, the unicorn's shimmering coat and mane shone softly, reflecting the light of the stars. Amon breathed an appreciative sigh whenever he looked at her radiant beauty.

The companions had traveled four hours when they reached the end of the Sand Sea. The moon had risen into the sky, a round globe of startling intensity, brightly illuminating their surroundings. Rock ledges rose out of the ground at sharp angles at the edge of the sand, making a wall of steep cliffs filled with deep hollows and narrow crevasses.

"The light from this moon will help us walk among these rocks," the bear said, searching the rugged landscape. "Somewhere along this edge there should be a wide opening. It is the northern end of the waterway that used to fill the Sand Sea, so it shouldn't be too hard to find. I would like to find it and follow it a little way in before we stop for some sleep."

This announcement caused Amon and Ranor to exchange sideways grimaces at each other.

Sanii, hearing what Baynor said while coming in for a landing, did a midair swoop. "I'll be right back," she called. After a few moments, she returned, landing on a rock ledge above their heads.

"Good news," she announced to everyone. "Baynor, you have

guided us well; the old waterway is only about one hundred paces to our left. On top of that, these cliffs are home to lots of food, and I am starved after so long a flight."

Finding the opening to the canyon, the animals quickly realized that this pathway was not an easy one. The old waterway's smooth and sandy floor was covered with scattered rocks, which increased in number until there was nothing but rock piled on top of rock. These rocks gradually grew in size until they were giant boulders piled together at the bottom of a steep cliff.

"A waterfall!" Amon groaned, and his feet started to ache at the sight of it. The path they needed to follow began at the foot of the now dry waterfall.

Overhearing Amon's groan, Baynor responded with a grunt of his own. "I guess it would be better to find a spot to rest here for the night. We should wait for the sun to help us through these rocks."

They found a circular cove with a soft sandy floor just off to their right as a resting place. After a short meal cooked by a driftwood fire, they relaxed, drinking some of the wood fairy nectar that had been given to them for their journey. Making themselves as comfortable as they could, they fell quickly to sleep, bringing to a close the events of a long day.

* * *

The sun had risen and set seven times since Necros had taken over the city, but to Prince Naibor it seemed like an eternity. Since the night of the sacrifice, he had been a prisoner in his own chambers. He was brought food and drink on a regular basis and even given the chance to walk in the garden outside of the banquet hall, but he was watched at all times by two Daimos guards. These Daimos were still in their wraithlike form, which allowed them to maintain a constant vigil and be aware of their master's every evil whim.

The prince had just finished his breakfast when the door to

his sitting room opened. Without turning to look behind him, the prince knew Necros was there.

"You're eating well, Prince. Not even any scraps left for you, Elbanor," the sorcerer commented to the raven on his shoulder. Elbanor eyed the empty plate and squawked with disappointment.

"Keeping up your strength just in case, Prince? That is good." The sorcerer gave a satisfied nod, and with a raspy cry, the raven left his shoulder and flapped over to the window ledge.

"Why are you keeping me alive, Necros?" Naibor demanded, angry with himself for having pleased the sorcerer. "You know I will not serve you."

"All in good time, my prince, all in good time."

The raven gave several raspy croaks from the window. "You are right, Elbanor," Necros replied to his black-winged servant. "It is a lovely day to show the prince the city." The dark king gazed maliciously at the prince. "You will come with me, Naibor. I want to show you what the city of Amuron has become."

With quiet defiance, the prince folded his arms and turned his back on the deadly king. "No. I will not go."

"Such disrespect," the sorcerer continued in his cold, flat mocking tones. "We will have to teach the prince a lesson, Elbanor. Chain him!"

The prince felt the icy fingers of the Daimos guards as they manacled his hands behind his back. Then he was turned around to face his enemy while they placed a collar around his neck and attached a chain to the front. The prince grimaced inwardly. He was once again under the sorcerer's control.

The raven clucked with laughter while eyeing the prince. Leaving the windowsill with quick wing beats, Elbanor took advantage of Naibor's chains and raked his sharp talons over the top of the prince's head before returning to his master's shoulder.

The prince tried to dodge the raven's attack, but he was unable to maneuver fast enough with the Daimos holding him. Naibor felt the sting of the scratches as the claws dug into his scalp, and the slow trickle of blood as it ran down the side of his face.

"Bring him!" the sorcerer commanded, and Naibor was forced to follow behind.

As they walked through the halls, Necros made a game out of having the Daimos pull strongly on the chain around Naibor's neck. This action caused the prince to go sprawling face-first to the ground. By the time they reached an awaiting carriage at the front of the palace, Naibor's nose was bleeding heavily and the shoulder he had attempted to fall upon was badly bruised.

Riding in the carriage through the streets, Naibor was shocked to see the changes that had taken place in the city. The Daimos had randomly gone through the city, wantonly burning and destroying both shops and homes. The prince passed by whole blocks of houses that now lay in blackened ruins. Other homes appeared untouched, but the streets surrounding them were strewn with whatever plunder the Daimos had not wanted. It looked to him as if the city had been ravaged by the violence of war, but all of this had happened during the chaos of one night—the night of the sacrifice.

Returning to the sanctity of his quarters after the ceremony, Naibor had thought the night of horror was finally over. He soon learned that for the Daimos, the night had just begun. Now, for the first time, he was seeing the extent of the damage. Naibor thought that he hadn't cared for the city of Amuron. As a city, it had seemed plain and at times unrefined. He sadly realized how wrong he had been. The prince took offense at each broken window, every ransacked home, and all the burned-out buildings.

When the carriage reached the lower parts of the city, Naibor noticed that tents and work shacks made of thrown-together materials had been set up. These buildings were used either by the Daimos as crude shelters or as cookhouses for the women to work in. It was here, in this part of the city, where Naibor began to see the misery of the people.

Lines of heavily guarded and chained men were marched by

the prince on their way to do some type of forced labor. What they all could be doing Naibor was at a loss to know. The men walked in silence with their heads hanging down, looking both tired and anxious. One or two of the prisoners looked up eagerly when they passed by where some of the women were making bread, but their hopes of seeing someone they recognized were in vain. There seemed to be few women about, and the prince wondered where they could be. He guessed wrongly that they must be with the children.

The city seemed strangely quiet amid the faint sounds of hammering, and Naibor was sickened by the sight of it when the carriage made its way to their destination. It was then that the prince realized they had taken the parade route to reach the arena.

The sorcerer smiled coldly when he noted his intended irony not being wasted on the prince. "Ah! Here we are," he said, with a grand sweep of his hand, "at the home of my new temple."

At the far end of the arena, the prince could see the beginnings of a building being made. Guide markers shot into the air like the ends of long spears. Planks of wood stretched out and up, like a skin around a skeletal frame, to hold the liquid coa as it was poured to become thick walls of blackstone. Lying between the prince and the sorcerer's creation was a scorched and broken field, like the hide of some animal eaten away by disease.

Giant forges melting the coa brought in from the open mines outside of the city belched fire and black smoke into the air. Teams of dirty men shoveled, carried, and sifted through the dirt to find the hard black rock needed for the fires. Other men were strapped to large wheels, plodding around in circles like workhorses to grind the hard stone so it could be melted quickly. The Daimos shouted threats and insults at the men while they worked, cracking their whips menacingly and enjoying the misery about them. It was not a pleasant sight, and it was one the sorcerer knew would pain the prince to see.

"See how well the people of the city work for their new king?

The city of Amuron has become a city of slaves with me as their master, and they have you to thank for it," Necros gloated.

The prince looked around him with renewed despair. The sorcerer's words worked like poison in his soul, and he struggled to keep his anguish hidden. The heat, smoke, and conditions of the men working around him filled him with a panicked rage, and he grabbed on to the edge of the carriage until his knuckles went white.

The hideous sorcerer eyed the prince with a look of triumph. "Do not worry, Prince. It will soon be over. My temple is almost complete. Then I will take the unbelievers—every man, women, and child—and one by one sacrifice them on an altar. And you, Prince, will have the pleasure of watching as they all die."

CHAPTER 11

The sun shone down mercilessly as Captain Regg dug into the caked dirt with his fingers. Breaking off a chunk, he threw it into the pile next to him. Sweat streamed down his face and into his eyes, but he did not bother to wipe it away. The sound of chains jingling down the line and the whispering of voices caused him to stop and look over his shoulder. A prisoner was being escorted in his direction by two guards. Seeing who the prisoner was, the captain quickly returned to his digging. He did not want to seem too interested or glad to have the man they brought in shackles back beside him. Pretending to be involved in his work, Regg heard the Daimos unshackle the man behind him. Then he felt the tug of the chain on his own ankle as the prisoner was chained back into line with the rest of the workers.

"Next time you die, unbeliever." After spitting in disgust at the old man, who now knelt in the dust, the guard retreated.

"Graypah, are you all right?" Captain Regg whispered, looking at the old advisor with concern in his eyes.

Graypah had been taken away and punished as an example to all other unbelievers, as they were called, who did not obey the rule of no talking. For two days he had been tied to a post and starved outside of their living quarters for all to see. Graypah nodded, smiling his reassurance to the captain, while he started to pull at the earth with his bare hands.

Regg marveled at the old man. He had been beaten and starved, and although his body did not look like it could take much more, his eyes still burned with a strong and determined spirit.

"It was not without reward." The words came to Regg's ears, but when he looked over at the old man beside him, he never would have guessed he had said anything.

"What?" the captain asked, looking around.

"The punishment was not without reward. I now know what Necros plans to do, and we have not much time."

"Quiet!" a voice ordered down the line with the crack of a whip, and for a while, nothing was said between any of the prisoners. Then another whip crack sounded, along with curses, and a voice shouted "Keep working!" as several of the guards ran over to where a prisoner had collapsed from exhaustion.

They both looked over with pity to where the prisoner was being beaten. Sensing for the first time that they were not being watched, Graypah risked speaking again.

"As Captain Zai confirms," he said gravely, "Necros is building a temple in the arena. It is being built out of the coa we are now digging from the ground. When the temple is complete, Necros plans to sacrifice every one of us who is not a Daimos on an altar."

"How do you know this, Graypah?" Regg asked in horror.

"While I was tied to the post, the Daimos used the news of this death to taunt me."

The sorcerer was planning to murder them all. Captain Regg's mind reeled at the news, and he pounded the dirt with his fists in frustration. He felt so incompetent. Here he was, the captain of the guard, sworn to protect the city and those living within its walls, and he could offer no protection. Soon all of them were going to die, and he was shackled along with the rest of them, watching helplessly and doing nothing as men were being beaten.

Captain Regg was troubled by another thought. "Does that

mean—" he began, only to be interrupted by the return of the guards. Afraid that Graypah might have to suffer more punishment, the captain had to wait for another opportunity.

Not long afterward, a short break was called. The captain and Graypah used each other's backs for support while they rested, and Regg once again summoned up his courage to ask his question. "Does that mean we will become like them, the Daimos, when we are sacrificed?"

"No, my friend," Graypah answered with his eyes closed. "Necros cannot summon our spirits after we are dead. It is just his way of getting rid of those he does not need anymore."

* * *

The next day, when the bell tower rang out ominously at midday, Prince Naibor made his decision. Rising slowly from his chair, he made a crude attempt at straightening out his appearance and strode determinedly to the door. The wraiths that guarded him were there, as expected. "I am going to my father's room," he stated to the hated figures.

The Daimos barred his way for a moment before allowing the prince to push past them on his way to the high king's chambers. They followed after him and remained standing on guard in the hallway after Naibor went inside.

Nothing had changed since the prince had last visited this room, except maybe his resolve. The lamps of perfumed oil to mask death's odor were still lit, and his father lay undisturbed on his bed, covered by a silken burial cloth. This puzzled the prince. Someone must have refilled the lamps since he had last been here, but whom? They could not burn for so long by themselves. His father had also remained unchanged, and even though Naibor let out his breath in relief, this made his decision even more difficult. With a heavy heart, Naibor approached his father's side for what he thought to be his last time.

"Father, the time has come for me to lay your body to rest," he whispered, choking on the words as he said them. "I promise that you will be taken to the resting place of the kings when all of this is over." Looking down at the lifeless features of his father's face, Naibor realized the greatness of his loss and wept with grief upon his father's chest.

After he had gained some composure, the prince gathered up the king's body into his arms. He intended to take him outside to the royal tomb beside the Hall of Hearing, but when he turned around, he found he was not alone. Standing by the curtain to the outer chamber was a small elderly woman.

"My lord, I'm sorry to have intruded, but may I ask where you are taking the king?"

"Who are you?" Naibor inquired, puzzled by her presence.

"Your servant, my lord. I have lived long and served in the high king's palace since I was a little girl, like my mother before me," she answered proudly.

"Yes, I know that; your face is familiar to me. But what is your name, and why are you here?"

"My name is Edra, and I have come to fill the lamps," she said, holding up her pitcher of oil as proof. Then she blurted out suddenly, "Please, my lord, do not take the king away." She looked at him imploringly with knowing eyes that rested comfortably in her kindly, wrinkled face.

"I have come to lay him to rest, Edra," the prince informed her simply.

"But he is not dead, Prince!" she replied likewise.

Naibor looked down at the body in his arms, not daring to believe her words. "Surely he is dead, Edra. Look at him!"

"I know him not to be dead, my lord. He has been poisoned by the sorcerer," she said, spitting the words out as if they filled her mouth with a bitter taste.

The possibility of this made Naibor's knees weak, and he put his father gently back down onto his bed.

"How can this be, Edra? Why would Necros not kill him?"

"The Stone of Wisdom, my lord—it would protect him from the evil powers of the accursed one. A sword or a knife the Stone of Wisdom cannot protect against, but something as foul as a sorcerer's magic cannot take the life of Aii's anointed king. Think on it, my lord, and you will know it to be true."

"Yes, you are right. The Stone of Wisdom is believed to have such powers, but yet my father lies here in contradiction to all you have said."

"He may not have been able to kill the high king, but this blasphemer has other powers. He has used them to keep the king from harming him."

"Edra, I thank you," the prince said with a warm smile as he accepted the wisdom of her words. "But where did you come from, and how did you get in here? The door is guarded by two Daimos. Do you have powers that I do not know about?"

She squeezed out a laugh that sounded like a sneeze and shook her head. "I have no power except what life has taught me through the years, my lord. And I need no power except the strength that comes from having faith and hope."

Naibor looked thoughtfully at the woman before him, who talked more like an advisor than an older palace servant. He was still perplexed about how she had entered the room, so he questioned her further. "Is the door unguarded, Edra? Have the Daimos left?"

"I came not by the door, my lord. I entered another way. I came by way of a secret passage within the walls of the palace."

"A secret passageway?" Naibor scoffed, trying not to laugh. "I don't believe it! Edra, I am the high king's son, and I know nothing about secret passageways in the palace."

"That does not mean they do not exist," she replied, undaunted. "Do you know about an ancient queen who was really a powerful foreign sorceress?"

"Was she not Necros's mother?"

"Yes, but not his birth mother. It was she that taught him the foul arts. This evil woman, when she was high queen, had false walls built in front of the old. She did this so that she could have secret passageways throughout the palace from which to spy on others and to keep control."

"How do you know this?" Naibor asked, incredulous.

"The servants, who were here at the time the walls were put in, passed the secret on to their children as a warning that they could be watched by their masters. I learned about it from my mother."

"So for years servants have been creeping around through these passageways, spying on their masters?"

"Oh no, my lord," she said with her peculiar abrupt bursts of laughter. "Many servants did not believe in the secret, and if they did, they knew not where the entrances were. But I, my lord, was given a vision in a dream, not more than a new moon ago, of a map and of traveling in the passageways. I then searched for this map, because I felt in my heart an urgency to do so. Eventually I found it in a chest filled with tools of the black arts hidden in the master tutor's study. I felt guilty about it at first, my lord—looking about and searching among another's belongings—but when I found that the court tutor kept a chest full of forbidden things, I did not feel so bad."

"You are an amazing woman, Edra" was all Naibor could find to say. "Do you have the map with you?"

"No, my lord; I did not know I would find you here today. But I can take you to it."

"All right," the prince said, casting a nervous glance toward the outer chamber, where the Daimos stood on guard outside the door. "You lead the way."

Nodding reassuringly, Edra led Prince Naibor through the curtains and into the outer chamber. The wall at the back of this room was covered with large squares of smooth colored stone that repeated itself in a pattern. The secret doorway was hidden by the squares of the pattern. Large support beams made of wood stood in each of the corners. In the back left-hand corner, Edra ran her hand up and down the wall beside the wooden beam, and a door magically appeared, swinging inward toward the passageway behind.

A shiver ran down Naibor's spine when he saw the dark opening. Edra had to bend slightly to step through the small doorway. She then turned and motioned for the prince to follow her inside. A childhood fear of dark and unknown places haunted Naibor for a moment before he too stepped into the passage.

Using the limited light that shone through the open doorway, Naibor could see that the passageway was both high and narrow, while being reasonably dry and airy. The door closed, sliding back perfectly into the wall without leaving a crack. They were left completely in the dark.

"Follow me, Prince," Naibor heard a voice say from somewhere close in front of him.

"Edra, I can see nothing at all. Have you a torch?"

"Oh no, my lord, I do not use a torch for fear of being discovered. I know this passageway well enough. I will not lead you astray."

There was only room enough for one person to walk in the passage at a time, so it was not difficult to follow behind Edra without getting lost. They had gone a surprisingly short distance when Edra announced that they had arrived at their destination. Once again she caused a door to open noiselessly in the wall.

The light from the room was soft and flickering, and looking in, Naibor realized that Edra had led him to the palace prayer room next to the high king's chambers. That was why it had taken so little time to reach it. Stepping into the room, Naibor heard the soft sound of movement beside him. Turning toward the sound, he saw a young woman standing before him with shoulder-length golden hair and large eyes that were a rich, deep brown. She was wearing the clothes of a merchant. Her embroidered short-sleeved tunic, of a vivid gold color, was long and had side slits. It fell to cover her baggy gold silken pants. She looked slightly embarrassed to be standing where she was.

"Taila?" Naibor asked, unsure if it was she. He had met her formally when she was a girl and then only seen her a few times since.

"You remembered," she said with a quiet smile.

"Of course, you are Janii's younger sister," he replied, finding her beauty soft and natural compared to her sister's more refined appearance.

"It was so long ago that we met, I was not sure that you would. I think I was only about ten years old."

"What are you doing here?" he inquired, looking at Taila while casting a sideways glance toward Edra, feeling she must have had something to do with it.

"Well, it is a long story." Taila dropped her eyes and fiddled with the gold signet ring on her finger.

"Come. Let's sit down." Drawn by curiosity, Naibor motioned to a comfortable chair before sitting down in the one across from it.

"I am really Janii's half sister," she began, taking a steadying breath. "My mother remarried when Janii's father died of an illness. She then married my father—a craftsman who is skilled, knowledgeable, and handsome, but not of nobility. I, therefore, am not considered part of the royal lineage, which means I am unable to participate in the Celebration Games. When Janii was chosen to compete in the games, I grew bitter. I have always been loved and treated fairly by my family. I also have had many privileges that others have not, so I had no right to feel this way.

"As the Celebration Games approached, I concentrated on what Janii could not do, rather than what she could. I convinced myself that she was sure to lose. So when the day of the games came, I chose not to go in support of my sister. I did not wish to go and watch her be defeated.

"After the parade left for the stadium, I suddenly realized how selfish I had been. I had not even said good-bye or given her my kiss as a blessing. I hadn't talked with her at all during the week before the games, and I felt ashamed. To make amends, I went to prayer to pray for her and all the competitors, and while I was in prayer, I felt a terrible evil all around me. I do not know how to explain it except to say that I felt the evil sweep through my house as if it were searching for something with a great longing and hungering.

"After the evil presence left, I got up and went outside into the streets to find out what had happened. The city seemed alive with screams of terror, but I did not see anything unusual until I approached the arena. It was there that I first saw people behaving strangely and acting savagely toward others. I realized then that they must have been taken over by evil spirits. I watched while helpless citizens and poor frightened children were taken captive by their former neighbors, and I knew I had to hide or I would be taken captive too.

"I ran back to my home only to hear loud yells and the sounds of things being broken coming from inside. Looking in a window, I found that my house had been taken over by Ix people. So I hid in a stable, and in my fear and grief, I somehow managed to fall asleep. When I awoke, it was dark and quiet, so I chanced a look outside and saw a line of people, the ones possessed, walking toward the palace. They seemed to be acting even stranger than before, so I followed them to see what was going to happen next. When they entered the Hall of Hearing, I decided to follow using the palace entrance. As I drew near the side entrance to the great hall, I saw you being led like a prisoner by two red-robed men. I tried to hide between the outer pillars and the door, but as I stepped back, I found someone else hiding there. It was Edra, and somehow we managed not to be seen. After they had taken you inside, she whispered to me that my eyes should not see what was going to happen in the hall that night. Pulling me by the arm, she led me here. And I have been hiding in the king's prayer room ever since."

Naibor looked at Taila with wonder, and then he felt uncomfortable. Her story had deeply moved him. He realized they had more in common than he cared to admit. Unfortunately, he found he could not be as honest with her as she had been with him. She made him think of Janii, and of Janii's beauty and what he had done to her. Feeling the shame of his actions, the prince turned to Edra and asked to see the map.

What Naibor did not know was the affection Taila had felt for him, and surprisingly still felt, ever since they first met. She had been only a child at the time, but she had made up her mind then and there that someday they were going to fall in love. Even while he had wanted to court her sister, Taila had not cared, because she dreamed that someday they would be together.

Relieved to be turning his attention back to the reason he had come, Prince Naibor watched Edra go over to a decorated urn on the mantle. She reached inside, took out a wrapped scroll, and brought it to him. Gingerly, Naibor untied the cord around the scroll and unrolled the soft cloth to reveal a faded piece of parchment inside.

"I cannot see in this light," Naibor said, trying to make sense of the document resting on his knees.

The prince rose and went to the side of the room, where two candles sat on a sideboard. Laying the map down, Naibor used the weight of the heavy brass candleholders to keep the scroll from rolling together again. Edra followed the prince to assist him, and Naibor made room for her beside him.

"We are here then?" Naibor asked Edra for verification while pointing to a room with his finger.

"Yes, Prince," she nodded, smiling as he shared in her secret. "And this thick black line is the passage you were in." She showed him by rubbing her finger over the line. "The hands"—she tapped one of the tiny representations—"point to where the latch is hidden to open the doors, and the pictures are drawings of the doors themselves. These numbers tell how many paces there is between the doors, and the arrows show the direction. To open a door from the inside of the passageway is simple; all you need to do is push on the door and it will unlock and swing toward you—although a few of the doors swing outward. Hold the latch down when you are on the other side, and the door will close behind you."

"I would like to take this with me to my room, if I may, Edra?"

Naibor inquired, and Edra responded by bowing slightly and moving away from the table. "I will make a copy of it and return it to you tomorrow in my father's chamber, at the same time as we met today."

"Yes, my lord," the servant woman replied.

Large panels of wood hid the door out of the prayer room, and once Naibor found the latch, he stopped to say good-bye and risked looking again at Taila. Janii's beauty was strong and demanding, while Taila's beauty was gentle and refreshing. She stood there before him, and in the subtle light, her beauty beckoned to him, making him forget momentarily about Janii. He thought instead about how nice it would be to be in love with this woman—to have the comfort of her kisses and the warmth of her embraces. He stopped himself. Remembering what he had done to Janii, he would not allow himself the pleasure of loving another. Feeling foolish, he quickly left the room, forgetting to say his good-byes.

* * *

Sunlight peeked playfully in and out from between the thick-billowing clouds building in the sky, as if the sun were still sleepy and not fully awake behind the soft blanket of white wool. Amon felt much the same way. He was not comfortable lying on the hard ground, and neither was he ready yet to commit to the day. Noticing that the others were all involved in their own activities, he decided to lie where he was a little longer.

Rolling over on his side, allowing some of the warmth from his blanket to escape, Amon looked at the rocky cliff at the end of the ravine. The climb looked difficult, but the youth was anticipating the view from the top. For a moment he wished there still was a waterfall, and he tried to imagine what it would look like with water cascading down its sides.

The morning air was cool and refreshing rather than cold. Heaving a sigh of resignation, Amon stood and tried to stretch the stiffness from his body. After scrubbing a handful of water from his water bag over his face and into his hair, he was ready for the day's adventures.

Most of his traveling companions were watching Princess Janii at the base of the old waterfall. The unicorn looked to be performing a peculiar type of dance, jumping in graceful leaps and bounds from one rock to another around the sides of the cliff. Amon wondered briefly what she was doing until Prince Ranor caught his attention. The badger was closer to him, on a shelf of rock not far off the ground.

Moving methodically along the ravine wall, Prince Ranor kept poking his head into the variously sized crevices. The birds nesting in the cracks of the cliff flew quickly to the air, crying out in startled protest.

Amon was about to call out a greeting when several of the birds dived toward the badger in an attack. "Look out!" the youth warned.

Prince Ranor turned and backed snugly into a badger-sized crevice. The birds swooped by before climbing into the air for their next dive.

"Just what we needed!" Ranor exclaimed, eyeing the pot Amon was banging on to scare away the birds.

"What do you mean?" the youth asked, confused but triumphant as the discouraged birds finally flew off.

"For the eggs," Ranor replied, revealing his prized possession of four speckled eggs in a nest beside him. "Follow me! Maybe we can find some more." Working their way along the ledge, Amon and the badger managed to collect seventeen eggs in all.

"This is great!" Amon said proudly, looking into the pot with a wide grin when they arrived back at the area where they had left their belongings. Some of the eggs had broken in their travels, but that did not matter.

Amon relit the fire, which took him longer than it should because he was impatient from hunger, and cooked the eggs in the pot, stirring them all together after he had carefully removed most of the shells.

"Delicious," the badger said, eating his share with a satisfied sigh and a smack of his animal lips. "I don't know about you, but this is what I call breakfast."

Amon thought about the dry biscuits he had been having for breakfast, and he savored the eggs all the more. "What is everyone up to this morning?" he asked after finishing off his last mouthful.

"Janii is trying to find the easiest way up the cliff for us," Ranor answered, turning his snout this way and that as he looked about. "Sanii is high above us, scouting ahead, while the others, I presume, are offering their advice on the least perilous way to reach the top of the ravine." Seeing the others starting to return to camp, he added to the youth, "You had better start packing up."

A short while later, all seven of them stood looking up at the rugged rock wall at the end of the canyon. The old waterfall rose above them to the height of at least eight men. It was both rocky and steep, but it was the only way out of the ravine because the rest of the walls in the canyon were too sheer.

"I have been searching the sides of this cliff," Baynor said, looking up at the cliff, "and I think it will be easier for me if I take the second route you proposed, Janii, over there to the left, where the rocks are larger and the sides less steep."

Prince Baynor noticed Amon kicking at a stone in the soft sand and asked, "What do you think about the climb, Amon?"

"I am not sure I can carry the supplies and Prince Ranor safely to the top," the youth replied honestly with his eyes downcast.

Taking a moment to think the problem through, the bear prince made a suggestion. "What if you leave the supplies behind and tie a rope to your waist to pull them up afterward? Will that help?" Amon approved with a nod of his head and a bright smile.

"Well, it looks as if I'm the thorn in the bush once again," Ranor moaned, knowing along with everyone else that he would not be able to make the climb.

Getting an idea, Princess Sanii spoke up. "Ranor, why don't you let me carry you to the top of the cliff? I should be able to carry you in the sack without any difficulty."

Horrified at the thought of hanging helplessly in the air, Ranor quickly responded by saying, "I don't know, Sanii. I don't think badgers were meant to fly."

"What is the matter, Ranor? Don't you trust me?" the golden eagle asked, holding her regal head to one side while she eyed her friend the badger.

"No! It's not that, Sanii! It's just that, truthfully, I am more comfortable on the ground than in the air." Ranor's animal instincts made him want to dig for cover.

"It's either that or be left behind, Ranor. You will be fine," Baynor said encouragingly, playfully giving the badger a shove in the side with his paw.

"Not much of a choice," Ranor muttered under his breath before he agreed. Backing into the sack that Amon used to carry him, the badger prince closed his eyes before announcing, "Hurry and get on with it before I change my mind."

Beating her wings, Sanii rose quickly into the air. There was a strong updraft rising from the ravine below that would help her rise quickly into the air after her dive, even with the extra weight of a badger beneath her. Circling around over the top of the cliff wall, she flew back to the mouth of the ravine and then down along its length before grabbing the sack in one powerful swoop. Lifting Ranor swiftly from the ground, she carried the swinging sack up to the top of the cliff and dropped it gently back down, several feet away from the edge. Ranor, afraid of losing his breakfast, remained in the sack until his head stopped spinning.

"Well, that's one of us at the top," Baynor noted happily, "Lead on, Janii."

"I will follow you up," Tayii told the unicorn, flicking her tail in anticipation.

"And I will go behind you," Tybor added to his sister.

"You go after Tybor, Amon. I will wait till everyone is at the top before I make my climb," Baynor stated.

Janii, with grace and confidence, began her ascent, stopping at intervals to check on the progress of those behind her. Tayii, with her agility had no difficulty. Tybor struggled only momentarily at the top, where he clambered a bit to get over the edge.

For Amon the climb was exhilarating. The rocky passage up the cliff was a new experience and therefore a challenge. Every height reached with a new foothold was a triumph, and his heart raced wildly from the effort he exerted and excitement he felt.

When he reached the summit, Amon looked around cheerfully with a wide grin, breathing hard. Surrounding him was a vast upland, covered for the main part by grasses and patches of pine trees mixed with spruce. They had reached the lower hills of the mountains, and before him, rising majestically in almost a semicircle to his right was the Khist mountain range. Amon's eyes opened wide at the sight. Never in his lifetime had he imagined the magnificence of the mountains before him. He could barely take in the wonder of it all as he looked this way and that, his heart beating with joy.

"Quite a sight to see, aren't they?" Tybor commented to the youth, looking with him at the mountain range with a gentle wag of his tail.

"I never dreamed I would be this close to the mountains," Amon replied in hushed tones, knowing that they were to travel closer still. Turning away from the mountains, the youth brought his eyes back to the cliff so that he could concentrate on Baynor's climb. The route Baynor had chosen was less steep but much rockier. Giant boulders at the bottom turned into jutting rock formations that formed a bizarre staircase for the bear to climb. Using his powerful muscles, Baynor propelled himself up the side of the cliff to join his friends.

"Ah, the Eastern Mountains," the grizzly bear said, stretching himself up to full height in an attempt to get a better view.

Now that they were out of the shelter of the ravine, a fresh breeze blew around them. The light wind lifted Baynor's shaggy fur in gentle ripples as he stood gazing upon the mountain peaks in the near distance.

"Do you know which way to go from here, Baynor?" the badger inquired.

"Yes. To reach the Gate of Awakening, the second gate, we must keep Ur on our right and travel almost north. Are we ready to move on?"

"Almost," Amon answered. "I still need to bring up the supplies." The youth quickly hauled their baggage up to the top, and they started on their way.

Climbing steadily through the open hills and trees, they gained height with the sun as it climbed behind the clouds now filling in the sky.

"Did you know," Ranor asked Amon during one of his stints on the youth's back, "that in some tribal folklore Ur is known as the Footrest and Sol, the mountain behind it, is the Seat of God?"

"What does that mean?" Amon asked.

"Not much," Ranor replied, "But stop for a moment and I will show you. This gap in the trees gives us a clear view."

Looking off through the opening, Amon could clearly see Ur, a large knoll of rock that was round and steep on all sides but flat and bare on top. It sat like a giant bud of stone waiting to bloom into a mountain. Behind it loomed Sol, the largest and highest-peaked mountain of the range.

"Well, certain tribes," Ranor explained, "thought Sol looked like a huge throne. See the way the sides of the mountain can look like arms, and how that indent in the middle could be a seat? The mountain throne was meant for God. Ur, the rock in front of the throne, was the footrest."

"Yes, I can see it," Amon replied as the view before him appeared to take the form that had been described. "But it doesn't look that comfortable to me," he added with a laugh.

As they journeyed deeper into the mountains, the group of seven stopped on several occasions to rest, breathing in the cool and pine-scented air. The day had clouded into gray, shrouding the mountaintops around them in mystery.

"Are you sure you can hear it?" Baynor said, asking Ranor for confirmation, making sure they were heading the right way.

"Yes, I am sure," Ranor informed him after listening for a moment. "I can definitely hear water running beneath the ground."

"Good. That means we should find the canyon soon."

The trees had closed in thickly around them, and as they came to the top of an incline, the land briefly levelled off. Over to the right they could now clearly hear the sound of quickly moving water echoing off the sides of high, moist walls.

Amon tried to see the water at the bottom of the narrow and deep chasm, but as yet he was unable to. As they moved up the long mountainside, following the slowly widening canyon, the inquisitive youth was soon not disappointed. Gushing down from an unseen source, the water raced white and frothy, foaming over rocks in a chorus of surges and splashes that caused a fine spray of mist to rise up and dampen the air. Clinging to the rocky sides of the canyon were colored varieties of moss, making the cold, gray rock appear stained with reds, blues, and greens.

The wood that surrounded them was mostly coniferous. Layers of fallen needles lined their path, making the ground soft and silent to walk on. They moved quietly as they climbed, preferring to thoughtfully enjoy the richness of the experiences around them.

The forest was alive with both the sights and sounds of other creatures. Birds chirped and flitted in the tree branches around them, and small rodents scampered hurriedly down holes as they approached. Squirrels called out warning signals from the safety of the treetops, loudly proclaiming their annoyance at having been disturbed.

Several hours later, the wood ended when they reached a mountain plateau. The plateau consisted of a large, flat field of broken rock covered with patches of green and brown moss. The lower mountain slopes now spread out around them, and to the east the enormous rock walls of Mount Sol opened like arms to welcome them. The wind blew stronger, and after a few drops of rain, the clouds clinging to the mountain peaks released their hold and floated off into the pale blueness.

"Not much farther now," Tybor said comfortingly to Amon as they huddled in a group for a breather. "There is a haven, a rest stop for travelers, at the foot of Ur."

"I will sleep well tonight," Amon replied, panting along with the wolf as they made their way across the rocky ground.

Off to their right, the canyon had grown into a deep gorge with the river racing wildly far below. Ahead of them in the distance, Amon could make out something that looked to cross over the precipice to the other side at the foot of Ur.

"There is the Gate of Awakening," Sanii shouted as she dived from out of the sky.

"Where?" Amon asked, confused, seeing nothing that looked like a gate.

"The bridge, Amon," the bear explained over his shoulder, "is the second gate."

"Is that the bridge over there, which crosses the river at the bottom of Ur?" He pointed for verification.

"Yes, that is it," Baynor answered with a grizzly grin.

"It doesn't look like a bridge from here," Amon stated, straining his eyes to see ahead.

"The Gate of Awakening is a most unusual bridge," Ranor told him from the ground by his feet. "But I won't spoil the surprise for you. You will have to wait and see for yourself."

Soon Amon was able to clearly see the Gate of Awakening, and he stopped in appreciative wonder. From glistening white stone, a marvelous flying horse had been carved, spanning the chasm as a bridge. The sculpted beast leaped from one side of the canyon to the other. Its glorious head stretched forward as it flew, while its forelegs were tucked up against its muscular torso and its massive wings swept back in an upward arc. The horse's chin and knees melded with the rock on this side of the canyon, while its back hooves and flowing tail rested firmly against the far side. It was certainly a spectacular sight!

"Where did it come from? Who made it?" the enthusiastic youth asked, never having seen anything quite like it.

"No one knows" was the disappointing answer.

"What do you mean?" Amon asked, turning to Janii, who had spoken.

"It's a mystery, Amon. No one knows for certain where the stone came from, how it got here, who carved it, or even how the bridge was placed over the river. Just think! Who could mine a stone so large and then transport it up into the mountains? And how was it fitted so exactly into place and attached to the sides of the canyon? It had to be carved before it was put into place; otherwise, how could the underside of the bridge have been carved when it hung over the gorge? If you can answer these questions, Amon, then you can answer what scholars have puzzled over for centuries."

"It seems to me more of a miracle than a mystery," the wolf added playfully.

Finally they came to the head of the great stone bridge. An impressive obelisk, made of the same white stone as the gate, stood to one side. It was about the height and width of a man and it had letters carved vertically into it, but Amon could not read the strange characters.

Tayii looked at the youth's puzzled expression and read the word aloud. "It says, 'Space.'"

"Space?" Amon muttered to himself. "What is that supposed to mean? I guess it is another mystery."

Wanting to be the first to cross the unusual bridge, the youth volunteered to take up the lead. Striding up the stone ramp of the horse's smooth nose to the forehead, Amon could feel the tug of the wind as it flowed over and around the great stone beast. Reaching the summit between the ears, he looked down the flowing mane, which made a stair to the horse's back. Even though the statue was a comfortable width to walk on, there was no railing down the neck of the horse.

Starting down the first few steps, Amon tried not to look at the dizzying drop beneath him. Instead he looked ahead to the large stone wings that rose up on either side. Once between the wings, Amon found that he was protected from both the feel of the wind and the sight of the river gorge beneath him. When the others reached him, Amon continued his descent over the hind quarters and the full-flowing tail to the other side of the canyon. Stepping off the bridge, Amon was overjoyed. It was almost as if he had actually soared over the expanse of the deep river by riding on the back of a great winged horse.

On the other side of the bridge there was another obelisk, just like the first, but with different letters carved on it. Without hesitation, Tayii read the obelisk. "This one says, 'Time.'"

Shrugging, the youth could make no sense of it.

"Come on!" Sanii called from above. "The resting place is over here on the left." She led them to a lovely grassy nook on the hillside at the bottom of the mountain butte.

The haven was not what Amon was expecting. Having been raised in the city, he was surprised to see that the haven was a sheltered cave that had a fire pit of stone built inside its entrance. The haven was supplied with dried food and firewood, as well as some woven hammocks strung up on hooks.

Outside of the haven, facing both to the south and the west, were decorative stone benches, providing a place for travelers to sit and admire the view. There was also a natural spring bubbling forth from the hill into a stone basin. Although Amon was tired, he sat on a bench with his back to the mountain, deep in thought.

On the soft grass close by sat the wolf. After a while, Tybor cocked his head to one side and asked the youth, "What are you thinking about?"

Realizing after a moment that he had been spoken to, Amon

answered, "Oh, I um … I was just trying to figure out what the name 'Awakening' has to do with the flying horse."

"I believe 'Awakening' has more to do with the chasm and the joining, or coming together, of time and space than it does with the horse figure," Ranor explained, coming over to join in the conversation so he could share his ideas.

"Oh," Amon replied with a weak smile, hoping to convince the badger that he had understood his explanation, even though he felt more confused now than he had to begin with. "How much farther is it to Berroc?" he added, changing the subject.

"We have five gates left to travel through … so we should reach Berroc on the fifth day," Tybor replied, looking over for verification at Baynor, who was swatting at an annoying bug with his large forepaw.

"Yes, I think it will take us the five days," Baynor concluded, with a hint of disappointment in his voice. "I had hoped to get there sooner, but I have a sense that Berroc cannot be reached any quicker."

"That means it will take us thirteen days before we can be back at Amuron," Amon remarked with dismay, remembering the vision of his younger brother.

"We can return by the East Road, Amon. That should save us two days," Baynor pointed out, secretly hoping that this would grant them enough time to right the wrongs of the evil sorcerer.

CHAPTER 12

The embers from the fire were still warm when the travelers were ready to start their next day's march. The sky was bright and clear, and the day a little cooler than the one before. Amon looked up at the rocky butte that awaited them and appraised the journey ahead. In the early morning shadows, it didn't look like an easy climb.

"My poor feet," Ranor moaned, shifting his weight from one paw to another, "They weren't made for climbing mountains."

Amon smiled at the badger as he placed the strap of the freshly filled water bag over his neck and across his shoulder. "Well, you could always ask for a lift from Sanii," he teased good-naturedly.

"It's about a six-hour march altogether to the seat of Mount Sol, Ranor. First we have to climb up and over Ur, and then climb two hours up another sheer cliff before we reach the third gate," Baynor informed his friend. "Amon's suggestion is not a bad one. We can meet with you at the top of Ur."

"All right, I will go with Sanii," the badger said, shaking his head in disbelief at what he was saying. "But please, Sanii, fly gently if you can."

"I will see what I can do," the eagle replied after preening a feather on one of her powerful wings.

The fur on the back of Ranor's neck stood up as he backed into the sack and waited for Sanii to pick him up. "The takeoffs are the worst," he grumbled miserably, closing his eyes.

With natural grace, the eagle princess took to the air before swooping down and grabbing the sack with her extended talons and lifting the badger into the air. "Look, Ranor!" Sanii called to her companion. "Look around you at the glorious heights, touched by the wind and the sun and the feet of eagles. It's so beautiful! I could stay up here all day, floating and gliding on the air."

Ranor tried to open his eyes, but the wind blew into them, making him blink. The mountains seemed to sway unsteadily as he hung in the air, and he withdrew protectively away from the front of the bag.

Sanii let out a cry of joy from her soul before she descended. The call came back to her in echoes from the surrounding walls of rock.

Moments later, Ranor was happily feeling the warmth of the dirt beneath his claws. Even though the flight had been a short one, he still felt relieved when his feet were back on the solid ground.

Looking down from the flat top of Ur, the badger watched his friends follow the bear up the steep hill at a brisk pace. Amon was riding on Janii's back so that he could keep pace with the others. The trail switchbacked across the rocky sides, making the climb longer but less perilous.

"You certainly have an advantage over the rest of us," Ranor commented to the eagle standing beside him. "It will still take them some time to reach us."

"An advantage you are just beginning to appreciate now that you are back on the ground," Sanii said with a sound that could be interpreted as a chuckle.

When the seven had regrouped at the top of the hill, Baynor took some time to scout the surrounding area while the others rested from the climb. Wandering near the edge of the hill, the grizzly caught traces of a scent that disturbed him. He sniffed at the earth several times, confirming his suspicions. Lifting a twitching snout, he searched the wind but could smell no immediate danger. Since the only scent he detected was old, he hoped they would be able to proceed without any trouble. Returning to his friends, he found they were ready to continue.

"How does the trail ahead look, Baynor?" Janii inquired.

"It should give us no trouble," the bear answered hopefully, deciding not to mention the scent he had found and alarm them unnecessarily.

"Are you coming with me, Ranor?" Sanii asked, eyeing her friend quizzically.

"No, thank you, Sanii. Since we are going downhill, I should be fine; however, I will probably need a lift when it comes time to climb up to the seat of Mount Sol."

"Very well, I shall fly on and meet with you later."

The descent down Ur became an almost pleasurable romp for Amon and the animals. The wind was light and refreshing, and the sun shone down warmly, inviting them to forget their troubles and revel in the glories of the day. They unconsciously began to travel faster, each looking forward to reaching the valley that spread out between them and the rocky sides of Mount Sol.

The meadow they were entering delighted their animal senses. They found themselves surrounded by succulent grasses amid which insects buzzed lazily by and sang droning melodies. Among the grasses grew an abundance of varied and colorful wildflowers. The flowers nodded merrily in time with the wind, attracting butterflies and hummingbirds that hovered in the air.

Without warning, Tybor gave the yip of a pup and raced after some brush fowl nesting in the long grass. Clucking in alarm, the large birds rained down feathers as they hastily flew up out of harm's way. Tayii started to join her brother in the chase, but she changed her mind when something else caught her eye. She began leaping and pouncing at various rodents who were calmly sunning themselves and were now darting madly for cover.

Janii, who had been nonchalantly munching at the tasty grasses as they walked down the hill, decided it was time to get rid of the itch in the middle of her back. She chose a fragrant patch of flowers, laid herself down upon them, and began to roll in a rather undignified manner.

Ranor decided that if his friends were having fun, then so could he, and he began to root around among the brush and then to dig merrily.

"What are you digging for, Prince Ranor?" Amon asked him, curious.

"I'm not sure," he replied gleefully, looking up at the youth while the dirt behind him continued to fly. "I'll let you know when I find out."

Baynor, surprised by the sudden gaiety of the group, gave in to the frivolity when he discovered trout in a gently flowing stream at the bottom of the valley. "Watch out for things, Amon," he told the youth with a wink before wading into the water and concentrating on catching some fish.

"I will," Amon assured him, but it wasn't long before he was busy making a fire to cook the birds and rodents his companions had caught and brought back to him.

Even Sanii, who soared above them and was ever watchful, had caught a warm updraft and was gliding peacefully up into the heavens with her eyes closed. She noticed that her friends had stopped traveling, and since most of them were hunting, she presumed they had stopped for lunch. She was not yet ready to eat and was enjoying her flight, so she let the ground slip slowly away beneath her.

On the far side of the meadow, the bear on the lower slopes of Mount Sol was not so carefree. On the wind he scented many things: smells that worried him—smells that disturbed his pleasant morning. A strong smell of unicorn: no threat. A male wolf, alone: no threat. A badger: no threat. A female cougar: troublesome. A human: more trouble. These smells were strangely mixed together. This confused and irritated him. Normally he would not bother with these creatures. The badger he might chase away, enlarging the animal's home to use for his own den, but he didn't like any of them in his territory.

He was thinking about going to investigate when he caught the one scent he could not ignore. This scent drove him to action. It angered and infuriated him, driving away his previous confusion. He tore down the slopes in a rage. What male bear would dare enter his territory? What male bear would dare challenge his authority? No male bear, as long as he was living and healthy and in the prime of his years!

Baynor was relaxing on his haunches by the stream, licking the fish from his paws, when the bear attacked. Hearing a roar, he looked up to see the bruin charging toward him from across the stream. The quickness of the attack left him with no time to prepare for the onslaught. The charging bear threw himself up in front of Baynor, plunging the teeth of his snarling muzzle into the soft folds of flesh around Baynor's throat. The violent strength of the angry bear caused Baynor to fall off balance to the ground, crushed by the weight of his opponent.

Rolling over on his side, Baynor tried to shake the bear off while trying desperately to get to his feet. Using the strength and weight of his muscles, Baynor smashed a paw down onto the other bear's head, hoping to get him to let go of his neck. After several such attempts, the bruin finally let go, and they both regained their footing to continue the battle standing at full height. The two bears roared and snapped fiercely at each other, using their claws both as weapons and as protection.

Amon and the other animals, hearing the sound of their fight, stopped what they were doing and hurried to Baynor's aid. Reacting instinctively, Tayii pounced onto the attacking bear's back. She gave the bear a throaty howl of rage in his ear, ensuring that he knew she was there, before digging in her claws.

Feeling the weight and the claws of the cougar on his back, the bruin backed cautiously away from Baynor. Lowering himself to the ground, he snapped from side to side at Tayii. He then tried to get rid of the cougar by shaking himself. Tayii, with a screech, tumbled and rolled to the ground, not having latched on with her teeth.

Now it was Tybor's turn. Growling viciously, he dived in, barking and nipping at the bear's hind feet. The bear turned, trying to get at the attacking animal, but the wolf was too quick for him, dodging and biting just out of reach. Joining in the fray, the badger added to the bear's misery. Ranor's sharp teeth struck the bear each time he went for Tybor, until it looked as though the bear was chasing his tail as he attempted to get rid of his adversaries.

As the bear was angered to the point of madness, his mouth frothed with fury. Choosing to ignore the challenges of the annoying wolf and badger, the bear charged again at Baynor. Baynor readied himself but still received a swat across the side of his head that left his face bleeding under his left eye.

From the sky there came a cry. Looking up, the attacking bear saw an eagle coming straight at him, diving in for the kill. He dodged, and the eagle just missed striking the top of his head. Undaunted, the persistent bear went for Baynor again. The mature bruin hurtled his massively strong body at his foremost challenge, causing Baynor to be knocked once again to the ground.

Rearing up in the excitement of his victory, the mountain bear was suddenly struck forcibly in the side. Howling, he reeled in pain. The stabbing pain was so intense he could hardly see the unicorn that trumpeted and lowered her horn for another attack.

Now that he was hurt, the bruin struck out in fear to protect himself. He savagely swatted at the enemies surrounding him, but the snapping wolf, snarling badger, hissing cougar, diving eagle, and charging unicorn proved to be too much, even for such a seasoned and courageous bear as he. With one last cry of outrage, the bear turned away from the onslaught and ran for the comfort of the rocky slopes of his beloved mountain range.

Amon watched the retreating bear from a safe distance to ensure he would not return. "He's gone," he told the others when he joined the group surrounding Baynor.

"Is everyone all right?" Baynor asked loudly, in an attempt to settle everyone down and to keep them from fussing about his wounds.

"We're fine," Tybor replied. "It's you we are worried about."

"Yes, well, you needn't be, because I am fine as well. Just a few cuts and bruises—that is all. What we need to do now is continue on with our journey without any further delays." So saying, the bear turned from his friends and headed toward Mount Sol without another word.

* * *

Using the morning light coming through the open shutters, Prince Naibor laboriously copied the map before him on the desk. He stopped only to move his fingers, easing the stiffness in his hand. Several hours passed before he was satisfied with the results. Putting down the pen, Naibor watched with a half-smile as the last ink strokes dried on the paper. He had been successful. Not only had he copied the map, but he had also been able to get both Janii and Taila out of his mind for a while. Leaning back in his chair, Naibor moved his shoulders in an attempt to relieve the ache between them and closed his eyes. For the first time in a long time, he was able to relax and actually rest.

It seemed on the previous evening that he could not stop thinking of Taila. This confused and frustrated him. He had loved Janii and lost, and now he no longer wanted to love, but it seemed that the harder he tried to forget Taila, the more she occupied his mind.

Feeling exhausted early in the evening, Naibor had gone to bed. He had not slept well, and when he woke in the morning, he still felt troubled and anxious. Hoping to be able to concentrate and expend his energy on something, the prince had set about copying the map.

As the prince leaned back in his chair, the importance of the map began to dawn on him. For the first time since Necros had taken over the city, he finally had some freedom from the sorcerer's imprisonment. The map gave him the ability to move around the palace without the watchful eyes of the Daimos and, therefore, the knowledge of Necros. This also meant that he could escape from the palace into the city. Lurching forward, Naibor grabbed the map to confirm his theory.

"Yes," he murmured to himself while searching the paper and its hidden secrets. "Many of the passages run throughout the servant areas, and there is even one leading into the kitchen and one leading outside! Ha! I have finally got something to use against you, Necros."

There were still several hours left before midday, when the prince was to meet with Edra, so he decided to use the map and attempt the passageways on his own. He had no difficulty deciding where to go. He needed to find out more about his enemy. Naibor's destination was therefore Elbanor's study library. Having committed his route to memory, he concealed both copies of the map in the pocket on the inside of his loose tunic.

When Prince Naibor was younger, he chose for himself a room away from the other royal chambers. Naibor always liked the fact that it was close to the back stairs, and he enjoyed the anonymity it brought him when he wanted to sneak out of the palace unnoticed. In fact, the room was really intended to be used by an important or favored guest. For this reason, the prince's private chamber had a secret passage connecting it to the hallway and the back stairs. This was most fortunate, but it was also a little unnerving to think that all this time someone could have been using the passageways to secretly observe his own private affairs.

The stone facing to the right of the fireplace was where the door was hidden. Naibor still found it difficult to believe the door actually was there even after he was staring into the unlit opening. Once inside the passageway, Naibor found he was uncomfortable with the darkness around him, and his progress was slow for fear he would bump into something. Feeling disoriented, he forgot to count his paces as he followed the length of the hallway. When he came to a turn in the wall, the prince quickly took up the count again. According to the map, he would soon reach a set of stairs going down into the blackness. Ten paces from the turn, he stretched out his right foot and found a void in front of him. He had reached the stairs. Carefully bringing his foot down, he felt for the lower step until he was standing securely on it with both feet. He went down each step in this manner until he came to a stop at the bottom.

Going over the map in his mind, Naibor knew he had to exit through a door that was not more than five paces away on his left. The door led into the banquet hall, and this worried him. Necros often ate in the banquet hall, along with the barbaric Ix people. The black sorcerer also spent a good deal of his time pacing the length of the adjoining balcony while he was thinking, or when he was in especially foul moods. Naibor had witnessed both such instances when he had been out in the courtyard "getting some air" with the Daimos. Naibor could not afford to be caught by Necros using the secret passageways. It would ruin all his plans against the sorcerer. Going into the banquet hall would require some risk, but he did not have much choice. The passageway went no farther.

Listening intently at the door for a few moments, Naibor could hear nothing except the pounding of his own heart. Growing impatient, he pushed on the wall, hoping to release the locking mechanism. The door swung silently inward, and he watched as the room behind it slowly revealed itself. The banquet hall was empty of all but its garden of milky white and jeweled stone. With a sigh of relief, Naibor stepped into the room. He pressed on the hidden latch, and the door vanished behind him.

Moving swiftly now that he was in the open, the prince hurried to the glass doors at the end of the room. Using them as cover, he looked cautiously into the hallway, half expecting to see two Daimos standing on either side of the doorway as they did outside his chambers. Once again, no one was in sight and all was quiet, so he risked crossing over to the kitchen. Finding it empty as well, he entered the large but cluttered room. Fearing he would be discovered at any moment, the prince wasted no time in finding the new door leading to the safety of the secret passageways.

The passage from the kitchen led straight into the heart of the palace, making only a few turns along the way. Naibor was now traveling at a faster pace within the dark halls. Confident in his memory of the map and his knowledge of the palace, he soon came to the place where the main library was on one side and Elbanor's study was on the other. He pushed on the door and then waited for a moment in the blackness. Nothing happened!

Thinking perhaps that he had counted wrong, he went over the paces again in his head. Sure that he was right, he pushed harder on the door. This time it moved slightly, but in the wrong direction. Realizing this was one of the doors that swung outward, the prince worried that there might be a spell on the door to keep it from opening.

Hoping he was mistaken, Naibor tried again. He used his shoulder to push against the door, opening it just wide enough to wiggle his hand through. He felt along the bottom edge to see if anything had jammed the door, but he could feel nothing unusual. Frustrated, he could see very little out of the crack except for a few books piled nearby.

Not giving up, the prince threw his body weight at the door and was rewarded. It opened reluctantly, accompanied by the sound of tumbling books. Ducking into the room, Naibor found a large pile of books and papers that had been piled against the back of the door. Naibor frowned at the sight. Elbanor must have had suspicions about someone being in his study after Edra's visit.

Looking around, Naibor whispered to himself, "I wonder where I can find the box that Edra found the map in?"

The prince hardly knew where to begin looking. The room was as it had been the day he had asked Elbanor about a sorcerer—full of books and papers that were in a seemingly disorganized pattern throughout the room. Edra had mentioned that the box had been hidden, so he expected to have difficulty finding it. Instead it lay in a cleared space on top of a table covered with books and several unfinished scrolls. The wooden box was black and shiny and covered with carved symbols. The lid was closed, and it had a plain golden clasp that was not locked. Naibor reached down to open the box but hesitated; he was not eager to open it.

From somewhere in the room, a clock chimed, and Naibor jumped. He realized he still had an hour before he was to meet with Edra. Quickly opening the lid, the prince was disappointed. All that was in the box were a few small, dried animal bones and some scrolls. Reclosing the lid, Naibor began to read what was written on the bindings of the books lying on the table. Several were in foreign languages, while others were inconsequential, but two titles caught his eye. One was *Ancient Rituals and Sacrifices*, and the other was *Common Sorcery*. After scanning a few pages in each, Naibor decided that these books were of significance.

The prince was about to leave, after searching for almost the entire hour, when he noticed a pile of important-looking papers. The papers were letters sent to Elbanor during the years of Necros's banishment. This was exactly what Naibor had been looking for—something specific about Necros. Grasping the pile, he placed the papers with the maps inside his now bulging tunic. There was only one other book he wanted, and he knew that he could find it in his father's chambers.

Returning to the open passage door, Naibor looked at the pile of fallen books and realized they no longer were a barricade against intruders but a signal that someone had entered the room.

CHAPTER 13

Naibor had just pushed the items he had taken from Elbanor's study under his bed, out of sight, when he heard an impatient rapping on his door. Hurrying to open the door, the Daimos presented his food to him on a tray. The prince frowned at his broth soup and chunks of dried bread—a sure sign that food in the city must be becoming scarce.

"I will eat this later," Naibor informed the black-robed Daimos while taking the tray and placing it on the mantle over the fireplace. "I am going to visit my father." Once again they followed Naibor like shadows, stopping outside when he entered the high king's chambers.

First Naibor checked on his father and found him undisturbed. So pale and still he lay. The scene unnerved him. Suppressing a shiver, the prince turned from the bedchamber to search for *The High King's Laws*. The book, which he had snubbed and scorned in his younger years, now offered him the hope of finding a way to fight against the sorcerer.

Naibor found the book lying open on a table under a window that overlooked a small private garden. Just then Edra entered from the passage, carrying oil with her for the lamps. Before turning to acknowledge the older servant, a passage caught his eye, which gave him an idea. Taking note of the page, he closed the book and tucked it under his arm before speaking. "Edra, here is the original map. I have made a copy of it." He handed her the scroll.

"Will you join us for lunch, Prince?" she asked, taking the map while smiling up at him with her deep-set eyes.

"No, thank you, Edra. My lunch is waiting for me back in my room. The Daimos might become suspicious if I don't return to eat it." His explanation was partly true. His main concern was that he did not feel confident about seeing Taila. "Besides, I have some work to do before tonight."

"Tonight? What is tonight?" Edra inquired.

"I'm going into the city. I want to find out how far Necros's plans are progressing and whether there is anything I can do against them."

"That is good. Our prayers will be with you. Some unseen help might yet come to us," the small woman confided before she moved the curtain aside to enter the inner chamber. "I will expect you for lunch tomorrow, then, to tell us what you have seen." She did not wait for a reply. The curtain swayed gently as it closed behind her.

The prince stood there for a moment watching the movement of the curtain. He did not want to further involve Edra and Taila in his plans against the sorcerer or endanger them any more than he already had. He always felt uncomfortable dealing with others, but he also knew he could not fight the sorcerer on his own. With a deep sigh, he went to the secret door in the wall and left the high king's chambers. Naibor had one more place to visit before returning to his room.

Traveling along the dark passageway with his newfound skill, Prince Naibor reached another door and stopped. He gave the door a push, and it swung inward silently, allowing the prince to enter the Hall of Hearing. The hall was dark. None of the pillar lamps had been lit. Only the phosphorescent chandeliers glowing from above illuminated the shining surfaces in the great hall.

The table from the night of the sacrifice was still in the center of the room. Although it was an unpleasant sight, it encouraged the prince that he would find what he was looking for. Searching behind the white pillars on the far side, Naibor was not disappointed. Lying on a side table were the death masks that the Daimos had used during the ceremony. Naibor smiled to himself, almost laughing at their gruesomeness. A death mask would provide the perfect disguise for tonight, along with his black hooded robe. He hoped that if he was seen while on his mission, the Daimos would think he was involved in a ritual of some sort and therefore leave him alone. He couldn't remember exactly what *The High King's Laws* had said, but it was something about evil disguising itself. Well, tonight he would be the one disguised!

Once back in his room, Naibor sat at his desk and began to go through the materials he had acquired. He did not spend much time with either of the sorcery books, finding the accounts of the rituals and the spells both frightening and unpleasant. Instead he was drawn toward *The High King's Laws*. It was a book that he had disregarded for many years, thinking it was foolish and outdated. These were the laws he feared would restrict his freedom and enslave him to tradition. On several occasions, when he had dutifully tried to read the book, the truth of the words had admonished him, reminding him of the things he should be doing, but his pride had gotten in the way, and he had not wanted to change.

Now he found himself reveling in what he read. The words were alive with wisdom. He was sorry that he had not spent more time learning from the book while he was growing up, but now was a time for action and not a time for remorse.

After many hours of study, Naibor looked up wearily and noticed the sun going down. The books and papers he had gathered helped him to feel that he now knew a little more about what he could expect from Necros.

One of the letters addressed to Elbanor revealed much of the sorcerer's treachery. It read,

My Dear Elbanor,

I am encouraged to find your skill in the arts growing. Do not be discouraged by the pain you feel when practicing sorcery. Eventually you will be able to control the burning fire of the power you are using, but it takes much time and practice. The day of my return is fast approaching. I have foreseen it, and the young prince is the key! Continue to turn him against the high king's laws and to use the spell of discouragement to poison his soul. In time, all will be ready. Time is our ally, and we must wait and use it for our preparations to make sure nothing stands in our way! Time is their enemy, and before long it will have run out!

Necros

The last light of the sun vanished quickly, having barely made an appearance during the gray haze of the day. Finishing what was left of his cold vegetable broth and hard pieces of bread, Naibor prepared himself mentally for his excursion. First he would check on the stores of food, and then he would see if he could locate the various camps.

Glancing out the window, he saw it had grown dark. Naibor knew his time for action had come. Gathering up his robe and the mask, the prince silently prayed that Necros would not come to visit him tonight. A locked door would not keep the sorcerer out.

Using the passageways, as he had earlier that day, he made it safely to the kitchen. He left through the back door and went down the steps into the darkness of the night. Once in the courtyard, from where the animals and Amon had previously escaped, Naibor put on his black robe, lifting the hood to cover his face. The mask he secreted inside a pocket for later use. He then entered the storeroom. As he expected, little of the food remained.

"Well, Necros, you obviously are running low on fresh supplies," Naibor grumbled to himself, somewhat irritated. The prince had hoped to sneak some food into the various camps in an attempt to help the prisoners. He now had to admit that the food would have helped more to assuage his guilt than anything else.

From the courtyard, Naibor slipped into the stable. His horse greeted him with a quiet nicker, eagerly extending his nose in the prince's direction.

"Hello, old friend," Naibor whispered to the animal, gently patting him on the shoulder from outside of the stall. The horse responded by pushing his nose into Naibor's other hand, seeking a treat. "I'm sorry to say I have nothing for you or anybody else tonight," he added regretfully. "You don't seem so badly off though. Someone has been looking after you." He noted there was clean straw on the floor, as well as some fresh hay and water.

Almost without thinking, the prince grabbed one of the small waterskins he often took with him on his excursions. Naibor was tempted to take the horse and ride for help, but he wasn't really sure if it would do any good. There were several cities that would come to Amuron's aid if he asked, but this was not a normal battle. He would be asking the cities to make war against his own people. And there was also the problem of the sorcerer. Swords and armies did not seem to be enough to use against the powers of Necros. He would just have to deal with the sorcerer in whatever way he could.

After leaving the stable, Naibor moved as silently as an imagined shadow through the city streets. He reached the Market Section without incident, and after confirming where the women were being held captive, he continued on to the Military Section. The city was deserted and in darkness, except for the areas where the prisoners were being kept. The Daimos had housed themselves around these areas, lighting the lamps on the light posts only on these streets.

Several slow hours passed, but Naibor still felt he had not gained enough information to return to the palace. He wanted, if possible, to get closer to the men's barracks and find out how closely they were being guarded, even though sneaking into one of these areas would be difficult.

Nearing the outskirts of lamplight, Naibor put the mask of death on under his hood, hoping the deception of his disguise would work if he was seen. Hugging what pools of darkness he could find, Naibor proceeded among the houses of the Daimos.

Pressing his body against the planks of the nearest building, he stopped to catch his breath at a road that crossed his path. Unexpectedly, the sounds of merrymaking drifted toward him on the night air. The rough laughter was so out of place that it made the small hairs on Naibor's skin jump.

Trying to get a sense of how close he was to the barracks, Naibor peeked out from the space between the two buildings where he was hiding. His adrenaline was pumping, and sweat dripped into his eyes from behind the hot mask. The barracks were in the center of this section. Across the street and a little to his left, Naibor could see a large house, more of a canteen, from which the happy sounds emitted.

His initial response was to leave quickly and try again from another direction, but he found himself curiously drawn toward the canteen. Hearing the approach of a patrolling guard, the masked prince quickly stepped back into the shadows. Naibor saw the guard come to a stop on the road right in front of the dark gap between the two buildings where he was hiding. The guard seemed to be listening intently for something, and Naibor did not even dare to breathe.

Almost as if he knew someone was there, the guard turned slowly around on the spot and stopped to peer into the gap. Suddenly from the canteen there was a loud crash followed by drunken laughter. The noise caused the guard to lose his concentration. With an annoyed tug on his uniform, the guard swung back toward the road and continued on his way.

Listening to the retreating guard, Prince Naibor took a moment to calm his racing heart. When all appeared safe, he dashed across the street. He was now two houses away from the canteen. He took off the mask and wiped his wet face on his sleeve before urging himself on.

Circling behind the buildings, Naibor was soon facing the rear corner of the canteen. He knew it was foolish to get this close to a place so crowded with his enemies, but he just could not picture the Daimos having a good time. The apparent contradiction of the situation drove him mad with curiosity, and he had to investigate. Creeping forward down the side of the canteen, Naibor tucked himself under a window, hoping the meager shadow would be enough to conceal him.

While he listened to snatches of the conversations and goings-on inside, a wry smile spread over Naibor's face beneath his mask. It suddenly became obvious why the Daimos were making so much noise. They were all uproariously drunk! The Daimos couldn't hold their liquor. He realized with great pleasure that this meant they had a weakness.

To confirm his suspicions, the prince risked a peek in the window he was crouched under. The same hard, cruel, and wicked Daimos that ruled the city by day had now been reduced to harmless, smiling idiots. Patting one another on the back, they laughed loudly, slopping their drinks as they tried to drink them down. By this point in time, most of the Daimos lay sprawled against the walls or on the floor, having already had more than their fair share of drink.

A sudden shout from the road caused Naibor's heart to jump. Another guard had come to relieve the previous one on patrol. Naibor had been concentrating solely on the occupants inside the canteen and had not heard the sound of their approaching footsteps. Only now, as the two guards greeted each other at the end of the building, did he realize how close they were and how exposed he was. He did not even have time to get out of sight. Pressing his back against the wall, Naibor tried to slide quietly away from the light of the window and more into the shadows. As he was looking in the direction of the guards, Naibor's foot accidentally hit an empty bottle that had previously been discarded. The noise instantly caught their attention.

Thinking quickly, Naibor slid down to the ground and pretended to be a drunken Daimos. He grabbed the bottle he had hit with his foot before the two guards reached him. After pouring the meager amount remaining across his chest, he held the bottle loosely in his hand by his side to use as a weapon—if they were not fooled into thinking that he had been drinking from it.

"What is this?" Naibor heard one guard ask as they came to stand over him. "A Daimos in ceremonial mask?"

"What Daimos are you?" the second guard inquired gruffly.

Naibor responded by muttering and rolling his head to the side.

"Drunk!" the same guard replied, spitting out the word violently. "I don't like this," he continued, gesturing in the direction of the canteen. "Daimos should only drink at appointed ceremonies. These Daimos have lost both their dignity and their nightly awareness."

"We work hard all day to keep the unbelievers working. It is nice to have a break," the first guard said defensively.

"We cannot be effective in such a state," the other countered, with a hard edge to his voice.

"Necros does not stop it," the first disagreed.

The second guard growled in reply before adding, "I curse it. It is unnatural. We are creatures of the night; we see more, hear more, and feel more after the sun goes down. By day, we are almost numb in comparison. Drink weakens us—takes away both our strength and our senses. It is not for the Daimos!"

The first Daimos wisely refused comment.

"I will report this one to the captain," the other said, still plainly irritated, and he reached down to remove the mask.

"No!" the first one stated firmly. "I will do it. You have been relieved."

Fortunately for the prince, who desperately tried to appear unconscious throughout the conversation, the other Daimos obeyed and left.

The remaining guard, after giving him a hard kick in the leg, leaned down and whispered close to his ear, "Sleep now. But if I find you here in the morning, I will take disciplinary action myself." Walking briskly back to the road, he resumed his patrol.

* * *

Almost giddy with relief, Prince Naibor hesitated only briefly after the second guard retreated into the night. Swiftly moving from one dark patch to another, the prince soon reached the officers' quarters. Before him, in square formation, were the soldiers' barracks. Now that he was here, Naibor wasn't sure what to do next. There was no sense in doing anything rash; he had already had one unfortunate incident, and he did not want another, so he tried to come up with some sort of plan.

While he was thinking, the prince heard a mournful sound come from the closest barrack. Listening intently, he heard it again—a low moan. The sound was of someone in pain. Naibor wanted to investigate further, but he considered he could be mistaken. *Maybe it was just a drunk Daimos.*

Another moan followed the previous one, and the sound was so pitiful that Naibor decided to chance being seen. Cautiously peering into the open area, Naibor gasped. There, in front of a barrack, was a man, bound tightly, hanging from a post. Losing all fear of being caught, the prince left the relative safety of the shadows and strode toward the man in the lighted courtyard.

"What are you tied there for?" Naibor asked with a soft voice, looking up at the poor man with compassion.

The man stared in horror at the grotesque mask staring up at him. Fearing that a Daimos had come to further torment him, he dared not make another sound.

Naibor, reading the man's face, realized who the man thought he was. Not wanting to take off his mask, he whispered, "I am not a Daimos. I am a friend." But the man still showed no response.

"Here, let me give you some water," Naibor said quietly, wanting to ease the man's suffering. Stepping up onto the small step that the Daimos had used when tying the prisoner to the post, he poured some water from his bag onto the man's closed lips. The man just stared wide-eyed in fright.

"What's the matter?" Naibor lowered his waterskin in exasperation. "Aren't you thirsty?"

Suddenly getting an idea, Naibor raised the water to his own lips and took a drink. "There, you see? Nothing is wrong with the water. Please, I want to help you. Please let me give you a drink."

The man nodded slightly. Relieved, Naibor poured the cool, refreshing liquid into the prisoner's open mouth. The man drank greedily for several moments. When he had finished, he looked at Naibor and asked in a hoarse whisper, "Who are you?"

"An angel in disguise," the prince answered, not wanting to reveal his identity.

"I believe you," the man said. "Daimos don't use the word 'please.'" He smiled feebly.

"Why are you up there?" Naibor was glad to have finally earned the man's trust.

"You don't know?" The man looked at the masked stranger incredulously. Naibor's silence gave him his answer.

"This is what the Daimos use as punishment, and as an example to the others, for anyone who gives them trouble. They call it the stick. They tie you to a post without any food or water —sometimes after they beat you, and sometimes until you die. I am being punished only for two days."

"But what did you do?" Naibor asked, horrified by such cruelty.

"I asked for some water." He gave a halfhearted laugh while tears rolled down his cheeks.

"Here. Drink the rest of mine," Naibor instructed, emptying the water from his bag into the mouth of the grateful man.

"Where are the guards?" Naibor inquired after returning to the ground, aware of how exposed he was.

"In the guardhouse," the man answered, using his eyes to point the way.

Naibor followed his eyes to a building at the corner of the square. "Why are they not outside patrolling the courtyard or watching over the prisoners?" he asked, thankful they were not.

"They don't need to," the prisoner replied frankly. "They are more afraid of us in the day, when we are all together out in the open.

They seem weaker in the daylight than they are at night. At night they just lock us in the barracks and leave us alone. When they first captured us, they had a guard at every door. Now we are too tired and half-starved to be any threat."

"But I met some guards patrolling the streets on the outskirts of this camp, so there must be some attempts at escape?"

"Could be, but I haven't heard of any. It is rumored that the Daimos fight a lot among themselves. I even heard they burned one of their own houses down. Could be they are policing their own."

"Yes, that could be it," Naibor agreed, smiling beneath his mask. So far tonight had been very informative.

Thinking about policing gave Naibor another idea. "Are any captains being held prisoner in these barracks?"

"Yes. Captain Zai and Captain Regg are together in the barrack across the square."

Naibor could not believe his good fortune. "The barrack on the right?"

The man nodded.

"How can I thank you, my friend?" The ropes holding the prisoner had given the man red welts and lacerations across his body. Confronted with the man's pain, the prince spoke his feelings aloud. "I wish I could cut you down."

"No! You can't cut me down!" the man protested, worried the stranger might try. "When they found me free they would beat me to death, and all my friends would suffer because they would be accused of rescuing me. No, I thank you for the water. You were an answer to my prayers, and you have renewed my hope. You may go in peace."

Without another word, Naibor turned and headed toward the guardhouse. As he moved stealthily forward, he formed a rough plan in his head. So far tonight he had used his disguise to his advantage. He hoped he would be able to use it successfully once more.

Wanting to get a look at his adversaries, Naibor sneaked around the building to a small side window. Inside were five Daimos guards.

Four of them were playing cards, but their minds did not seem to be on the game. The fifth was watching them play, amused by what he saw. None of them seemed to be very alert. Two were smoking leaves that were considered harmful, and there was an empty bottle of alcohol on the table. Noticing that the front door had been left open, Naibor decided to move closer to hear what they were saying.

"These nights are almost as bad as the days. What kind of life is this?" one of the Daimos said, throwing down his losing hand of cards. "I'm as much a prisoner as they are," he added, jerking his head toward the courtyard.

"Would you prefer it to be like the way we were before?" the Daimos across from him asked, scowling.

"No, not like that!" the first answered with a shudder. "But sitting here isn't doing me much good. I'd rather be out raiding villages, murdering unbelievers, or participating in rituals and ceremonies. These people have made it too easy for us. Scared like rabbits they are. No fight!" He spit phlegm at the floor to punctuate his words.

Taking his cue, Naibor entered the guardhouse. "Perhaps if you paid more attention to your duties, the night would not seem so dull," he challenged.

Turning in surprise, the Daimos saw a commanding figure wearing a ceremonial mask standing in the open doorway. Instantly they jumped up in front of the table, trying to cover their sins.

"Who are you? What do you want?" the guard, who had been watching the game, growled in defense, annoyed at having been caught so lax while on duty.

"Don't you speak to me like that, or I will report you!" Naibor snapped back.

"For what?" the same Daimos asked innocently, backing down a little.

"For drinking and smoking while on duty," Naibor bluffed, hoping these were offenses.

The Daimos in the room shifted uncomfortably, trying to look as orderly and respectable as possible.

"Give me the keys!" the masked prince demanded, now fully in control.

"What for?" the first guard asked, a little suspicious.

"I need a prisoner for a ceremony the Ix people are having tonight."

"Which prisoner?" the same guard asked, smiling grimly while he went to get the keys. Putting them into Naibor's outstretched hand, he eyed him with envy.

"I will choose one," Naibor said, quickly thinking up his next line while closing his hand around the key ring. "In the morning you can guess which one is missing."

The Daimos in the room laughed and grinned at one another, and in their minds they imagined the hideous proceedings of the ceremony.

Leaving the guardhouse, Naibor almost laughed himself, knowing that in the morning the only thing they would find missing would be their keys.

* * *

Captain Regg lay awake and restless on his cot in the barrack where he was a prisoner. His head pounded and his leg ached from the seemingly endless hours of toil during the day.

"You don't look so good, Regg," Captain Zai said with a grin, trying to make light of their misery.

"Neither do you," Regg returned, turning to look at his friend sitting beside him on the floor between his bed and the next. Both men were bone weary and underfed, but except for sunburn, various bruises and lash marks, and a few new calluses, scratches, and blisters, they were still strong, and they knew it.

"It's Graypah I'm worried about," Zai whispered back, and together they both looked with concern toward where he lay.

The old advisor lay weak and shivering on his bed against the opposite wall, while another man from the barrack tried to comfort him and attend to his needs.

"He has kept our spirits up, always giving us reason to hope. He was so confident that some help would come to us and that Amuron would not be forsaken, its people left to die at the hands of a sorcerer. Now he is sick, and we can do little to help even him. Curse these Daimos and that sorcerer Necros," Regg added.

The man attending Graypah got up and left. The advisor had finally fallen into a light sleep.

"It's getting late," Regg commented to Zai. "It's time we tried to get some sleep."

Zai nodded in agreement. Getting up to lie down on his bed, he stopped when he heard the sound of a key turning in the lock. Regg looked at Zai with surprise, and Zai returned his look with a furrowed brow. The whole room suddenly became tense. This was not a sound they expected to hear. They worked hard until the sun went down, and then they were left to rest until morning.

The long room was dark. They could light only one lamp in the room, to conserve the lamp oil, and the doorway lay entirely in shadow. The prisoners watched in silence as the door opened. A black-robed figure entered, quickly closing the door. The frightening figure strode forward, turning his head this way and that to look at each of the prisoners. Captain Regg swallowed hard when he saw the death mask stare straight at him and come to a stop.

The robed figure then removed his hood and mask. "I must talk to you, Captain," Prince Naibor said.

Captain Regg stared in disbelief and then quickly recovered from his shock. "Yes. Come and sit. Captain Zai is here too."

The prince looked over and nodded a greeting. He did not know the head of the city guard as well as Captain Regg, and he would not have recognized him either. His hair was dirty and hung in his eyes, and his normally small, trim beard had blended in with the hair growing on the rest of his face. Captain Regg also looked dirty and disheveled. His eyes were darkly circled and sunken in his heavily lined face.

"Good. I was hoping we could come up with a strategy to save the city," Naibor confided to the captains.

Hearing a feeble cough and movement in the room, he looked over his shoulder and saw a man hurry to the side of a cot. "Who is it?" the prince inquired, feeling he knew the wan face of the man on the bed.

"It's Graypah, Prince, and he is very sick."

"Graypah! Do you think he is well enough for me to talk with him?"

Captain Regg shrugged but did not stop him.

The prince went quietly to the old man's bedside and took his hand. The other man attending him moved away to let them talk privately.

"Graypah," he whispered softly. "It's Prince Naibor."

The old advisor opened his eyes and looked lovingly up at the prince. "Naibor," he said with a sigh, "the high king's son. I love your father with all my heart, and you are his only son. I have loved you all these years as I have watched you grow from a boy to a man."

Naibor smiled tenderly. He wondered if he knew anyone else so kind.

"You have got to save the city, Prince," Graypah said suddenly, as if he had just remembered something important.

"I know, Graypah. I will," the prince promised.

"You are the only one who can kill the sorcerer," he insisted.

"How, Graypah? Do you know how I can fight against Necros and the Daimos?"

"You will find the answer soon, Prince," the old advisor smiled assuredly. "The answer will come to you."

There was a pause, almost as if he expected the answer to come at that very moment, and his eyes glowed confidently. "Evil shall not overcome. Necros awaits his doom," he continued weakly, closing his eyes. "Save Amuron. It's time, Prince." His voice was barely above a whisper. "It's time you showed everyone who you really are."

As Naibor watched, the breath of his father's dear friend left his tired body. All that made Graypah who he was went to rest where his heart had always been. Clutching the advisor's thin body tight in an embrace, Naibor wept. The room became filled with the solemn movement and murmurs of those in mourning.

After a while, Naibor joined the two captains, silently sharing their loss. "When did he become sick?" Naibor asked with an unsteady voice.

"Just yesterday. He must have caught a chill in the night, and they still worked him today in the cold wind. He barely made it back to the barrack at nightfall," Captain Regg told him with anguish in his voice.

"So sudden then!" Naibor was surprised.

"Yes, it is a good thing you came when you did, but how did you get here?" Regg asked, recognizing the strangeness of it.

All the events of the night swirled in Naibor's head as he tried to organize his thoughts. Focusing on the important details, he explained how he happened to sneak out of the palace and what he had learned about the Daimos.

"This is important news!" Captain Regg said in summation. "We suspected that the Daimos might be more vulnerable during the day, and now we know they have little tolerance for alcohol as well."

"We must find some way to use this information to our advantage," Captain Zai added. "Together we should be able to come up with some sort of plan."

"Yes, that is what I was hoping too. There are still many details to work out, but I must leave you now. It is getting late," the prince said, rising from the bed. "When I return, we will hopefully find a way to stop the sorcerer."

"I wish there was some way to contact you, Prince," Zai said regretfully.

"If we could think up a signal of some sort," Regg agreed.

"Do you have one of those devices that makes things in the distance seem close? A looking glass, I think it is called?" Zai asked, suddenly getting an idea.

"Yes, I have one. Why?"

"Can you see as far as the arena with it?"

"Yes, I think so," Naibor answered, waiting for Zai's explanation.

"During the day I have been working on the roof of Necros's temple. If we need to contact you, I could tie a piece of black cloth to one of the metal spires."

"Good idea, Captain," Naibor said, pleased that they were now working together. "A black cloth shouldn't attract unwanted attention, and I should still be able to see it with the lens."

They stood there awkwardly for a moment, not knowing how to end such an unusual evening, until Naibor found himself saying, "May the Lord of Goodness watch over you and guide you on the right path."

The captains looked about as surprised as he was by his sudden use of a traditional blessing. Naibor was not one to use the traditional sayings, and he was not even sure how he knew them, but somehow the words seemed comforting to them all.

"Yes, and the same to you, Prince," the captains returned, watching him quietly leave their barrack in his disguise.

"He is our hope then," Captain Zai commented after the prince had left. "We may yet be able to save Amuron."

Captain Regg looked thoughtful for a moment, and then he looked over at his friend and fellow captain. The light of renewed hope shone within the eyes of Zai, where before there had been defeat and loss.

Captain Regg smiled in reply. Remembering Graypah, he echoed the advisor's words. "Even one man's faith is enough for hope."

CHAPTER 14

The sun was shifting over to the west in the highest reaches of the sky when the animals met up again on the seat of Mount Sol. As earlier arranged, Ranor had gotten a lift from Sanii up the steep cliff face. The others had followed Janii, trusting her to choose which of the available rocks, ledges, and crevices would make the easiest route for them to climb. Baynor, choosing his own path, had gone up ahead of the rest, still sullen and keeping to himself.

The third gate they sought was located at the back of a wide plateau of rock that stretched between the arms of the semicircular heights of the mountain. This gate was known as the Gate of Darkness and Light and was so named because one had to pass through the interior of the mountain to get to the other side. To avoid the uncomfortable silence that had developed, all eyes looked thoughtfully at the shiny metal door that marked the entrance into the mountain.

The door of the third gate was impressive, towering to more than three times a man's height and as wide as ten men across. A picture was etched deeply into the face of the metal, filling its entire surface. Amon's eyes danced as he admired the picture before him. In the center of the door was a majestic steed rearing back on his hind legs. The horse was balanced on the upper peak of Mount Sol, with the rest of the Khist mountain range spread out beneath. The muscles of the horse rippled and his nostrils flared, while his mane flowed wildly behind him. Seated on the excited animal was the figure of a mighty champion whose glowing body radiated power and strength. With one hand, the champion steadied his mount; with the other, he held the fiery ball of the sun raised to the heavens. The champion's face shone with joy, and his eyes were filled with confidence and assurance. The sight was inspiring.

Baynor looked away from the gate and then at his friends, and he felt ashamed. "Friends," he began, addressing the group, "I have to apologize to you for my foolishness, and I have a confession to make before we enter into the mountain."

"Let me guess," Tybor jumped in before he could finish. "You want to tell us that you knew there was a bear somewhere in the valley and you did not warn us."

"That's right! Did you know there was a bear in the area as well?" Baynor asked, puzzled, looking directly at the wolf for clarification.

"Give my nose some credit. Most of us were aware of the same weak scent you found back on Ur. It wouldn't have mattered if you had warned us, Baynor, because you were the only one in any danger."

"What are you saying, Tybor?"

"The bear would not have bothered any of us while we were passing through his territory. It was your scent, the scent of another male bear, that caused him to attack. We are as much to blame as you—maybe more, because we were not alert and watching for any possible danger. We should have been able to warn you before the bear attacked."

"But he would have attacked even if you had warned me ahead of time."

"Exactly!"

"And we could not have chosen another route, because this is the path to Berroc."

"Exactly!"

"And you came quickly to my rescue. If it had not been for you, I could have been seriously injured. For that I am grateful, and I am grateful also that you are such good friends!"

"Exactly!" Tybor said in conclusion.

"Now, if I could have your assistance, Amon?" Baynor inquired of the youth. "Could you see to this cut on my face? It is stinging badly."

In reply, Amon dug greedily in his bag for the medical supplies. Despite Baynor's wincing and growling, Amon managed to wash the badly torn wound and apply some ointment to protect against infection.

"There, we are done," Amon soon announced to the group with relief, packing away the things he had been using.

"Good! Time to move on," the contrite bear added, thankful the whole ordeal was over.

"How do we open the gate?" Amon marveled again at the size of the door.

"There should be a handle of some sort," Baynor informed them, and everyone carefully searched the metal surface.

"Here it is!" the eagle exclaimed, and looking to where she pointed with her beak, they could all make out a ring craftily hidden by the picture on the door.

"Go ahead and give it a pull, Amon," the bear instructed.

The youth grabbed the ring and pulled hard, expecting the door to be as heavy as it looked, but the door swung open easily, as if floating magically through the air.

It opened to reveal a large tunnel the same dimensions as the door. The rocky sides of the tunnel were unnaturally smooth and did not vary in size or shape as they went straight into the heart of the mountain. The deep darkness of the tunnel seemed to go on forever. The only bit of light was the pool of sunlight that ended a few short paces away from where they stood.

"Oh dear!" Sanii exclaimed, ruffling her rich brown feathers with dismay. "I just realized I won't be able to fly."

"Why don't you just fly over and meet us on the other side?" Amon suggested.

"Impossible," Baynor said, trying to explain what was not explainable. "If she did that, she would not be able to come to Berroc with us. There is only one way to Berroc, and that is by passing through all seven of the gates. Berroc can be reached no other way."

"Thanks for thinking of me, Amon," the eagle said gratefully, cocking her head to look up at the youth with one of her large, round eyes. "I'll just have to put these scrawny things called legs to use."

"On to Berroc then," the wolf urged, stepping forward through the gate with the others following. "And by the way," he whispered secretively to Sanii, "I happen to think you have a lovely pair of scrawny legs."

"Why, thank you," she replied with a laugh, strutting forward proudly.

They had taken only a few steps inside the tunnel when the door to the gate swung back silently into place—leaving them entirely in the dark. They were now shut inside a passage that ran beneath a mountain of rock, with nothing but their instincts to guide them. Strangely, they felt no fear, and a quiet settled around the travelers. The gates were sacred places, constructed according to Aii's wishes to be used by his followers. Nothing evil or unholy would go near them. They knew that they were safe inside the gate and that nothing would be waiting in the darkness to harm them.

"I can't see a thing," Janii realized, sounding somewhat surprised.

"I'll light a torch," Amon volunteered.

The animals heard the sounds of the youth digging into his pack, and then they saw the sparks from the flint. At last a flame lit up the darkness. Holding the torch high, Amon started to lead them down the tunnel, but the fire soon went out. He tried again, but the same thing happened.

"I don't know what's wrong," the frustrated youth said. "It won't stay lit."

"That's all right, Amon," the unicorn said kindly. "The smoke was stinging our eyes anyway."

"It seems the gate has an appropriate name," Tybor announced into the surrounding blackness.

"I'll lead the way," the mountain cat ventured. "This darkness doesn't bother me."

"Can I walk beside you, Princess Janii?" Amon asked the unicorn, feeling uncomfortable without any light.

"Certainly," she replied. "We will follow behind Tayii."

"And I will walk behind you, Janii," Baynor decided. "That way I won't have to worry about stepping on anyone."

"This is horrible," Sanii muttered. "First I'm grounded, and then I'm blind."

"Stay close to me then," the badger advised from beside her. "I'll help you out."

"It seems you have the advantage over me this time," she added to Ranor in reply. "You are much more at home in tunnels than I."

"And I'll follow behind the both of you, taking up the rear," the wolf told his companions, with his alert ears listening to the darkness.

"All right," Tayii said after the others had taken up their positions. "Are we ready?" Hearing everyone's affirmation, the panther started off into the depths of Mount Sol.

They began their journey through the darkness at a slow pace, afraid of bumping into one another. Then, after a while, they became accustomed to the sound of their own movements and those of the others within the walls of the mountain. This allowed them to make judgements about the speed at which they were traveling and adjust how close they were to one another.

On and on they went through the infinite blackness. They soon lost all sense of time, so that the hours turned into days and the days into a lifetime. When they were tired, they stopped for a rest, munching on whatever food supplies Amon carried with him. When they felt they had traveled a day's journey, they decided to sleep. Waking was no different from sleeping. Nothing changed. All that surrounded them was the mountain of darkness.

"Umf," grunted Baynor when he woke up.

"Is that you, Baynor?" Tybor's voice asked groggily. "Do you know how long we have been asleep?"

"Well, it feels like I slept for several hours, but how would I know? It could have been only a few minutes."

"Judging from my stomach clock," the wolf replied, "I'd estimate about four hours."

"Sounds about right to me," the large bear agreed, shifting his bulk. "If we ever want to see the light of day, we should get moving again. Who else is awake?" Baynor asked the darkness, giving himself a shake.

"I am," Janii said.

"So am I," answered the panther.

"I think I hear Amon snoring," the unicorn added with a quiet nicker.

"It's not me!" Amon spoke up defensively, his voice still husky from sleep.

"It's Ranor," Sanii explained from beside her sleeping companion. "A snoring badger, imagine!"

"Well, wake him up," Baynor instructed with his throaty laugh. "It's time to go."

Tybor pushed at the badger with his muzzle to rouse his friend. "Ranor, wake up!"

Ranor gave a little grunt, and then with a groan he rolled off his back and onto his feet. "What's up?" he asked with a yawn.

"Everybody but you," Tayii noted, and her companions laughed.

Shortly afterward, they resumed their march. Sanii, with a lift up from Amon, had taken to riding on Baynor's back, finding it too difficult to walk far on her taloned feet. By the time the travelers had cast off their sleepiness and had settled down to a good pace, Tayii called a halt from her position at the head of the group.

"What is the matter?" Baynor called to her with concern.

"Nothing," she informed those behind her. "We have reached the end of the tunnel."

The others pushed their way forward and indeed found they could go no farther. Blocking their path was what felt like another metal door. They were elated with the thought of having finally reached the end of their dark journey. Excitedly they pushed on the door, only to find it didn't open.

"Oh, not again," moaned Amon. "Why is it none of these gate doors want to open?"

"Perhaps there is a ring, like the first door, or even a latch that we need to find," Janii suggested.

They felt over every inch of the door, but they could feel nothing.

"Something is etched on the door like the last one," Amon observed. "I'll light a torch so we can see it."

Once again the youth lit one of the torches. The light was dazzlingly bright, and they were blinded until their eyes slowly adjusted. Etched into the door was a picture of the shining sun.

"Well, it's what we hoped to see," the grizzly snorted at the irony. "But this isn't how we hoped to see it!"

With the aid of the lighted torch, the group searched the door again, hoping to find a way to open it, but they searched in vain. Then, as before, the torch flickered and went out, leaving them lost in the pervasive blackness.

"Do you think we could have taken a wrong turn?" Sanii asked aloud, thinking her feet couldn't possibly take her much farther.

"I'm sure we didn't," Tayii answered. "There was no change in the sound of our echoes in the tunnel or in the air surrounding us. I feel sure I would have noticed if there had been."

"I didn't notice any changes either," the badger agreed.

"Then I am sure we are in the right place," Baynor concluded, having faith in his friends. "We will just have to rest here and try to think of a solution."

Listening to the sound of the animals settling down into comfortable positions, Amon leaned his back against the cool metal. Sliding down to a sitting position, he felt the wall slip away from him as the door to the gate silently opened.

"Hey!" he cried out in surprise, his body lying half outside of the tunnel and half inside.

The others turned to see the blackness give way to a shade of light gray.

"What did you do, Amon?" Baynor asked, rising to his feet with the others and walking outside into the fresh breeze. "How did you open the door?"

"I don't know." He got up and wiped himself off. "The door just opened when I leaned against it."

They stood together on the circular edge of a cliff facing eastward. They were now on the other side of the Khist mountain range. Above them the sky stretched out cloudless, brightening in shades from gray to blue. Beneath them lay a steep mountainside, some hills, and a forest of trees lost beneath a layer of haze. Beyond the trees they could just make out something dark and flat, which they knew to be the sea.

Out on the very edge of the line of the sea, a glow of pale orange announced the arrival of a new day. While the group of travelers watched, the shimmering globe of the sun appeared. As it rose slowly above the waters, the world they faced was flooded with light.

"The answer is clear to me now," Baynor realized, thoroughly enjoying the sight before him. "The door opens with the rising of the sun. It truly is the gate of Darkness and Light." Turning, he found the door had closed behind them.

"It is so good to be out in the daylight again." The unicorn expressed how she felt with a soft sigh and a light toss of her mane.

"Yes, and I think we deserve that rest," the bear added with a full yawn. "At least now we can keep track of where we are going and how far we have come."

Comforted that they had made it through the third gate, the group settled down to rest and to sleep for a few more hours in the early light of a new morning.

*   *   *

The morning shadows were still long when the seven travelers looked around them and assessed their situation. The cliff they were on, besides providing them with a spectacular view, unfortunately had sheer sides that plummeted beneath them for a distance that was at least double the height of the walls of Amuron. Their only means of getting down was by using a basket attached to a rope and pulley system on the south side of the cliff. Going over to inspect it further, they found that the basket was big enough to hold only an individual man-sized passenger. Everyone but Janii and Baynor could comfortably use it.

For Janii, this did not present too much of a problem. Her nimble feet seemed designed to cling to the sheerest of mountainsides. Baynor, however, was not as fortunate.

"They use systems like this in Amuron for lifting up buckets of hot coa when they are working on the wall." Amon, recognizing the apparatus, smiled enthusiastically. "The basket works this way." He demonstrated by pulling on the rope to make the basket move up and down. Realizing that the animals could not work the rope, he added, "I can send down whoever is in the basket."

"Hold on to the basket to steady it while I jump in," said Tybor, volunteering to be the first. He easily leaped inside.

Amon let the wolf down in the gently swaying basket and then repeated the whole procedure for Tayii while Baynor watched.

"I'm too big and heavy for that basket," Baynor concluded apprehensively.

"Considering the options, you haven't much choice," Janii said, attempting to encourage her friend. "I'll wait up here until you reach the bottom."

"It would be easier if I could fly," Baynor replied dryly, giving Sanii an envious glance. "But it does seem to be the only way. What about you, Ranor?"

"I have already discussed it with Amon, and we will go down together. I am too small to get in and out of the basket on my own," the badger explained.

"Then I guess it is my turn to try," Baynor sighed with resignation. Testing the basket with his paw, he caused it to rock back and forth.

Lowering the basket slightly, Amon made it easier for the bear to get in.

"Once I'm settled, lower me down as quickly as you can," Baynor instructed the youth as he half sat, half straddled the rim of the basket with the bulk of his body. "All right, I'm ready," he stated, looking both awkward and uncomfortable on his precarious perch.

In an attempt to gain some balance, Baynor stretched his front paws upward and grasped onto the rope as the youth sent him down the side of the cliff. Although Amon was letting him down quickly, the journey seemed to be taking a long time. Wanting to see how much farther he still had to go, Baynor risked looking over the side. This movement was enough to tilt the basket, causing his weight to shift so that he toppled headfirst halfway over the side.

"He's falling!" Janii cried out in alarm from the top of the cliff.

CHAPTER 15

Hanging half out of the basket, Prince Baynor tried desperately to hang on and not make any sudden moves. It was no use. The side of the basket could not support all the bear's weight. It further tipped until it upended, sending its passenger crashing to the ground with a quarter of its journey still unfinished.

"Baynor!" Janii shouted out. "Amon! Hurry! Bring the basket back up and follow behind with the medical supplies." She then urgently ran to the side of the cliff and leaped down it to Baynor's aid. Sanii took flight, swooping down beside her.

Amon swiftly gathered the supply packs and then dashed to the basket with Prince Ranor. On reaching the ground, Amon quickly released the badger. "Is Prince Baynor all right?" he asked Janii when they gathered with the others around the unmoving bear.

"He is unconscious." There was a quaver in her voice, and worry filled the depths of her liquid blue eyes.

Tybor was busy licking the bear's face. "Baynor," he called softly between licks, "Baynor."

The grizzly bear gave a small grunt and moved his head away from the wolf's wet tongue.

"Careful," Tybor gently cautioned. "Move slowly, and let me know what hurts."

"Everything," Baynor complained with a low moan, rising slowly onto his four paws. "But I don't think anything is broken."

"I have checked you over as best I can, and I found no traces of fresh blood. As long as there are no internal injuries, I predict you will live." Tybor concluded his inspection with a hopeful wag of his tail. "What you need now is a mixture of herbs added to some tea. It will help to minimize the bruising and swelling. Let me see what you have in the medical kit, Amon."

Amon revealed the contents of the kit to Tybor. "This will do nicely," the wolf murmured, quite satisfied, before instructing Amon on how to mix up a concoction of the ingredients in just the right proportions.

"You will have to drink it cold," Tybor commented as Amon offered the herbed drink in a bowl to the bear. "It is better to take it immediately for best results. It would take too long to heat the water in this case."

"What is this stuff?" Baynor asked curiously, giving the strange ingredients a quick sniff. Deciding it didn't smell too bad, he began to lap up the liquid medicine.

"Humanly speaking, it has a rather strong and bitter flavor, but for a bear I'll wager it makes a pleasant appetizer," Tybor deduced, watching Baynor's bear lips curl back in a smile when he was finished.

They still had a long day's march ahead of them, down the side of the mountain and into the forest below, but they delayed their journey a while longer to give Baynor more time to recover from his fall.

Judging by the sun in the sky, it was still two hours from midday when the travelers began to descend the eastern side of Mount Sol. The trail was steep and switchbacked across rocky slopes covered in sparse brush.

"How do you feel?" Tybor asked, coming up beside the injured bear.

Baynor's bulky body filled up the narrow trail while he plunged heavily forward, half sliding down the slope as he walked. "My right front paw is tender when I put my weight on it, but other than that, I seem to be in pretty good shape."

"That was quite the fall you had. Luckily that fall didn't happen while you were still human. Being a bear had its advantages."

"If I weren't a bear, I would not have fallen," Baynor pointed out with a disapproving snort.

"Um, true enough," Tybor replied, and Baynor noted a tone of seriousness in the wolf's voice along with a look of concern in his deep brown eyes. "That brings up something that has been on my mind lately. There is something I would like to talk to you about privately. Wait here a minute." Tybor hesitated, and Baynor complied.

Perking up his ears, the wolf prince heard Amon approaching with the badger riding on his back. Turning, he looked at the youth. "You go on ahead of us, Amon. Baynor and I are going to slow our pace a little. Tell the others in front to wait for us where the trail leads into the trees."

Amon nodded between puffs of air. Then, with a wipe of his forehead, the youth crashed through the underbrush to go around them.

"I've been thinking about something that disturbs me, Baynor," Tybor said over his shoulder while continuing his descent down the mountain path with the grizzly following closely behind.

"What is it, Tybor?"

"The issue of our humanity. Do you think it will be possible to ever be human again?"

"I was hoping that question could be answered at Berroc." Baynor spoke honestly, although he secretly doubted that anything could be done.

Tybor looked around suspiciously and then stopped for a moment, listening to see who was within earshot. Satisfied that he would not be overheard, he lowered his voice and said, "I haven't said anything to anyone else, but if we have the chance to be changed back, it will be strange becoming human again."

"What are you saying, Tybor? Don't you want to become human again?"

"No, not so much that, but I will miss being a wolf. Do you understand what I mean?"

"Yes, and that scares me."

"It does?"

"I hadn't really thought about it, but now that you have brought the subject up, I realize how much being a bear is so much a part of me," Baynor confided emphatically. "It almost seems natural, and that's what scares me. This is not who we were meant to be, Tybor. We must not remain like this. We have got to do all we can to become human again. We can't settle for being animals. We have our whole lives to think about. I don't want to die a bear living in the mountains, and you must think about Sanii and how you are betrothed. You can't possibly think of marriage while you are still a wolf."

"You are right, Baynor, but it almost seems that the longer we remain animals, the less I think about being human. We must seek the help of Aii at Berroc. The sooner we get there, the better."

"I couldn't agree more," Baynor said heartily, wincing when he put too much weight on his sore paw.

Not far ahead, the others were waiting for them at the edge of the forest.

"Are you all right?" Janii asked with concern when they arrived, thinking their slowed pace was due to Baynor's injuries from the fall. "We can stop here and have some lunch," she suggested.

"No, I'm fine," Baynor replied, giving Janii a big bear grin and a wink. "I was hoping to reach the fourth gate by nightfall. I think we should keep going for a little while yet."

"Especially since it looks like rain," Tybor added, looking up at the gathering clouds.

"Indeed it does," Ranor agreed. The sky had turned sullen, and the wind had picked up, promising a good downpour.

"All right," Janii said, giving in somewhat reluctantly, still believing that Baynor was in more pain than he was willing to admit.

The unicorn led the group into a refreshing wood of mixed broad-leaved trees and conifers that spread out thickly around them as they headed away from the mountains. The approaching storm grew until the wind blew in strong gusts, swirling violently around them while grabbing at the tree branches, making them sway and hiss. The sky became dark, covered by giant, rolling black clouds that hung threateningly just over the tops of the trees.

"Shall we take cover?" Ranor asked, raising his voice to be heard above the noise of the wind.

"I don't know where we will find any," Baynor answered, a little disgruntled by the thought of the rain. Looking around him to either side of the trail, he added, "We are sure to get wet wherever we try to shelter."

The rain came and fell hard, making the boughs of the trees around the travelers bend in subservience. Nothing escaped from the storm's fury. The sky fell in sheets of water, soaking fur, feathers, hair, and clothing. Walking became difficult as the ground became soggy and covered in water. The wind blew the cold rain into their faces, making it hard to see, but they continued on as best they could until the storm abated. Even Sanii was forced to the ground, her feathers too wet for flying, so she rode on Baynor's back clinging to his damp, long shaggy hair.

After a while, the sky lightened and the driving rain subsided into heavy rainfall. Feeling the rain let up a little, the travelers searched for a place to rest for some refreshment. They soon found a large evergreen tree by the path and huddled under its large branches and dripping needles for meager protection.

"There is not much here," the discouraged youth told them, opening up the supply pack with chilled fingers. "There is a handful of bran, some travelers' bread, and a few berries, but that is all."

"It will have to do," Baynor remarked, aware of the pangs of hunger in his stomach.

Amon distributed what little food there was among the cheerless group, wishing there was some way he could make a small fire to warm them. Even though he was soaked to the bone and shivering, despite his hooded traveler's cloak, his companions looked so pitiful that he was moved to want to offer them some sort of comfort. He especially wanted to help the unicorn. This was the first time Princess Janii's glistening coat did not shine with its soft, radiant light. Instead she stood among her friends almost appearing to be a common mare. Her sodden mane hung in her face, sending rivulets of water down her nose, and her dainty legs and glorious tail were soiled up to her knees, having been splashed with muck. Suddenly he got an idea.

"My lady, let me cover you with this," Amon said, pulling his blanket out of the bag and holding it out to her.

Overwhelmed by his generosity, Janii replied, "But then your blanket will be wet tonight when you want to sleep."

"That doesn't matter," he simply stated. "I want you to have it, and I will sleep much better knowing that you do."

"Thank you, Amon." Bowing her head, she gratefully accepted his gift. The warmth of the blanket quickly radiated over her entire body as he threw the light fabric over her neck and down her back. "You will forever be in my prayers," she sighed.

"That was nice of you," Baynor commented to the youth.

Amon shrugged awkwardly at the praise. "I wish I had enough for all of you."

"I know." The bear nodded his large head in affirmation. "You have a good heart, Amon."

They rested as best as they could, huddling together to protect themselves against the elements, but they could not escape from the persistent wet and cold wind.

"I can't say I'm enjoying this weather," the miserable panther confided to her feathered friend, her whiskers drooping mournfully.

"Rain is always so much nicer when you are watching it from

inside a room with a warm fire," her winged friend agreed while the water trickled down off her back in big drops.

The wolf gave a sneeze and scanned the sky, "It looks like we will be traveling in the rain all day." Tybor's tail hung down low.

"Yes, but we will be one gate closer to Berroc at the end of it," Baynor offered encouragingly, giving Tybor a significant glance.

"Then let's go!" Ranor said impatiently. "I'm tired of standing around."

Leaving the limited shelter of the tree behind, the travelers continued on, and so did the rain. The animals and Amon were thoroughly wet, cold, tired, and hungry when they came within sight of the haven at the end of the day.

"I wasn't expecting another haven until after the next gate!" Baynor exclaimed, cheered by the sight, and the rest of the group exchanged expressions of delight. All agreed that a warm fire and a dry place to sleep was just what they needed.

In a clearing to the south side of the trail stood a small cabin made of logs. The weary travelers hastened forward until they saw smoke rising from the chimney.

"Looks like someone is already using it," the eagle observed, discouraged by the sight.

"I'll go and investigate," the wolf offered, jogging off in the direction of the building.

There were no windows in the cabin, so they stopped to watch Tybor from the trail, not afraid of being seen. Someone was watching them, however—someone who wished not to be seen and who watched them from the concealment of the forest shadows with a smile on his lips.

Tybor approached the haven cautiously, every fiber of his being alert for danger. Circling around to the back of the building, he hunted for clues about who might be inside. He found some large footprints in the mud, but they were full of water and the scent had been lost in the rain. He could hear no sound of movement coming from the cabin, but he could easily smell the cooking food.

The delicious aromas drifted out to him, tantalizing him. His nose twitched appreciatively, and he licked his muzzle as his poor stomach cried out in protest at having been empty for so long.

Going to the door on the east side of the building, Tybor stopped in his tracks. The door to the cabin was ajar. With a threatening snarl on his lips, the wolf stared at the door, listening, watching. Nothing moved, and he could hear no sound except that of the rain falling around him. Through the crack in the door, he could see a warm light in the fireplace—but nothing else. He moved forward a pace or two, and then another step. He could still hear only the sounds of the crackling fire coming from inside. There wasn't the sound of someone eating or preparing the food that he could smell all too well, and Tybor found that puzzling. Stepping right up to the door, he sniffed the air and listened for any signs of life. Finally he could stand it no longer. The smell of food was too great, and he could not hear or see anyone, so he pushed the door open with his nose and went inside.

The rest of Tybor's companions were becoming anxious. It had been too long since he had disappeared from view.

"What is taking him so long?" Baynor grumbled, expressing his worried thoughts aloud. "He should have been back by now. We should go and investigate."

But before they had the chance to move, they suddenly caught sight of Tybor tearing around the corner from the front of the building. He came charging toward them, running as fast as he could. The others, fearing he was being attacked, prepared for battle, but the steps of his feet were light and he was yelping excitedly.

"Tybor, calm down and tell us what is wrong," Tayii said to her brother with concern.

"Nothing is wrong!" Tybor cried out joyfully, bouncing lightly on his four paws before them. "Come and see for yourselves. I do believe we were expected. I had half a mind to leave you standing in the rain while I remained to enjoy myself. Ha ha! But I didn't; I came running."

"Tybor, please! Who is in the cabin?" Baynor asked, not at all sure he understood what the wolf was saying.

"Nobody, but come on!" he added empathically. "Why are you still standing out in the rain? Come on!"

"Is it safe?" Janii questioned.

"Yes, of course, but I'm not going to wait for you any longer!" With that the wolf prince trotted quickly back toward the cabin. He stopped at the door to give himself a final shake before entering the sanctity of the haven. His friends followed him inside, relieved to have a warm and dry place to relax for the night.

With a satisfied nod of his head, the person who was watching them from a distance slipped back into the woods as if he had never been.

Amon entered the cabin last, shutting the door behind him. Pushing back the hood from his eyes, he looked around the room and was surprised. What Tybor had been saying was right. Someone apparently had been expecting them. A feast of food had been prepared, and there were bowls set out on the table—seven bowls exactly! The youth removed his dripping cloak and hung it on a peg by the door before going over to the hearth at the back of the cabin to inspect what was cooking. Ten fish were roasting over the fire on an iron spit. Suspended from another iron arm were several pots. In one pot there was some hot mash for Janii. Another pot was filled with some deliciously thick fish chowder, while in another some goat meat simmered in a stew. Amon's mouth watered, and his stomach gurgled in anticipation.

On a table in front of the fireplace was a basket filled with fresh bread, a hunk of cheese wrapped in cloth, and some goose eggs. There was also goat's milk in a clay pitcher, as well as some sweetgrass tied with a string and a large wooden bowl full of fruit. Hardly knowing where to begin, the youth started serving the animals their meal.

"It looks like we arrived at just the right time," Baynor commented, hungrily eyeing the fish Amon took off the spit.

"If you had waited any longer, they would have been charred

black," Tybor retorted merrily, gobbling down a large portion of stew that Amon had dished out for him.

"At least I will savor the flavor when I eat my fish," the bear shot back, referring to Tybor's already empty bowl.

"This fish is good!" Sanii happily exclaimed, pulling at a piece from one of her clawed talons with her sharp beak.

Finishing his portion of fish, the badger prince started to eat the goose eggs Amon had put in his bowl. With delight, he carefully licked out all the gooey contents until there was nothing left but the shells.

After eating her fish and bowl of stew, the panther lapped down some goat's milk. Purring contentedly, she lay down to clean herself by the fire.

Sitting down on one of the wooden benches at the table, Amon heartily ate his chowder, taking in the comfort of his surroundings as he did so. To one side of the fireplace was a hand pump with a large wooden bucket full of water. Beside the pump sat a small table with a basin and towel for washing. Nestled on either side of the door were two wooden beds with down-filled mattresses. At the end of each bed was a large trunk containing thick, warm blankets made of soft wool.

When the youth finished his meal, the mountain cat made a suggestion. "Amon, there are some spare clothes over by the washbasin. You should really change out of the ones you are wearing."

Still feeling chilly, Amon welcomed the chance to change into something drier. In the corner, he pulled off his wet top, and in its place he put on a large and baggy rust-colored tunic. The youth kept his pants on when he realized his lack of privacy.

The bear noticed Amon's problem and offered some help. "You can change behind me, Amon. The ladies will look the other way." Coming over, he blocked the youth from view.

Seeing the ladies oblige, Amon changed as fast as he could into the loose brown pants he found lying next to the tunic. He then hung his wet things over a chair by the fire, along with the blanket

Janii had pulled off when she entered the cabin. Feeling his body warm to the food and the dry clothes, Amon went over to a bed to recline.

"What would be nice now is a little bit of music," the refreshed unicorn mused, crunching into an apple after finishing her hot mash.

Sitting up, Amon gave a laugh, and everyone turned to look at him. "I just remembered! I have my reed pipe" was the explanation he gave for his outburst. "I took it with me when I went for my guard duty at the North Gate. I had it in my back pocket, and then later, I stuck it into my bag. I completely forgot about it until now."

"Play us something, won't you?" Janii said, encouraging the youth.

Resting comfortably in the warmth from the fire, they listened in silence as Amon played a light, sweet tune that everyone instantly recognized. It was a simple melody—one they had heard frequently as children growing up in the palaces of Amuron. They closed their eyes, drifting off into pleasant past memories, until one by one they fell asleep, captured by the magic of the lullaby.

* * *

With one last look to see that everything was in order, Amon closed the door to the cozy haven and jogged over to join the others waiting outside on the grass. Their stomachs were full from a nourishing breakfast, and they were eager to start on their way.

The trail led them back into the seclusion of the forest. The sunlight pierced beneath the tall elm, spruce, and hemlock trees to where large ferns grew in abundance. The ground was soft and spongy under their feet, and the air was heavy with moist smells of dark earth, tree bark, and new plant life. The ferns caressed them with their wet fronds as they walked in single file on the narrow path. Soon they could hear the sound of running water over the chirps and twitters of birds in the surrounding trees.

Ahead of them down the forest path, they could see the trees end in a patch of sunlight where the river cut its way through the dense wood. Before they reached the riverbank, however, they had to pass between two large stones of granite, one on each side of the path. The stones were taller than they were wide, with one side of each stone sloping down toward them like the banks of a deep river. Chiseled onto each slope was a miniature version of a waterfall cascading down in an image of untamed power.

"These are the markers of the fourth gate, the Gate of Water," the wolf prince commented, pausing to admire them.

The grizzly stopped beside him and the stones, listening intently to the sound of the water coming to them through the trees. The sound caused Baynor's brow to furrow in a frown, and as he followed the others out from under the boughs of the trees and onto the riverbank, he shook his bear head slowly in frustration. The river, wild and white, raced nosily downstream, swollen almost to the top of its banks from the previous day's heavy rain.

The seven companions looked up and down the river with dismay. Their only way to cross the river was by a small boat that tossed and bounced about violently on the water, straining against the rope that tied it to the shore.

"We have come at a bad time. It will be nearly impossible to cross the river with the water running this fast," Baynor said, expressing his frustration with a bear howl.

"Is there a bridge we can use somewhere near here?" the unicorn inquired, her eyes widening at the thought of crossing the river in such a small and unstable craft.

"No, I don't think so. I have never heard of one," Baynor replied, disappointed he did not have another solution.

"What shall we do?" Janii asked, a shiver of fear running over her body. "Shall we wait until the water calms a little?"

Baynor thought for a moment before speaking to his friends. "It certainly would be nice to go back to the haven and wait another day until the water level lowers, but can Amuron wait another day?

Crossing the river now could be dangerous. Someone could get hurt, and we might not all make it safely across, but waiting could mean the loss of many lives back in Amuron. We have to trust Aii. He has called us to Berroc to help Amuron, and that is what we must try to do."

"But the current is too strong," the unicorn objected, taking an unconscious step away from the water. "If we use the boat now, the water will carry us down the river, away from our destination."

"What seems to be the holdup?" the eagle called out to her companions, flapping her wings behind her to land gracefully on a swaying branch above them.

"The only way to cross the river is by the boat. Unfortunately, it is too small to hold all of our weight at one time and, as Janii pointed out, the strong current will most likely pull us too far downstream," the bear explained.

"I know of another way to cross the river," Sanii proclaimed, turning to preen a feather on her wing while holding her friends in suspense. "A large, dead tree has fallen across the river not too far upstream. I saw it before I came to join you. I'm sure it would make a suitable bridge for all of you."

"Sanii, that's wonderful news!" Baynor exclaimed with relief, eager to continue forward.

The eagle led them up the narrow bank of the river, which twisted and turned, winding its way down from the mountains. They rounded first one corner and then the next, until they finally saw the fallen tree Sanii had spoken of.

The storm and the floodwaters had caused a large, barren willow to topple over, its old roots tearing up part of the riverbank as it fell. The trunk of the tree lay stretched across the river with its upper branches lying securely on the other side. The bottom half of their footbridge was underwater, but the top half was held out of the water by the large limbs and remaining branches protruding from the tree on the far side of the bank.

"Made to order, Sanii!" Baynor announced, thoroughly pleased, before she easily flew over to the awaiting bank. "Who wants to be the first to cross the bridge?" the bear inquired, turning to his companions.

"Allow me," Janii said, while daintily jumping past the clump of roots and dirt facing her. In moments she was standing on the opposite bank. "It's good and solid," she shouted back at them over the noise of the river.

Tayii and Tybor followed effortlessly in her footsteps. Ranor needed some help from Amon to get over the tangle of roots, but he too scurried across without any trouble. Amon went next, the rushing river making him nervous because he did not know how to swim. He looked down at the water, watching as it surged and frothed, climbing dangerously up the one side of the tree as it fought to find a way around the obstruction. The tree trunk was wide, narrowing only slightly at the top end. and after taking a few cautious steps, he quickly made it across. Baynor was the last to use the makeshift bridge. Avoiding the roots, he jumped onto the trunk from the side. Using his powerful claws to dig into the wood, he soon joined his companions.

"The Partner Stones are just ahead," the golden eagle cried out triumphantly after they had retraced their steps back down the river. "We have made it through the fourth gate!"

Sanii was right. In front of them was a duplicate set of stones, just like the ones they had passed on the other side. They were back on the trail to Berroc.

"I hope that's the last of our troubles," Janii whispered earnestly as they left the fourth gate behind.

A renewed sense of urgency began to rise in Amon and the animals as they journeyed closer to Berroc. It was almost as if they could hear Berroc summoning them, urging them forward. The animals unconsciously picked up speed until the badger and Amon had to ride on Janii's back to keep up.

They traveled through an airy wood that seemed sleepy and calm in sharp contrast to the way they felt. Pressing forward, they did not slow their pace until they arrived at the fifth gate, three hours before the eve of night. The gate before them was beautifully crafted and was called the Gate of Life. Supporting the gate were two square pillars cut from the same glistening stone as the Gate of Awakening. The gate itself was entirely made of a light-colored bronze and covered with an assortment of intricate and finely detailed metalwork of various flowering plants and wild mountain animals.

"It's beautiful," Tayii purred appreciatively, and even though she longed to stay and admire it, the pull to Berroc was stronger.

Amon muttered a prayer of thanks when the door to the gate opened easily, allowing them to pass through unhindered.

"We will continue on until nightfall," Baynor advised the others after Amon closed the gate behind them. "Then we can have a long night of rest and a good hot meal."

The day grew warm fast when they started on their journey the next morning. The wood thinned until there were pockets of trees among patches of open grassland, and by midday the travelers had reached the sixth gate.

The sixth gate, the Gate of Wisdom, was by far the most impressive and disquieting gate they had seen. The gate comprised two stone guardians—giant figures who were alarming to look at and hauntingly lifelike. A path lined with kneeling figures of stone, their faces hidden by their hands, led up to where they stood in the middle of a small sheltered valley surrounded by trees.

The group of seven approached the gate with reverence, moving as quietly as possible down the path, as if making a sound would wake the still guardians. The frightening figures loomed up before them to twice a man's height, looking down upon them with stern faces and cold, expressionless eyes. Their wings spread out full length behind them, framing the sides to the gate. Each of the guardians held a shining sword in one hand, their tips crossed at the top to make an archway over the entrance.

Amon looked down at the ground as he approached them,

shielding his eyes from their penetrating gaze. He felt their eyes pierce his inner being, searching the truth of his heart, and he cringed, wanting to get away from these strange lifelike representations as fast as possible.

Passing through the gate meant passing between the two statues underneath their raised swords. It became apparent to each of the travelers that if the guardians did not think one worthy of traveling to Berroc, they would find enough life in their stone limbs to use their swords and cut the traveler down as he or she stood before them. Passing through the sixth gate, therefore, demanded great courage—courage which suddenly failed Amon.

"I can't do it," he blurted out honestly, afraid for his life.

"I know you can, Amon," Baynor said to encourage the youth, coming up beside him.

"But the guardians will destroy me. I'm not worthy to pass through," he lamented with a shaky voice. All Amon could think about were his recent failures as a guard of the gates.

"None of us are worthy by our own right, but we have been summoned to Berroc, and that is where we must go. You must have faith in Aii. Trust him that he will let us pass."

"I want to, but I don't know if I can."

"Then we will walk through together, and if the guardians strike you down, then they must strike me down as well."

Amon was about to protest until he looked into the warm brown eyes of the bear and saw how much the prince respected and cared for him. Baynor's faith in him gave him the courage he lacked, and he agreed.

Taking a deep breath, Amon closed his eyes and grabbed onto the shaggy bear's shoulder. Letting the bear guide him, Amon walked forward until he heard Baynor say, "We are through."

Opening his eyes, the youth turned and looked behind him. With relief he could see the backs of the winged guardians. They had made it safely through the gate. Amon gave the bear a warm smile of gratitude, and in return the bear gave a nod of his great head while they waited side by side for the others to join them.

They watched as Tybor and Tayii came through the gate together, and then, as one, the remaining three—Ranor, Sanii, and Janii—all passed through.

When they had all made it safely to the other side, a wave of relief and intense joy flowed among them, causing them to fawn over one another as if they had been separated for years.

"Enough rejoicing," Baynor said, breaking up the short celebration, "Berroc awaits!"

At Baynor's words their eyes all burned with a deep sense of mission, and they readied themselves to race as one toward their final destination. Amon, with Ranor at his back, jumped up on Janii. Signaling to the group that he was ready, they started off at a run. Amon relaxed while he rode, enjoying the now familiar gait of the unicorn and the feel of the wind brushing over his face.

They ran at an easy pace, slowing every now and then to regain their strength before picking up speed again. The hours passed. By evening the land had changed to rolling hills, with only a few trees to be seen. When it became dark, they found that they were not really hungry and only minimally tired, so they continued on. Guided by the stars and moonlight, they finally came to rest on the rise of a hill. Before them in the deep, shadow-filled darkness was a wide valley. In the center of the valley, the soft light of the moon shone like a mist upon a ring of white stone, making it appear to be ethereal. They had reached Berroc!

The last haven of their journey was cut into a hill on the north side of the trail. It was a small dwelling made out of grass and wood. Inside the travelers found clean blankets on cloth mattresses of straw laid out on the floor. Some lamb stew was still warm in a pot over the dying embers in a fire pit, and some plain earthenware dishes were set up on a small wooden table next to a barrel of fresh water. They ate heartily, with Janii munching quietly on a pile of sweetgrass, before lying down to get some sleep, knowing that tomorrow they would enter the seventh gate into Berroc.

* * *

Amon dreamed many things that night. He dreamed about his family and again saw the faces of his parents smiling proudly when he told them of his first opportunity to guard at the North Gate. Then he was with the high king. The king seemed to want something from him, but Amon was not sure what. Repeating the words of the prophecy that Amon had received at his birth, the high king looked at him expectantly.

Next, from a strange place of darkness, he saw the decrepit sorcerer float toward him, and again he felt the evil presence that had surrounded him when he had hidden at the North Gate. Wanting to get away, Amon ran through the palace until he saw Prince Naibor. The prince led him to a door and told him to leave the city.

Opening the door, Amon saw his little brother crying alone and abandoned. In his dream he reached out to his brother, trying to comfort him, but he fell forward and found himself sliding down the side of a mountain, unable to stop. At the bottom, he found himself standing in front of the two stone guardians at the sixth gate, and as he walked through the gate under their terrible gaze, he saw them come to life and their swords come slashing down, and he woke with a start.

Lying on his mattress with his heart pounding, these images came back to Amon in the darkness of the haven. He became restless listening to those sleeping around him, and rising as quietly as possible from his bed, he moved toward the door.

Apologizing to his light-sleeping companions, whose hearing was more sensitive than his, he let himself out of the haven and stood breathing in the cool early morning air while trying to steady his nerves.

Dawn was just coloring the edge of eastern sky, and the valley of Berroc still lay beneath a blanket of fog.

Leaving footmarks behind him on the wet grass, Amon approached the ringed wall of white. When he reached the wall, Amon was a little disappointed. Although the wall was thick and high, it was ordinary looking and wet and cold to the touch. This, however, did not deter him from what he had set out to do. Falling to his knees in the damp grass, he set one hand on the stone wall and prayed for his family and the home he loved.

The sky had grown brighter and the fog had lifted when he heard Janii's voice call his name. Looking over his shoulder, Amon saw her come into sight around the hillock, looking for him. When the unicorn saw him, she called to the others that she had found him. Rising up from the ground, his knees a little stiff, Amon walked quickly toward the small group of animals that had now gathered at the unicorn's side.

"Are you ready to go with us through the seventh gate to Berroc, the Gate of Communion?" Janii inquired respectfully.

"I'm not going with you inside Berroc. I've decided to stay here and wait for you," Amon replied.

"We shouldn't be gone long," Baynor said, knowing the youth had made his decision.

Walking back together to the path, the unicorn stopped to whisper in Amon's ear before they parted. "May we find the answer to your prayers," she said softly, knowing they all hoped to find a way of saving Amuron.

Amon watched the others approach the seventh gate, which was an opening in the rock wall that surrounded Berroc. Inscribed into the rock around the door to the seventh gate were ancient words describing the significance of the sacred ground they were about to enter.

Passing through the Gate of Communion, the animals entered what was known as the Place of the Stones. The bottom of the bowl-shaped valley spread out before them, lush and green from the morning dew. Randomly dotted around the valley floor were variously sized white stone slabs that marked the graves of the past ruling kings and queens. On each of these stones was an inscription telling about their families and of their descendants.

In the center of the Place of the Stones was another smaller circle of white stone, the Place of Communion. The animals would have liked to spend some time reading the stones around them, but they knew that was not the purpose for which they had come. Continuing on, they entered the Place of Communion, which until now had only been entered by the high kings and high queens appointed by Aii. A quiet reverence filled the princes and princesses of Amuron as they stood within the white walls carved with all the characters, symbols, and names representing the Lord Aii.

In the center was a large stone sarcophagus. It marked where the first king of this land was buried. The sarcophagus lay raised from the ground upon four cornerstones. The first high king had requested that he be buried here in this valley to commemorate the spot where he had first met with the Great Lord of All, the Lord Aii, and received his anointing as king. Aii had blessed him and instructed him on how to rule the kingdom, as written in *The High King's Law.*

Sunlight dipped down into the small circle, shining into the eager faces of the travelers and onto the large stone tomb that lay in front of them. The animals were anxious, feeling like children who had entered a room where they knew they were not supposed to be. They waited patiently, looking around them at the names on the wall, at the stone before them, and up into the sky, but nothing changed. As time wore slowly on, their confidence waned and they began to be plagued by doubts.

"I'm worried," the unicorn said while she nervously twitched her ears back and forth, listening for any sound.

"Maybe we should let someone know we are here," the badger suggested, absentmindedly digging his nails into the soft grass-covered soil.

"Let who know?" the bear asked impatiently, turning away from the list of names he had just read through for the twentieth time.

"The Lord Aii, I suppose. He summoned us here."

"Yes, and therefore he should know we are here, but you are right, maybe we should try." Addressing the air around him, Baynor raised his muzzle heavenward, "Our great Lord Aii, we have come here to meet with a messenger from you concerning how we can help the city of Amuron."

Silence was the only reply.

"What's wrong?" Sanii asked with concern, cocking her golden head at an angle.

"I don't know," Baynor answered, perplexed.

"Maybe we came too late, or at the wrong time?" Tybor suggested, his tail drooping.

"Or maybe we did something wrong?" the panther added, looking over at her brother for reassurance.

"It doesn't make any sense," Janii said, circling the stone marker. "What should we do? Should we continue to wait?"

In response to her question, a glimmering light appeared above the sarcophagus, and it grew in intensity. It became a long line of light that stretched up to the height of the wall. Spreading from the center outward, it took on the shape of a body, until before them there appeared a figure consumed in a fire of iridescence.

"I am Orilian, a ministering spirit of the Lord Aii, and I am sent to you by him to bring you these words," the radiant apparition said. "You have let your circumstances cloud your faith in Aii. He has not abandoned either you or Amuron. Did he not send Nagala to you? Did she not tell you to come to Berroc and meet with a messenger from Aii? I am here!"

The messenger paused as if challenging them to deny his existence, and then he continued, looking down on the animals as they listened while crouched humbly before him in awe and fear.

"You came as instructed and had faith enough at the Gate of Wisdom to pass by the stone guardians; therefore, do not doubt yourselves or Aii anymore! This message must be given to Prince Naibor. He is to gather together the sorcerer's conjuring powder, his personal red spell book, and the amulet of the high king. They will provide the means for the evil one's destruction. I will meet with you at Binah, outside of the East Gate, when he has these things—but do not delay! Necros has the power to destroy all who are living inside the city of Amuron, and he soon will do so. Do you understand what I have told you?"

The six travelers looked up at Orilian, their eyes squinting at his brilliance, and Baynor spoke on their behalf. "Yes, we understand."

"Good," he replied, but his light did not fade. "There was another traveling with you. Where is he?"

"He is waiting in the haven outside the walls of Berroc," Baynor answered again.

"Deliver this message to him. He is to wait in the haven and not return to Amuron with you. He has yet to fulfil the prophecy given at his birth. The success of his mission depends on the success of yours. You will not require his help on your journey home. You must return with all speed, first by the river at the Gate of Water and then by the East Road. Be diligent in your task, and remember—Aii goes with you always."

As the animals watched, the luminous figure of Orilian diminished into a line of white light that shrank to the light of a glowing star in the night sky before finally disappearing altogether. For a moment there was a great ache within each of the animals—a longing to follow the light into the realm beyond. They felt as if they had been left behind in a world of dim shadows, in contrast to the vibrant light they had witnessed a moment before. Then the feeling passed and the world around them lightened once more. They knew that, for now, this was the world that they belonged in.

"Wait!" Ranor called out unexpectedly. "We didn't ask how, or even if, we could be changed back to human form."

It was true; they had forgotten to ask Orilian if there was a way for them to break the sorcerer's curse.

CHAPTER 16

Amon was waiting for them, sitting in the sunlight on the grass in front of the hut. He got up when the wolf broke off from the group and loped over to him. The youth wanted to ask him what Berroc was like and all about what had happened, but when he saw the glow in Prince Tybor's eyes, he decided not to. He remembered what Baynor had said to him about Berroc being a personal experience, so instead he asked, "Did you find a way to help Amuron?"

"Yes, there is still hope. We must leave immediately for Amuron, but you will not be coming with us, Amon." The wolf then relayed what the messenger from Aii had said.

"Did he say anything else?" the puzzled youth asked the wolf.

"Only that the success of your mission depends on ours, so your reason for staying here must be very important indeed."

Amon's eyes widened in shock; he was amazed that this could be true. On his way here he had questioned whether leaving his home behind had been the right thing to do. Now, when he finally had the chance to return, he had a special message from Aii saying that he was to stay behind and not return to Amuron at all.

Amon looked away from the wolf, not knowing what else to say. All he could think about was that they were going back to Amuron without him. The group of seven travelers would now be parting company.

"The supplies are all ready and packed, but I guess you won't need them," he said when the other animals came over to join them.

"No, but thank you, Amon," Ranor said, looking up at the youth with gratitude. "We could not have made it here to Berroc without you, and I am especially indebted to you for all your help."

"You have already been a great friend to us, and a guided servant," Janii said, trying to ease the sadness she saw in his eyes. "Now that it is our turn to help you, I hope we won't let you down."

"You won't," Amon replied, shaking his head while averting his eyes to the ground. Knowing that he had won their respect seemed to make this moment even harder for him.

"Take heart, Amon. We may have been called to help in different ways, but we are one in purpose. The city of Amuron depends on us all," Baynor stated, and then they knew that they could delay no longer and that it was time for them to leave.

"We will miss your company, Amon," Tybor panted, jumping up affectionately onto the youth's chest with his front paws. "Take care, and be careful," he added while Amon embraced him in a tight hug.

"Keep us in your prayers. Ours will be with you," the panther told him, laying her feline head against his leg with a quiet purr.

"May our Lord Aii bless you and keep you safe," the eagle said with a gleam in her eye. And with a sweep of her wings, she rose up into the blueness of the early afternoon sky.

"There will be much celebrating when we are together again and the sorcerer is defeated," Baynor promised as Amon threw his arms around the grizzly bear's large shoulders.

"This is very hard for me," the unicorn began, her voice soft with emotion. When Amon put his arms around her smooth white neck, a tear rolled down her velvet cheek. "Aii has chosen you well. May his goodness guide you and keep you safe until we are together again."

"Would you do me the honor one more time?" Ranor asked, his

striped face looking up from the ground from in front of the sack he had just carried out of the haven. "I'm going to fly with Sanii."

Amon picked up the badger in the sack and held him high in the air. Looking down at the youth and into his eyes, the badger prince added, "I am looking forward to the many stories we will have to share when we are back together again. Until then, remember: our friendship will not have lessened because of the distance between us."

Amon managed a weak lopsided grin in reply before Sanii swept down, taking Ranor with her into the air. Then, without another word, all the animals were off, running with gracefulness and with swiftness out of the sacred valley of Berroc.

Standing by the haven, Amon watched them leave, and he continued standing there even after the last of his former companions had disappeared over the top of the rise. He stood there for long, aching moments, and then, with a sigh, he entered the comfort of the haven, closing the door behind him.

* * *

Amon had made himself a small meal and was playing a favorite tune to himself on his pipe when he heard the sound of someone outside the haven followed by a loud knock on the door. Before the youth reached the door, he heard someone call out, "Greetings, emissary," with a voice unlike any he had ever heard. The voice was rich and strong and deep, and it resonated like the large temple bells back in Amuron. Amon opened the door cautiously and peered outside. Standing in front of the haven door was a giant of a man who towered at least a full three heads above his own, making him seem as if he were a child of eight years standing next to his father. As soon as the giant saw him, he bowed low and repeated with a large smile, "Greetings, emissary of Aii; I am Bartok."

Amon said nothing but continued to stare at the unexpected guest. He had long, thick, wild, and wavy hair the color of sunlight that he had unsuccessfully tried to tie back from his face with a thong. His facial features were strong and heavy, and his skin had been weathered into a soft leather of warm brown. His eyes were a dazzling color of azure blue—the same color as the water found in the lakes of the Khist mountain range. His size was further emphasized by his large, muscular build, over which he wore a vest and leggings made from the skin of a deer. Amon found him to be both an impressive and an alarming sight.

"Have you a name that I may call you, emissary?" Bartok asked the bewildered youth, breaking the momentary silence.

"My name is Amon," the youth replied, recovering himself. "But I'm not an emissary. I am from the city of Amuron, and I was told to wait here by Orilian, a messenger from Aii."

"And I was sent here to meet with someone and to take him to a special place, by that same person. Does that not make you an emissary?" Bartok asked, the lines beside his eyes wrinkling up when he smiled.

"I guess, but you can call me Amon; you don't have to call me 'emissary.'"

"Very well, my lord."

"Just Amon," the youth interrupted. "I'm not a lord either."

"Very well, Amon," the giant said. "Come, we should be on our way."

"Where are we going?" Amon asked after gathering up his traveling pack and a few other items before joining his guide outside of the haven.

"First to my home, and then to a place you will not have heard of. It is a place that has existed for over seven hundred years, but few know of it," Bartok answered as they walked along, Amon having to take two steps for Bartok's every one.

"Is it far?" the youth inquired, concerned that he would not be able to keep up with the large man's pace for long.

"Far enough. A journey of about a day and a half for you, but you must tell me if I travel too fast so I can slow the pace down. I am not used to walking with company. I spend most of my days alone." He said this not with any sadness or bitterness in his voice, but matter-of-factly, as if he was content to spend the rest of his life not seeing or talking to anyone else.

He was not content to be silent, however, and as they walked together, Bartok talked about everything he heard, saw, or could think of, but mainly he talked about the Khist Mountains.

"You seem to know a lot about these mountains," Amon commented when they stopped for a rest to allow the youth to catch his breath. They had been traveling roughly north along the line of the Khist mountain range, and Mount Sol was now behind them.

"These mountains have been my home for the past one hundred thirty-five years. I know just about everything there is to know about them."

"You certainly don't look a hundred thirty-five years old!" Amon blurted out in surprise, and he looked again at Bartok's face to see if there was something that he had missed. His guide did not look particularly ancient or youthful, but somewhere in between. Bartok's face was creased and had wrinkles, but there was also a healthy glow and strength to it, and his eyes were lit with a youthful exuberance that transcended age.

"I'm not," he said with a booming laugh that Amon fancied echoed endlessly off the rock walls of the mountains surrounding them. "I'm actually one hundred fifty-three of your years old." Then with a twinkle in his bright blue eyes, he added, "I should explain that my people age one year for every three of yours. That should help your confusion. I came over on a boat from my homeland when I was quite small. I was only six of my years at the time."

Amon looked at the massive man and tried to imagine what he meant by "quite small." "Where are the rest of your people now?" he asked, curious. "Are they still here?"

"No, most of them returned home many years ago. I stayed because Aii appointed me the keeper of the gates."

"The keeper of the gates," Amon repeated, thinking aloud. "Then you are the one who—"

"Yes, I am the one who made you welcome at the havens," Bartok interrupted, standing up and stretching his huge limbs. "That is part of what I do. But it is time we continued on. There is still so much for you to learn and see."

On the next part of their journey, they left the gentle slopes behind and began climbing over rockier ground. As they climbed, Bartok asked Amon all sorts of questions about his family and his home.

"My mother once told me, when I was a boy, that our home was in a beautiful city by the sea, but I don't remember it very well," Bartok told his small companion. "I don't think a city could be as beautiful as a place like this," he added with a smile, looking around him at the magnificent sights. "You did not mention if Amuron is a city of beauty?"

"Amuron is not known as a beautiful city. It was made to defend its ruler, but it does have some beautiful places. I think it is the people in it that make it beautiful," Amon added after thoughtfully considering what it was he liked about his home.

Bartok looked at him, his silence asking him to elaborate.

"The people make it a welcome and warm place to be in," Amon told him, thinking of the variety of interesting smiling faces that greeted him each day when he went through the city on errands. "Most people in the city follow the high king's laws, which Aii gave to us, and believe that we are all like one big family, where everyone cares and supports one another."

"It sounds like a city of great worth, Little One," Bartok replied affectionately.

"There is another city—the city of Aquar. It is down by the sea. Have you heard of it? It is supposed to be beautiful."

"Yes, that is where my people first landed their boats, but it was little more than a fishing village back then. That is where I go now when I am in need of supplies."

Their journey had taken them past rocky ledges and up steep slopes covered with wild flowers and long grasses. When they stopped for another rest, Amon saw Bartok look far off into the distance toward the sea as if he suddenly longed for home, but it was only for a moment. Then his giant companion continued giving him details about the surrounding landscape.

"Bartok? Why did your people come here and leave their home?" Amon asked him when he paused in his instruction.

"My people are artisans skilled in carving stone and wood. We came to practice our trade and to find new materials. We built many things for your first king."

Many hours later, after Bartok and Amon had rested several more times and had stopped to eat a meal, they came to a stop in front of a river that ran swift and deep across their path.

"I will have to carry you across, little one," Bartok said to the youth, and in the time it took for Amon to react to this news, Bartok had reached his strong arms around him and under his legs. Lifting his companion easily, the giant strode into the depths of the river. The water rose high above his knees, swirling quickly around his powerful legs.

"I normally jump this one," Bartok said when they reached the other side. He set Amon back down with a hearty laugh.

Several hours later, they had climbed high enough to reach a pass through the upper heights of the mountain. The pass was a flattened ledge of rock between a sheer cliff and a high ridge on the left side of their path. As they came around this ridge, they found themselves facing the top of another mountain.

"The mountain before us is Mount Rosh, the home of my people, the Raphacharii," Bartok informed Amon with delight and pride shining in his eyes. "Look down this side," he instructed, pointing with his finger to the lower slopes. "There is my winter home, the Castle of the Raphacharii!"

On a ledge of solid rock jutting out at the base of the mountain was a magnificent castle. It was like nothing Amon had ever seen or dreamed of before. The sight before him was breathtaking. Bartok had not lied when he had said his people were skilled artisans.

The castle was made from the natural colored stone taken from the mountains surrounding it, but it had been carved and shaped until it looked light and delicate despite its massive size. It had slim bridges connecting tall towers, and balconies that floated on top of columns. The entire castle, which was large enough to hold half the inhabitants of Amuron, was wonderfully accented with sculpted statues and intricate details.

"It is truly wonderful," Amon said in appreciation. "Is that where we are going?"

Bartok shook his head in reply, his fair hair further loosening itself from the thong in the process. "Another time, perhaps," Bartok added with a trace of disappointment in his voice.

Then he pointed to a pathway that followed around the side of the mountain, a little lower down from where they were standing. "There is a higher pasture a little farther north from here. That is where we are going."

Almost an hour later, Amon and his large guide entered the pastureland on an inverted slope that stretched along the mountainside. Grazing on the short grass was a flock of sheep, and nestled into the mountainside in one corner of the slope sat a stone cottage. Surrounding the cottage were a few other low-lying buildings, out of which wandered some wild chickens and a few goats waiting to be milked.

"This is where we will rest until Orilian comes to us again," Bartok explained with the heavy sigh of one who has labored long and is finally glad to be home. Then he gave a whistle.

In answer to his call, two dogs came happily running from where they had lain among the sheep, and a joyful whinny echoed off the upper slopes.

At the sound of hooves, Amon looked up to see a noble stallion come charging down from the heights. The beast was the largest horse the youth had ever seen. There was no doubt in Amon's mind as to who owned this horse. This steed was the only mount large and strong enough to carry a man the size of Bartok. He held his head majestically, arching his thick neck, and there was a wild look in his eye. His body was strong and muscular, and his four large hooves, which were covered with hair, moved sure-footedly over the rough ground as he descended toward them. His long mane danced like a free spirit in the wind, and in every aspect he matched the untamed look of Bartok. They both were powerful and frightening figures, full of fortitude and, by their very natures, one with the surrounding landscape.

"I think of these creatures as my children," Bartok told him with a twinkle in his merry eyes when he introduced the animals that had arrived.

"These two I call Hammer and Tong," the giant said proudly, kneeling to speak softly to each of the big dogs while he stroked their shaggy fur. "The sheep are the metal they work with, always shaping and molding. They are very skilled at what they do." The two dogs barked in reply to their master's words of praise.

"And this is Orros," Bartok said, addressing the stallion who had come to stand close behind him. The horse gave the giant a nudge so strong with his nose that Bartok was almost knocked off balance. "He is the son of the king of the mountain horses, and the last of his kind in this part of the world."

"I have missed you too, Orros," Bartok added with a laugh, giving the horse a couple of slaps on the side of his strong neck.

"Now it is time for dinner, and then sleep," Bartok informed all those around him as they moved toward the cottage. "But first—Hammer! Tong! The sun is setting. Go and see to your charges."

The dogs, with eyes alert and laughing, bounded away barking to gather the sheep together and herd them into the stable. Amon watched with amazement while the two dogs worked as one to bring the animals into a group and guide them toward the open door of the barn. By the time Bartok and he arrived at the cottage, the last of the sheep were being hurried inside.

"I will join you after I have checked on the animals and given them their food. Please make yourself welcome in my home," the giant told him, giving the youth a nod and a wink before he strode off to the barn.

Amon entered the mountain home of Bartok and looked around. The cottage was what he would have called large and roomy, but by his friend's standards, it was cozy. The first thing that Amon noticed in the cottage was the stone fireplace. It was built into one side of the building and was so large that Amon could have walked inside of it. He gazed up at the roof high above him, and then around at the large wooden furniture that was of simple design. The chairs were covered with either sheepskin or cloth cushions that had been filled with down to make them more comfortable. Carvings of animals made from wood or stone filled the cottage. Amon noticed that Bartok had small lifelike carvings of his friends Orros, Hammer, and Tong sitting on the large mantel over the fireplace.

With a yawn, the youth sat down utterly exhausted in a big chair with arms. Every muscle in his body hurt from overuse. Traveling with Bartok, he realized, was even more grueling than it had been traveling with the animals.

It was not long before Bartok finished with his animals and returned to the cottage, where he found Amon fast asleep in the chair. With a smile that filled his face with warmth, Bartok covered the youth up with a soft blanket before lighting a fire in the fireplace to keep them both warm through the night.

* * *

The animals hurried back to the fourth gate with all the speed they could muster. They reached their destination, the Miy River, in the afternoon on the second day of their return journey. Any concern they might have had about how they would travel down the river disappeared when they reached it. Moored next to the small boat was a larger and more stable flat-bottomed vessel made for hauling cargo up and down swift rivers. It was steered with a simple rudder at the back.

"Well, it looks as if everything has been taken care of for us again," Baynor marveled, eyeing the craft as the river flowed swiftly by them in a southerly direction.

The animals wasted no time getting into the boat. Baynor loosened the rope that was wrapped around a post and pushed off with his strong back legs before hauling the rest of his bulk into the craft. This action greatly distressed Janii, who, having a fear of boats, protested at the rocking of the vessel.

"This is terrible," she grumbled as the boat started off downstream, being pulled out into the river by the current.

"Don't worry, Janii; I'll make sure we get there safely," Ranor assured her from the back of the boat, standing next to the rudder. "I have steered boats before."

Grabbing the handle of the rudder in his mouth, the badger prince brought the sideways drifting boat around and kept it heading straight down the center of the river.

Ranor's confidence and apparent skill did not ease Janii's worries as she watched the land slip quickly by. There was no chance of her leaving the boat now, so the troubled unicorn braced herself for the ride. She looked at the trees with envy while they moved down the river; they stood so still and steady on the solid ground. Then even the trees were gone from view, replaced by the banks of the river, which grew up high around them, and for a while their only view was of its pale, powdered-clay sides.

They traveled for many hours, Tybor relieving Ranor when the river ran straight and letting Ranor steer when it curved its way through flatter territory. At times the Miy River was joined by other rivers and streams, making the water rough and fast for the strange river passengers. Poor Janii's look of elegance and grace was lost, replaced with the look of a forlorn creature living in misery.

The boat they traveled in came well supplied with wooden containers of food and water. They had lids that were easy for the animals to lift open with either the push of a nose or a pull of a paw. The river travelers were very thankful for these supplies, finding that the motion of the boat and the rushing water made all but Janii both hungry and thirsty.

While their voyage down the river continued, darkness came, and with it a night sky filled with bright stars. During the night, most of the animals had a turn at steering the boat while the others tried to sleep. Even Sanii came down from the skies to join them in some much-needed rest.

"Any idea how far we have come?" Janii asked Tybor, who was at the rudder. She felt relief at the sight of the first morning light.

"We are almost at the southernmost end of the Khist mountain range, and we are now heading into the foothills," he answered after studying the surrounding landscape.

This news encouraged Janii. The Miy River would soon run into Lake Ore, which meant the end of their river journey. After that, the Miy River split into two at the bottom end of the lake. Part of the river continued south, where it eventually ended in the marshlands, while a smaller river, the River Mur, headed toward the kingdom of Amuron and ran through its outlying districts. Unfortunately this river was too rocky and shallow for the boat to travel on.

Not long afterward, the boat slowed its pace and carried the animals out onto a large lake. Their long river ride had come to an end. After a short debate over the best spot to land the boat, they drifted over to the side and with a soft bump came to a stop.

"Ah, dry land! I could kiss you!" Janii cried out, leaping a little shakily onto the firm ground beside the boat before the others quickly joined her.

They started on their way south, and by midmorning their route along the River Mur had led them to the East Road, which connected the sea city Aquar with the city of Amuron. This meant that at top speed they could reach their home in a day and a half.

* * *

Prince Naibor slept the morning away, waking to the sound of the tower clock striking the chime eleven times.

"An hour before midday," Naibor said groggily to himself, while he sat up in bed and shook his head in an attempt to further clear his mind. He kicked at the clothes on the floor by his bed with his bare foot. They still lay where he had pulled them off late the previous night, before he had fallen into bed. Getting up wearily from his bed, Naibor rolled his black cloak up carefully, making sure the mask was hidden inside, and slid it under the bed, out of sight.

He had made it home the night before without further incident, but he had not easily fallen asleep. Even though he had been tired, the excitement of the night had kept his mind racing. It was not until the room began to lighten with the coming of dawn that he had drifted off into a light slumber.

Entering the bath area, the prince looked down at the square pool in the floor at his feet. He knew the tank of water next to the pool had not been heated by the servants to make it warm. Seeking to be refreshed, Naibor took a deep breath and quickly stepped down into the tub, immersing himself in the chilly water. Rising up again just as quickly, Naibor gasped for air from the shock. Shaking the water droplets from his hair and body, he climbed out of the pool and surrounded himself in the dryness of the awaiting bath blanket.

Naibor opened his wardrobe and looked inside. He was drawn toward his finer clothes, which marked him as royalty, and he fingered the rich quality material of his best coat while he made a decision on what to wear.

The prince knew the time when he would wear these clothes was fast approaching, but instead he reached for something simpler. He chose to wear a loose white tunic and blue merchant pants with a gold sash. He smiled to himself as he put the clothes on. *The royal colors!* The choice was subtle but still satisfying. For a final touch, he put a bit of oil in his hair to keep it from falling into his face.

He was about to leave the room on his way to meet with Edra and Taila, as they had previously arranged, when he heard a strange flurry of movement behind him. Turning toward the sound, Naibor saw an eagle enter his open window and land on the floor at his feet.

"Prince, I must speak with you; it's urgent!" the large bird said, panting with its wings open to cool down from the long flight.

Naibor stared with wonder at the talking creature but said nothing.

"Prince, I am Princess Sanii. Remember how I was changed along with the others in the cellar by the sorcerer?" The eagle princess cocked her head to one side to get a better look at the prince standing before her.

He still did not answer, so she continued, "Well, at that time the others and I were not changed as the sorcerer had intended. We did not lose our humanity, and we were left with the ability to speak."

Naibor remembered well seeing the intelligent looks in the animals' eyes when he had gone to the cellar to free Amon. "Are the others with you in the city?" he asked, wide-eyed.

"No, the others are on their way. Do you know the old sanctuary south of the East Gate, where there is an ancient well?"

"Yes, I know the place. Binah it is called."

"Yes, that is where we will take refuge. I flew ahead of the others to bring you a message. We have traveled to Berroc and have been told there is a way to save Amuron, but you must help us!"

"Tell me how I can help, Sanii," the prince responded, almost desperate for the answer.

"You must bring with you to Binah the Stone of Wisdom, the sorcerer's magic powder, and his red spell book. Do you know of these things?"

The prince nodded, picturing the objects in his mind.

"Once you have these items, a messenger from Aii will meet with us at Binah to give us further instructions."

"The Stone of Wisdom will be the easiest to obtain. The others will be more difficult," Naibor told her truthfully.

"We must stop the sorcerer, Prince. I hardly recognized the city as my beloved Amuron when I flew over it. Do you know what the sorcerer is planning to do?"

"Yes, and there is not much time left," the prince replied with urgency. "Necros is planning on sacrificing all the people of Amuron who have not been taken over by the evil spirits of the dead in his new temple, and it is almost complete!"

"We will help you if we can," the eagle volunteered.

"No, I think it will be better if I do this on my own. I'll try to get the sorcerer's things by tomorrow morning and meet with you outside of the East Gate before sunrise.

"If I am not at Binah by sunrise tomorrow, can you fly back here to meet with me?"

"Yes."

"Thank you, Sanii."

She ruffled her feathers and then turned to leave. "May the Lord Aii grant us time to save the city," she replied, flying off into the bright light of the day.

It was now up to Naibor. The fate of Amuron rested in his hands.

CHAPTER 17

Prince Naibor stared after the eagle, lost in thought. He had no idea how to get the powder and book from Necros. The last time he had seen Necros with these items, the sorcerer had them hidden in his robes.

As he stared out the window, he suddenly became aware of the temple off in the distance. Going over to the fireplace in his room, he grabbed the looking glass that had sat on his mantle ever since it had been given to him as a gift. Extending the folding tubes, he looked through the glass in the direction of the arena. The spires of the sorcerer's temple jumped up in front of the lens. The black iron spikes that stuck up into the sky like the ends of spears appeared to be much nearer. On one of the spires he could see a black piece of cloth fluttering in the hot steam of the cooling coa around it. Naibor searched the top of the structure with the looking glass, hoping to catch sight of the one who put it there, but there was no one in view. There did not seem to be anyone working anywhere on the temple. After one last sweep over the entire area, he lowered the lens from his eye.

"Already a signal from the captains," Naibor muttered to himself, strengthening his resolve. "Well, it is now or never." Replacing the looking glass on the mantle, the prince went over a quick plan in his head.

The clock tower was striking midday when Naibor left his room and demanded that his silent guards take him to Necros. One of the Daimos before him shook its head. The Daimos who guarded Naibor were still only in their wraithlike form, which allowed them to maintain their constant vigil and be aware of their evil master's every whim.

"If you don't take me to him, then I will go and find him myself," the prince threatened, aware that the Daimos could easily stop him if they wished.

When Naibor attempted to move past them, he felt the icy grasp of a Daimos on his shoulder. The hallway suddenly appeared to fold in on itself, and the ground to heave beneath his feet. At the same time, a wave of dizziness and nausea hit him so hard that his stomach attempted to wrench itself from his body. The world as he knew it had been thrown into chaos, and Naibor shut his eyes in an attempt to stop the rocking images and the shattering pain. As quickly as the dizzying effect had started, it stopped. Bent over almost double, Naibor slowly opened his eyes when he felt the tingling pain in his body subside and the churning of his stomach settle down.

How did I get here? he wondered when he found himself standing in a strange place. *Did Necros magically bring me here, or did I pass out and the Daimos bring me here?* It was no use asking the Daimos, who were still beside him; they would not answer.

He was in the middle of a square chamber. It was meagerly lit by oil burning in half-circle wells sticking out from the two walls on either side of him. He found the room suffocating. The ceiling was low and the walls close, in contrast to the light and airy rooms of the palace. There were four pillars in the room, made from heavy, square stone bricks that had strange markings painted on them. The floor was cut into three consecutive circles that rose like steps to the wall. Naibor could see only one entrance into the room, and that was the doorway in front of him, which was covered by a dark cloth.

The Daimos led him from the strange room into the narrow hallway outside. Directly facing him were two large doors, each adorned with a giant death mask made of brass. The Daimos opened these doors and brought him into a room unlike any the prince could have imagined.

The room he entered was dark and cavernous, and it was dimly lit with a strange orange glow. The cause of the eerie light came from the center of the room. Naibor swallowed loudly, unnerved by the unusual sight. In the middle of the black floor of coa was a wide ring of water, the entire surface of which was engulfed in low flames. The ring of flames surrounded a large square dais raised high in the air, with a flight of steps going up each side to the top.

The Daimos ushered Naibor forward toward the flames and a flat walkway that crossed over the burning water. The prince hesitated, fearing that when he reached the bridge, Necros would cause the walkway to collapse, causing him to fall into the fiery liquid. Naibor struggled to put the frightening image out of his mind. By focusing on his reason for being there, he quickly crossed over to the other side, feeling the heat of the fire rise from beneath him.

Urged on by the Daimos beside him, Naibor climbed the steps to the top of the platform. There he found the sorcerer sitting on a throne made of wood and black leather. The simple throne was accented with two attacking ravens made of silver on each side of the back of the throne, and two small silver human skulls at the ends of the arms. Behind the sorcerer on poles were two lanterns, also shaped like skulls. Fire burned in the open mouths of the lanterns, and the skulls' eyes danced menacingly from the flicking flames.

"Dear Prince, how nice of you to visit me," the master of the dead coldly addressed him. "You have the pleasure of being one of the first to stand before me in the great hall of my temple. Unfortunately you and the other inhabitants of Amuron will only have the privilege of enjoying my temple for a short time, while I, the new king of Amuron, plan on enjoying this temple for a long time to come."

Prince Naibor did not respond to the sorcerer's welcome. Instead he attempted to quell his emotions and gain control of his thoughts. In doing so, the prince found it gave him the opportunity to carefully observe his adversary.

The black lord appeared to be resting in his chair, but Naibor noticed that his body was stiff and tense. Even though the sorcerer spoke calmly, the prince detected a note of fierceness in his adversary's voice that was reflected in his eyes, and the ends of his fingers tightly gripped the tiny skulls at the end the arms on his throne.

"Why are you here, Naibor?" Necros snapped, dispensing with the pleasantries. "Why have you disturbed me?"

"I … I …" Naibor began, looking around the gloomy hall uneasily. "Is there someplace less oppressive where we could talk?"

The sorcerer scowled at the prince, clearly irritated by his presence, but he obliged by going over to the steps at the back of the platform. The prince, following the sorcerer, suddenly realized that the two Daimos that guarded him were gone, but just when his constant watchers had disappeared he did not know. Necros then proceeded to lead him down the stairs by floating effortlessly just above each step all the way to the bottom. When Naibor reached the floor where Necros stood waiting, a secret door swung outward from the middle of the stairs he had just descended. The opening revealed another set of stairs going down into the base of the raised platform. Again Naibor followed behind the floating sorcerer, until he stopped in front of the door to the inner chamber.

"I hope this better serves your purpose," Necros said, humoring the prince as they entered the room. "I have no more time to waste."

Naibor gave a mental sigh of relief when he looked around the room. He was in the sorcerer's chamber—a room filled with all sorts of magical paraphernalia, including the two objects he had hoped to find. There before his very eyes, on a wooden table in the center of the room, sat the sorcerer's red book and his sachet of magic powder. Naibor stared at the items, half expecting them to melt from view like a mirage, but they remained where they were, and Naibor had to take his eyes off them so that he did not arouse suspicion.

A raspy cry rang in his ear, and turning, the prince saw the raven form of Elbanor sitting on a wooden perch behind him.

"That is right, Elbanor," the black king said to the coarse bird, who cocked his black feathered head on one side in order to listen intently to every word his master said. "The prince has come to pay us a visit, but as yet he has given me no clue as to why. He did mention he wanted to talk to me, but he has said very little. I suspect that the real reason he has come here is to spy on us, but he has no need, as the temple will be finished tomorrow. I am going to show him the whole building before the sacrifice so that he might know the legacy he has left behind."

"No, I've come to make you a deal, Necros," Naibor stammered out, fearing that Necros had already read too much of his thoughts. "Give me the opportunity to convince the others in Amuron to worship you, and I will offer up my life to you as your sacrifice."

The sorcerer responded with cold laughter that rang hollow throughout the room. "Do you take me for an utter fool, Prince? I have no wish to change my plans for any deal you might have to offer.

"What is your real reason for coming here? Have you come for one last futile attempt to challenge my authority?" His face of terrifying mirth changed in an instant to a piercing glance that stabbed at Naibor's heart.

Keeping his eyes on the prince, Necros moved to the table in the middle of the room and stood next to it. Searching into Naibor's soul, the sorcerer's hands traveled over the various objects that lay on the surface, touching first one object and then another until, horrified, Naibor saw them come to a stop right over the very items that he had come for.

Naibor tried desperately to concentrate on something else in the room, trying to draw the attention of Necros away from the table, but all he could concentrate on was the pounding of his heart and the small smirk of triumph on the sorcerer's face.

Placing a hand on top of the red book, Necros turned to face the prince. “Have you anything further to say to me, Prince? If not, then leave. Tonight the Daimos and I are celebrating the completion of our hard labors with a banquet of sorts at the palace, and there are still some details and preparations to be taken care of.”

Naibor shook his head in reply, mystified by what he was hearing, and then his two Daimos guards returned silently to his side, seemingly from out of the air. Without another word spoken between them, Naibor was hurried from the room and taken back to his private quarters in the palace.

After the prince had gone, the sorcerer patted the book under his hand before he strode over to stroke the raven’s chest. “Well, Elbanor, what did you think of Naibor’s little visit? Yes, I did think it was quite entertaining and, of course, very enlightening. But as you already know, I have taken care of things. No, I am not troubled by his petty little plans; they amuse me, but I shall relish his death. I look forward to squashing him like an annoying bug. When his splattered blood covers the ground, I shall have my final victory here in Amuron. Then I shall begin my conquest in earnest, and I shall continue until every person in every town of this kingdom cowers at my name and kneels shuddering in submission before me.”

Elbanor caught Necros giving one more smile before he too left his chambers, but it was a smile of cruelty, and it was not a pleasant sight to see.

* * *

Naibor’s mind was still whirling when he entered the seclusion of his quarters only to find someone there waiting for him.

“Taila, what are you doing here?” Naibor asked with surprise.

She stood in the center of his room, looking a little lost and misplaced. “When you didn’t come and meet with Edra and me, as previously arranged, I worried that something might have happened to you,” she explained with color rising into her soft cheeks. “I came to see if you were all right.”

"I'm fine," Naibor casually replied, but then he looked into her infinite brown eyes. He saw in them all the care and deep affection she felt for him, which he hadn't seen at their first meeting, and he almost flushed in return.

He had an impulse to run to her, sweep her off her feet, and, while holding her gently in his arms, kiss her over and over again. How and why someone as kind and gentle as this would love him he had no idea. All he could think about were his flaws and shortcomings, not to mention how rude and unsociable he had been to her family and friends for years.

"I'm sorry I couldn't meet with you. I was with Necros," the prince apologized, relaxing unconsciously in her presence.

"He plans on killing us all, doesn't he?" Taila asked suddenly, with a mix of horror and concern on her face.

Naibor held her gaze for a moment, and then, responding to her insight, he answered her honestly. "Yes. He has completed the temple, and tomorrow he plans on killing all the people of Amuron he has taken prisoner."

At this news Taila lowered her eyes to the ground, and her body shook like a delicate flower petal crushed by the weight of a human hand. His heart went out to her, and he would have done anything for her in that instant.

"Is there no way to stop him? Is there nothing we can do?" She looked again at the prince, her eyes begging him for a way out.

He was about to tell her how Sanii had brought him a message, and that there still might be a way to stop the sorcerer, when he realized he would have to explain to her what had happened to her sister. He wanted to tell her, to get it off his guilty conscience, but he could not. He was too ashamed of what he had done and how he had behaved. He did not want to hurt her with the knowledge of what he, the man she thought she loved, had done.

He looked straight into her eyes again, and he marveled at her love. She looked so innocent and pure, like someone who needed his protection. He wanted to do something for her, offer her some hope, so he said, "I can't give you all the details, but I have a plan. There is something I am going to try."

"Edra said she thought you might know of a way to stop the sorcerer. I knew you wouldn't let us down." She was suddenly reassured.

"She did? What else did Edra tell you about me?" Naibor asked, wondering what the two of them had been discussing in private.

"Why, nothing," Taila told him innocently while her eyes sparkled mischievously. "We have spent most of our time in prayer."

"I am going back to the temple tonight in disguise. I need the sorcerer's book of spells and his magic powder, so I am going back to his temple to try to get them. Necros bragged to me that he was throwing a victory party here at the palace, so hopefully I will be able to get in and out of the temple without any problems."

"I'm coming with you, Prince," Taila announced unexpectedly. "And there is nothing you can say or do to stop me."

The prince found he was pleased by this announcement, although he did not know why. He guessed the reason was because he would not have to be alone. He had done everything else on his own, and he told himself it was nice to have someone along for a change, even though it greatly complicated things and increased the risk for both of them.

"All right," Naibor said, giving his consent, and they made their plans before she left the room, making it feel even emptier than before she had entered.

The hours dragged slowly by while Naibor waited for evening to come. He watched the dome of the sky progressively darken, making the shadows on the opposite wall grow long, until finally it was time for him to leave.

He met with Taila in his father's chambers, and they secretly hurried off together in the hidden passageways of the palace to the great hall, where they picked up a ceremonial red gown and a mask for Taila to wear.

Once outside in the darkness, in a night made black by a layer of clouds concealing the stars overhead, Naibor reached his hand out for Taila's. Their fingers met and entwined in a secure embrace. The feeling of her delicate hand in his made Naibor's heart pound even more than her presence so close beside him and the adventures they were about to face. Giving her hand a gentle squeeze of reassurance, the prince led Taila by the shortest route he knew of to the temple of Necros. They passed through the streets and laneways unnoticed, like two whispers floating on the cool breeze of the night, until they came to the place where the grand arena of the city of Amuron once stood.

Pressing their bodies against the wall next to the main entrance of the arena, they stopped to catch their breath and assess their situation. Peeking around the wall, Naibor tilted his head so he could see out from underneath his hood. Leading up to the temple was a laneway lined with skull-shaped lanterns like the ones he had seen beside the throne of Necros. In front of the temple, large tents had been set up for the Ix people, several of whom were standing about.

The temple itself was unguarded, but the sight of the ghastly thing was enough to keep anyone away. The slaves of Amuron had been forced, beaten, hurried, and terrorized while making the sorcerer's new home, and it showed. The dull black surface was not shiny and smooth, as it should have been; instead its surface was covered with lines and gashes, bumps and hollows. There were several windows in the front of the temple, but they were nothing more than crude holes that had no unity in either their size or shape. The temple also had four short, thin towers—one at each corner of the main structure of the building. The tops of these towers all leaned at awkward angles, making them appear as if they were about to topple over. Above the entrance, there was a platform for guards to stand on. The platform was protected by a parapet made from short pillars of blackstone that were connected by two rows of chains. Behind this rose the hump of a dome, surrounded by a row of tall spires placed about one shoulder width apart. Beneath the parapet there was an opening but no door—just a portcullis of iron whose bottom edge was a row of spikes. The prince could not help but picture in his mind the face of some horribly scarred and dying creature, on top of which sat a cruel crown.

This was the first real look Naibor had gotten of the new temple. He had not seen the completed temple before. Earlier that day, the prince had caught only glimpses of it as he was being ushered away by the Daimos. Now as he looked at it, his breath came in shallow, rapid little gasps. His palms began to sweat, and he realized that the sorcerer's creation frightened him.

Finished with his observations, the prince rested his head back against the comforting wall. Trying to sound calm, he said to Taila, "I warn you, it's not a pretty sight."

"I'm not here for the scenery," she whispered back, giving him an encouraging smile.

Naibor was reassured by the confidence she had in him. "It is time to put on our masks," the prince told her quietly, knowing there would be no turning back.

Taila answered with a nod, lifting the mask to her fine features, which were entirely swallowed up by the ugly thing.

"How do I look?" she asked, her sweet voice making a mockery of the horrible face that stared up at him.

"Terrifying," he replied truthfully, suppressing a shudder.

"Good, and you look equally repulsive," she responded, speaking to his mask-covered face.

"I am glad I brought you along," the prince added in a serious tone. "Daimos almost always travel in twos, and this way it will look less suspicious. It is important to appear as natural as possible. If we look like we belong at the temple, hopefully no one will question what we are doing. Are you ready?"

Taila gave another nod that she was, and in unison they strode boldly out into the laneway. Naibor heard her give a slight gasp when she saw the temple, but other than that she made no sound and moved with a fierce determination toward their destination.

The prince was proud of her and the courage she had to walk down this path with him toward unknown dangers, into the heart of their enemies' palace of death.

Some of the Ix people stared at them curiously, with a hunger in their eyes to know what these strange Daimos might be up to. Naibor and Taila paid no attention to them as they went by, and they kept on walking as if they didn't exist. They walked with purpose up the steps to the portcullis, where, unnoticed by anyone but Naibor, Taila momentarily hesitated before entering.

Inside the temple it was dark, almost as if the surrounding darkness of night had followed them in. The only bit of light came from the skull lanterns outside, showing them that they were in a vestibule with open doors to either side of them.

Taila looked over at Naibor, who, without a word spoken between them, quickly led the way through the door on their right. The hallway they entered was long and dark and lit only by a few burning wells of oil spaced too far apart on the walls to dispel the gloom. Despite it being difficult to see, they were pleased to find they were alone. The temple seemed to be empty.

They went forward cautiously. In the dim light, Naibor did not want to miss the hallway he was looking for on their left-hand side. When they reached it, they ventured forward again toward the two brass doors that marked the entrance of the great hall, where Necros had his throne.

When they stood in front of the glowering faces on the doors, Naibor and Taila both heard the sound they had been alert and listening for—the sound of someone approaching. They could clearly hear voices coming toward them and see the light of a swinging lantern gleam off the walls at the end of the hallway they were in.

Naibor panicked, having convinced himself that they were alone in the temple. At the sight of the light growing brighter with every moment, he lost his nerve. Pushing Taila through the curtain into the chamber on the other side of the hallway, he followed closely behind. Flattening themselves as much as possible against the walls on either side of the curtain, they became as still as the shadows around them, listening to the voices approach their hiding place. Sweat moistened the back of Naibor's neck when the light came to a stop outside the curtained doorway, and he prayed a silent prayer that they would not be found.

"Well, we have checked the temple as Lord Necros asked us to, and everyone has left as ordered," a harsh voice said.

"Yes, all the cells are empty, and I have locked all the doors," the other agreed.

"Good, then we must leave now."

"He has something special planned for tonight," the other one whispered with hideous glee.

"Shh, no more about that," the first one hissed quickly, as if they might be overheard. Then he added, "After we leave, the temple must be secured. Understand?"

"Yes, I will lower the portcullis so no one can get in or out," the second replied, smothering a laugh.

"Good. Come, let us go." Naibor and Taila remained motionless while both the light of the lantern and the sound of retreating footsteps diminished.

The prince was still trying to make sense of what the two Daimos had said when the stifling silence surrounding them was broken by the harsh grating sound of iron falling to the ground in a final loud, ringing clang!

CHAPTER 18

Naibor looked over quickly into the worried eyes of Taila, each of them realizing with horror that they had been locked inside the sorcerer's temple.

"We're trapped," Taila said, flinging herself at him, nearly collapsing in his arms. "What are we going to do?" she cried, lifting her masked face up toward him.

Naibor carefully removed her mask, and he gently stroked the side of her face with his hand. There was fear in the pools of her eyes, and he noticed that her bottom lip trembled ever so slightly. At his touch, she dropped her eyes and backed away from him, ashamed of the way she had just acted.

"Don't worry; we will find a way out," Naibor said tenderly after taking off his mask. "We can't give up yet. The sooner we get those two items we came here for, the sooner we can start to find a way out."

"Okay," Taila said, regaining her composure, "Where do we go from here?"

"From here we go through those doors across the hall," he replied.

Pushing the damp hair from her face, Taila stood calmly before him. "All right, I'm ready." Her momentary panic was over.

Pushing her fear aside, she hoped she could now deal with whatever difficulties they might have to face.

Now that they were alone in the temple, they secreted their masks inside their robes before entering the great hall. It was still as Naibor remembered it—dark and foreboding. Without knowing why, the prince felt strangely calm and confident.

They reached the back of the dais without incident, but their next challenge was to find the hidden door to the private chambers of Necros and then find a way to open it.

"It was right in the middle of the bottom steps," Naibor told her, the frustration showing on his face while they searched for it. The hard coa steps were seamless. There was no sign of any opening.

"Do you remember if he said any magic words to make it open?" Taila asked, climbing up the steps a little way to see if she could spot anything from another angle.

"No, it just seemed to open all on its own when I reached the bottom of the stairs," Naibor explained, continuing to push on the steps and to tap on them in case he heard anything different when he did so.

"Well, I don't see anything from up here either," Taila said, discouraged, and she walked slowly back down to where Naibor was standing.

When she got to the bottom, Naibor couldn't believe his eyes. A doorway suddenly appeared outlined in the steps before magically opening. Thinking quickly, they jumped behind the door, fearing that someone might have heard them. They waited in breathless silence until it was apparent no one was coming to investigate.

"It must have been triggered when you came down the steps," Naibor whispered to Taila, and coming out from behind the door, they peered together down the private stairs.

"You want to wait here?" Naibor asked, knowing what her answer would be.

"No," she smiled, and leaning over, she gave him a quick kiss.

It was a light kiss, a kiss given in friendship, but to the prince it meant more. The kiss confirmed to Naibor that Taila cared for him, and it helped him to realize that he cared for her. The painful memories of rejection and loss he had experienced in each of his relationships immediately crowded into his mind. He had lived most of his life being afraid of making new relationships and dealing with feelings of self-doubt. All it had gotten him, he now realized, was loneliness and isolation. He looked again into the deep, honest brown of her eyes, and he longed for something more. Instead of fearing her love, he welcomed it and even found comfort in it. It was the first time in a long time that Naibor felt he was worth loving and that he could allow himself the chance to get close to another person. He smiled a thank-you back at Taila with his eyes, and inwardly his heart rejoiced.

The door to the inner chamber was not locked, and knowing he would not get another chance, Naibor opened it. He breathed a sigh of relief when he found not even the pesky Elbanor in the room. His perch was empty. With a final nod to Taila that it was safe, they silently entered the sorcerer's chambers and shut the door.

"They are still here!" Naibor exclaimed in a triumphant whisper, and going over to the table, he grabbed up the red spell book and the sachet of magic powder. Turning toward Taila with them in his hands, he said, "Now all we need to … do … is …"

Naibor was about to say "escape" when his words were swallowed by a pounding in his head. The walls began to lean at awkward angles and the floor to tilt beneath his feet. He heard Taila cry out over the noise in his head, and he saw her try to steady herself as she too felt the dizzying effect of the room as it seemed to bend in an unnatural way. Then he saw the two wraith Daimos of Necros materialize behind her, reaching for her with arms outstretched. He wanted to yell out a warning, but it was too late; they already had her firmly held between them.

The prince heard a loud snap and a crack, like the breaking of something unnatural, as Necros appeared in the room with a raven on his shoulder. The room immediately settled down to its former state, and the booming in Naibor's head slowly subsided. The prince felt as if he were going to be sick. The juices in his stomach churned and swirled, and looking at Necros, he was filled with despair and renewed fear.

Naibor expected the sorcerer to laugh at him and to gloat over the fact that he had caught them, but Necros did not give them even a pretense of mirth. He stood before them the embodiment of evil.

The prince swallowed several times, trying not to lose control. He had managed to place the powder of the black sorcerer in a pocket inside his robe before Necros arrived, but the book had dropped back onto the table in front of him when the room had first begun to rock and heave.

During the uncomfortable silence that filled the room, the red book rose up from the table and floated over to Necros. The cruel conjurer snatched the book from the air and flipped through it as if he were looking for an appropriate spell—one that would make them suffer horribly for what they had done. Elbanor ruffled his feathers impatiently while his master turned the pages, and then the harsh fingers snapped the crimson binding closed with an air of finality.

"Well done, Naibor," Necros said with almost genuine approval, "but this book will not help you with what you plan. I know what you hope to do with this book and my magic powder, but it will do you no good."

Naibor looked at the sorcerer in shock, visibly shaken and disturbed to hear that the sorcerer already knew what he had been sent to do.

"I know about your many visits to your father in his chambers, and that you intend to try to break the spell that he is under," Necros continued confidently. "But even if you knew how to undo the spell that holds your father captive, your attempt to overthrow me would be futile. He would just be killed along with the rest during the sacrifice tomorrow night."

After a sickening pause, Necros moved toward Naibor and continued maliciously, "I have decided that I will make a deal with you after all, Prince. I will trade you this book for that pretty creature standing over there." Casting Taila an indecent glance, he thrust the book into the bewildered prince's stomach.

Naibor looked from Necros to Taila and then back again to the sorcerer, searching hopelessly for another option.

"Take the book, Naibor," Taila encouraged. "Don't worry about me."

Naibor looked down at the book, not daring to take it.

"Yes, take it and go, Prince. The two of us want to be alone," Necros said wickedly.

Naibor looked again at Taila. He knew that his only hope to help Amuron was to take the book, but he also knew Necros. Hoping she would forgive him, he took the book and hurried out the door.

* * *

Prince Naibor tried to hurry up the steps and away from the sorcerer's chamber, but his feet did not cooperate, and he kept stumbling. He kept looking back down the stairs to the doorway at the bottom, not wanting to leave Taila behind. Desperately clutching the items he had obtained from his evil adversary, the prince forced himself to continue on with his next task.

"I cannot help Taila by staying here," he told himself. "I must get the Stone of Wisdom and take these items to Binah."

It did not take him long to retrace his steps back to the front of the temple. To his surprise, he found the portcullis open. Naibor could not understand why Necros was allowing him to leave the temple. He felt sure that Necros wanted him to leave, and this worried him. He wondered why the sorcerer was so eager to see him flee the temple with his spell book and conjurer's powder.

The night was still as black as it had been before, but this time Naibor did not fear being seen. Traveling as fast as his legs would allow him, Naibor hurried back to his home. When he arrived he knew without a doubt that he had been tricked. The palace was empty! The celebration that Necros had told him about was not taking place. It had been a trap, and now the sorcerer had Taila. There was no time left for indecision. The prince knew that Necros had to be stopped, and he had to be stopped now!

Walking with purposeful strides through the familiar hallways of the palace, he headed toward his father's chambers. The wall lamps had not been lit, and none of Necros's servants were about, including the two Daimos guards that he had as constant companions.

All was dark and quiet when Prince Naibor reached the quarters of the high king. Entering the outer chamber, he pushed his way past the curtain to where his father lay so still and unchanged upon the bed. It seemed that his father had been like that as long as he could remember, and only in his dreams had he been alive and laughing.

As he looked down at his father, the amulet of the high king caught his eye. Softly radiating a warm glow in the lamplight, it beckoned to him. For so long he had wanted to wear the Stone of Wisdom as proof of his worthiness. His pride had deceived him into thinking that if he wore the Stone of Wisdom, the people of Amuron would recognize him as the rightful heir to the throne. The desire to wear the amulet had been a consuming desire that had blinded him, partly leading him to the desperate situation he now found himself in.

Reaching forward, he held the amulet in his hand so that he could look into the heart of the stone. The soft, inviting colors danced gaily as he gazed thoughtfully at it for a moment. All his worries and fears vanished, and he almost laughed aloud as he held it. The truth of the stone suddenly seemed to shine clear. For the prince, it was like clearly seeing his own reflection, which up until then had always been cloudy and unrecognizable. The wisdom of the stone came from knowing who you were in the sight of Aii.

"With the help of the Lord Aii, Amuron will be saved from the sorcerer and I will be able to redeem myself," the prince realized. Knowing he had his father's blessing, Naibor took the amulet gently from around his father's neck and then kissed him on the forehead before leaving the room.

Naibor's next destination was the prayer room beside his father's chambers. He went to the door down the hall, turned the glass knob, and stepped inside. Catching sight of something out of the corner of his eye, the prince ducked out of the way just in time.

"Oh it's you!" Standing next to the door with relief was the small, but tough, elderly servant woman. She was holding a brass candlestick over her head, ready to strike again if necessary. "Sorry, my lord," she apologized with a twinkle of mischief in her eyes while lowering the candlestick. "I wasn't expecting anyone to come through the door. I kept waiting for someone to come in through the secret passageway. I have been worried, since Taila has not returned and the hour is so late."

"I'm sorry to have frightened you, Edra," Naibor said, throwing his tired body into one of the large, comfortable chairs. "We have a lot to talk about. I have some news to tell you. Taila has been captured by Necros." Unable to bear the burden of guilt any longer, he confided to a kindhearted and caring Edra all the events that had occurred since he had gone seeking a sorcerer to help him win the Celebration Games.

The conclusion of their talk came many hours later. "We will have to risk it, Edra. I believe we have no other choice. I'm sorry to have to involve you. It would be better if you were to escape now, but I need your help."

"My lord, you know I already agreed. The best way to defeat evil is to stand up against it, and sometimes that requires the help of others," she said reassuringly. Giving him a motherly smile, she blew out one of the two remaining lit candles when she finally saw the prince close his tired eyes.

After the prince fell asleep in the chair, both physically and emotionally exhausted, Edra continued in prayer for a while. They had worked out a plan of action against the sorcerer that would require the efforts of their allies Captain Regg and Captain Zai.

His meeting at sunrise with the animals at Binah would have to wait until after he had met with the captains. Although Naibor was greatly distressed that Taila was a prisoner of Necros, there was little more he could do about it now. They had prayed together that Taila would be protected. He hoped that he would be able to rescue her when he fought against the sorcerer tomorrow.

* * *

After Prince Naibor had gone from the chamber, Taila was left to face Necros on her own. She looked down at the cold stone floor—anywhere but at the vile sorcerer standing so close in front of her. She glanced at the doorway where Naibor had left moments before, with a look of loss and dismay that could not be hidden from the sharp eyes of the predator that watched her every move.

This was what Necros had been waiting for—some sign of where to attack his prey. He licked his pale lips greedily, eager to ravage his next victim. "Prince Naibor has given me everything," Necros said slowly, savoring every moment and emotion he was able to evoke. His voice was dangerously precise, hard-edged, and cold. "First he gave me his father and his friends, then the city, and now you. Victory is mine."

"You have not won yet," Taila said, boldly lifting her head in challenge to the sorcerer's words.

Necros reveled in her resistance, the mock smile on his lips as vicious as his reply.

"You still have so much faith in him, don't you? But you know so little about him. I assure you your faith in him is quite misplaced." Necros paused. "What is it you like about him so much? His princely appearance? Appearances can be deceiving, you know. Or perhaps you are attracted to the poor maligned and misunderstood prince—the one who needs you to care for him?" Necros circling around as he spoke, using his magic to draw the life and feeling from her body with every word.

"Your belief that Naibor cares for you as much as you care for him has enabled the prince to fool you completely. He has been working with me all along. For years we have been in communication. He was the one who contacted me to help him overthrow the kingdom. He brought me secretly into this city for the purpose of murdering your sister and her friends. The prince never told you what happened to your sister, did he? Never mentioned a word? No?"

Taila stood silently, defenseless against the sorcerer's numbing power.

"That is because he had me destroy them. They are gone, and you will never see them again." He grinned evilly with satisfaction when Taila started to softly weep. "Then he had me poison his father, but the Stone of Wisdom kept his father from dying."

"That's a lie," Taila cried out, tears of grief flowing unhindered down her cheeks. "You said yourself that he has gone to try to revive his father. That is why he wanted the book and the powder."

"But that was all just part of the plan to trick you," he said with a mocking laugh of glee. "Those objects mean nothing to me. I can easily remake my powder, and I have several copies of the spells in that book." A new pouch of powder and another book of spells materialized on the table in front of Taila to emphasize his point.

"The exchange was what I would call something for nothing," he continued with a tone of pity in his voice. "Those objects he took are useless to him. Did you honestly expect Naibor to be able to use them? He cannot even understand the spells in the book, let alone read them, and he does not know the words of power to make the powder work. I'm afraid they were just props used in our little play staged against you."

"No. No, it can't be true! You did not even know about me until tonight."

"I knew about you hiding in the palace, just as I knew about you using the secret tunnels. There is no use fighting against the truth, Taila; Naibor led you here to be captured by me. In fact, we met earlier today to discuss how we would get you here—by letting you believe he had a plan."

"Why didn't you just come and get me in the palace, then?" Taila countered stubbornly.

"Naibor thought it would be more fun this way. Knowing how much you care for him, the prince used your feelings for him to gain your trust. Why do you think the temple was so conveniently empty when you came here tonight and this chamber so easy to enter?

"My dear, you must accept what has happened to you and the city of Amuron. There is no need for tears. Tomorrow night during the ceremony, to demonstrate the strength of the new power controlling this city, Prince Naibor and I shall stand side by side when all the unbelievers of Amuron are sacrificed—and together we shall rejoice."

"Then I shall die, proud to be sacrificed with the rest of my people." Taila tried to hide the quaver in her voice. Wiping the tears from her cheek, she bowed her head, allowing her silken hair to fall down and cover her face.

Necros could tell she believed him. He was satisfied that he had turned her against Naibor, but then he had another idea. He would be even more satisfied if he could make her his companion. "But it doesn't have to be that way, Taila," the evil sorcerer continued with a voice that was now soothing and comforting.

Taila looked up at the sudden change.

"I will spare your life and those of any others in the city you like—your parents, perhaps? You need only to stop resisting me."

"No."

"But you have not even heard my proposal. I am not as cruel as you may think. I have much to offer, and besides, you did not even stop to think about what I could give you."

"I want nothing from you." Taila started shaking, more afraid of the sorcerer now than she had been before.

"You and I both know that is not true. You can't honestly tell me the lives of your parents mean nothing to you? Their lives can be easily spared, you know, along with those of the rest of your family. What would that be worth to you? Nothing?"

Her lips parted slightly, but no sound came out.

"Well, I have a suspicion that their lives mean a great deal to you. And I am willing to spare your family." He paused, reaching up a black-nailed hand to stroke one side of her neck. "All you need to do is consent to be my wife."

Taila looked at the sorcerer, her eyes round from shock. She swallowed, trying to keep down the down the bile that rose in her throat.

"I, unlike Prince Naibor, have noticed how beautiful you are. I can give you anything you want—gold, jewels, all the riches of world—if you will become the queen of Amuron. It has been a long time since Amuron has had a queen." The table behind the sorcerer instantly became covered with all the fineries he had mentioned, and he motioned with his hand toward it.

"You don't have to answer me right away," Necros said, taking a step forward, closing the small gap that had separated them. His body now pressed against hers, and his cool breath brushed across her neck as he looked down into her face. "My proposal was sudden. You need time to think it over. But remember, my dear, you have seen only one side of me—the side I show to my adversaries." Stroking her hair with his fingers, he added, "I can also be very gentle and giving, not always so frightening."

Taila stood as still as a statue, her heart racing as a tide of hysteria threatened to overwhelm her.

"Come!" Necros instructed, guiding her to the table. "Sit down and eat." He helped her into a chair while the material goods on the table disappeared to be replaced with a sensuous feast.

Taila stared at the food on the table, hardly seeing it. She shook her head slightly, knowing she wouldn't be able to eat. Then, with a meek smile, she quietly said, "Some tea would be nice. Fruit tea is my favorite."

"Try this." Necros handed her a steaming goblet that had appeared in his hand.

As she took the goblet from him, she looked into his eyes, but there was no compassion in them. "If I agreed to be your wife," she asked, after taking a sip of the hot tea, "would you let all the people of Amuron go?"

"But, my dear, then there would be no one to sacrifice at the ceremony tomorrow," he casually replied as he sat down at the table opposite Taila and began eating.

"You could sacrifice Prince Naibor," Taila suggested softly after taking several more sips of tea.

The hand of Necros stopped with a forkful of food on the way up to his mouth. "You are a delight," he laughed wickedly. "If you want to kill Naibor, then I certainly will give you the opportunity."

Putting down his fork, Necros looked at Taila thoughtfully and then announced, "Twenty! Twenty people of Amuron I will spare, if you consent. I will line the people of Amuron up, and you can choose any twenty you like. And I guarantee you the offer I make is a generous one."

"Yes, twenty is a generous amount," Taila agreed, hoping to further please the sorcerer with her words, while her heart sank at the low number.

"Then you consent?" Necros said, forcing her to make a decision.

"Can I have more time to decide?" she asked weakly.

"You have had enough time. You must decide now!" Necros said with an edge of impatience in his voice, and his eyes gleamed like two polished black stones.

"Yes," Taila consented in a whisper that was barely audible.

A profane smile briefly crossed the sorcerer's face. He rose up from his seat at the table, and raised his goblet of wine in the air. "To the new queen of Amuron."

Taila lifted her goblet weakly in reply. She felt all the strength drain from her body. Just as she was going to drink the rest of her tea to steady herself, Necros pulled her up from the chair toward him by the wrist. Holding her firmly, he kissed her lips and then released her. The kiss was cold, hard, and ruthless.

Visibly shaking, Taila watched while the sorcerer went to get Elbanor from his perch on his way out of the chamber. She barely heard him call out that the ceremony would be after first light tomorrow as she collapsed to the table, sobbing in anguish.

* * *

"My lord," Edra called out quietly, gently shaking the prince in his chair. "My lord, it is time."

The prince awoke with a start. Grabbing firmly onto the arm of the person shaking him, Naibor waited for his eyes to focus. "It is almost sunrise," he heard the servant woman say.

"Thank you, Edra," Naibor replied, realizing what those words meant. Rising up from his chair, he prepared to face the day. "Did you get some sleep?" he inquired, concerned about the woman's strength.

"Don't you worry about me," she said, patting him on the arm. "We have other things to worry about today."

The prince nodded his agreement. He took the sorcerer's book and powder from the inside of the cloak he had not bothered to remove, as well as the high king's amulet, and handed them over to Edra. "The eagle, Princess Sanii, should come to my room when I don't meet with her this morning at Binah. Please give these to her for me, and tell her I will go to Binah as soon as I am able," the prince gravely instructed. "I will be loading up the wagon behind the palace, and you can meet with me there afterward."

"Let me just put these items in this cloth before I go," Edra told him while wrapping them up in an embroidered linen cloth she had taken from a side table.

"I brought you some fresh water in a pitcher. It's on the washstand, along with some dry biscuits and some fruit compote."

Giving the prince an encouraging smile as she went out the door, she added, "May Aii go with us."

Naibor splashed some water on his face and ran some through his hair and over the back of his neck, but he was not hungry. He went to the window and opened the wooden shutters and the glass panels behind them to have a look outside. Dawn was approaching, and the sky was slowly growing brighter. The air, however, was full of moisture, and it hung suspended around him in a misty gray. Naibor smiled to himself. The morning fog was a welcome sight. It would help to keep his plans secret from his enemy.

He checked the inside of his cloak to confirm that the death mask was still where he had hidden it, and it was. He was going to need it one more time for his biggest bluff yet. Having gotten a guard's uniform from the room next door, he changed into the black clothes.

His heart pounded just thinking of what he planned to do. There was so much at stake, and the level of risk was great, but he also knew that this was his only chance to stop Necros. This was to be the day of reckoning.

CHAPTER 19

The prince wrapped himself in his cloak and the silence of the surrounding fog as he headed toward the stables. The high-spirited horse inside shifted nervously when the dark figure approached in the dim light. "It's me, old friend," Naibor whispered softly to his horse, who took a few more minutes of reassuring before he settled down enough to let the prince lift the latch and enter the stall.

"That's right; it is me. And I even brought you this sticky mess, otherwise known as a biscuit with fruit compote." The prince felt the hot breath from the horse's nostrils as the horse closed his soft lips over the handheld offering,

While the horse was munching on the biscuit, Naibor gently guided his mount out of the stall. He quickly bridled the horse and strapped him into the appropriate harness for pulling a small wagon. Snorting in disapproval, the horse began to struggle against being constrained.

"You are a military horse," Naibor reminded the muscular stallion, attempting to maneuver the protesting horse backward. "You have been trained to pull wagons of heavy equipment and personal chariots, as well as to carry a rider; the least you could do is act accordingly." Puffing with exertion, the prince leaned on the horse's side to catch his breath when he had completed the job.

Edra met him, as soon as she was able, outside of the wine cellar door. He was loading the wagon with every barrel he could roll, every crate he could lift, and every bottle he could carry. Naibor almost didn't recognize her when she arrived, and he smiled with approval at her disguise.

She had stopped in the prayer room to fix her appearance before coming to meet with the prince. The neat and tidy servant woman, whom Naibor knew, had been replaced by an old and weary woman of many sorrows. Edra had freshly powdered and then soiled her face with ashes, darkening the shadows under her eyes so that she appeared tired and worn. Her hair stuck out from under an old kerchief that she used as a dusting rag, and the clothes she wore were ripped and fraying from overuse and long years of wear. She absentmindedly tugged on her shirt to straighten it with her dirty hands, and then, with a giggle and a deep sigh, she remembered to leave it the way it was.

"Almost ready," he whispered to her after he put the ramp he had used for loading the wagon back inside the cellar and closed the door.

"How did things go with you?" he asked while splashing some strong wine on his face and clothes. He took several mouthfuls of the potent liquid and spit them out beside the wagon.

"Fine," Edra replied, holding her nose and sneezing out her little laugh as the prince helped her up into the wagon. "They await your arrival."

"Then we had best not keep them waiting for too much longer," he added. With one last check to see that the contents of the wagon were secure, he jumped up into the front.

With a flip of the reins and a quiet signal to the horse, he started the wagon rolling. They headed through the thick fog toward the military barracks, where the men prisoners were being held captive. Just before they entered the square, Naibor gave a conspirator's nod in Edra's direction and slipped on his mask. Driving right up to the main guardhouse—the one inhabited by the Daimos—the prince stopped the wagon in front of the door.

"Let's make this convincing," he commented in Edra's ear before hopping down from the wagon with a whip in one hand and a bottle and cup in the other.

"Easy, you stupid woman!" the masked prince yelled out into the damp air.

The seemingly pitiful woman was struggling to carry several heavy bottles toward the guardhouse, and at his harsh words, one of the bottles accidentally slipped and crashed to the ground.

"Did I not tell you to be careful?" Naibor screamed, lunging toward the woman. He raised an arm to strike her.

"Here! You! What is going on?" A Daimos demanded, flying down the steps from the guardhouse toward them.

The masked Daimos stopped his assault on the poor woman when the other Daimos approached. "This unbeliever," Naibor scowled, "is trying to destroy your gift from Necros. Necros has ordered me to deliver to each guardhouse a portion of this wagon's contents for the celebration after the sacrifice today."

The Daimos looked from Naibor to the wagon and then back to Naibor again, but he said nothing.

"Would you like to try a little? It's good stuff. It's from the palace stock," the disguised prince informed him, pouring a little shot into the cup and offering it to the Daimos.

The Daimos licked his lips at the offer, but he said with disappointment, "I'm on duty."

"This little bit won't hurt," Naibor pressed, feeling the man struggle with his decision. "Who's going to tell?"

The Daimos broke down and took the offered drink. "It's still early, but you'd best get this stuff 'round to the back before anyone else sees it, or it will be broken into an' drunk before the ceremony even begins, if you know what I mean." The two of them shared in a laugh.

Naibor did know what he meant, and that was just what he hoped would happen.

"And you plan to do this all on your own, with only this feeble woman to help?" the Daimos inquired, shaking his head in disbelief.

"Well, to tell you the truth, I could use a little help from some of the male prisoners."

"Fine, take as many as you like. It will get the job done faster. Leave the old woman with me. I will see she is taken back to her camp."

"The old woman stays with me!" Naibor objected sternly. "She's not getting off that easy. She's still being punished for the horrible job she did shining my boots."

The Daimos, with another laugh, took the bottle and cup offered to him by Naibor. He poured himself another drink and finished it in several big gulps.

"These barracks over here," the masked prince continued, pointing in the general direction of where the two captains were being held, "are there any strong men housed in it?"

The Daimos just smiled momentarily to himself, and then, with a shrug, he turned to leave. Going back up the steps to the guardhouse, he called out behind him, "I will send someone to open the door for you." He then vanished inside the building.

"So far so good," Naibor whispered secretly to Edra. His breath mingled with the fog while he checked the supply of alcohol they had unloaded from the wagon.

Moments later, a nervous and young Daimos came down the steps toward them from the guardhouse. His eyes darted quickly to the left and right as he appraised the situation before hurrying off toward the barrack that Naibor directed him to.

Naibor still had the set of keys he had taken the last time he had ventured out to this camp, but he did not want these Daimos to know that. They were an important part of his plan.

"I'm looking forward to the ceremony today," the young Daimos nervously chatted, taking the masked Daimos into his confidence. "It's a good thing Necros ordered all the prisoners to be locked up until the ceremony. We don't want any attempts at escape," he continued, his eyes wide at the thought, before unlocking the door to the barrack.

Naibor nodded absentmindedly, pretending not to pay attention, while the high-strung Daimos shared this useful information with him.

Captain Regg, seeing Prince Naibor enter the barrack, quickly rose up from the bed, where he had been uneasily watching the dim morning light through the shutters make patterned shadows of bars on the opposite wall.

"Eager to meet your doom, unbeliever?" the prince shot out, cutting Regg off before he could call out his name.

"No, I … I …" Regg stammered, seeing the young Daimos guard follow Naibor into the room.

"I will take this one," Naibor said with his voice full of scorn, nodding in Regg's direction. "He still has some life left in him. And this one over in the corner," he added, pointing at Captain Zai. "Come with me!"

"These two should be enough with the old women," Naibor commented, impatiently ushering the prisoners out the door before him with a shove.

While the young guard was making sure the barrack door was locked and secure, the masked prince went over to the wagon and pulled out two bottles of potent wine. "Here! Guard! This is for your trouble," he said, shoving them into the delighted recipient's hands.

"Thank you," the excited youth gratefully said to the dark Daimos while cradling his treasure in his arms.

"Have a drink with your friends, but make sure you don't tell anyone where you got it," Naibor warned him in low menacing tones. "Understand? Or making you miserable will be part of my fun during the celebration."

The smile instantly disappeared from the youth's face. "I won't tell anyone where I got it. You have my word," he assured the disguised prince before returning to his own affairs.

"Have you a plan to use against the sorcerer?" Zai inquired quietly after the young Daimos had gone.

The prince nodded, but he did not answer until he had moved the wagon out of the main camp to a more private and less visible location. Then he took a few moments to quickly outline his plan with the two captains. The day was still gray and cloudy as they talked. Fortunately the fog had remained dense, making their situation seem somehow unreal and dreamlike. The air was full of damp echoes, and the world surrounding them was nothing but sifting patches of gray light mixed with indistinct shadows of darkness.

"Captain Zai, I'm leaving you in charge of freeing the men in this camp and getting as many as possible to the West Gate without being seen," Naibor informed him, handing Zai a group of keys off the key ring he carried, which fortunately had been separated according to camp.

"Captain Regg, Edra, and I will continue on to the other camps, leaving our precious gifts behind. Hopefully we can get as many people as we can out of the city before the ceremony at noon. Captain Regg and Edra will meet with you at the West Gate after the wagon is empty. This alcohol will hopefully cause enough of a distraction until I can create a larger distraction by challenging Necros at his temple. If this doesn't work, may Aii have mercy on our souls."

In response, Captain Zai jumped down from the wagon. In a salute of friendship, he clasped Naibor's inner arm momentarily by the wrist. The prince then signaled to his horse, and they left Zai in charge of a task worthy of a captain of the People's Guard.

* * *

Back inside the guardhouse, the Daimos in charge went into the kitchen, where another half-dressed guard sat sleepily at the table.

"What was all that going on outside?" his fellow guard asked when he entered the room.

"Can you keep a secret?" the subcommander inquired while sitting down at the table.

The other made a face in reply.

"That masked Daimos out there is delivering presents from Necros for after the ceremony. His wagon is full of bottles and barrels of our favorite drink."

"Gee, I wish I had some of that right now," the other commented, looking longingly toward the window, where he could just catch sight of the front of the wagon.

"Shh … fool! We can steal some for ourselves later, but for now we don't want the others to find out."

His companion nodded, smiling cunningly. Shifting in his seat, he added, "I've heard about that masked Daimos; he has caused some trouble around here lately. It's rumored he is a favorite of Necros because he wears that stupid mask."

"All I know is that he scares me. I couldn't read his thoughts. He blocked me out of his mind completely, almost as if he wasn't a Daimos at all."

Normally this news might have disturbed the subordinate guard. A Daimos able to close his mind from another commanding Daimos would be very powerful and therefore a threat. When the Daimos had been in their wraithlike form, their only means of communication had been focusing their thoughts at one another. Now that they inhabited the citizens of Amuron, only the strongest Daimos could use their thoughts to communicate by using Necros as a catalyst to provide them with power. The sorcerer was the only one who could fully use his mind powers to command them by sending out orders and simple instructions that resounded inside their heads, but today there would be no communication. Necros's attention was needed elsewhere, and he did not want any distractions.

"You won't be able to communicate mentally with anyone today. Necros has closed his mind to us while he prepares for the ceremony," the subordinate guard explained.

"That must have been the reason," the guard in charge agreed, still feeling that there was something strange about the masked Daimos.

"It is our commanding Daimos that scares me," the shirtless guard interjected, breaking the momentary silence.

"What about the commander?" The first Daimos inquired, looking over his shoulder as if he suddenly expected him to appear in the doorway at the slightest reference.

"Don't you remember? He ordered us to tell him immediately if we saw the masked Daimos again," he reminded him. "And if we do that, you know very well that the commander will take Necros's gift from us and lock it up somewhere. He probably won't even let us have it during the celebration. You know how he hates drink."

The Daimos in charge nodded his head slowly in agreement, his eyes narrowing in thought.

"When do you expect the commander back?" the other guard asked.

"I expect him to be at the temple all day, and I don't want to disturb him."

"Well then, I had best grab a few bottles for myself to put away for later, don't you think, Subcommander?"

"Not so fast," the Daimos in charge cautioned. "I will be the one punished if the commander finds out, and I will be sure to name you as an accomplice if I do. I don't like to suffer alone, and your misery will be sure to ease my pain." He gave a threatening look, making sure his coconspirator fully understood.

"After the ceremony, what can it matter?"

The temporary commander shrugged before answering slyly, "All this talk has suddenly made me very thirsty."

Sharing a laugh, the two went to check and see if the masked Daimos had left them a good share of the wagon's contents.

* * *

The women's camp was located in the Market Section of the city, and Naibor was both shocked and surprised at the sight of the camp when he arrived in the meager early morning light. In comparison to the men's camp, the women's camp was disorganized and disheveled and appeared to be without orderly supervision. Most of the women prisoners were housed in a large building previously used to hold the livestock brought to the market for auctioning. Others were kept in large tents, which were grouped together in the center of one of the wide-open areas in the market. They were guarded by female Daimos, who occupied several of the more expensive merchant homes and shops.

Stopping the wagon in the main section of the camp, they found a group of the female Daimos already having a party of their own in front of one of the more elaborate homes.

"Hey! No men allowed in the women's camp, Daimos or otherwise," one of the female guards shouted at them with authority, putting down her bottle and striding over. "Not that I mind personally," she added with a wink, coming close to Naibor, who had dismounted from the wagon.

"I am the subcommander who is in charge; state your business," she announced firmly, and then, lowering her voice so only Naibor could hear, she added, "and then let me know what I can do for you."

Naibor cleared his throat nervously. This female Daimos made him very uncomfortable. "Necros has ordered me to deliver to each camp a portion of this wagon's contents for the celebration after the ceremony today."

"Ha!" the female Daimos laughed with disbelief, swaying her body from side to side as if listening to music only she could hear. "That doesn't sound to me like something Necros would do." Licking her lips, she sized Naibor up with a smile. "You would not believe the stories I have heard from men trying to get into this camp—male Daimos just like you. Now, what makes you think I am going to believe your story?"

"You don't have to. I'll just leave you a few bottles and then be on my way," Naibor said, thinking quickly. He waved a hand behind him so those in the wagon would start to unload the precious cargo.

"I have an even better idea. Why don't you leave a few bottles for my friends, and then we can have our own private party together—just you and me?" she teased, pressing herself tightly up against Naibor's body. "But first let me see the man behind the mysterious mask." She slid her hands up his body and grabbed the mask.

She was just about to pull it off when Naibor firmly grabbed her hands and said, "But then there would be no mystery."

Disappointed, the woman moved away from Naibor and demanded, "What is your name, Daimos? Answer me or I will call my commander and have you arrested."

Naibor paused, his mind racing. If he backed down now, she had him. The only things these Daimos seemed to understand and respond to were threats and authority. So he countered her attack. "Call her and I will call mine, and you can explain why you have detained me from my work."

"You're bluffing," she said coolly. "I happen to know that your commander is at an important private ceremony, while mine is only making preparations for today's ritual and might welcome a distraction."

"You are lying as well," Naibor challenged, trying to sound annoyed while behind his mask he bit his lip apprehensively. "I'm sure your commander won't be pleased to see you celebrating so early while you are on duty."

"Ha!" the Daimos snapped back in frustration, her anger rising. "Too bad for you, you are not my type," she snarled. "So do what you have come here to do and leave quickly! I've already been too generous with my time." With that she returned to her friends.

They quickly unloaded a smaller amount for these women Daimos, who already seemed to have their own secret supply; but before getting into the wagon, Naibor got an idea.

"I have some friends back at the men's camp who may be more your type," Naibor remarked casually, going over to the subcommander. "They may not be allowed to come visit you, but there is no reason why you cannot visit them. I'm sure they would enjoy your company. They have been complaining lately about certain hardships they have had to endure."

The women laughed loudly in reply, giving one another knowing looks and playful shoves. "I bet they have been suffering," one of them replied with mock pity.

"What makes you think we would be interested in something like that?" the Daimos in charge asked fiercely, still angry at Naibor's rejection, but a couple of the women had already gotten up on some pretense and left the group.

"I am not guarding this camp alone, ladies," the subcommander hissed at several others who began to leave. "The next one who tries to leave will have to fight me," she threatened, smashing an empty bottle against the ground at her feet, and the women returned to miserably take up their guard positions.

"It looks like you could guard this place on your own," Naibor commented truthfully to the subcommander, who was smiling over her victory. "Don't the women unbelievers give you any trouble?" he inquired, trying to appease her anger.

"We never have any trouble with the women," the subcommander bragged, pleased with her apparent superiority. "The children are housed in the next camp, and the women know that if they give us any trouble, the children will suffer. We had to use several children as examples in the beginning, and after that the women did whatever we told them to do. You men are too soft—not ruthless enough."

Turning her attention toward the gifts the others had unloaded from the wagon, she went over to inspect the contents. Finding something that she liked, the female Daimos gave a laugh of pleasure.

"Well, I guess it won't hurt if a few more of you ladies want to leave for a bit of company, but at least five should stay with me," the subcommander stated with sudden good humor. "Just make sure that those you are guarding remember our agreement: either they continue to cooperate or they do not get to see the children before they die."

Wanting to leave before the subcommander's mood changed again for the worse, the masked Daimos leaped up into the front of the wagon. Giving her a curt nod of his head, he quickly drove out of the camp to the outskirts of the market.

Now it was Captain Regg's turn. Climbing down from the wagon, out of sight from the women Daimos, the captain took the necessary keys from the prince and grabbed a long, slender-necked bottle. Eager to engage in his own private battle, he swung the bottle several times through the air. His plan was to knock out the Daimos guarding the women's camp in his own way and lock them up together in a horse enclosure after releasing the prisoners. Assuring the prince with a nod that he was ready to put things right, he hurried off to free some of the captives of the city.

* * *

Elbanor, with a quick flap of his black wings, left the sorcerer's temple through an open window, flying into the misty morning air. He was not pleased with his master. He could not understand his lord's decision to marry the girl. She was pretty enough and all that, but there were more important things for him to attend to at this time. He secretly thought the whole idea was foolish, especially this close to the sacrifice.

The raven sat on top of one of the slim temple towers, his favorite perch, preferring to spend some time alone. The morning air, however, was too cold and damp for just sitting and thinking, so he decided instead to go and check on the city. With a raspy cry, he set off, every methodical stroke of his wings causing the wet feathers on his back to shine with iridescence.

Heading toward the women's camp on his usual route, he wished that Necros hadn't closed down his method of communicating with the Daimos. Reaching the camp, he looked below him, and all seemed quiet—much too quiet!

Where are the guards? he wondered with the wind ruffling his feathers while he circled in low over the middle of the camp. Then he spotted several empty bottles of wine lying about, and he flew down to investigate. Giving one of the empty bottles a shove with his black-toed foot, he croaked out his disappointment. He knew of the Daimos weakness for drink, and also of the results.

If the Daimos have been drinking, they will be uncontrollable and useless when it comes time to move the prisoners for the sacrifice, he thought to himself, angry at their weak-minded insubordination.

Squawking loudly several times, he hoped to be heard by one of the guards, but no one responded. Frustrated, he flew off to check on the condition of the men's camp, only to find that things there were much worse.

Flying into the heart of the camp, Elbanor was appalled to find women Daimos carousing with the men Daimos at the main guardhouse, and they were anything but quiet! The rest of the Daimos were so intoxicated that they had spilled out of the guardhouse and onto the grounds in front. Some couldn't even stand up, while others were stumbling blindly about.

Infuriated, Elbanor was about to turn around and report the whole disgraceful lot to Necros when something by the West Gate caught his eye. Curious, he went to see what was going on, but before he even reached the gate he was horrified by what he saw.

The prisoners were escaping! Groups of men and women were hurrying cautiously through the fog down the road, slipping quickly through the open gate and then huddling together, barely visible, in the trench below the city walls. Quickly beating his wings, the raven headed back toward the temple. He had to warn Necros before it was too late.

CHAPTER 20

The winged princess glided in low through the mist over Binah after returning from her second visit to the palace. She entered the abandoned building through the open bell tower and quickly dropped down to the wooden floor beneath her.

"Who's there?" a deep voice growled from the damp darkness behind the doorway leading into the next room.

"It's Sanii," she answered. Using her beak to pick up the cloth bag she had been carrying, she joined her friends in the other room.

The other animals pounced on her with questions and concerns when she entered.

"Did you meet with Naibor? Is he coming?" Janii asked, lowering her head to be on eye level with the eagle.

"No, I didn't see him, but he sent a servant woman with this parcel. It has the items we need in it."

"It could be a trick," Baynor said suspiciously, his hackles rising. "The woman could have been the sorcerer in disguise."

"No, I don't think so. She showed me the items in the cloth before she gave it to me, and they looked authentic. She also said that Naibor would meet with us here as soon as he was able."

"But can Naibor be trusted?" Tybor wondered aloud, restlessly pacing the floor.

"I don't think we have a choice. We will just have to wait," Sanii concluded.

"I'm tired of waiting," Tayii stated, giving a sleepy blink of her large cat eyes. Leaning back, she stretched her front legs out in front of her, extending her powerful claws as she eased the tension from her shoulders. "I think I should go into the city to scout around and see what we are up against. With this fog, I will be able to blend into the shadows. Sanii has given us some idea of the situation from her trips into the city, but I may be able to add to it."

Sanii and Ranor both quickly volunteered to go along.

"Now hold on a minute," Baynor said, sitting down on his haunches while addressing his friends. "We all can't go, as much as we would like to. For one thing, we all need to be here when Naibor arrives; and for another, it's too dangerous." He paused for a moment, thinking. "It might be wise, however, if the three of you do go into the city, but for different reasons. Tayii, from the reports Sanii gave us yesterday, it would be helpful if you scouted out the camps that the prisoners are in. Ranor, we need someone to watch for Naibor by the East Gate. Sanii, I know you have to fly low in this fog, low enough to be seen, but if you could make another quick survey of what is going on in the city, we should be better prepared for when Prince Naibor arrives. And, please, all of you be extra careful," the bear needlessly cautioned his friends, knowing that they would be.

"On my way into the city, I'll fly by the gate and let you know if I see any guards or anything else that looks like trouble," the watchful eagle promised her two companions.

"Thank you," the badger said gratefully to his winged friend, and she winked an eye at him in return. "I'm glad this time I get to stay on the ground," he added to the panther beside him.

Flying out of the bell tower, Sanii wheeled slowly around in a circle, waiting for her friends to appear beneath her on the ground. She saw them come out at the back of the old sanctuary, using a door with broken hinges that was stuck half open in the dirt. As she watched, both Ranor and Tayii headed toward the trench that surrounded the city. It provided a natural cover for both of them to travel in. Once they reached the trench in safety, she flew on ahead to make sure there was no danger waiting for them at the East Gate.

The East Gate, like each of the main gates, was built into an arch in the wall between two guard towers. The gate consisted of a heavy iron portcullis that could be lowered or raised in front of the two thick wooden doors. For further protection, the doors were covered with sheets of hammered metal.

Sanii flew down to join Tayii and Ranor near the ramp leading up to the entrance.

"I've checked both of the towers, and I could see nothing. The gate is unguarded, and only the portcullis is down, so you should have no trouble getting into the city," she informed them.

"I will meet you back at Binah," the eagle added over her shoulder as she flew off into the cloud-filled sky.

"Well, let's get going," Tayii said impatiently, looking up at the high towers above her. She had never realized before just how foreboding the city she had grown up in could be.

They climbed together up the bank to the front of the gate, and the badger slipped easily under the portcullis. Tayii followed, but being unable to go under the gate, she had to squeeze herself through the bars.

"What I need is to find a good spot to keep an eye on the road," the badger mused. "Not that I can see much in this fog."

"What about in the guardhouse?" Tayii suggested.

"Worth a try," he agreed, going over to investigate.

The door was slightly open, and after poking his head in and having a look around, he went inside.

"Not bad," he nodded, appraising the situation to the sleek panther that had come in behind him. "I could use the stool to climb up onto the table, and then balance myself against the wall to look out the window. That way I could get a clear view of the road without being seen."

"It's a good strategy," Tayii agreed, "but not very practical for a badger." Smiling to herself, she pictured him balancing awkwardly on his hind legs. "I was thinking more of you lying in the doorway," she explained, and then, taking the opportunity to tease him, she quipped, "In fact, you could probably even stand in the middle of the road. It is not likely that anyone will take much notice of a common badger."

"I'm anything but common," Ranor replied with a snort. Then, looking out the doorway, he added, "You're right, of course. This will do nicely, and you had better get going." But before his feline friend could slip by him, he stopped her to say, "You know that I care for you a great deal. I would be greatly distressed if anything were to happen to you."

"I'll be careful," she said, looking into his eyes, and before he could say anything more, she trotted off down the road, leaving him on duty in the doorway of the guardhouse.

Keeping south of the area surrounding the arena and the sorcerer's temple, the panther continued following the road farther into the East Quarter. She passed the Traveler's Inn and the different trade shops until she turned up a main street that led to the market. This part of the city was a maze of small streets crowded with rows of houses and filled with a variety of merchant shops. Twitching nervously in the dampness, she stopped to check exactly where she was. She knew this part of the neighborhood well, but the emptiness coming from the open doorways, and the debris lying in the laneways, made it seem unfamiliar and uninviting.

Before she went on to the other camps, Tayii planned to visit the quarters of the People's Guard. Located between the market and the arena, this was where Sanii thought the children were being held. Choosing the quickest route she knew of through the back streets, she hurried on her way.

The People's Guard had their main quarters set back from the street in a large building with two levels. Attached at the back of this building were two other sections separated by an open courtyard. One of these sections was used for holding prisoners, and the other was for stabling horses. Surrounding the area was a high stone wall that had an iron fencing around the top. The only way inside the enclosure was through two tall iron gates at the entrance.

As Tayii got closer to the camp, every fiber of her body became tense and alert. Using all of her stalking instincts to make sure that she wasn't seen or heard, she slowly circled the wall, looking for the most inconspicuous place to enter. Over by the stables, Tayii found the perfect place. Next to the wall was the roof to a building, which she hoped by its location was a supply shed. Backing up a bit, she sprang up lightly onto the wall. Then, effortlessly and without making a sound, she leaped over the sharp iron spikes onto the flat tin roof of the building.

The wildcat was just about to jump down into the courtyard when she saw two Daimos guards come out of the building used for prisoners. Engaged in conversation, they walked over in her direction. Flattening herself to the rooftop, she backed away from the edge, hoping they would not see her.

"I've had enough," one of them said angrily, banging the pails he carried loudly together. "Lookin' after horses is bad enough, but those stinkin' children is worse. That bite one of 'em gave me still hurts."

"Shuddup idiot," the other one grumbled. Entering into the stables, they conveniently left the door open so that Tayii, with her panther ears, could easily hear what they were saying.

"Ten of us stuck here on guard duty while everyone else is up at the temple celebratin'," the first one continued, ignoring his companion's obvious disinterest. "Then the subcommander sends us out back to check on things. The troublemakers are all locked up in the prisoners' barracks as usual. Wha'd he expect?"

"I told you to shuddup," the other one replied harshly, clearly annoyed, but his companion kept right on talking.

"Hate them lit'l beggars. I've had it in my mind to poison 'em all," he said with a chuckle. "And kill all these 'orses while I'm at it. I don't care that Necros wants 'em alive for raids on villages."

"And I'd kill you if I had a chance!" the other snarled.

The first just laughed when he heard this. "Go ahead," he baited. "Try it. I'm only twice your size, and I'd snap your neck like a twig."

By the momentary silence, Tayii could tell that the other Daimos had wisely backed down. After finishing with the horses, they came back out of the barn, with the big Daimos still loudly voicing his opinions all the way back to the main building.

Once more the panther princess crept to the front of the supply shed. She was preparing to jump down a second time when another sound stopped her. This time she could hear a wagon approaching the camp from the north. As Tayii listened, she saw a wagon break through the foggy haze and roll to a stop close to the end of the shed. She froze to the spot with her ears flat back. Her heart thumped wildly, pumping adrenaline through her veins, and she tensed her feline muscles, ready for action.

Fearing the worst, Tayii was relieved when she heard two voices in quiet conversation. Wanting to see who it was, she sneaked in a crouched position over to the fence. Looking down, she was surprised to see Prince Naibor.

The prince had taken his mask off and was relaxing in the back of the wagon, talking with what appeared to be a tattered gray-haired woman. "It is getting late. I'm glad this is the last place we have to deliver Necros's precious cargo," Naibor told her with a wide grin.

"You made a lot of Daimos happy," the woman commented with an abrupt little laugh.

Naibor nodded, but his mind was on meeting with the animals and defeating the sorcerer. "After we finish here, I will be ready to meet with Necros," he said with nervous bravado. "I wonder what the animals would say if they knew what they were waiting for."

"You have done what you have set out to do," she replied, looking up at him with her eyes shining proudly.

"I still have a hard time believing that we fooled them—that the disguise worked."

"There was no reason for it not to work; they weren't expecting any treachery," she added encouragingly.

"Well, that little gift you gave the animals should hopefully put an end to this charade," the prince said, hoping she didn't know how frightened he really was.

Tayii, from on top of the roof, couldn't believe her ears. Naibor had betrayed them again! He was working for Necros, and they had planned something horrible for her and her friends at Binah. He had to be stopped! Springing down over the wall, the panther landed on the prince, knocking him to the floor of the wagon.

The horse lurched forward in fright, and Edra threw herself at the reins before the frightened animal took off at a gallop with them in tow. It took all her strength, leaning back with the reins wrapped around her arms, to keep the stallion from bolting.

"Naibor, you traitor!" she screamed at him, and in her fury, her voice broke into a vicious snarl. "I will do whatever I have to do to stop you," she hissed. She raised one of her powerful paws in the air and held it threateningly over his head with the scythe-shaped claws extended.

"Tayii! Don't!" Naibor pleaded, recognizing her voice despite the panther's anger. Trying to ward off the blow, the prince raised his arms in front of his face.

"Tell me what the animals are waiting for," she demanded. "What plan have you worked out with the sorcerer against us?"

"There is no plan," Naibor gasped as he felt the nails from her remaining paw rip through his clothes and into his skin. "We were pretending to work for Necros so we could help the prisoners. Right now Captain Regg and Captain Zai should be helping them escape through the West Gate."

"I don't believe you," she growled, her tail lashing from side to side. "What about the Daimos guards?"

"I have a Daimos mask inside my robe. I wear it so no one recognizes me. We were delivering alcohol to the guards as a diversion," he explained, the weight of her body making it difficult for him to breathe. "Tayii, you've got to believe me!"

"Please, my lady, he's telling you the truth," Edra added earnestly, still holding tightly to the reigns.

"Show me the mask!" Tayii ordered, getting off the prince just enough so that he could reach inside his robe.

"Here." Hoping it would be enough to convince her, Naibor pulled the death mask out and showed it to her.

Tayii was about to release the prince when she heard the strong flap of wings. Looking up, she saw Sanii land on the iron fence above them.

"Tayii, what are you doing?" the eagle asked, keeping her voice low as a reminder to everyone else to keep their voices down. "The prince is on our side."

"I'm not so sure," the panther said, showing Naibor her sharp set of teeth and laying her small, round ears flat against the sides of her head. "Did you see any prisoners being helped to escape by the West Gate?" She was glad to have some help with her dilemma.

"Yes. Please just let him up," Sanii said, and Tayii allowed the prince to get up. He winced from the cuts the large cat's claws had made in his chest.

"I am sorry, Naibor. Are you all right?" Tayii asked with concern, backing up to give him some more room.

"I could be worse," Naibor told her truthfully, pressing his shirt against the deep scratches in an attempt to stop the bleeding. "But you two had better get out of sight when we enter the camp to deliver these bottles. This is my last stop before going on to Binah. I was hoping, with Edra's help, to somehow sneak the children out of here."

Looking at the panther and eagle, the prince wondered if there was any way they could help to speed up his plans. Briefly explaining to the newcomers what had happened at each of the other camps, the prince realized this was to be the greatest challenge yet.

"I think I may have a solution," Sanii said hopefully, before outlining her proposal to the others.

Naibor thought her plan was a little bold, but he also knew that any plan they came up with would require taking risks. It was their lack of time that put their plan in action.

Tayii leaped back over the wall, and Sanii flew along with her to further investigate the camp. Prince Naibor and Edra saw them off and then brought the wagon around to one side of the front gate, where they would not be seen. Helping the servant woman down from the wagon, the prince gave Edra a nod of encouragement while handing her the last set of keys.

The horse nickered quietly while she unlocked the gate and slipped inside. Running as fast as she could beside the shrubbery along the wall, Edra headed toward the jail. As she neared the building where the prisoners were held, she was met by the panther and the eagle.

"All the guards are in the main building," Tayii happily reported.

Edra, a little winded from her run, nodded her kerchiefed head in reply. Finding the key to open the lock, Edra went in while Tayii and Sanii waited for her outside.

As Edra walked down the row of cells in the dreary light coming through the windows, her heart went out to the children when she saw their miserable faces looking out at her.

"Who are you?" one of the boys asked. "You're not like them."

"That's right. I'm not like them," she said, giving the children a warm smile as she tried to push her displaced hair back from her face. "My name is Edra, and I'm here to help you escape and get you safely out of the city. But first I need five very brave children to help me play a game against those who have locked you up in here. Now, who wants to help me?" To her surprise, almost all the children put up a hand. "Well, who is the oldest then?"

"I am," said the same boy who had first spoken to her.

His size belied his age. Edra had a good look at the small boy. He had a thin frame and large, serious eyes set in an impish face framed by a shaggy mane of thick, dark hair. Despite his appearance, Edra felt him to be sincere.

"Good," Edra replied, pleased she had gotten this far. "And what is your name?"

"Venn," he told her.

"Venn, I need you to choose, very carefully, five of your bravest and fastest friends for an important job. The safety of all these children depends on it. Can you do it?"

Venn nodded and then picked out three boys and two girls close to his own age. After telling the rest of the children to wait a little longer and to trust Venn and his friends, Edra let the six children out of their cells and led them to the back door.

Stopping for a moment before the door, the kindly servant woman explained to the children, "The cruel sorcerer that has taken over our city has turned some of my friends into wild animals. They are waiting for us outside. But I want you to know that they would not hurt any of you, so you don't have to be afraid when you see them."

The children promised her that they would not be afraid, so she opened the door, and together they went outside. It took only a few moments for the animals and the children to become acquainted, and then they all gathered around the servant woman to discuss the tasks they were going to perform. Eager to play their part outlined in the plan, the children suppressed their laughter and fidgeted until Edra sent them on their way.

While Venn and his friends headed for the main building, Edra let the remaining children out of the prison. They followed her as quickly and quietly as they could to the front gate, with the bigger children helping the smaller ones. Once there, the prince helped load everyone onto the wagon. Tayii hid so the children would not be frightened any more than they might already be, and Sanii flew to the top of the wall so she could keep watch over the children until they all made it safely to Naibor. When the last of the children had gotten into the wagon, the eagle flew over to the main building to signal the other six that it was time.

* * *

The heavyset subcommander was sitting at a table in the large kitchen, picking his teeth, when one of the Daimos hurried in to give him the bad news. One of the children had escaped. The subcommander was a hot-tempered man and was easily agitated. This news was the very type of thing to start him on one of his raving rampages.

"What do you mean one of the children has escaped?" the subcommander demanded, his round face reddening as he got up and rushed into the hallway behind the one who had brought him the news.

"I saw one run by me when I was … Look! There goes another one!" he shouted, pointing to the end of the hall by the stairs.

"Another one?" The subcommander roared, clenching his large hands into fists. "Well, get after them!"

The Daimos obeyed by running down the hall after the child while the fuming subcommander went to find out what was going on and to get some help. Charging up the stairs at the opposite end of the building, he burst into the living quarters where the remaining Daimos were relaxing. They immediately all jumped to their feet when they saw what kind of a mood he was in.

"I've just had a report that some of the children have escaped," the subcommander informed the shocked faces before him through clenched teeth while the veins in his broad neck visibly pulsed. "What do you know about it?"

"We just took a head count," one of the Daimos said, pointing to his partner for verification, "And they were all locked in their rooms."

"You two," the subcommander barked, turning to the two

Daimos that Tayii had seen from the supply shed roof. "What about outside?"

"All locked up tight," the big one answered, producing the keys so he could not be accused of having lost them.

"Well, that doesn't explain why one just ran past me, does it?" the Daimos in charge asked, his face making him look as though he were about to explode. As if on cue, Venn stuck his head in the room and stuck his tongue out at them.

All but one of the Daimos rushed toward the door after the boy. One had to stay behind to help the subcommander, who in a fit of outrage had collapsed onto the couch, gasping for water.

"I'm going to beat them black-and-blue for this," the subcommander choked out as the Daimos handed him the glass of water before leaving to join the others in the chase.

The subcommander tried to remain calm as he listened to shouts of "There's one!" and "Over here!"

"What's going on!" he bellowed, hearing the occasional crash and thud along with the sound of running footsteps, but no one answered. "Why haven't you caught them yet?" he yelled, but then, as he listened, everything became quiet.

He called out a few of the guards' names, but none of them replied. "Where could the idiots be?" he grumbled under his breath, hoisting himself up off the couch.

He went to the door and looked out into the hallway, but he could see and hear nothing. In his desperation, he tried using his mind to call the Daimos, but he knew it was no use. Necros had closed down the link between them.

Wandering angrily down the corridor, the subcommander went back down the stairs to the main floor. Peeking into this room and that, he searched for some sign of both the Daimos and the children. He had almost returned to the kitchen, where this whole fiasco had started, when he heard a low whistle behind him. Turning his bulk around surprisingly quickly, the subcommander saw the same impertinent boy who had stuck his tongue out at them. The boy was standing in the hall just two doors down from him.

"You!" the subcommander bellowed, storming down the hallway after the boy, who laughed at him and then ran away. "Come back here! Stop!"

Venn ran past the stairs and down to the end of the hall, where he stopped for the moment before entering a door on his left.

"Ha! Got you now," the commanding Daimos shouted triumphantly to the boy. "That's a dead end. You need keys to get out the back door."

Following closely on the boy's heels, the subcommander chased Venn through the doorway and into the first open jail cell, where he cornered him. He grabbed the thin boy by the shoulders and shook him. "Where are the other children and the Daimos?" the large man demanded, his eyes bulging out from his face in his fury.

The Daimos who were locked in the other cells called out to the subcommander to warn him, but they were too late. They had lost their chance. At the sound of an animal's angry cry, they knew the panther they had all previously faced had run into the cell behind the commanding Daimos and trapped him.

Seeing the muscled panther preparing to pounce on him, with her teeth and claws bared, the subcommander tried hiding behind the boy in a feeble attempt to shield himself. Then he got what he thought was an even better idea.

Throwing Venn away from him, straight at the carnivore, he cried out, "Eat the boy!"

Venn veered away from the large cat's snarling jaws, moving quickly over to the side of the cell to get out of the way.

"Get the boy, kitty cat," the subcommander purred, watching in frustration as the boy slipped easily out of the cell and past the snarling beast. "He's the one you want, not me. Go get him!" But at the subcommander's slightest movement, the panther charged forward and took a swipe at him—just missing.

Flattening himself against the wall in fright, the subcommander was confronted with an even greater horror. The boy was about to swing close the door and lock him in the cell with the panther. The subcommander, with wide eyes, pleaded with the boy and shook his head slowly back and forth. The boy, with an air of satisfaction, just shook his head in return. Then, with another hiss and a growl, the panther lunged at the terrified subcommander. The commanding Daimos closed his eyes and gritted his teeth, awaiting his imminent death.

When nothing happened, he slowly opened his eyes to find the panther standing calmly beside the boy outside of the cell. With the push of one hand, Venn shut the door to the cell with a clang while he playfully scratched the panther behind her ears with the other.

"What's going on here?" the subcommander shouted, his nerve returning when he realized he had been tricked.

Edra, coming down the hall, counted along the way. "Ten!" she proudly announced. "That's all of them then. Very good work. And you are sure they can't get out?"

"No ma'am," Venn replied with a good-natured grin. "Even if they have keys, the locks only work from the outside, and the bars are too close together for them to be able to reach out and open the doors that way. I tried it once when they left a key in the door, and even I couldn't open it."

"Good!" Edra said with a satisfied smile, and leaving the prisoners alone, they went outside to join their friends and make further plans.

There were still some children locked up in the main building, so while Venn and his friends went to set them free, Edra went to the stables to hitch up another wagon. Not long afterward, they all met at the front gate.

"Edra, I'm going to leave you in charge of the children as we planned," Naibor said, covering the horses' hooves with the special socks the guard used when they wanted to make as little noise as possible. "I have got to go to Binah with Sanii and Tayii." He strode over to the woman and gave her a large hug, almost pulling her out of the wagon as he did so.

"Aii will protect us," she said with a reassuring nod of her head to the prince. After checking to make sure all the children were settled, she signaled to Venn, who was driving the other wagon, and they started on their way toward the West Gate.

"That's strange," Naibor heard Sanii mutter from where she sat on the wall behind him.

"What's strange?" Naibor asked, turning to look up at her.

"I just saw a raven that was flying straight for us, but when it saw us, it veered away to the right as if it didn't want to be seen," she explained.

The fog had retreated into the low-hanging clouds, which seemed to hang like a damp shroud over the city. Looking up, Naibor could just make out a dark spot against the gray clouds, flying toward the arena

"Sanii!" Naibor called out urgently. "That raven! It's going to tell the sorcerer about the escaping prisoners! He is a servant of Necros."

"Don't worry; I'll stop it," she said, and in a flurry of wingbeats, the eagle hurried after the disappearing raven.

CHAPTER 21

During the rest of that night, Taila waited sleeplessly in the private chamber of Necros, her mind raging through a storm of emotions. Time seemed to go by both torturously slow and frightfully fast. She could not believe that she was about to become the wife of such a repulsive and terrifying sorcerer. How could she have consented to such a thing, even for the lives of twenty people?

Taila thought about escaping, running, and hiding, leaving Amuron forever, but she knew she couldn't abandon her home or the people she loved. Her whole reason for agreeing to marry the sorcerer was so she could hopefully find a way to help some of them. Taila wanted to save twenty people from being sacrificed, but she did not know how she would choose from among them. She wondered if she would even have the strength to stand in front of them as the new bride of Necros. In her desperation, she briefly thought about taking her own life and about trying to kill the sorcerer, but she knew she was incapable of doing both of these things.

This was all Prince Naibor's doing. It was his fault she was in this mess. How could she have been so foolish to have believed him and even cared for him? He was the one who deserved to die, not the people of Amuron. Taila hated him. She would rather marry the dreaded Necros than still be in love with the prince. She wished it would all be over with so she wouldn't have to face it anymore. She had to stop thinking about it. It was too horrible. Utterly exhausted, Taila laid her head down on the table in front of her and closed her eyes, trying to keep the coming events from her mind.

"Lord Aii," she prayed, "Please help stop this marriage from happening, or give me the strength to endure it so that I may help as many people of Amuron as possible."

The hour of the ceremony eventually arrived. The small carved clock in the chamber announced each passing hour with the strike of the chime, almost as if it had been counting out every moment for that very purpose.

The door to the underground room flew suddenly open, forced abruptly aside to admit the floating sorcerer. "All is prepared," he announced, landing close to his intended bride, and to Taila it sounded as if he were proclaiming her doom.

Standing forlornly in front of a large gilded mirror hanging on the wall over a small washing table, Taila risked looking at his reflection in the mirror. He looked even fouler than before. The look of desire in his eyes made Taila feel naked and defiled, and she shuddered when he held out his hand to her. "May I escort you to the top of the dais?"

When her knees threatened to buckle, Taila thought that the sorcerer might need to carry her. Without answering, she allowed herself to be led out of the chamber and up the steps to the top of the platform.

Volkas, the leader of the Ix people, and several Ix women were there when they arrived, as well as a large group of Daimos forming a ring around the top step of the dais. Necros's throne had been removed and replaced with a gilded black table. In front of the table, a circle of white powder had been poured onto the floor of the dais, and extra lanterns had been brought up to brighten the area of the ceremony.

"Volkas will have the honor of officiating over the marriage," Necros explained, going over to speak privately to the short potbellied man who grinned horribly at her. The Ix women giggled and whispered secretly among themselves.

"Let us begin the ceremony," Necros said with triumph. "Prepare the bride."

Two of the woman approached Taila and covered her hair with a black cloth and her face with a black lace veil.

"You make a beautiful bride, my dear," Necros said approvingly, looking at her indecently. "All dressed in black and red," he added wickedly, referring the red robe she had put on the night before as part of her disguise, as if she had dressed to please him.

One of the Ix woman started beating on a drum, and she was guided by another into the white circle, where Necros joined her. Taila watched, biting her lip under her veil, while Volkas went to the table. A golden basin and a towel, a knife, a leather thong, and a golden goblet were on the table.

The squat leader sprinkled some powder into the basin and then he brought it over to them with the towel over one arm. "First we will wash our hands," Necros explained.

The sorcerer's soulless eyes watched her, waiting for her to obey. Dipping her hands into the chilled water, Taila felt a cold shiver course up her spine. Seeking to placate the sorcerer, she quickly rinsed her hands and removed them from the basin, drying them on the provided towel. Barely taking his eyes off her, Necros followed her actions.

"Next we will slice our wrists and have our arms tied together," Necros explained while Volkas went to the table and gathered up the knife and the thong after replacing the bowl and towel. "This will symbolize our joining, made complete by the mixing of our blood. The Ix people will then dance around us, giving us their prayers of blessing. While they do this, they will try to pull us apart, but the thong will hold us together, symbolizing the strong relationship we two will have. And after we have proven that we cannot be pulled apart, we will drink from the cup to celebrate our joining. To end the ceremony, Volkas will untie us, and then you will be my wife."

Taking the knife from the Ix leader, Necros held the handle out to her and said, "Here, you may cut me first."

Taila's hands trembled as she reached to grab the long, slender knife. The sharp blade flashed coldly in the dim light when she touched the handle, but she couldn't will her shaking hands to pick it up.

"I can't," she said, not daring to look up at the sorcerer.

"But you must," he replied. Taking her hand in his, Necros forced her fingers around the handle. Then, with his hand still firmly around hers, he placed the blade against his flesh. He was just about to push down and make a cut when his two silent specters appeared holding a dead raven in their hands.

"How could this be?" he thundered in an outburst of anger, crushing Taila's fingers against the knife handle with his powerful hand before he let go of her.

"Elbanor—dead?" he shouted. "Show me!" He hurried over to the Daimos that held Elbanor.

Taking the dead bird from them, he carefully inspected the body. Then, as he passed his hand over the bird and spoke words that Taila could not hear, the body of Elbanor disappeared and was gone forever.

"You deceived me!" he exclaimed while turning his attention violently back upon Taila, who had fallen to her knees in pain and bewilderment. "The marriage ceremony is off until after the sacrifice," he announced, struggling to get his anger back under control. "I can have no further distractions until that time. I should have known that with the coming of their death so close, the people of Amuron would make one last attempt to stop me. I should have known, but my thoughts were elsewhere. I was not thinking of hate or death, and what these things have taught me.

"But I think you knew that, didn't you?" he said, still speaking to Taila from where he stood next to the black servants. "That is why you consented to be my wife. I would be foolishly flattering myself to think otherwise. You thought you could take my mind off the city with your beauty and your charm, while they plotted and planned against me." Darkness and hate spilled from his eyes as he looked at her, preparing for her torment.

Suddenly Taila could feel invisible fingers wrap around her slender throat and squeeze in a grip of death. Pulling the veil and black cloth from her head, she tried to grab at the unseen hand, but it was useless. She couldn't breathe. The blood throbbed in her neck, and her head began to pound. Falling forward onto her hands, she gasped for air, but it was no use. The room blurred as she fought for consciousness.

She heard a voice that seemed to come from far away. "For your treachery, I deny you the freedom of the twenty people I offered you." Then, as she collapsed to the floor, she was released.

"You will pay for this later," Necros said savagely, watching with satisfaction while she gulped down big breaths of air.

Taila briefly felt the icy hands of Naibor's former guards grab her before blackness finally engulfed her.

Reestablishing his contact with the Daimos, Necros realized what had taken place in the city while he had been concentrating on the wedding ceremony. Responding immediately, the ruthless sorcerer called on the many Daimos he had working for him in preparation for the sacrifice at the temple. Giving them orders, he mentally told them what he wanted to be done, and they quickly obeyed.

"The fools! To think they could escape me so easily," Necros commented coldly to the Ix leader, who stood grinning wildly beside him while his people busily removed the wedding items from the dais and replaced the sorcerer's throne. "I have some surprises for them, and for Prince Naibor, but I must be ready for when the prince comes to me." He took a seat. "Take the girl and the high king to the sacrifice area," the lord of death calmly instructed his two wraith servants, who remained standing beside the unconscious figure. "That will set the stage for when the prince arrives. Then, my dear

Volkas, you will have the pleasure of witnessing my revenge over this kingdom, and afterward all surrounding it shall be mine!"

* * *

Heading off in the opposite direction the wagons carrying the children had gone, the prince ran along the streets at a good pace with the panther beside him. They had not gone far, however, when Naibor decided to make a short stop.

"This cloak—it's slowing me down." He took it off and threw it and the mask into a heap by a doorway. "That's better," he said, taking in several breaths of air before they started off again.

The winged princess had already been to the East Gate by the time they arrived, so Ranor was waiting for them on the road. Tayii surprised the badger by greeting him with a tender lick on his snout.

"By the way," Ranor said to Naibor, watching while the prince turned the lever to open the portcullis, "the raven is dead. Sanii said she caught him and he died in the struggle, so for now the sorcerer doesn't know about the escaped prisoners."

Naibor acknowledged the news with a nod of his head. He had no words to say, knowing in his heart that Elbanor, his tutor, the renowned court historian, had already lost his life long ago to the evil sorcerer.

After Naibor opened the gate, they hurried off together down the ramp and then back along the inside of the trench toward Binah.

Binah was the oldest known temple of Aii, built many years before the city of Amuron. In times past, it had been a haven for weary travelers, and in troubled times it had been a refuge for farmers and their families from outlying areas. Now it had been abandoned for the luxuries and protection given by the city, but it was still a sacred place to some who knew of its significance in the earlier history of the kingdom.

Stepping into the temple past the broken door, Naibor followed the panther and the badger through the back of the building to the sanctuary, where the others were waiting. Naibor felt a little awkward seeing the animals all together for the first time since their transformation in the wine cellar. Looking at them, he wondered for a moment what it must be like, but he couldn't imagine.

"I'm sorry to have kept you waiting, but I—" Naibor began.

"I know, Sanii told us," Baynor told him, still unsure of whether or not he could completely trust the prince. "But there is still a lot to be done to free the city of Amuron from the sorcerer."

"I agree, and that is why I am here," Naibor replied. "Do you know what is to be done now?"

In response to Naibor's question, a streak of glowing white appeared and grew in size until Orilian stood towering above them, filling the sanctuary with his brilliant light.

"Prince Naibor, son of the high king of Amuron, you are the one that can answer that question," the frightening figure solemnly told him. "Have you the items that were requested of you?"

Naibor looked over at the animals, and the bear brought him the parcel. He opened it and showed the items to the radiant messenger.

"Place them on the altar," Orilian instructed, moving back so Naibor had room to do so.

Orilian raised his arms toward the heavens, and a sword in a finely filigreed scabbard appeared in his hands. Drawing the sword from its sheath by its hilt of gold, the shimmering blade reflected the light of its owner. Returning the sword to its scabbard, Orilian placed it on top of the three items Naibor had previously put on the altar. He held his hands over the objects, and the entire room was momentarily filled by a flash of blinding white. Then, as the light faded, even Orilian seemed to dim. Lying on the table was a dark scabbard, and next to it was the Stone of Wisdom, which appeared unchanged. The sorcerer's belongings had vanished.

"Prince Naibor, you have gone against the Lord Aii and invited evil into this city. By using your royal blood in a covenant with a sorcerer, the people and city of Amuron have become enslaved, and Amuron has become a foul place. The laws of Aii have decreed that you are the only one who can save the people and city of Amuron, by breaking the bond of the blood covenant. To do this, you must use this sword to destroy the sorcerer, but you have not much time. Lives have already been lost, and the sorcerer will claim the lives of many more if you delay in your task. Be warned! If you fail, this land and all surrounding it will be cursed, and all life in it will eventually be destroyed."

Naibor looked at the floor for a moment, not having anything to say, but he knew what he must do. Walking with purposeful strides over to the altar, Naibor picked up the sword and slid it out of its accompanying scabbard. Tainted by the sorcerer's foul objects, the sword now appeared a dull gray, but the blade was sharp, and it was lightweight and easy to handle. After slipping the blade back into the sheath, Naibor attached it to the belt of the black guard's uniform he had been wearing underneath his robe. Turning from the altar, he took another moment to look into the eyes of each of the animals to silently promise them redemption. Then, with a grim look of determination on his face, he left the sanctuary.

Baynor, not wanting to miss the opportunity a second time, quickly asked Orilian before he left them, "Do you know if we can be returned to our former selves?"

"I do not know the will of Aii concerning this," the messenger replied, but their disappointment caused him to add, "Faithful servants of Aii, take heart. Our Lord is great. He hears your prayers and knows the desire of your hearts."

Then, as his light began to fade, he took the high king's amulet from the table, saying, "There is another who has need of this."

* * *

Amon awoke to the sounds of a rooster crowing outside his window, along with the deep vibrations of Bartok's voice bursting into song. Lying in his cot, the youth smiled, thinking that because of the noise of the rooster crowing and Bartok singing the whole mountainside should now be awake.

The door to the cottage opened just wide enough for Bartok to poke his head through. "Time to get up, little one," the giant gently said to him. "A working man cannot spend his time in bed, especially when there is work to be done."

"All right," Amon sighed, getting up with a yawn and a stretch. "Just don't send the dogs in like you did yesterday."

Amon had spent two days with his gracious host, and he had found him to be both entertaining and informative. The youth had learned from the giant all about the life of a shepherd and what it was like to live in the mountains, and he was surprised to find that he enjoyed the solemnity of his surroundings.

After he had washed and dressed and had eaten the rest of the porridge left in a pot hanging over the fire, Bartok entered the cottage, his face even more aglow than usual.

"Come, little one! Orilian has been here, and it is time for us to go."

"Orilian, the messenger of Aii?" the youth asked with amazement, struggling to get his boots on. "Where are we going?"

"We go to prepare for battle" was Bartok's astounding reply.

"Battle? What battle?" a confused Amon asked the giant as he grabbed up his traveling cloak and ran out of the cottage after his big friend.

Bartok's normally relaxed face was set with purpose and conviction. "The battle against the evil that has taken over the city of Amuron," he answered gravely, going to the front of the barn, where the great horse Orros was saddled and ready to ride.

Giving the youth a reassuring grin, Bartok swung himself up onto the horse. "We will ride together," he said, reaching down to help Amon up onto the saddle behind him. "Now I will take you to the place I told you about when we first met."

With a quiet word from his master, Orros went around the cottage and then up the steep mountainside behind it. Amon felt awkward and uncomfortable bouncing on top of the horse's back. His long legs seemed ridiculously short for such a large beast, but he had no fear of sliding off with Bartok's arm within reach.

From the top of Mount Rosh, Orros took them down the other side, heading in a southward direction. By midmorning their path was blocked by a massive wall of rock and dirt that had slid down from the opposite sides of two mountains.

"Is there a way through?" Amon asked, looking up at the imposing barrier before them, sensing that was their intention.

"There is for you," Bartok answered mysteriously, and riding up beside the wall, he urged the horse slowly forward. "If we look carefully, we will find the opening. Otherwise your eyes trick you into thinking that there is no way through."

A small opening appeared at the middle of the wall between where the tapered ends of the two rubble mounds crossed in front of each other. From any other perspective, the two piles of mountain debris gave the impression of being one great, continuous wall.

Bartok guided Orros through the narrow opening, turning the horse sharply to the left around one wall and then to the right around the next. On the other side of the landslide stretched a long, still valley filled with short grass but little else. Ordinarily Amon would have found a hidden valley nestled between mountains a pleasant place to be, but there was something strange and unnaturally quiet about this valley. The booming silence echoed around them. Nothing moved, almost as if the entire valley were holding its breath. Amon looked back at Bartok apprehensively, feeling the hair on his skin began to rise.

"The valley you see before you is the valley of the Sleeping Lyoai," Bartok informed Amon with excitement shining in his eyes. "This is the special place I told you of. Very few people know of its existence. But you, Amon"—Bartok placed his large, weathered hand proudly on the youth's shoulder—"have an important part to play in its significance."

Bartok's words had a strange calming effect on the youth. The nervousness he had felt all morning in his stomach was gone, and he was suddenly filled with a building sense of anticipation.

They rode on for a while into the heart of the valley, veering off a little to one side when they reached the first of a series of old, worn rocks lying partially under the ground.

Stopping Orros and dismounting, Bartok asked his companion, "Do you know what this is?"

Amon jumped down from the horse and looked closely at the broken slabs and lines of the large stones, which were half hidden by the dirt and grass. "It was a building of some sort," he concluded after recognizing that the rocks created a pattern.

Bartok nodded in affirmation. "It was a temple. A long time ago, before the kingdom of Amuron existed, this valley was lived in by a people who worshipped Aii in this temple. They were a wise and just people who reveled in the glory of the goodness of life. One day a warrior tribe came to their land and challenged them to a battle. The warrior king made an oath with the people of this valley, telling them that they had three days to decide whether they would fight or agree to be taken captive as slaves.

"The people of this valley always fasted and prayed before they fought in a battle. The challenging king knew this and used it against them. Breaking his oath, the warrior king attacked the people of this valley with his armies before the third day, killing every man, woman, and child while they were unarmed and still at prayer. The warriors collected everything of value they could find and then celebrated their victory by destroying this temple.

"The spirits of the people killed here cried out to the Lord Aii for justice. They asked to stay in this world until their deaths could be avenged. Aii granted that their spirits would then sleep in this valley until an appointed time when they would be called upon to fight against a foe that no man could fight."

Amon stared wide-eyed at the temple remains before him, and an unconscious shiver ran up the length of his spine.

"What can you tell me about the enemy Amuron faces?" Bartok asked the youth, coming up beside him.

Amon took a moment to think, trying to piece together all that he knew about the situation before he answered. He remembered clearly the night of Prince Naibor's betrayal, and the vision of his poor brother as a prisoner. He also remembered seeing the black cloud approaching the city of Amuron when he was escaping. "The city has been taken over by a powerful sorcerer—one that has the power to control the evil spirits of the dead."

The giant looked earnestly at the youth for a moment before he said, "The Lyoai are the spirits of the followers of Aii. They are the only people who can fight against the Daimos—the evil spirits that the sorcerer called to take control of the city of Amuron.

"The Sleeping Lyoai are the spirits of the people who were killed here in this valley. Their spirits would not rest until they could avenge their deaths, and so they lie here waiting for the justice promised them long ago by the Lord Aii.

"That day has come, Amon. That is why we are here," the giant told him with emotion in his deep voice. "We must awaken the Sleeping Lyoai!"

Amon's heart pounded wildly in his chest as he thought of the two spirit armies. "How do we awaken them?" the youth asked with his voice barely above a whisper.

"Orilian has given me these two things," Bartok said, drawing the items carefully out of a pouch he carried. "This horn is for me to call them with, and the Stone of Wisdom is for you to guide them with. They will follow whoever wears it."

"The high king's amulet!" Amon exclaimed. "But why are you giving it to me when you could guide them much better?"

"It is not my battle, little one. It is your city and your people who are in danger. But it is my privilege as keeper of the gates to awaken them, and that I will now do. Are you ready?"

Amon was not at all sure he was ready, but he nodded anyway.

"You have a brave heart, little one," Bartok told him softly, and then he gave Amon the Stone of Wisdom to put on. "Trust that the amulet will give you the knowledge you need to take the right paths safely back to Amuron."

Holding it in his hands for a moment, Amon noticed how clear and brilliant the Stone of Wisdom shone in its center. Closing his eyes, he took a deep breath before putting the amulet on over his head. Opening his eyes, he was surprised. He expected to feel different, but instead he felt resolute and calm.

"Now you are ready for battle," Bartok concluded, and lifting the horn to his lips, the imposing giant blew a strong, unwavering note.

The note was answered in echo after echo off the surrounding mountainsides.

A strong wind rushed through the valley, breaking the stillness. Looking about him, Amon noticed the valley was no longer empty. Spread out before him was a silent army of transparent figures dressed in their armor for battle and seated on horseback. Amon could see their swords and spears and helmets gleam dimly like small flickers of light seen from a long way off. They sat as they should have sat years before, waiting to defend themselves and their lands against the warrior tribe who betrayed and slaughtered them. They looked at Amon with their grim faces, waiting to do battle, but strangely Amon found he was not afraid.

"I will need to ride Orros," Amon pointed out, and Bartok, without objection, helped him into the saddle of the great horse.

Urging Orros forward, Amon lifted the amulet high before speaking to the spirits surrounding him. "My people have need of your army. They are suffering at the hands of a sorcerer and his army of Daimos—an army they cannot fight against but you can. The Lord Aii has allowed me to wear this amulet as a sign to you that in following me you will find the justice that you have long awaited."

In answer to his words, he heard the echo of horns once again, but this time Amon knew it was not Bartok who had caused the horns to blow. The Lyoai army was now his to command. The formidable army parted before the youth, creating a passage for him to ride through.

When he reached the other end of the valley, Amon turned back to wave at the giant standing far behind him. For a moment he thought he saw the Lyoai woman and children standing among the temple ruins, but they were not there for long, and Amon was not really sure he had seen them.

The giant, however, was solid enough, and after waving his farewell, the youth gripped the horse's mane and saddle tight.

Leaning slightly forward in the saddle, Amon cried out, "All speed, Orros!" Needing no more encouragement, the stallion charged forward. The silent army closed ranks, following Amon in a desperate ride down the mountainside.

CHAPTER 22

Prince Naibor walked up the short road that led to the main entrance of the arena. He could see the hideous temple before him through the opening of the broken-down gate. Once again the portcullis over the gaping entrance to the temple was open, beckoning him to come inside.

Somehow knowing he would not find Necros in his throne room, the prince headed toward the competitor's entrance at the back of the arena. Going through the rear entrance, Naibor was glad to see that his instincts had been right. The prince took a moment to calm his nerves, attempting to straighten out his appearance as best he could. He wanted to appear confident and prepared when he stood before the sorcerer.

Here, at the back of the temple, Necros had built a large open theater for his nightly ceremonies. Tiered seats supported by square columns surrounded the area. In the middle of the theater were four square stone pillars, standing at the corners of a rectangular base made of blackstone. The pillars were covered with inscriptions and held large metal wells for burning oil. Between these four pillars lay two stone sacrifice tables, spaced some distance apart.

Prince Naibor could see Necros from where he stood hidden behind the tiered seats. The sorcerer was standing at the head of one sacrifice table, and the Ix leader, Volkas, was standing at the other. They each held a knife poised over the heart of their intended victim.

"Necros!" Naibor shouted out, challenging the sorcerer as he came out into the open. The prince drew his sword.

"Naibor, my dear fellow, I was expecting you," Necros informed him grandly. "Two of your loved ones are waiting here for you," he added, motioning with his free hand to those lying on the tables.

Moving forward so he could see who Necros was planning to sacrifice, Prince Naibor hid his dismay when he saw Taila and his father lying on the tables. Even though the sorcerer had paralyzed their bodies with a spell, Naibor could tell by their eye movement that they were both conscious.

"I've come to destroy you, Necros, and put an end to what you have done," the prince announced to his foe, trying to keep his anger under control while raising his sword again.

"Of course you have," the evil one continued, baiting the prince. "But before you do, consider this: if you kill me, then Volkas will kill Taila, the woman I believe you love; but if you rescue Taila, then your father will die. You now know, of course, that I have revived him from the original spell he was under."

The sorcerer paused, relishing Naibor's dilemma as he looked from one table to the other, unable to choose between his father and Taila. "Oh, and I think you should also know that the prisoners you so bravely sought to free from the city have walked into a trap and so serve as a sacrifice to me anyway. Right now they are being miserably slaughtered by an arm of Ix people who were coming up the West Road on their way to the sacrifice. Ironic, isn't it, that those coming to witness the deaths of the people of Amuron get to lend a hand in their destruction."

The loss Naibor felt at these words made his heart heavy, and his hesitation to act fed the sorcerer's hunger for vengeance.

"Knowing that, you will now die!" the lord of the dark arts said with finality, spitting out a spell that made his face distort when he spoke the deadly words.

The prince felt a wall of heat hit him, but then it was gone! The sword in his hand burst suddenly into hot orange flames that leaped from the sword and flew with great speed back toward the sorcerer.

The sorcerer screamed and gasped for a moment, dealing with the pain. His entire body was engulfed by the burning flames. Using his sorcery, Necros fought with the deadly fire. When he gained control, the cruel flames diminished and became nothing more than an outline around his body. Then, with victory sizzling in his eyes, they were gone. The black sorcerer, however, was weakened by this attack, and the knife that both he and Volkas held splintered and fell to the ground in pieces.

A look of surprise crossed the sorcerer's face, followed by a look of outrage. Summoning the strength of his power, the lord of darkness changed in form as he grew in size, becoming a raging storm of wind and black clouds. Rising up into the air, the menacing clouds moved in a churning mass toward the prince.

The hot wind whipped Naibor's face and tore at the clothes on his body. Looking up at the dark cloud, the prince saw, with horror, two large eyes staring down at him. They were the sorcerer's eyes, and they were lit with the burning light of an eerie orange glow emanating from the middle of the storm.

An orange liquid began to fall from the foul cloud in big drops of rain. Naibor watched as a drop of the glowing liquid hit the ground, scorching the grass black. A drop fell onto his arm, and he cried out in pain when it burned through the cloth of his shirt and into his skin. Naibor dropped his sword and used his arms to protect his head from the poison rain until they were badly burned and bleeding.

A booming laugh thundered from the cloud, and Naibor cautiously looked up to find the rain had stopped. "Fool!" The swirling mass rumbled as the wind picked up again. "I am Necros, the lord of death. What can you do to fight against me?"

A bolt of lightning shot out of the blackness and came sizzling down, narrowly missing the prince. Then another bolt flashed down, and another. The searing energy bolts exploded when they hit the ground, shaking the earth with their impacts while sending rocks and dirt flying up into the air.

The blazing light blinded Naibor's eyes, and the roaring cracks of deafening thunder ripped through his head. The prince struggled to keep his balance against the violent winds and the shuddering earth while he dodged more of the sorcerer's powerful lightning. He picked up his sword and swung it helplessly in an attempt to protect himself against the powerful bolts that crashed down from the skies. Naibor knew he was weakening. He could feel his strength draining as he tried to stand against the raging of these unnatural elements.

Naibor realized the sorcerer was toying with him. The prince knew that this would not last much longer, but he couldn't think what to do. How could he fight Necros with the sword when the sorcerer wasn't in human form? When Necros threw his next bolt of lightning, the prince held up the sword directly in its path, hoping the sword would again direct the sorcerer's power back at him. The force of the energy made the dull blade glow bright, but it was also too strong for Naibor. The prince was knocked backward off his feet, and the heat and pain traveling from the sword into his arm caused Naibor to throw the weapon away from him.

Clinging to the ground, Naibor listened as the sorcerer's laughter echoed in the thunder around him. Looking up, he saw the blackness moving closer toward him. The prince could see the look of death in the sorcerer's floating eyes. Reaching across the burned grass, Naibor tried to grab the sword lying nearby. He was running out of time. The next bolt of lightning surely would not miss. The prince could feel the tingling in the air around him as the sorcerer prepared for his final blast. Feeling his fingers grasp the sword, Prince Naibor gathered what strength remained. Rolling quickly to one side, Naibor stood up and with both hands threw the sword with all his might right into the heart of the storm as it closed in upon him.

The approaching cloud stopped, hovering over the prince in the air. The wind became silent and calm. The evil eyes stared blindly before the orange light grew dim, disappearing into the swirling blackness. The storm cloud shuddered and receded back into the sky, shrinking in size while growing darker than it had originally been. Then, all at once, the boiling mass erupted violently, madly exploding in flashes of light that sent out spears of lightning piercing the sky in all directions. The lightning ended in a final great crash of thunder that shook both the ground and the air. A deadly wail in the wild wind followed—a scream of anguish and defeat. The scream died to an echo as the storm cloud broke apart and disintegrated, ending in a swirl of smoke that floated away out of sight.

Without a word, Volkas turned and ran from the theater.

Letting the Ix leader go, the prince rushed over to the sacrifice tables. "Are you all right?" he asked with concern. "Are you both all right?" He looked anxiously from his father to Taila as they sat up. Freed from the sorcerer's spell, they both nodded to him that they were fine.

"And what about you?" The king inquired of his son. "Are you all right?"

The prince looked at his arms. The burning had stopped, as well as the bleeding, but there were ugly black marks where the sorcerer's rain had touched his skin. As Naibor was wondering what to use to wrap up the burns, the black marks suddenly began to fade and disappear. As they stood watching this miracle, new skin formed over the wounds without leaving any scars. The burns were completely healed. "I seem to be fine," he answered, somewhat amazed, not knowing what else to say.

The high king smiled with relief and threw his arms around his son.

As the two embraced, Naibor began to apologize. "Father, I'm sorry. I almost destroyed both you and the city."

"I know," his father said holding him tight. "But what is done is done, and the sorcerer is dead." Then, holding his son at arm's length, the high king looked into his son's eyes and pronounced, "You are forgiven."

Leaving his father, the prince went over to where Taila stood. There were tears brimming in her large, warm eyes.

"Taila, I worried every moment while you were with the sorcerer. If he harmed you in any way, I'll never forgive myself."

"No, I'm all right," she replied, allowing him to wrap his arms around her.

Looking down into the deep wells of her eyes, he leaned forward to kiss her, but he stopped when he heard his father call out, "Naibor!" in a warning.

Turning to see what was wrong, the prince saw a large group of Daimos enter the sacrifice area. As he readied himself for their attack, they suddenly fell to the ground helpless. Then, as Naibor continued to watch, the evil spirits of the Daimos left the bodies they had been using. He saw their shadowy gray forms rise up and begin to swirl around slowly in a circle.

The people the Daimos had held hostage got up weakly from the ground, looking around with fear and bewilderment. They tried to sneak away unnoticed, only to have the Daimos attack them as they tried to get away. Naibor heard them hiss menacingly and howl with cold voices. They swooped down upon one unfortunate person and violently hurled him through the air.

"What is happening?" Taila asked apprehensively, watching a group of the hideous and cruel specters of death come flying toward them.

"They have no master to guide and rule them, so they are out of control," the high king explained while the Daimos encircled them. "They are more deadly now than they were before."

"Are you going to destroy us too?" one of the Daimos screamed at Naibor in anger, still keeping his distance.

Realizing that the Daimos seemed to be afraid of him, the prince wondered how long their fear would last.

"How can we stop them?" Naibor whispered to his father, trying not to appear worried. He could hear shrieks and screams coming from the city, and he imagined the harm and havoc they were causing.

"If I had the amulet, perhaps," the king answered, giving his son a concerned look when one of the more daring Daimos moved threateningly closer.

Naibor moved in front of his father and Taila in an attempt to protect them. The Daimos, however, suddenly became completely still and quiet, as if they were listening to something. Naibor listened too, and he thought he heard the sound of horns blowing faintly in the distance.

The Daimos gathered together in the open area behind the temple and waited. They appeared worried by the sound, but they did not seem sure of what to do.

This action made Naibor even more uneasy. Then he heard the sound of horns blowing again. This time the horns were loud enough to be right outside the city walls. Naibor thought he heard the sound of horses' hooves as well, but he wasn't sure, because other sounds much closer to him caught his attention. The Daimos in front of him started shrieking and fleeing for their lives in all directions. At the same time, the sorcerer's temple slowly began to shake and break apart, crumbling piece by piece to the ground.

"We'd better get out of here," Naibor said when one of the pillars next to the sacrifice tables fell with a shattering crash dangerously close to where they were standing.

The three of them headed toward the closest opening between the seats of the theater. As they were about to go through, the columns holding the seats gave way, collapsing in a pile of rubble that blocked their exit.

Hearing the excited cry of a horse, they turned and saw someone charge into the theater on what was clearly the largest horse they had ever seen.

"Amon!" Prince Naibor exclaimed, hardly believing his eyes when the youth rode up beside them on the giant beast.

"I've come to return this amulet," he told them while taking the Stone of Wisdom from around his neck and giving it back to the king to wear. "The amulet let me know where you would be."

The high king nodded his thanks to the youth, replacing the amulet around his neck. "Then you also know that the sorcerer is dead."

The youth verified this with a nod of his head.

"Amon, do you know what is happening? Do you know who was sounding the horns?" Naibor asked, bewildered.

"Yes. It was the Lyoai!" he explained with a wide smile and shining eyes, speaking so quickly in his excitement that the words almost tripped over themselves. "They have waited a long time to avenge their deaths by being called to fight against the Daimos. Two days ago, in the secret valley of the Sleeping Lyoai, they were awakened; and using the high king's amulet, I led them here riding on Orros. They blew their battle horns as we approached the city, and then again as we rode through the open East Gate. At this very moment, the Daimos are fleeing from the Lyoai and this world, never to return again!"

Hearing a loud snap behind them, they turned and saw the dome of the temple crack down the middle. From where they stood, they felt the dome shudder—resisting to the very end. Then, collapsing in the center, the dome splintered into pieces, falling in a shower of rock and gray dust.

"The horns of the Lyoai are also the cause of the temple's destruction," Amon continued. "The Lyoai are destroying the sorcerer's temple because their temple was destroyed long ago. Nothing else could bring down these walls built of blackstone."

"This is good news!" Naibor shouted above the noise of the destruction, watching as one of the towers at the front of the temple fell with a great rumbling roar to the ground. "But we had better find another place to talk. It is not safe here with the temple falling."

"The back way is still clear!" the high king called out, pointing to the entrance Naibor had come in by. Together he and the prince and Taila hurried toward the opening, while Amon stayed to turn Orros around.

Springing out of hiding from behind a pile of broken stone, Volkas chased after Naibor and the others, holding a knife with a long, cruel blade.

Seeing the Ix man and what he was about to do, Amon quickly jumped down from Orros and ran with top speed to stop him, knowing that if he tried to warn the others, he would be too late. With a lunge, the youth managed to grab Volkas's arm just before he thrust the knife into Naibor's back.

At the sound of Volkas's angry cry, the others turned and watched, horrified, while Amon struggled with the Ix leader, trying to knock the knife out of his hand. Even though Amon was younger and taller, Volkas was an experienced fighter, and he managed to the break free from Amon's grasp and stab him viciously in the chest. Amon crumpled to the ground with a gasp, unconsciousness overtaking him as blood spilled from his wound. Volkas, clutching the blood-covered knife victoriously in his hand, ran back into the theater.

"Amon! No!" Naibor cried out in sorrow, resisting the urge to run after the Ix leader. Falling to his knees beside the youth, Naibor checked on his condition. "He's alive, but the wound is deep and he is bleeding badly," he informed his father and Taila, who stood beside him, full of concern.

"We had better move him into the athlete's training center," the king advised, checking to see if the entrance had been blocked. Relieved to see the opening was still clear, he added, "We will be able to help him better there."

The prince, with a nod of his head, was about to lift the youth and carry him out of the crumbling theater when he heard Orros neigh excitedly. Looking toward the sound, Naibor saw Volkas trying to catch the magnificent stallion by the reins. The king of the mountain horses, with an angry snort, reared up onto its powerful back legs, kicking out wildly with his front hooves.

Dodging the large hooves of the beast, Volkas slowly backed up, waiting for just the right moment to run in and grab the reins. Not taking his eyes off the horse, he moved dangerously close to one of the remaining pillars by the sacrifice tables. The shaking pillar began to lean precariously on an angle toward the Ix leader. Volkas, realizing his mistake too late, was unable to escape as the pillar collapsed on top of him, crushing him underneath. Orros, with one last kick and a powerful leap, was unharmed.

Naibor, giving a weary sigh, carefully moved Amon to the safety of the training center. Taila quickly went to get the horse, who responded to her quiet urging and soft voice.

Carrying Amon to the room for treating injured athletes, the prince gently laid the youth down onto one of the cots. His father, finding the necessary cloths and disinfectant, quickly brought them over to the bedside. Placing the cloths over the wound, Naibor managed to slow the bleeding, but he feared the youth had already lost too much blood. Covering Amon up with a warm blanket, he noticed how pale the youth was and that his breathing was labored.

The high king placed a comforting hand on his kneeling son's shoulder. "There are others who need your help in the city," he reminded his son.

"Not now, father," Naibor whispered, focusing his attention on the youth. Amon had regained consciousness, but his eyes were glazed over, and he did not seem to know where he was.

"I will stay with Amon," the king gently urged. "The people need a leader to guide them, Naibor. My time has passed. It is your time now."

"They won't follow me, father," Naibor said sadly. "They hate me for what I've done."

"Then you must leave this city now and never return if that is what you believe," the king replied, moving away from his son's side impatiently. "But you are wrong, Naibor; they will follow you. When they look at you, they will see you as you are now, not as you were before. You have overcome both your fear and the sorcerer. Now you must let go of the past and look to the needs of the city."

Looking into his father's eyes, Naibor knew he was right. Even though the battle against the sorcerer had been won, there was still a lot that needed to be done. "Where has Taila taken the horse?" he asked, getting to his feet.

"To the stables at the back," the king proudly answered his son.

Leaving Amon in his father's capable hands, Naibor left the room and went to find Taila. He found her and the large horse outside of the enclosure where his father had told him they would be.

Approaching them slowly, Naibor allowed Orros some time to get used to him. Taila kept stroking the horse's neck as the now bright sunlight shone down around them. Her face looked troubled and worried.

"Taila, what's wrong? Can I help? Are you ill?" the prince inquired with concern.

"Oh, Prince!" she cried out in distress, turning away. Not able to face him, she leaned onto the horse's side. "I need to ask for your forgiveness."

"Forgiveness? Forgiveness for what?" he asked, privately wondering what injury she could possibly have done to him.

"When I was with the sorcerer, he told me terrible things about you, and I believed him. He said that you and he had plotted together to take over the city, and that you had my sister and the other competitors killed. I was so angry with you for what you had done, I wanted you dead. I am so ashamed of myself for thinking what I did. I never should have believed his lies," she mournfully said, shaking her head. "I knew when you came to challenge the sorcerer that I was wrong about you. Can you forgive me, Naibor?"

"I forgive you, Taila," Naibor said, looking deeply into her eyes while taking her hands in his. "You can't blame yourself. I know the kind of power Necros had. When I was with the sorcerer, I hated everything and everyone around me, including myself.

"Now I must ask you to forgive me," he said, kissing each of her hands tenderly before he released them. "Not all the sorcerer told you was a lie. His lies contained some truth to make them more believable. I wish I had told you this before; perhaps you would not have suffered so much if I had. But now I will tell you the truth."

Taking a deep breath, he began. "I was the one who brought the sorcerer into Amuron. I foolishly thought he would help me become high king, but he just used me to take over the city by telling me what I wanted to hear."

"I know," she shyly said to the prince. "I mean, I guessed that you were the one who brought the sorcerer into the city, after I saw you being escorted into the great hall for the ceremony on the night the city was taken over."

"Oh," Naibor replied sheepishly.

"There is something else you should know, Taila. Janii and the others were not killed. Instead the sorcerer turned them all into animals."

"How horrible for them."

"I thought so too at first, thinking that it probably would have been better if the sorcerer had killed them, but I don't believe that anymore. They are not the dumb witless animals that Necros intended them to be. Somehow they didn't lose their humanity, and they can speak. I have seen them, and they helped me defeat the sorcerer. Amuron owes its victory as much to them as to me. We need to trust in the Lord Aii that they can be changed back to their former selves. You have a lot to forgive me for, Taila; many have hated another for a lot less."

"I forgive you, and I don't hate you," she said, giving him a golden smile.

He looked at her and wanted to fall on his knees and weep, shout, and laugh for joy, but instead he leaned forward and gently touched her lips with his in a momentary kiss. Orros stomped his foot impatiently, reminding the prince of what he had set out to do.

"I'm going to ride to the West Gate to see what I can do to help,"

Naibor explained, breaking the sweet silence between them. "Want to come along? I'm going to need all the help I can get."

She responded by giving him another smile as bright as the sunshine around them.

"Good," he replied, grinning back at her like a young schoolboy in love.

Leading the horse to a bench, Naibor swung himself up into the saddle.

"You really didn't think I'd let you leave me behind, did you?" Taila said with a laugh, climbing onto the bench and then up onto the horse's back with Naibor's help.

"I'd have been disappointed if you did," he replied, and urging the horse forward, they left the compound, riding out into the city.

CHAPTER 23

The bear prince and the other animals were discussing what they should do after Prince Naibor left the sanctuary when they heard a sound at the main doors to the temple. Someone was trying to get in! The animals were instantly on the alert.

Listening intently, they heard someone moving around the building, trying to find a way in. Their mystery guest rattled all the windows to see if they could be opened, but they were all locked and covered over with heavy shutters.

"Whoever is out there, they have almost reached the open door at the back," Tybor commented to his friends, with his hackles raised and a snarl on his lips.

"I'm ready for a fight," Baynor growled, rising up on his hind legs.

"Me too," Janii agreed, standing her ground, and her horn flashed momentarily in a stream of light coming from an unseen source above.

They heard someone enter through the back way and then hesitate after taking a few steps forward.

"Prince Naibor," a voice whispered. "Are you there?"

It was a man's voice, and it seemed familiar to Prince Baynor.

Moving through the empty rooms, they heard the man trip over something in the dark. "Ow," he complained, obviously in pain. Then, with a slightly irritated voice, he called for Prince Naibor again.

"I know that voice," Baynor realized, lowering his body to the floor.

Entering the sanctuary cautiously, Captain Regg gasped and stepped back a few paces when he saw the threatening faces of the animals staring at him.

"Is anything wrong, Captain?" the bear asked with concern, wondering why he was searching for Prince Naibor.

"Edra said he was with talking animals, but I never imagined anything like this," the captain muttered under his breath, misinterpreting Baynor's question as he wiped perspiration from his brow.

Then, looking around in utter desperation, he blurted out, "We're under attack! We managed to get all the captives of Amuron safely out of the city, and we were moving them down the West Road when we were met and attacked by several hundred Ix people. We tried running back to the gate for some hope of protection only to find the portcullis down and the doors locked. Now we are trapped between the walls of the city and the army of warriors. Edra told me that the prince was here and that he might be able to help. So taking one of the horses that we had hitched to a wagon, I rode down around the South Gate of the city hoping to find him."

"Is Prince Naibor here?" Regg asked, looking around, secretly hoping that he would come out of the shadows.

"No," the bear answered, "he is no longer here, but we can help you, Captain. The sorcerer changed us into what you see before you, but we are citizens of Amuron, and we are willing to fight to help save it."

"All right," the captain said, needing no more convincing. "Let's go."

Captain Regg galloped quickly back toward the West Gate with the unicorn, bear, panther, and wolf following close behind. The badger flew once again with the eagle overhead.

When they neared the gate, the animals could see the battle was not going well for the prisoners. The Amuron men were outnumbered almost two to one by the Ix warriors who fought with them partway down the road.

The Ix men were advancing, striking, and stabbing savagely with the spears they had been carrying to use in a tribal dance after the sacrifice. The Ix women fought alongside the men, using the personal knives that all the Ix people carried. Screaming out war cries, they made sure that their wounded adversaries did not rise again.

The Amuron men weren't completely defenseless against the ruthless warriors. They were armed with the swords that Captain Zai had thought to sneak out of the armory before they left the city.

A barrier had been made by placing the wagons on their sides, to protect the women and children back by the trench. It was obvious, however, that the prisoners could not hold up against the onslaught from the Ix warriors much longer. Despite their valiant effort, the men were weak from having been starved and beaten, and many casualties already lay on the ground.

Riding on the remaining horse, Captain Zai was trying to draw off some Ix men from the main attack when Captain Regg and the animals rushed in to join him.

"Just in time!" Zai shouted to his friend Regg while the Ix People fell back and engaged the newcomers in battle. Pushing forward into the center of the onslaught, Zai and Regg slashed with their swords at the wall of spears and men.

The animals fanned out and attacked from different directions. The bear, with his strength and powerful claws, charged at the fighting Ix men, knocking both spears and warriors to the ground. The unicorn, with swiftness and agility, battled with quick kicks and her pointed horn. The eagle attacked from above, dropping down from the skies with lightning speed and perfect timing just as an Ix warrior was about to strike a deadly blow.

While the eagle was striking from above, the badger was attacking from below. After being carefully dropped to the ground, Ranor made good use of his teeth and speed. Darting expertly in and out between the legs of his enemies, he bit and tripped as many as he could. Wasting no time, the panther cunningly circled around and pounced on the Ix warriors from behind, overpowering them with her fierceness. The wolf, with battle cries of his own, used all of his cunning to help the injured escape death when they found themselves in trouble from a brutal attack.

For a while, the animals succeeded in helping the prisoners defend themselves against their adversaries, but they were still outnumbered, and the warriors fought relentlessly. At the sight of an evil cloud hovering over the temple, the Ix people took it as a sign that the battle was theirs to take, and their zeal renewed.

Tayii suddenly found herself surrounded by a circle of spears with no way out. Ranor, rushing in to help, was pinned to the ground by a dying prisoner. Baynor was tiring and bleeding from a cut in his shoulder. He fought beside Captain Zai, who had a large slash across the top of his arm. Janii and Sanii were both trying to free Tayii. Tybor, concerned for his friend Ranor, was trying to find out what happened to him. Things were becoming increasingly grim when they heard Baynor cry out with a roar.

Captain Regg fell from his horse. He had been hit in the stomach with a spear. Baynor and Zai had just begun to work their way toward him when they heard another cry that stopped everyone in their tracks. It was a cry of death—the sorcerer's death! The fighting suddenly came to a stop, and all eyes turned toward the city.

The look of victory, and the excitement of battle, vanished from the faces of the Ix people as they looked toward the temple. They watched as the black cloud convulsed and broke apart, signaling the sorcerer's defeat. Waiting until the last shreds of the storm floated away on the wind, the bold Ix warriors were now filled with fear, and they turned and began running back down the road the way they had come.

The people of Amuron gave a weak cheer of relief when the Ix warriors fled, but the men were too exhausted to pursue them. Dropping their swords, they looked with dismay at the number of the dead, and then they hurried to help the wounded. Baynor and Zai rushed over to help Captain Regg. There was nothing that could be done. The spear wound in his side was too severe, and the captain of the guard died even as his friend Zai held him in his arms.

"What shall we do now, Captain?" one of the men asked Zai, coming over to stand beside him for instructions. The captain, overcome with grief, couldn't answer the man.

After a few moments, Captain Zai stood up and wiped the damp hair from his face. Putting his grief aside, he began the weary task of separating the dead from the wounded and making the best out of a bad situation.

Leaving the battlefield, Baynor moved to a vacant spot where his friends came and joined him. Tybor and Tayii had managed to find Ranor and help him out from underneath the body of a fallen citizen of Amuron. Ranor limped along slowly with a broken front paw, but otherwise he was all right. Janii had also been wounded. A red line of blood ran down from a nasty gash she had above one of her hind legs, but she could still walk.

Looking around, Baynor assessed the situation. The women and men of Amuron were in a state of shock and grief, both from the battle and from their previous imprisonment. They had few supplies and little strength left. He wished there were some way he could help them, but there was not. His animal appearance had only seemed to further frighten the people when he had attempted to help, and he couldn't blame them. They had had enough of anything to do with sorcery.

"I think we should return to Binah," Baynor commented to his friends. "There is nothing more we can do here," he said sadly.

They all agreed, but just before they started to leave, Captain Zai hurried over to them.

"I don't know who or what you are, to tell you the truth, but I want to thank you. Many more people would have died without your help," he said to them, not knowing if they understood what he was saying. "Captain Regg probably could have explained to me more about you," he added, looking off into the distance for a moment. "But he is not here, so I hope in the future that we will meet again under better circumstances."

"Thank you for your kind words, Captain," Baynor replied, catching the captain's look of amazement when he spoke, "but I do not think you will see us again. There is no place for us in the city of Amuron."

"May the blessings of Aii go with you then," Captain Zai added. And hearing someone call his name, he turned and ran back to see what he was needed for.

The animals walked along beside the trench, not saying anything to one another but being comforted in their sadness by one another's presence. The battle was over, but they could not share in the victory. What Baynor had told Captain Zai was true. As animals, they did not belong in the city. Their lives would have to begin anew.

Ranor had to move even more slowly now that he had a broken paw. Sanii, being too tired after the battle to carry him, walked along beside him with the others. As they approached the South Gate, they heard the sound of horns blowing and stopped, wondering what it could mean. After listening for a moment, they somehow knew that the horns were a sign of help and not of more trouble, so they continued on.

Passing over the ramp leading up to the South Gate, the animals could now hear the sound of unnatural screams and wails coming toward them from inside the city wall. The sounds made their hair rise, and looking toward the gate, they saw the haunting spirits of the Daimos come at them through the closed doors and the surrounding wall of blackstone. Rushing around and past them, the animals saw that their hideous faces were filled with fear. The Daimos kept looking behind them in terror as they fled like a cold cloud of smoke over the ground.

Following them through the walls, the Lyoai charged after them on their transparent steeds. Their faces were set with a fearsome fury. They chased after the Daimos, trampling them down with the pounding of hoofbeats, sending them back to their deathly realm beneath the ground. The evil wraiths disintegrated into swirls of darkness that sank down slowly out of sight until there was nothing but a whirlwind of dust and dirt beneath the feet of the horses. Unfurling their banners, the Lyoai army rode in a circle around where the last of the Daimos had disappeared. With their banners proudly streaming out behind them, the shadowy riders then rode off in a line to the south, until they too faded from view.

The animals' spirits rose in knowing that the city was now truly free, but they were all utterly exhausted when they finally reached Binah.

"At last, some rest," Ranor sighed, collapsing to the floor of the sanctuary and shutting his eyes.

"I think I'll join you," Tayii whispered to the already sleeping badger. She lay down beside him, and with the hint of a purr she closed her eyes.

"I'm so tired," Janii murmured with her head drooping. "I can hardly keep my eyes open." Lying down on the ground, the unicorn was careful not to reopen her wound.

"It seems like I haven't slept in years," Sanii agreed, fluffing up her feathers.

"Must have been all the excitement," Tybor said with a big yawn, stretching out on the floor. "This rest is just what I, being a doctor, would have ordered."

"Seems a little strange to me that we should all be this tired," Baynor muttered, looking around at his friends, who were all blissfully sleeping. Then, with a big shake of his bear head, he could resist the urge no longer. Lying down, he curled up his shaggy body and fell into a deep sleep.

* * *

When Prince Baynor woke up, he felt strange and a little dizzy. He lifted a hand to his forehead, quickly took it off again, and looked at it. It took him a moment to realize what he was seeing, but then he fully understood. He had a hand! He was human again! Getting up, he looked around at his sleeping friends. They were all human again too!

"Janii," Baynor called out gently to her when she was beginning to stir, and she opened her eyes.

"Baynor, you're …" she cried out in surprise. "And so am I. Oh, Baynor!" she sighed with relief as he helped her to her feet and embraced her.

"Just look at us!" Princess Janii continued, speaking joyously while they stood at arm's length, holding hands. "We are still in our clothes from the banquet, and they look as fresh as when we put them on. How's that for a bit of magic?" she added with a smile and a giggle of delight.

"You've never looked lovelier," he said, admiring her beautiful face, and reaching up a hand, he felt her silky hair. It was as if it were the first time in his life he had done these things. "I'm never going to stop looking at you from this moment on."

As their friends woke up, they exchanged embraces with each of them, along with tears of joy and laughter.

"For a moment, I thought I was dreaming," Prince Tybor said, first giving a kiss to his sister and then tenderly kissing his bride to be, "but this is better than any dream."

"And I can truly say it feels good to stretch my legs," Prince Ranor added, stroking his beard while giving Princess Tayii a smile and a wink.

Along with the rediscovery of their sensations and feelings of being human, they also discovered that the injuries they had received as animals were still with them now that they had returned to human form. Baynor had a scar down his cheek from when he was attacked by the bear at Ur. He laughed it off, saying he could always cover it up with a beard and that he was quite comfortable having a furry face. The wound in his shoulder from the battle, however, was still bleeding and quite sore when he moved it, painfully reminding him of the situation they had just left. The cut in Princess Janii's hip was severe and would have to be properly treated with herbs to prevent infection, and Prince Ranor's hand was still broken.

Prince Tybor attempted to help them as much as possible with the few supplies that remained in the old refuge of Binah. After he had supported and bandaged up Prince Ranor's broken hand and inspected and washed both Baynor's and Janii's wounds, they decided to return back home to the city through the East Gate. Their plans to enter the city, however, were soon to change.

CHAPTER 24

Riding with Taila on Orros, Prince Naibor called out to the small groups of men and women who wandered wearily and dejectedly through the streets of the city. These were the people that the Daimos had formally inhabited. The prince told them that they were needed and that they could make amends for the damage the Daimos had done. Most of them visibly brightened at the idea of helping, but some of them ran away frightened or with shame when they saw the valiant-looking prince riding on the magnificent steed.

By the time they reached the West Gate, Prince Naibor and Taila had about sixty people following behind to help. Instructing one of the men with them to open the large doors and raise the portcullis of the gate, the prince looked toward the battle area. The fighting had ceased, but Naibor could see that their help was still needed.

Riding forward down the ramp from the gate, the prince addressed the citizens before him. "The sorcerer is dead, and the Daimos have been banished from this world, so Amuron is once again free from evil. I have come, as well as those with me, to lend a hand and help you back into the city."

"Your help is welcome," Captain Zai stated as he greeted the prince. "But to be honest, I wish that your help had arrived sooner."

Naibor dismounted and helped Taila down from Orros, and with a heavy heart he listened while Zai reported what had happened during the battle, including the loss of Captain Regg. This was another unexpected sorrow for the prince, but for now his grief would have to wait.

Working together with the people of Amuron, the prince and Captain Zai buried the dead and prepared to return into the city. After loading the wounded into the wagons, they started moving everyone back toward the military barracks. To Naibor's dismay, they soon saw a large group of riders coming toward them from the south.

The approaching riders came to a stop near the south end of the city, but they were still too far away to be identified. Standing next to Captain Zai, Prince Naibor watched and waited for what seemed like endless moments until six riders rode out from the rest of the group and came galloping toward them.

"Let's hope they are friends," Captain Zai stated into the ear of the prince. "If they come to challenge us, we will have to surrender."

Naibor looked around at the people standing behind him and nodded to the captain in agreement. The faces of the citizens of Amuron were full of apprehension and pain as they stood silently watching the approach of the riders.

"Naibor, look!" Taila exclaimed, coming over and squeezing his arm. "Don't you recognize those riders?"

As they rode closer, Naibor's face became filled with a look of joy and amazement. He did recognize the riders, but he could hardly believe his eyes. It was Prince Baynor and the others!

"Baynor!" the prince called out when they reined in their horses beside where he and the captain and Taila were standing.

"Janii!" Taila cried out as the princess leaped down from the saddle and quickly embraced her sister. "It's you; it's really you!" Tears of joy flowed down her cheeks.

"It's so good to see you!" Janii exclaimed, giving Taila another squeeze. "I thought I might never see you again."

The crowd behind them, realizing they had nothing to fear, began to cheer and gather around the newcomers.

"The king of the sea city Aquar brings you greetings and aid," Prince Baynor told them, raising his voice over the excitement of the crowd.

"Return the king's greetings and tell him they are most welcome—and so too are all of you," Naibor stated formally to the others as they dismounted, while Baynor rode back to the king of Aquar.

The crowd broke out into another cheer as the king of Aquar rode up with a group of his strongest seamen and wagons filled with supplies. The king and his men followed Prince Naibor on the giant horse back to the newly reclaimed barracks, which by evening they had turned into a large camp and a hospital for the wounded.

As soon as he could, Naibor returned with Orros to the competitor's compound to check on Amon. The afternoon shadows were becoming long when he met Prince Tybor in the corridor outside of the room where Amon lay resting. Naibor had earlier told Tybor about Amon's injury, and the gifted healer had come to see what he could do to help the youth.

"How is he?" Naibor asked, concerned.

Tybor shook his head sadly. "There was very little I could do for him. I did everything I could. His bleeding has stopped, but the knife wound did too much damage." He paused, and looking at Prince Naibor with his youthful face full of sorrow, he added, "He might live for another day or two, but that is all. I love the boy, but I could do no more than ease his pain."

To Prince Naibor, the words were like a knife wound to his own heart. First they had lost Graypah, then Captain Regg, and now Amon. So many lives had been lost because of his greed and shortsightedness. How could he possibly make right all the things that had gone wrong?

"Can I see him?" Naibor asked, moving closer to the door while he brushed away the water that blurred his eyes.

"His family is with him now. They somehow heard that Amon was hurt and that I had come here to try to heal him. They arrived shortly after I did. Your father is also with them …" Prince Tybor left off speaking when he realized the prince wasn't really listening.

With a polite nod of his head, Naibor turned and walked sadly back down the corridor the way he had come. He went out into the exercise area and collapsed onto a bench and buried his head in his hands. He sat for a long time, dealing with his grief, until he slowly became aware that he was not alone. Hearing Orros nicker quietly from down the field, he looked up and saw a giant standing next to the mountain horse.

"I am Bartok. I came for my horse, Orros," the giant explained. "Orros tells me that things are not well with Amon. Is he near death?"

"Yes," Naibor replied with regret, seeing concern for the youth clearly in the giant's face. "His wounds are severe. He has not long to live."

"You are sure of this?" Bartok inquired, his thick brows meeting in the middle of his forehead.

"Yes. One of our best healers told me so."

"Then allow me to take him to Berroc. There the Lord Aii may heal him," Bartok advised.

"But it takes seven days to get to Berroc; you would never get there in time," Naibor protested.

"I may enter Berroc without passing through the six gates. I am the keeper of the gates," Bartok explained. "Amon has worn the Stone of Wisdom, so he may enter into the Place of Communion. Our Lord has a plan for this one's life, and he will die if he stays here. He may die if I take him, but there is also a chance that he may live. It will be his only chance."

Naibor needed no more convincing. He reentered the building and hurried to the room where Amon lay. After knocking softly on the door, Naibor opened it and was relieved to find only Tybor inside with the youth.

"He is resting comfortably," Tybor informed him, gathering his things to leave, but when Naibor began to lift him off the cot, he forcefully tried to stop him. "Naibor, what do you think you are doing?" he asked, alarmed.

"There is a chance his life can be saved," Naibor told him. "Someone is here that can take him to Berroc to be healed. I can't answer all your questions now. You've got to trust me."

Prince Tybor obliged, and gathering up an extra blanket and some supplies, he followed Naibor outside to where Bartok sat waiting on Orros. At the sight of the giant, Tybor had some momentary misgivings, but when he saw how gently Bartok took Amon from Naibor's arms, he was reassured.

"Here, I have an extra blanket to wrap him in, and this liquid should help sustain him on the journey," Tybor said, handing the items up to the large man.

"Thank you, healer. He will need both," Bartok told him, and making sure Amon was lying as comfortably as possible, he started off to the only place where Amon's life could still be saved.

* * *

Leaving the city by the East Gate, Orros traveled back to the wilderness that he and his master knew so well. Running like a horse with wings, his feet floated deftly over the ground with a speed that outmatched the strong evening wind. Night came as they traveled over the mountain terrain. Passing through forests of trees and crossing rocky plateaus, they leaped across swift streams and deep rivers, but not once did the mountain horse slow his pace; nor did his sure feet falter.

During their journey, Bartok protected Amon as much as possible from the chill of the night air, cradling him in his arms. Remaining unconscious, the youth stirred only when dawn approached and he began to cough, struggling to breathe.

"Drink this, little one," Bartok instructed softly, giving the youth a drink from the skin bag Tybor had given him.

"Bartok?" Amon murmured, a weak smile catching up the corners of his mouth. "I did it. The Lyoai are free."

"I am proud, Amon. You did well," Bartok assured him, tears slipping down the weathered lines of his face. "Sleep now. You soon will be well," the giant promised the dying youth, pulling the blankets closer around him. "Hear my prayer, Lord," he added to the sky above him, but little life remained in Amon's body.

Running like no ordinary horse could, Orros knew in his heart his need for speed. Listening to every labored breath that Amon took, he gathered his strength from the lively mountain air and the solid ground beneath his feet and raced on.

Twilight was again descending when they reached the valley of Berroc and rode through the ring of white to its center, but Amon's spirit was no longer with his body.

"Lord, have mercy," Bartok said heavyheartedly as he lay the lifeless body of the youth, still wrapped in blankets for warmth, on the stone in the center of the Place of Communion. "I give you your servant," he added, looking down on the pale face in the dim light. Not wanting to leave, Bartok waited, breathing in the sacred silence that surrounded him. Then he turned and went out through the door.

Leaning his back against the cold stone wall, Bartok looked toward his mountain home high up on Mount Rosh, hoping to gain some comfort as the light from last rays of the sun faded around him.

* * *

The early stars had just begun to brighten against the ever darkening sky when Bartok heard the sound of movement behind him. Turning, he saw the figure of Amon standing in the open doorway.

"Little one!" Bartok exclaimed in a ringing shout of joy. "You are well again!" He went over and clasped the youth by the shoulders just to make sure he was real.

"Yes," Amon agreed with a small laugh. "And I don't even have a scar," he concluded after searching under his shirt.

"Praise Aii!" Bartok added with awe. "He has answered our prayers."

"I'm at Berroc!" Amon marveled, taking note for the first time of his surroundings. "How did I get here?" he asked, a little confused,

"Orros and I brought you. Don't you remember?"

"Not really. I remember faces and voices mostly," Amon replied, thinking back. "I remember seeing the faces of my family and the high king. I also remember the sound of the wind and the beating of a horse's hooves, and then darkness: nothing but darkness—like floating in a sea of endless night. Then I heard a sound, but I don't remember clearly what the sound was. It could have been a voice or even music, but afterward I was surrounded by brightness—such a light that I thought even my body was glowing. Then I suddenly had this urge to get up and walk. So I got up, and here I am. And that's all I remember," he concluded, grinning happily. "I also am very hungry."

"Then let us go home." Smiling back, Bartok handed the youth what food he had with him and whistled for Orros.

Responding quickly, the mountain horse came charging up from the far end of the valley. When he saw Amon, he neighed with delight and gave a couple of leaps in the air.

"I'm happy to see you too!" Amon said affectionately, hugging what he could of the horse's huge neck before he was helped up into the saddle.

Proudly holding his head and tail high, the mountain horse, with a light step and an easy pace, carried his two riders underneath the glistening canopy of starlight back to his home.

* * *

The day after the sorcerer's death, Prince Naibor called a day of mourning and repentance for all the people of Amuron. At first light, the prince—on horseback, with his father riding on one side and the king of Aquar on the other—led the citizens in a solemn procession through the streets.

Gathering outside the old arena wall, they wept for their many losses, and a short ceremony was given to remember those who had died. Prince Naibor then led the people in prayer. They prayed together with one heart that they might be better devoted to Aii in the days to come by rededicating themselves to the laws in the high king's book.

And it was to be, as recorded in the city's history, that every year on that same day, all the people of Amuron would gather together in front of the main gates to the old arena and dedicate themselves once again to the Lord Aii. A new arena was later constructed outside of the city above the East Gate, ensuring that the city would remain safe if anyone attending a future Celebration Games had any evil intentions.

Over the next few days, weeks, and months, the city of Amuron was reborn. Families were reunited, and old friendships were reestablished and strengthened. Among those who had returned to the city with the king of Aquar was Dame Lucianii. She had managed to escape during the chaos of the city's capture and borrow a horse from an outlying villager. She then had ridden, as fast as Aii could lend her speed, to the coastal city for help. No one was happier than Prince Baynor to see his mother alive and well again, and to hear about her daring adventure.

Two weeks after the king of Aquar had ridden to the aid of Amuron, a group of Raphacharii arrived at the city gates. The artisans had learned about the fate of Amuron after their ship had docked at the seaport of Aquar. Thinking that they might be able to help, they had brought with them the tools of their trade. The people welcomed their services, and under the advisory of the high king, they teamed up with the skilled tradesmen of the city. Soon they were working hard to rebuild and beautify Amuron.

The king of Aquar stayed for most of the month, and then, with great fanfare from the people of Amuron, he returned home with his people. The Raphacharii remained several months longer, wanting to complete their work. When it came time for them to leave, with personal gifts of gratitude from the high king, the city of Amuron was much more renowned for its beauty than it had been previously.

Although many citizens left the city after it was freed from the sorcerer, Amuron soon began to grow and flourish. Once again it became time to name a new high king.

"The people want you to become their new high king, Naibor," his father announced when they were standing together on the terrace outside of the banquet hall after an evening meal.

"There must be someone else," Naibor said, rejecting the idea. "What about one of my former competitors?"

"None of them are interested. They now say they no longer wish to compete."

"Well, neither do I. Besides, there isn't even a place to compete in. Have you seen the old arena? There is nothing left but a big mound of dirt over where the sorcerer's temple was buried."

"I know that, and so do the people. If the people are unanimous in their decision, then *The High King's Laws* declares that there is no need for a competition, as long as the leader chosen is bound to uphold what is written in the book. I think their choice in you is a good one."

"You're my father," Naibor commented dryly.

"And I'm also the high king—for now."

"I'm engaged to be married; I don't think now is a good time."

"Does Taila not want you to become high king?"

"When I ask her about it, she says it is my decision to make, but I don't feel ready. I used to think being a high king was easy, but now I have learned what it is really like. I just don't know enough about how to rule an entire kingdom."

"You will never know enough, but you'll have the Stone of Wisdom and the laws of the high king. You can also appoint advisors, and"—he chuckled—"I will still be around."

"To be fair to the people, you should announce your decision by the end of this week," the high king advised.

"All right," Naibor said, giving in to his father's persistence. "By then I will have made my decision."

CHAPTER 25

Amon stayed with Bartok for three months in the stone cottage and continued learning from his host about mountain life.

"It is time for me to leave now," Bartok announced one morning while they stood together on the mountainside watching the sunrise.

"Leave?" Amon said with amazement, looking up at his companion, who stood looking toward the east. "Where are you going?"

"Home, little one. It is time I returned back home over the sea," Bartok replied peacefully, the sun warming his brown cheeks. "You are to become the new keeper of the gates in my place. I can teach you no more. The rest you will have to learn as time goes by."

"But you can't; I mean … I can't!" Amon blurted out.

"At Aquar, some Raphacharii have a ship," Bartok continued calmly. "They will be returning home before the winter weather comes, and I will be leaving with them. This will be your home now."

"But what about the animals?"

"They are yours to care for, all except for Orros, who will come with me on my journey."

"Then you really are leaving," Amon said sadly. "I know you said you were, but I was hoping you wouldn't."

Bartok looked down at the youth affectionately and nodded that it was so. Then, with a merry twinkle in his mountain-azure eyes, he said, "Do not worry, little one; you have already accomplished in your life what those twice your size tremble at the thought of doing. Aii has chosen you as the next keeper of the gates, and I have faith that he has chosen well. You have already worn the Stone of Wisdom, and now you will wear the sister stone, the Stone of the Gates." Reaching underneath his tunic, he took off the amulet he had hidden there and gave it to the youth.

Holding the amulet in his hand, Amon stared at it with disbelief. Hanging from the finely woven silken gold chain was a sparkling clear stone, lesser in size than the Stone of Wisdom, with seven jewels surrounding it to represent the seven gates.

"This stone will let you know when you are needed. You may pass through any of the gates at any time without fear while you are wearing it," Bartok instructed his successor.

"I also have this to give you," the giant added, reaching into a pocket of his tunic. He took out a small carved wooden box and held it out to Amon in the palm of his large hand.

Amon took the box and examined it. It was made of an oiled black wood and was the size of his fist. Inlaid on the cover was a blossom made from a light-colored wood, but other than that, the design was simple.

"Did you make it?" Amon asked.

"No. It was given to me after I helped a sick traveler once long ago, when I was no more than your age. The traveler told me that the seeds inside the box were over a thousand years old. He had searched all over the world for the place to plant them, because they would only grow wherever the blossom that was pictured on the cover grew. He never was able to find a blossom like it, and he hoped I might have better success in my travels; but I, as well, have never found any blossom like it, and I fear that the blossom grows no more. Perhaps while you are on your journeys …"

Seeing how important it seemed to his mountain friend, Amon promised to keep the search up.

"Come! There is something else," Bartok added secretively, leading the way into the back of the barn.

Amon followed, curious. The back of the barn was usually where the supplies for the animals were kept, but Amon noticed the supplies had been moved. In one corner, bundles of straw had been used to make a small enclosure. Without making a sound, Bartok beckoned to Amon to look into the enclosure. Hearing a small rustle in the straw, the youth peered into the pen. Not believing his eyes, Amon looked again.

"Bartok! There is a baby unicorn in there!" he whispered in disbelief. "Where did it come from?"

"Hammer found her with a broken leg. She had somehow fallen down a cliffside. Her mother left her because she was not able to get up, and she was dying, so I brought her here. I kept it a secret from you until I was sure she would live. Her leg is almost healed, but she cannot return to the wild. Her contact with us would make her own kind reject her, and she couldn't survive in the wild without another unicorn to teach her how. So, little one, she is yours. When she is older, you can use her to ride to the gates."

"But everyone knows it is impossible to tame a unicorn."

Bartok gave a hearty laugh, causing the glistening animal to leap excitedly in her stall while tossing her horn high in the air. "That is true of wild unicorns, but this one is already tame. Go to her and you will see," he instructed, watching as Amon climbed in.

Speaking softly to the timid beast, Amon squatted down low and held out his hand to her. She looked at him with her large eyes, sniffing the stranger without moving closer. Then, as Amon remained calmly where he was, still holding out his hand, she reached out with her delicate, soft nose and touched his fingers. Deciding he was friendly, the unicorn allowed him to move closer. Eventually Amon was stroking her neck and mane.

"There, you see! If anyone can teach her to be ridden, it will be you, Amon. You have ridden a unicorn before. You know how a unicorn moves and how it runs. Show her you know this, and together you will learn to ride as one."

"Does she have a name?"

"I call her Tazur, after a small white wildflower that grows on the hillsides back in my homeland. This one small flower fills the whole land with a hint of perfume whenever the breeze blows fresh," he related, his eyes glowing with the memory. "But you may call her what you wish."

"No, Tazur is a perfect name. Thank you, Bartok."

After placing a few items in his sack, Bartok whistled for Orros. The time had come for them to say a final good-bye.

"Good-bye, Orros," Amon whispered to the king of the mountain horses as Bartok leaped up onto the horse's back. "These mountains and I will miss you."

In reply, Orros gave him an affectionate nudge with his nose while looking straight into Amon's eyes as if promising not to forget him.

Looking up at Bartok, Amon said, a little awkwardly, "I have so much to thank you for. I don't know where to begin."

"Knowing that you are here in my place—that is enough," Bartok answered, his smile deepening the creases in his warm and weathered face. His confidence in the youth clearly showed.

Amon felt a tug at his heart as he watched them head off toward the edge of the mountain plateau. Turning once more, Bartok called out, "Take care, little one. I hope the day will come when you will visit me in my homeland."

"I'd like that," Amon shouted back, wondering if he would ever get the chance.

Then with a wave and a merry laugh, Bartok and Orros descended for the last time the side of the mountain where they had lived for many years to journey on toward the eastern horizon and the land their ancestors had called home.

* * *

Seven days after Bartok had left, the sister stone that Amon now wore around his neck began to shine, and he knew that the new high king of Amuron was on his way to Berroc. Packing up a push wagon with supplies, the new keeper of the gates went to each of the havens, making sure they were properly supplied for when the king arrived.

Waiting at the last haven, Amon decided to speak to the new high king when he returned on his pilgrimage from the Place of Communion.

"Greetings, Lord Naibor," Amon called out, dropping down on one knee in a formal bow when he saw the high king leaving the white walls of Berroc.

"Amon!" King Naibor exclaimed, happily striding over in surprise when he saw the youth. "It's good to see you again!"

They stood appraising each other for a moment.

"I'm glad to find that you were healed from your wound," the high king added. "When you did not return to the city, there was some concern."

"I have been staying in the mountains," he explained. "They are my home now."

"I was hoping you would return to the city so I could reinstate your former position as a guard of the gates, but it seems that you have your own gates to look after," King Naibor stated, proudly acknowledging the youth's new position. "I hope that you will come to visit Amuron. It has been rebuilt, and with the help of some Raphacharii, it has become quite a beautiful place. I don't think you will recognize it."

"I had planned to go and visit my family soon," Amon informed him, knowing he would enjoy a short visit.

"Do you think you could come as early as next week? My coronation is in ten days, and I would like for you to be there if you can."

Amon said he would, and as promised, he arrived in the city the day before the coronation. Wandering through the streets, the youth couldn't help but admire the changes that the Raphacharii had made to Amuron. The city, once proud because of its strength and fortitude, was much more inviting and engaging than in the past. Modest homes were adorned with carved wood accents or painted clay tiles. Main streets leading into the city from the gates were bordered with decorative half-walls made of mixed stone. Trees had also been planted throughout the city, and in places where people usually gathered, gardens and benches had been added. Amuron had changed to a city reflecting the character of its people—cordial and colorful, as well as practical and hardworking.

The gates between the sections inside the city had designs added around their archways, and pairs of statues had been placed beside each entrance. Amon found statues of mighty warriors outside the entrance to the military section, dancing children made of bronze at the entrance to the market section, carved athletes in front of the competitors' compound, and many more, but the one that impressed and moved him the most he found in front of a high wall covering the main entrance to the old arena.

A monument built of stones stood there, inscribed with the names of those lost during the sorcerer's short reign. On top of this monument was a lifelike statue made to honor the memory of Captain Regg. The youth looked up at the captain with a joyless grin, finding it strange to see him carved in stone rather than in person. He had wanted to say good-bye to the captain and explain why he had again left his post at the North Gate. He could almost hear what Captain Regg would have said if he had: "To be a guard of the gates means knowing what is truly important during a crisis." He knew in his heart that Captain Regg would not have been disappointed with him.

Realizing that not all the changes in the city had been good, Amon turned and left the area with a sigh of sadness. It was time for him to go and visit his family. He was eager to see them again, even though he felt strangely nervous after having been away for so long. The prophecy seemed to have come true. He wasn't sure about the great and guided servant part, but he did bring his family both sorrow and joy.

On the day of the coronation, festivities were being held throughout the city. It was a glorious day. The air was vibrant and alive, and the sky an endless blue. Banners and ribbons displaying the royal colors could be seen fluttering and waving everywhere. Bands of musicians played in the streets, encouraging the crowds that watched to join in and dance to the lighthearted music. Acrobats and jugglers performed in colorful costumes wherever they could find a space. Vendors with carts of food followed the crowds, offering fresh fruits, baked breads, and tasty sweets, filling the streets with their delightful aromas.

Several young pages pushed a wagon loaded with gifts for the new high king through the city. Each family added to the wagon as it went by until it was piled high. All the inhabitants seemed to be in a joyful mood and to be enjoying themselves, especially after so much suffering and all the hard work that had been done to rebuild the city.

Amon found himself wandering through the Market Section. The center of this section had been enlarged into a wide open space, the shops and homes having been burned to the ground during the Daimos raid. Flat stones now covered the ground, and a raised platform had been added in one corner for performers. In the middle of the square, water fell from a flowing fountain, while the rest of the area was enhanced by miniature gardens in front of carved reliefs.

Amon was laughing at the tricks of some trained dogs when he heard the blaring of horns and the crowds in the market parted for the approach of the small parade. A group of military men dressed in their finest marched by blowing horns and carrying banners, inviting the citizens to follow them to witness the ceremony for the new high king.

Leaving the market area, Amon followed the crowd to the Palace Section. The coronation was going to be held on the lawn outside of the Hall of Hearing. Platforms with rows of seats had been set out to accommodate the crowds on both sides of the fountain. The sound of water splashing in the main fountain was almost drowned out by the noise of excitement and anticipation in the air. Amon moved as close to the steps as possible, preferring to stand beside the seating platform to get a good view.

Another platform had been set up on the steps of the great hall, where the ceremony was going to take place. The seats at the back of this platform were filled by the king's advisors, each of whom was wearing robes displaying their family colors.

To begin the ceremony, a band of musicians played processional music. In response to the music, the military marched in patterned lines down the field in front of the crowds. Captain Zai and Amon's father, who replaced Captain Regg, led the march. The crowds applauded when the two captains stopped at the bottom of the stairs in front of the king's platform, ending the march. The rest of the guard, with bright swords at their sides and banners held high, dispersed themselves to stand evenly throughout the crowd.

A trumpet sounded, silencing the crowd, and all those in attendance rose to their feet. The large doors to the Hall of Hearing were then opened wide, and the reigning high king and his son, Prince Naibor, left the hall. They were escorted by the impressive Palace Guard, who lined the steps down each side of the platform. Both Naibor and his father came to stand side by side in the middle of the platform. They were dressed in their ceremonial finest, but it wasn't their outward appearance that impressed those watching the ceremony so much as the look of gracious authority on their faces. Before he spoke, the high king motioned for the crowd to be seated.

"On this day, before Aii, you, the people of Amuron, will receive a new high king. You have made it known in a unanimous decision that you choose Prince Naibor as my successor. Are there any who disagree with this decision? Now is the time to bring forth your charges against the prince if there are any."

Nothing was heard from the surrounding crowd except the gentle flapping of banners. After waiting an appropriate amount of time, the king continued. "Since there are none who disagree with this appointment, can I then have public confirmation?"

The advisors at the back of the platform stood up, and the senior advisor came forward to address all those in attendance. "The advisors representing the different royal houses agree with the appointment of Prince Naibor as the new high king of the city of Amuron and its surrounding kingdom."

"The King's Guard also agree, and we give our lives in protection of the high king and his family," the leader of the Personal Guard called out, while the guards lining the steps went down on one knee in a salute.

"As does the guard sworn to protect the city," both of the captains at the foot of the stairs said in unison. They then walked up the steps, placed their swords at the feet of Prince Naibor, and saluted him.

"And so do the people," shouted the crowd.

"Then may the Lord Aii bless high king Naibor," Naibor's father announced, and he then took the Stone of Wisdom from around his neck and placed it around his son's. A great cheer rose from the crowd for the new high king of the kingdom of Amuron, and he was presented with the cart of gifts.

After a short acceptance speech, high king Naibor sat down in a throne that was placed at the front of the platform, while the crowd came up in families to give and receive their personal blessings. Tables covered with food and drink were then brought out onto the lawn, and all were invited to feast. Later, music and lanterns were added, along with a space for dancing long into the night.

Amon enjoyed watching the ceremony, but he decided not stay for the celebration. He would congratulate the high king later, when all the excitement had died down. As he turned to leave and head back toward his family home, a large hand on his shoulder stopped him. "Amon?" he heard a deep voice inquire, and turning to look behind him, the youth saw Prince Baynor and the other lords and ladies of the city.

"I told you it was he," Prince Ranor proudly remarked to the others.

"You look well!" Tybor exclaimed with a mixture of joy and relief. "How is your wound?"

"I'm completely healed," Amon affirmed. "And you," the grinning youth continued, "you have changed back into your former selves, lords and ladies. You are no longer animals." He looked at the princes, dressed handsomely in their formal attire, and the princesses, with their beauty and flowing gowns.

Breaking their initial shyness, Janii went over to Amon and gave him a big hug. The others quickly joined in, giving him a warm reunion. "I am so glad we got to see you before we left the city," Janii told him.

"What do you mean?" Amon inquired. "Are you not going stay and help advise the new high king?" he wondered, knowing it was customary.

"No, we have declined King Naibor's offer. We decided it was for the best," Baynor explained.

Hearing a loud cheer from the crowd after someone's speech at the feast, Ranor proposed, "Let's find a better place to talk, shall we?"

"How about the upper balcony at my family's home," Tayii suggested. "It will be far enough away from the crowd that we won't be interrupted, but close enough to the festivities that we can still see what is going on."

They all agreed, and when they were comfortably seated on the balcony, they resumed their talk.

"The city has changed so much that it hardly seems like home, and strangely enough, we all miss the mountains," Tybor informed Amon from his seat next to Sanii. "So when a visiting Raphacharii told us about a castle they had built in the mountains, we decided to go and live there—after he gave us his blessing. We will be leaving tomorrow."

"Then this isn't another good-bye," Amon said happily, and he explained to them about what had happened to him after they had first parted company.

"Then we will prepare the castle and make it ready for you when you come down the mountain for the winter," a delighted Janii promised with a heartwarming smile.

When the colorful party lanterns had been lit on the palace lawn, Amon gave a cheerful farewell to the small group on the private balcony. He was pleased that they would eventually see one another again.

Amon spent a week with his family before it was time for him to leave Amuron and return to the cottage in the mountains to prepare for the winter. On his way home from the city, the new keeper of the gates followed the original route that he and the others had taken to Berroc.

As he neared the first gate, he fondly remembered the wood fairies Nita and Ari and his wonderful wood fairy dream. The vision of the glade filled with the laughing voices of the fairies and the brightly colored flowers hanging from the surrounding trees made Amon feel full of joy. Walking along the trail, he could almost taste the sweetness of the fairy nectar and smell the fragrant air of that day. While these visions drifted through his mind, he remembered Nita sitting on a blossom while playing her wood pipe. Trying to remember the tune she had played, he suddenly realized that the blossom she had sat on was the same as the one on the box that Bartok had given to him.

"They're the seeds of wood fairy trees!" Amon cried out with amazement, and picking up his pace, he hurried to reach the gate.

When he arrived, it was just as he remembered it. Nothing looked like it had changed, but the air was now cooler with the coming of winter.

"Nita? Ari? Are you there?" Amon called. "Nita! Ari! It's me, Amon. I need to talk to you. I came here last spring with my friends the talking animals when we were traveling to Berroc. Please, if you are there, I need to talk to you."

"Oh, do be quiet," Amon heard a tired little voice implore. "Winter is almost here, and all respectable wood fairies are sleeping. Come back in the spring." It was Ari's voice, but Amon could not see him.

"No! Wait!" Amon shouted, worried that the invisible wood fairy had left. "I have some seeds for wood fairy trees."

"Impossible," Ari said, faintly appearing at the top of the gate. "There are none of the seed-bearing trees left. They died sooo … long ago now …"—the fairy stopped in midsentence to yawn, accompanied by a slow stretch—"that I can't remember how long it's been."

He was just starting to fade from view again when Amon took out the box. "No, look! They are in this box with this blossom on its cover. I was told that the seeds inside are over a thousand years old and can be planted only where this blossom grows."

The wood fairy gasped and flew down closer. "It can't be," he said with wide-eyed disbelief. "Show me the seeds."

Opening the box ever so slowly, Amon, along with the wood fairy fluttering beside him, looked inside. Lying close together in fine, sandy-colored dirt were ten slim seeds half the size of a man's thumbnail. They were covered on the outside with a shimmering gray sheath the same color as the bark of the trees beside the gate. Inside each of the sheaths lay what looked like tiny transparent jewels the color of sunlight.

"True wood fairy seeds!" Ari proclaimed with a look of delight on his pointed wood fairy face. Suddenly bursting out in laughter, he cried, "Hee, Hee. I'm a father!" and he did a backflip. "Wait till I tell Nita," he said gleefully, floating quickly up to her tree before disappearing inside.

That very fine fall day, Amon, with instructions from an excited Nita and Ari, planted the seeds where, in an almost forgotten time from the past, wood fairy trees used to blossom.

Amon stayed for a small ceremony of wood fairy songs given at the end, but by the time it was over, Ari's little head was bobbing along with his musical snores and Nita could hardly keep her eyes open between yawns. Promising to return in the spring, he listened to their cheerful good-byes and their merry laughter as they floated up invisibly to the trees beside the first gate.

Amon could still feel the tingle from Nita's tiny kiss on his cheek while he journeyed back to his home in the heart of the Khist mountain range, taking along with him a fresh supply of fairy nectar. The leaves had left the trees, and the animals had dug deep into their burrows, but Amon carried a song in his heart, as well as a peacefulness that had never existed there before.

With the coming of the cold winter winds, Amon knew it was time to move to the castle of the Raphacharii to spend the winter in its sheltered valley. So with the help of Hammer and Tong, who knew the journey well, he moved his family of animals down the side of the mountain. Tazur was timid and shy when she left the barn for the open expanse of the mountains, and she stayed quite close beside him on her lead. The sheep and the goats were carefully ushered down the slopes by the dogs whose guidance they knew so well, while he pushed a cart that contained a few personal items and clucking chickens in crates.

As promised, Amon was cheerfully greeted by his former traveling companions with a round of hugs and some kisses when he finally reached the castle of the Raphacharii. After they had helped Amon settle his animals into their winter home, they sat down together for supper and talked late into the night.

Amon enjoyed spending time with his mountain friends and watching their families grow. One winter while they were all together, gathered in a common room around a roaring fire, something unexpected happened. Tybor and Sanii's eldest daughter was playing a game on the floor with Janii and Baynor's eldest son. The game involved sticks made into patterned squares and colored stones for jumping. Janii's daughter was clearly winning when the two of them got into an argument. Tybor was just about to intervene when his daughter suddenly turned into a wolf and growled fiercely at her opponent before turning back to her former self.

"Oh! I'm sorry," she cried out, bursting into tears. "I didn't mean to do it."

Recovering from his shock, Tybor went over to comfort his daughter. "Has this happened before?" he asked.

"Yes," she sobbed, "but only when I get really angry. When I get mad, I go to my room, and sometimes I change into a wolf. Do you know what's happening to me, Father?" she asked, trembling in his arms.

Tybor wasn't completely sure, and neither were any of the others, but it became apparent that as each of their children grew toward adulthood, they gained the unique ability to change into specific animals at will. At first they could change only when they were angry or in danger, but later, when they developed control, they could change whenever they wanted. They were the first of their kind—a changeling race that would inhabit the Khist mountain range for many years to come.

Over the years, the mountain companions noticed that Amon was not growing any older. He remained young and robust while they began to gray and have less energy. They debated the many reasons for this. Tybor was convinced it was from drinking all the fairy nectar. Baynor felt it was because Amon was the keeper of the gates and wore the Stone of the Gates. Janii was certain it was because he had been brought back to life by Aii in the Place of Communion. Whatever the reason, Amon was sure to outlive them all and live for a very long time to come.

* * *

The spring after his coronation, High King Naibor gave the people cause for another celebration by marrying the Lady Taila. As a high king, Naibor was well loved by the citizens of Amuron. He was known as a king that cared about the needs of his people. Edra remained a servant at the palace, and while she was officially not one of the king's advisors, every now and again Naibor could be found sitting in the servants' kitchen, talking with her late into the night.

King Naibor liked to spend his days wandering or riding through the streets of Amuron, talking with the street merchants or visiting with the guards at the gates. There were many times when his wife, the Lady Taila, accompanied him on these outings. They had five beautiful children together, the eldest being a girl, followed by three boys and then another girl. Naibor had the longest reign of any high king in the history of the kingdom of Amuron, remaining high king for five successions, until finally he passed his title proudly on to his eldest daughter. For many years, even after Naibor was no longer high king, he and his wife could be seen holding hands and laughing together while they strolled contentedly through the city streets. A large ceremony was held in Berroc when Lord Naibor eventually passed from this world into the next and he was buried, along with the previous high kings, at the Place of the Stones.

About the Author

Michaela Peters has been a child educator for more than twenty-five years. She has one daughter and two dogs and happily lives in a small town in southern Ontario.